Praise for *Lemon Tart*
The Reviews Are In—and They Are Delicious!

"**I couldn't put it down!** I love, love, love this book. Sadie is more lovable than Regan Reilly, Goldy Bear, and James Qwilleran—all rolled together!"

—Whit Larson, http://www.MormonMomCast.com

"*Lemon Tart* **was delicious!** Sadie's curiosity, determination, and good old-fashioned pluck made her one of the most delightful characters I've ever met in a book. Finding that all my guesses about whodunit were wrong made for an exciting and clever ending to a satisfying mystery."

—Julie Wright, author of *My Not-So-Fairy-Tale Life*, http://www .juliewright.com

"Josi Kilpack's new book *Lemon Tart* takes everything I love about a culinary mystery—the food, the humor, the intrigue—and blends it all at high speed with a dash of spice in the form of our main character, Sadie. **A must-read for those who enjoy well-crafted mysteries.**"

—Tristi Pinkston, http://www.tristipinkston.blogspot.com

"**Mystery-lovers will be entranced** with Josi Kilpack's cozy mystery, *Lemon Tart*. Amateur sleuth/busybody neighbor Sadie Hoffmiller is funny, quirky, and just the person to uncover the right clues and get her neighborhood back to normal. With a little romance and a lot of yummy baking, I had fun trying to guess whodunit until the very end."

—H. B. Moore, award-winning author of the *Out of Jerusalem* series and *Abinadi*, http://www.mywriterslair.blogspot.com

"*Lemon Tart* **is an absolutely scrumptious culinary mystery.** It not only kept me guessing, but also had my taste buds demanding I make the included recipes. I'm very excited about this new series by Josi S. Kilpack!"

—T. Danyelle Ferguson, http://www.queenoftheclan.blogspot.com

ENGLISH TRIFLE

OTHER BOOKS BY JOSI S. KILPACK

ENGLISH TRIFLE

A CULINARY MYSTERY

JOSI S. KILPACK

DESERET
BOOK

SALT LAKE CITY, UTAH

To my Breanna—Thank you for being you and blessing my life every day.

Love ya, Babe.

Library of Congress Cataloging-in-Publication Data
Kilpack, Josi S.
  English trifle / Josi S. Kilpack.
      p.   cm.
  ISBN 978-1-60641-121-6 (paperbound)
  1. Cooks—Fiction.   2. Mothers and daughters—Fiction.   3. Manors—Fiction.
4. Murder—Investigation—Fiction.   5. England—Fiction.   I. Title.
  PS3561.I412E54 2009
  813'.54—dc22
                                                                                    2009007829

Printed in the United States of America
Sheridan Books, Chelsea, MI

10   9   8   7   6   5   4   3   2   1

CHAPTER 1

Is it just me or does it feel like the staff wants us to leave?" Sadie Hoffmiller asked after the door of the sitting room shut behind them.

"It's just you, Mom." Breanna sat on one of the damask-covered settees and kicked out one leg so that she slumped into the seat. She managed to look perfectly bohemian in the elegant room. "They're probably anxious to get back to their regular routine."

"Hmmm, maybe," Sadie replied, but she wasn't convinced. If not for the fact that Breanna had a lot to deal with right now, Sadie would have tried to dissect the situation a little more; however, she could sense that with their departure only minutes away, her daughter was on overload. Sadie didn't want to add to her stress.

Instead, she sat down across from Breanna as if being in the sitting room of an English estate was an everyday occurrence instead of an unforeseen shift in Breanna's possible future. That Breanna hadn't known Liam was heir apparent to an earldom when she fell in love with him hadn't made the adjustment any easier, but it *had* become the reason they'd come to England in the first place. Liam's father—William Everet Martin Jr., ninth Earl of Garnett—had been

1

ill for several months and Liam needed to see to some matters of the estate, necessitating he travel to England a week before Christmas. Sadie and Breanna had been invited to join him between Christmas and New Year's, while Breanna was out of school, in order to meet the earl and tour the country of Liam's birth. They'd spent one night at Southgate before leaving to see nearly everything else in England, returning only the night before last. Sadie couldn't imagine how they'd have thrown off the staff's routine when they'd been at the estate for such a short time. "It just seems to me that they're in a hurry for us to go back home."

"Well, they've got their hands full with the earl. I'm sure having guests—and foreign guests at that—is nothing more than an irritation."

Liam had had an extra week to adjust to his father's declining health, but admitted that he hadn't even recognized his father; he'd aged tremendously in the four years since Liam had seen him in person. Breanna suggested they forgo the sightseeing, but Liam assured them that the earl wouldn't want them to spend the week hovering when there was nothing any of them could do.

"Is Liam okay?" Sadie asked. She'd seen very little of him since their return to the estate. Once Liam's father passed on, Liam would inherit the title of earl, and the weight of the impending responsibility sat heavily on his shoulders now that the fun portion of the trip was over. He'd spent nearly every moment either at his father's bedside or in the library, poring over the history and accounts of the earldom, wanting to learn all he could before he returned to his other life in Portland, Oregon, where he supervised the bat exhibit at the Washington Park Zoo.

Breanna looked at her hands in her lap. She was wearing a T-shirt that said *Keep It Clean, Keep It Green.* "I don't know," she said quietly. "He's not sure when he'll be able to come back home. If he could, I'm sure he'd stay here."

Sadie wasn't so sure he *couldn't* stay—he was going to be an earl after all; why worry about something as inconsequential as his job? "It must be hard to leave with his dad still so sick," Sadie said sympathetically. Both of Sadie's parents were gone now, and losing them had been second in heartache only to her husband's premature death almost twenty years ago. Nothing quite compared to losing people close to you even if, like Liam and his father, there had been half a world between you for most of your life.

Breanna let out a breath and nodded.

"And how about you?" Sadie asked, peering at her daughter in the hopes of reading her expression should she choose not to be forthcoming. "How do you feel about leaving?"

Breanna flicked her green eyes up to meet her mother's, then stared back into her lap. She shrugged one shoulder like a thirteen-year-old girl, instead of a twenty-four-year-old woman facing the decision of a lifetime. Would she one day marry Liam and live the rest of her life as the Countess of Garnett? It was a subject she'd avoided talking about. For Breanna—earthy, easygoing, and hardworking—to consider living a life full of social functions, obligatory friendships, and a lifestyle disproportionate to that of her neighbors, would be difficult. Her world was nothing like this one. For a moment Sadie thought her daughter might be ready to discuss it now that the visit was almost behind them, but then Breanna's face broke into a smile. "Let's see," she said, a tease in her voice. "How do I feel about leaving?" She tapped her chin with feigned consternation. "I simply can't wait to eat a freaking Ho Ho."

"A Ho Ho?" Sadie said, pulling back in pure disgust. "We've

been surrounded by the finest of English cuisine for the last week and you want a Ho Ho?"

"The very words *English cuisine* are pretty much an oxymoron. It's bland, it's weird—mushrooms for breakfast? Come on! They served pigeons for dinner at that one place in York, Mom. Can you honestly tell me that a Big Mac isn't screaming your name about now?"

"Those were Cornish hens," Sadie reprimanded. "And they were delicious. The rosemary sauce was nothing short of amazing."

Breanna waved her hand, as if unwilling to even consider the possibility. "Hostess and McDonald's are not multibillion dollar companies for no reason." Breanna smiled as if she'd won the argument. "Oh, I liked the English trifle from the other night—that was delicious."

Sadie couldn't help but smile at the memory. She made the layered dessert every Christmas, but had never had it with real ladyfingers and custard pudding made from scratch. "It was excellent, wasn't it?" She couldn't wait to go home and make it herself to see if she could match Mrs. Land's. Now that she'd actually had real English trifle, she knew what to shoot for.

Breanna nodded as the door opened. Sadie straightened in her chair, all things forgiven and all senses on alert because there was food on the tray! Scones, clotted cream, strawberry jam, and tea, to be exact—a cream tea, for which Devonshire was famous. The scones—pronounced so that *scone* rhymed with the word *gone*—were not the deep-fried American kind, rather they were like a sweet biscuit that fairly melted in your mouth. Grant, the butler, placed the tea tray on a small table. "Your final tea," he said as he righted the tea cups on the saucers. "As soon as you finish here, you'll be on your way to Heathrow. Your bags are being loaded as we speak."

Aha, more proof that the staff was practically pushing them out the door. Their flight didn't leave until ten o'clock tonight—nearly seven hours from now—and it was only three hours to London. Why the rush? But she simply smiled at the man, watching his expression carefully.

"We can pour," Sadie said when he reached for the teapot. It felt funny to be waited on all the time and she took every opportunity to be self-sufficient. "And I hope the driver is okay to wait for a little while; we'd hate to rush." She thought she caught a flicker of irritation in Grant's expression, but he nodded his head and took a step backward toward the door, as professional as ever.

"Of course," he said. "I'll let the driver know he can turn off the engine."

Grant nodded once more when he reached the door, reminded them to ring the bell by the fireplace if they needed assistance, and then left the room. As soon as he was gone, Sadie leaned forward. "They weren't even going to shut off the engine," she said smugly. "They'd probably send us out there with Dixie cups and the scones wrapped in a napkin if they could."

"Mom, please," Breanna said, reaching for her scone. "Can we just enjoy these last few minutes?"

Oh, fine, Sadie said to herself. She was willing to put off nearly anything when there was food in need of savoring. She picked up, split, and jammed a scone before topping it with a dollop of clotted cream.

"Are you sure you want to bother with the scone at all?" Sadie asked, raising her eyebrows toward the treat in her daughter's hand. "Seeing as how these scones aren't loaded with trans fats or preservatives? I mean, they don't even have any artificial coloring, for goodness' sake."

"The scones," Breanna said, pronouncing the word like an American, "I like. But that cream stuff is nasty."

"That *cream stuff* is called clotted cream," Sadie corrected as she put the halves of her scone back together, making a sandwich—which was how the English ate their scones. "And Devon is famous for it."

Breanna looked up and lifted her eyebrows. "The very words *clotted cream* make my point: it even sounds gross. And talk about unhealthy—it's like pure butterfat."

"And what do you think butter is made of?" Sadie asked, but then she promptly ignored her daughter's reply, putting up her hand to block any further complaints as she took her first bite, allowing the cool cream, sweet jam, and smooth scone to combine perfectly in her mouth. She chewed slowly and carefully, savoring every moment. When she opened her eyes, Breanna was grinning at her.

"You're such a food junkie," Breanna said.

"Agreed," Sadie said before taking another bite.

It was several minutes before she finished a second scone, set down her cup of tea—peppermint, since she thought real tea tasted like wet socks—and let out a satisfied breath. "Our last tea in England," she said sadly. "And I never did wrestle the scone recipe away from Mrs. Land."

"Whatever," Breanna said dismissively. "You'll go home, spend two weeks baking scone recipes you find online and end up with a recipe that blows Mrs. Land's out of the water. You can call them 'Sadie's Scrumptulicious Scones' or 'Scones to Die For' or something like that."

Sadie cocked her head and smiled at the compliment. "You know me too well."

Breanna nodded and leaned back in her seat. She looked at her watch—a waterproof, multifunctioning black monstrosity that was as feminine as a chainsaw. "Where's Liam?" she asked.

Sadie shrugged. He'd texted Breanna, telling them to wait for him in the sitting room, but that had been nearly fifteen minutes ago. Sadie eyed the two scones they'd left for him and wondered if he'd notice if she ate one. Would he even have time to eat both scones with the staff in such a hurry to be done with them? And yet, when she'd put on her jeans this morning she found them a bit harder to button up than they'd been when she had arrived. At fifty-six years old she no longer had the metabolism of her youth and needed to have limits. But it was so hard! And how often was she going to have a cream tea in Devonshire? Sadie gave in and grabbed a third scone. Breanna didn't seem to notice, so Sadie quickly prepared it and then savored every bite. When it was gone, the last scone called to her, but this time she ignored it. She couldn't eat *all* of Liam's scones.

In order to distract herself from that last baked confection, she reviewed all the amazing things they'd done and seen that week. She and Breanna had made a list on the airplane from the U.S. and had diligently sought out things from some of their favorite books and movies set in England. They'd toured Tintagel, the ruins of King Arthur's castle in Cornwall, Ascot where Eliza Doolittle attended the races in *My Fair Lady*, Alnwick Castle in Northumberland which was used as Hogwarts in the Harry Potter movies, and they even took the Jack the Ripper tour in London—creepy. Sadie felt sure they'd gotten everything on the list, but reviewed it in her mind one last time, mostly to keep herself from the final scone. Instantly, she sat up.

"We need to take a turn about the room," she said excitedly. She didn't wait for an answer, instead she moved to her daughter's side and pulled her to her feet.

"What?" Breanna asked, looking at her strangely as she stumbled to get her balance, nearly dropping the scone in her hand as she did so.

Sadie was already tugging her toward the perimeter of the room.

"Remember? It was on our list—taking a turn around the room like Miss Bingley and Elizabeth in *Pride and Prejudice*." She waved her hand through the air in a regal fashion. "I'll be Caroline Bingley and you can be Elizabeth—although with your bad attitude, maybe you should be Caroline."

"I don't remember us assigning characters when we put it on the list," Breanna said before taking a bite of her scone.

Sadie gave her a dirty look, ignoring the commentary. Breanna shook her head but fell into step beside her mother, standing nearly five inches taller than Sadie thanks to the genetics she'd inherited from her birth parents. They walked slowly, scanning the collection of paintings and antique furniture on the interior wall as they made their way toward the far end of the long, narrow room. They'd been in this room twice before, but hadn't inspected it too closely. It was only fitting that doing so should be part of their final moments at Southgate estate.

When they neared the far wall, they turned and found themselves looking out the window furthest from the door. It was one of three floor-to-ceiling windows covered in elaborate folds of the same fabric used on the settees she and Breanna had been sitting on earlier. It had rained off and on all week, and had just started to sprinkle again, giving the view of the garden a watery look. Breanna popped the last of her scone in her mouth.

"I wish we'd had more time to walk through the gardens," Sadie said as they walked toward the window and she looked out upon the meticulously kept shrubs and bushes. "It's too bad it was so wet."

Breanna suddenly stopped, and since Sadie's arm was linked through Breanna's she was pulled to a stop as well, and none too gracefully either.

"Why are you being so difficult?" Sadie said, tugging on her daughter's arm again.

Breanna didn't respond. Instead she lifted a hand and pointed toward the curtain panel just to the right of the window.

The curtain was pushed out from the wall, nearly a foot. Poking out from beneath the folds of the heavy pleated fabric were the toes of two black leather shoes. A glass-fronted china cabinet, which stood between two of the windows, kept that particular curtain panel from being easily noticed. It was a perfect hiding place for whoever had chosen to do just that.

"Hello?" Sadie asked after several seconds of silence.

No response.

She and Breanna shared a look and Sadie felt annoyance rush through her at the idea that they were being spied upon. They'd have overheard her suspicions about the staff wanting them to leave. How embarrassing.

"Alright," she said in her schoolteacher voice, directing her comments toward the shoes that hadn't moved. "We can see you, so come out. Is that you, Liam?" Liam didn't strike Sadie as the practical joker type, but it was the only explanation she could think of.

No answer. Not Liam.

Breanna took a step back, pulling her mother with her, and although Sadie's chest prickled with apprehension, she refused to give into it. She pulled herself up to her full five and a half feet and raised her chin. "This isn't funny," she said. "So just make it easy on all of us and come out."

Nothing.

Taking a deep breath, and ignoring a new tremor of fear, she took a few steps forward and in one motion pulled the drapes back in order to unmask their uninvited guest.

Sadie sucked in a breath and didn't move.

Breanna screamed before clamping both hands over her mouth.

The man impaled and subsequently pinned to the wall by what looked like a fireplace poker did nothing but stare at the floor with his face frozen in shocked horror, a blossom-shaped bloodstain on his chest.

Sadie's American English Trifle

1 yellow or white cake mix (can use pre-made pound or angel food cake), cut into cubes
1 package Danish dessert, raspberry or strawberry (can use Jell-O)
1 packet Bird's brand custard mix (can use a large box of vanilla pudding)
1–2 cups frozen strawberries, thawed (Shawn prefers raspberries)
2 bananas, sliced
1 cup whipping cream, whipped

A couple of hours before assembling the trifle, prepare the cake mix, the custard mix, and the Danish dessert according to the package directions and allow to cool properly.

In a trifle dish or glass bowl layer all ingredients in the following order—cake cubes, Danish dessert, custard, fruit, and bananas. A trifle dish will usually allow two layers; a glass casserole dish will only allow one. Top trifle with whipping cream and refrigerate until ready to serve. Don't layer trifle more than six hours before eating or cake will get soggy and bananas may brown. Serves 8.

*If using Jell-O instead of Danish dessert, allow time for Jell-O to set up in refrigerator before serving, about 4 hours.

*Bre's chocolate trifle: chocolate cake, chocolate pudding, and crushed Oreos instead of fruit. Yummy!

CHAPTER 2

Sadie stumbled backwards, grabbing Breanna's arm as she did so, and unable to catch her breath for what felt like several seconds. She stared at the man while her brain argued over what she was seeing.

A dead man?

No way. Not here.

That poker isn't there for decoration.

Once Sadie fully absorbed the sight before her, she began walking backward again—away from the man behind the curtain though she couldn't stop staring at him. The light in the room reflected off the brass handle of the poker, drawing attention to itself as if there were any way they wouldn't notice. She bumped into Breanna who was frozen in place, reminding Sadie that she wasn't alone. Breanna's wide eyes kicked in Sadie's motherly instincts, even if her curiosity didn't want to leave just yet, and she grabbed Breanna's arm.

"Come on," she said as she tugged Breanna toward the door. Breanna finally pulled her eyes away from the body and took her shaky hands away from her mouth as they dodged furniture on their way out of the room. The slamming of the door behind them echoed off the marble floor and vaulted ceiling of the foyer. Sadie's heart was pumping in her chest as she and Breanna stumbled to a stop on the marble floor.

A fireplace poker? She asked in her mind as she scanned the huge area for help, feeling very small and vulnerable in the cavernous room. *Was it really a poker?*

Maybe she should go back in and take a second look, just to make sure. She shook away the thought. *What is wrong with you, Sadie Hoffmiller?* she demanded of herself. She had Breanna to take care of right now. *Focus, woman, focus!*

The holiday decorations that had seemed so festive and quaint during their stay now looked garish. The red ornaments on the two trees flanking the marble staircase, and the red leaves of the poinsettias spread throughout the room, reminded Sadie not of the holiday season that was coming to an end, but of the bloodstain on the chest of the man pinned to the sitting room wall. Deep red. Fresh. Her stomach tightened at the realization that the body hadn't been there—hadn't been dead—for long. She and Breanna had enjoyed their tea without any idea they were in the company of a corpse. How disgusting. The memory of their final tea was definitely ruined forever.

"Help!" Sadie yelled, though the word caught in her throat that had gone dry. She swallowed and tried again. "Someone?"

In the center of the foyer was a wide staircase that led to a landing before branching into two narrower staircases, leading to the upper east and west wings of the house where the bedrooms and family suites were located. A garland-wrapped balcony rimmed what could be seen of the second floor, but no one was on either level.

"Please," Sadie called. "Help us!"

The silence that echoed back was eerie and Sadie shivered as her mind considered their options and her heart raced with adrenaline. Breanna's hand was still in hers and she didn't seem in any hurry to let go. Sadie gave her daughter's hand a squeeze, her way of assuring Breanna that everything was okay, just before Breanna leaned forward, bracing her free hand on her thigh. "I think I'm gonna be sick," she said.

Sadie immediately identified a nearby chair as somewhere Breanna could sit down, but with a dead man on the other side of the wall it seemed an unwise choice to stay so close—especially out in the open. She couldn't help but feel a little like Bambi and his mother in the meadow. Instead, Sadie put an arm around her daughter's waist and pulled her toward the far side of the staircase. "Come on," Sadie said. "Let's find a staff member."

On their first day at the estate she'd noticed that staff disappeared on the far side of the staircase and although there was a call button in nearly every room of the house, Sadie wasn't about to wait for them to come to her. She'd asked Liam for a full tour of the house when they first arrived, curious as to the setup of utility areas such as staff rooms, kitchen, and laundry facilities—but he'd said that in order to respect the privacy of the staff, he could only show the public areas. Though these weren't the circumstances Sadie would have chosen, she was eager to see the servant portion of the house all the same. And they'd certainly find someone to help them down there. She was sure of it.

Exactly as she'd suspected, on the far side of the stairway, beneath the stairs themselves and hidden behind one of the towering Christmas trees, was a door. It wasn't green, but all the same Sadie was pretty sure it was the proverbial green baize door that separated the servant area from the main house—all the Regency romance novels she'd read lately mentioned that door. Since beginning a new relationship with a new man—Detective Pete Cunningham—she'd developed an odd hunger for the British romances where morality still held some merit but allowed room for a little passion all the same.

Sadie opened the door, leading Breanna and herself onto a cement landing at the top of a short flight of stairs. Centered at the base of the stairs was a set of swinging doors like the ones that divided a restaurant kitchen from the eating area. A narrow hallway separated the stairs from the door and small windows in the door showed a bright room on the other side, though the Plexiglas was too scratched to see much detail. It had to be the kitchen, and imagining that the cook was likely in the middle of preparing dinner, the kitchen seemed the obvious place to find someone to help them.

"Just a little further," Sadie urged Breanna, who was decidedly paler than she'd been when they left the sitting room.

Sadie helped Breanna down the stairs and pushed through the doors into what looked like a pantry for dishes. Shelves and shelves of glass-fronted cabinets held a wide variety of dishes, some ordinary and some quite elegant. A rolling ladder, similar to one in the library, allowed access to the higher items. Through another doorway opposite of where they stood, Sadie could see into a large kitchen, but what caught her attention was a small desk and chair tucked into one corner of the dish room. Sadie steered Breanna toward it, pulled the chair clear of the desk, and helped her sit down. Breanna leaned forward, resting her elbows on her knees and her head in her hands.

"Take deep breaths," Sadie said, brushing Breanna's long dark hair off of her neck while scanning the area for a bucket or bowl in case Breanna's shock got the best of her and she threw up.

"I'm feeling better," Breanna said behind the veil of her hair, but her voice was weak, and Sadie wasn't going to take any chances.

She heard footsteps and when she looked up, Mrs. Land, the house-keeper and cook as far as Sadie could figure, appeared in the doorway of the dish room. Her penciled-in eyebrows lifted to the middle of her forehead. "What are you doing here?" she asked with alarm. "It's not allowed."

"Can you get me a bowl or something? She might be sick."

The woman paused for a moment before she disappeared, returning a moment later with a large silver bowl. She handed it to Sadie, who put it on the floor in front of Breanna. Another cook with Asian features joined Mrs. Land, her face equally shocked as she looked at the two of them. Both women wore what looked like black hospital scrubs covered with black aprons—rather clean and flour-free for two women obviously working in a kitchen—but Sadie's mind was still a whirl of thoughts and she was unable to distract herself from what had brought her here in the first place.

"There's a man in the sitting room," she said fast, trying to explain why they were there and why Breanna was suddenly weak in the knees.

"Um, a man?" Mrs. Land asked carefully, sounding confused, cluing Sadie in on the fact that she'd left out some rather pertinent information.

"He's dead!" Sadie spat out in order to make sure she said it. It was a surprise to hear that the words even worked on her tongue and she found herself questioning it all over again. Had he really been *dead?* Was it truly a poker stuck through his chest? Even though she knew the answers, it was quite another thing to really believe those answers.

Mrs. Land pulled back with a gasp when the words registered

with her, while the other woman's eyes went even wider and she put a hand to her mouth. "Who's dead?" Mrs. Land asked.

"The man in the sitting room. He's got a poker clear through his chest, pinning him to the wall. I think—" Sadie cut herself off as she realized she hadn't yet considered if she recognized the man. It took only a moment to realize she knew who he was. His name was John Henry, and he served as the earl's personal nurse. Sadie had seen very little of him since he was usually at the earl's bedside and Sadie hadn't spent much time there. However, regardless of how seldom their paths had crossed, realizing she knew who he was caused the room to tilt beneath her feet a little bit.

The two women continued to stare at her, but she was loathe to tell them the identity of the corpse who had been their coworker. Her neighbor, Anne, had been murdered only a few months ago and the shock of it still hadn't faded. She did not want to be the one responsible for announcing a similar situation for these women.

"Have you seen Liam? I need to find him. Someone needs to call the police." She couldn't believe that only four months after coming face-to-face with murder for the first time, she was facing it again. What were the chances?

Mrs. Land just stood there—as did the other cook. Then Mrs. Land seemed to shake herself out of it. She moved toward the door, then stopped when she was even with Sadie. She turned to face Sadie, who pulled back because Mrs. Land was so close. "Um," she glanced toward the other cook and spoke in a whisper. "Please don't let her follow me." Then she turned to the other woman. When she spoke, it was in the kind of tone Sadie would use to speak to a small child or a pet. Far too calm for the circumstances. "Stay here—the earl will be expecting his dinner at eight."

Even with his nurse dead in the sitting room? Sadie thought to herself. *Can't they order pizza just this once? Can you have pizza delivered to an English estate? Do they even have pizza delivery in Devonshire?*

Mrs. Land pushed through the double doors while Sadie pulled her thoughts back to the situation.

"Wait!" Sadie called after her, realizing she'd just been left in charge. But Mrs. Land was gone.

With the doors swinging shut, Sadie looked at Breanna, who was still bent over and taking deep breaths. Breanna lifted her head to look at her mother. "I'm okay," she said, attempting to use the desk to stand. Sadie knew that Breanna's embarrassment of appearing so delicate was bothering her as much as anything.

Sadie hurried to her. "No, no, don't stand yet," she said, pushing her gently back into the chair. "Can you text Liam and tell him where to find us?"

Breanna nodded, and leaned forward again, digging her phone out of her pocket in the process and seemingly relieved to have something to do.

Sadie turned to face the other woman who continued to regard her with shock, tears forming in her almond-shaped eyes. Though she'd dropped her hand from her mouth, she looked pale beneath the light brown color of her skin. The two women stared at each other; Sadie tried to force a smile, though the muscles in her face resisted.

"Hi," she finally said after a few seconds had passed and she couldn't think of anything else to say. She put out her hand. "Um, I'm Sadie Hoffmiller, I don't believe we've met."

The woman remained silent, blinked once, then turned on her heel and began to run. Sadie paused a moment before taking off after the woman. On the left side of the large kitchen was a door, and

Sadie was navigating her way around the butcher-block table when she realized the other woman was headed toward it.

"Wait," Sadie called out even as she questioned herself on why she was becoming involved. "Stop."

The woman reached the door just as Sadie caught up with her and grabbed her arm. The woman's hand was on the doorknob and she made a whimpering sound in her throat.

"Please, stay here," Sadie pleaded in a breathless voice. She hadn't yet recovered from the shock of finding the body and was in no condition to chase down the assistant cook. Mrs. Land's words rung in her ears: *"Don't let her follow me."* Was it only *following* that was the problem? Was it alright if she left? Somehow, Sadie didn't think so and the other woman's desire to get out sent off yet more alarm bells in Sadie's head. The police would be coming, they would need to talk to everyone. She tightened her grip on the woman's arm. "Please wait for Mrs. Land to come back."

"I can't," the woman said, her accent different from Mrs. Land's or Grant's, but still British. Sadie had learned during this trip that in England, a person's speech not only revealed where they were from, but also what class they belonged to—but of course Sadie didn't know how to decipher it. The woman's dark eyes filled with tears as she looked at Sadie. She was a petite woman, trim and young. She wore a black scarf over her equally black hair. Devoid of makeup, her complexion was as flawless as any Sadie had ever seen. "He made me promise if something happened, I'd disappear."

"He?" Sadie repeated. "He who?"

"Please," the woman begged, openly crying as she tried to twist and pull her arm away; a sob broke through. "Please, I have to go."

Sadie didn't know what to do. "But—"

"Please," the woman said again, and this time her voice was

shaking, her eyes wild as tears streamed down her face. In that moment, sympathy overwhelmed sense. Sadie didn't know how this woman was connected to John Henry, but the absolute terror on her face made it impossible for Sadie to detain her. The woman looked surprised for the briefest moment when Sadie let go.

"My name is Sadie Hoffmiller," Sadie said again as the woman turned the knob and pulled the door open. "Is there anything I can do to help?"

The woman seemed even more surprised by that, but then her face fell. "No one can help me with this," she said before disappearing through the door.

CHAPTER 3

The woman's cryptic comments hung heavily in the air, but only a few moments passed before Sadie turned back to the kitchen, one of the largest—and cleanest—kitchens she'd ever seen. Countertops and sinks extended along one of the four walls, glass-fronted refrigerators and freezers along another, with ovens and stoves along a third. A huge butcher-block table stood in the center of the room, with a couple stools tucked underneath. A nearly full garbage can meant someone needed to take out the trash, but every other aspect of the kitchen was shined and polished to perfection—not what Sadie would have expected for what was essentially a commercial kitchen churning out food for a household and its staff three times a day—four if you counted high tea; five if elevenses were added to the list. She reflected on the details for only a moment before remembering that Breanna still needed help. Sadie found a dishrag in a drawer near the sink and ran it under cool water before ringing it out, hoping that the tight feeling in her stomach brought on by letting the assistant cook leave would disappear in a few moments. She hoped she hadn't made too horrible a mistake.

"Lean over again," she said when she returned to the dish room and found Breanna sitting up. Sadie moved Breanna's hair out of the way and laid the cloth over her neck. "Deep breaths," she said, while smoothing out Breanna's hair. Within a few seconds, Breanna's shoulders softened and her response helped relax Sadie as well. She took a deep breath while a thousand questions swirled through her mind. Who was the woman she'd just let go? What was her relationship to John Henry? Why didn't Mrs. Land want the assistant cook to follow her? Why did Mrs. Land insist on leaving in the first place? What if she was the murderer and Sadie had let her go?

"I texted Liam," Breanna said. Her voice sounded better. "He hasn't texted back."

"I thought all he had to do was say good-bye to his dad before we left," Sadie said. "He's been up there all day, hasn't he?" She hadn't minded waiting for him while they were enjoying their tea, but now his absence was unnerving. Why hadn't Mrs. Land returned yet?

Breanna nodded and looked up at her mom, worried. "He wanted as much time with his dad as possible—he's been on the phone most of the day. Do you think he's okay?"

"I'm sure he's fine," Sadie said—but mostly because she was a mother and that's the kind of thing mothers told their daughters when their daughters turned to them for help.

"I'd feel a lot better if he were here. Should we go find him?"

"I'm hoping Mrs. Land found him for us," Sadie said, looking at the double doors separating them from the main part of the house with a curious kind of longing. *What was going on up there?* She hated being left out of the rising action she had no doubt was taking place up there in the sitting room.

Breanna sat up and leaned her head back, placing the rag on her forehead as she closed her eyes again. "Maybe that's why he hasn't responded; maybe he's calling the police."

"Maybe so," Sadie said, looking at her watch. They were supposed to leave by 4:30. It was 4:26. "How are you feeling?" Sadie asked, placing the back of her fingers against Breanna's cheek. It didn't feel too hot or too cold; she hoped the shock had passed.

"Better," Breanna said, opening her eyes and looking around the dish room. "I've never seen a dead body before," she said, removing the rag as she straightened up. "At least not a human one."

Sadie, however, had seen several in her lifetime. Perhaps that made it a bit less traumatic for her, or maybe she was just being strong for her daughter. Either way, she wasn't nearly as unnerved as she imagined most people would be. Her curiosity, however, was fit to be tied, but she was determined to keep it together. "I think we should return to the foyer. I'm sure Scotland Yard will be here soon."

"Was it John Henry?" Breanna asked carefully as she looked up at her mother once again.

Sadie nodded. "I think so."

Breanna stood slowly, testing her balance before taking a step. Sadie stayed by her elbow in case she was needed, but Breanna seemed to have recovered and she walked back through the double doors on her own. "I didn't imagine one of the things I'd do in England was make an official statement to the police about the dead body of the earl's nurse," Breanna muttered as they headed up the concrete steps. She held tightly to the handrail, moving slowly and carefully.

"Do you think we'll make the news?" Sadie asked. She didn't mean to sound excited about the prospect of being on television, but if the story made the international circuit her friends might see her. Did the Associated Press pick up international stories? What would people back home think about Sadie being involved in another murder investigation?

When they exited the second doorway and stepped onto the

main floor, Sadie expected to encounter pandemonium. Mrs. Land crying or shouting, Grant trying to comfort her while Liam directed the police on where to go and who was who. She imagined more servants would be milling about, wringing their aprons and holding back tears. Instead, they rounded the Christmas tree and found the foyer empty—as silent and unoccupied as it had been when she and Breanna left it eight or nine minutes earlier.

They both stopped in the empty hall and looked around. For a brief moment Sadie wondered if they'd come out the wrong way, into a different foyer that looked exactly like the last one. The one thing she hadn't expected to find was this—empty silence. She looked toward the sitting room door; it was closed. A shiver raced up her spine.

"Hello?" Sadie called out, not wanting to move. "Mrs. Land?"

No one answered and the mixture of fear, anxiety, and downright annoyance began bubbling. "Oh, for heaven's sake." Sadie marched into the center of the room so she could see up onto the balcony and down the hallways that led toward the library on the right and the formal dining area on the left. Not a single person was in sight. She took a deep breath and yelled at the top of her lungs: "Isn't there anyone here but us?"

Her words echoed back to her but that was the only answer she received. After a few more seconds, she looked back at the sitting room door. Maybe Mrs. Land and Liam were in there? Could the stone walls keep them from being able to hear her? Her eyes drifted to the front doors that would lead them to the car that was supposed to take them to London.

Breanna had pulled her phone from her pocket again and dialed a number. After a few seconds, she pulled the phone away from her ear and scowled. "Voice mail," she said, looking at her mother and pushing the phone back into her pocket. "Where is everyone?" She looked at the door to the sitting room. "Maybe they're in there."

Sadie nodded, turning away from the idea that making their flight was even a possibility. Together they went to the door and Sadie pulled it open slowly, listening for the discussion between Liam and Mrs. Land that she expected to hear. When she didn't hear any voices, Sadie poked her head around the door frame. The room was empty.

"You've got to be kidding me," Breanna said, glancing behind them as they entered the room. They both stood just inside the doorway for a few seconds, trying to accept what they had found— or not found. In the two days they'd been at Southgate, the staff was constantly around. The feeling that they were never alone was now contrasted with the fact that they seemed to be the only people here. The butler, footmen, and maids that seemed to be hovering everywhere had now disappeared completely.

In tandem their eyes traveled toward the back of the room, but the glass-fronted china cabinet that had hidden John Henry from them during their tea still obscured their view. Sadie reached for Breanna's hand and carefully headed for the back of the room if for no other reason than to verify what they had seen. When the curtain finally came into view, they stopped in their tracks.

"No shoes," she muttered as Breanna sucked in a breath. Sadie dropped Breanna's hand and, in eight quick steps, she reached the curtain that now hung in pleats against the wall like all the other curtain panels in the room. Sadie took a breath and pulled back the fabric—just as she had the first time—but this time all that greeted them was the textured wallpaper. No body, no blood.

A missing chunk of plaster was the only indication that John Henry had been there at all.

CHAPTER 4

S ilence.

Sadie couldn't believe it and blinked several times to make sure the scene in front of her didn't change. It was as shocking to *not* see the body this time as it had been to *see* the body the first time she'd pulled back the curtains.

"Mom?" Breanna said with a question in her voice, reminding Sadie she wasn't alone. She turned to look at her daughter, whose eyes were wide as she too stared at the hole in the plaster. "Where did he go?"

A battle waged itself in Sadie's mind as she looked from her daughter to the missing plaster. Her first thought had been to start searching for the body, Mrs. Land, Liam, and Grant, but seeing Breanna's pale face made her next thoughts much more practical. There was little chance that John Henry had *accidentally* skewered himself with a fireplace poker behind a curtain panel in the sitting room or that he had simply walked away on his own. Therefore, Sadie could conclude that there had definitely been a murder, which meant there was definitely a murderer—and now a body snatcher as well.

"Let's go," she said, taking Breanna's hand and heading out of the sitting room, frantically trying to beat her curiosity into submission by flogging it with the reality of the situation and her abilities to accomplish anything by staying. *This is dangerous—it's not safe—I'm not a real detective—we'll miss our flight—Breanna doesn't need this— anyone willing to move a body is seriously disturbed and not someone with whom we should stay in the same house.*

"Go?" Breanna repeated from behind her as she took hurried steps.

"Grant said the car was ready," Sadie said. "They already packed our bags and we've got a flight to catch." She was the mother here, the older and wiser individual, and she needed to make a sensible decision for the two of them.

They were nearly to the front doors when Breanna stopped and pulled her hand from Sadie's grip. "Mom," she said, already shaking her head. "We can't leave."

"But we certainly can't stay," Sadie said, turning to look at her. "It's not safe."

"We can't leave without Liam," Breanna said.

"Liam can catch another flight."

"Someone has to call the police."

"Couldn't we just leave a note?" Sadie offered. "Or call the police on our way to London?"

Breanna gave her a look that said a note wasn't going to cut it. "Mom," she reprimanded, "you know we can't do that."

Sadie raised one hand to her forehead and put the other one on her hip as she let out a breath. "Well, I don't know!" she said in frustration. "We most certainly did not put this on our list of things to do while in England and I'm afraid I have no idea what we do now."

"Okay," Breanna said, taking the role of reasonable adult for the moment since Sadie had so efficiently relinquished her right to play the part by throwing a tantrum and admitting she didn't know what to do. "What would we do if we were at home?"

"And found a dead man in the sitting room who then disappeared along with the rest of the staff and your boyfriend?" Those kinds of things didn't happen at home. Well, actually her neighbor *had* been found dead in her backyard a few months ago, but it still felt very different from this, and by the time Sadie showed up on that scene the police were already investigating. Her eyes met Breanna's. "I guess I would call the police," Sadie said.

Breanna patted her mother's arm. "Good answer. I'd do the same thing, so, since we agree, that's where we should start. We *did* see a body and someone has to report it." She fished her phone out of her pocket and stared at the numbers. "Does 911 work in England?"

"No, it's 999 in the UK," Sadie said, looking toward the door of the sitting room, wondering if she dared leave the room. When she looked back, Breanna was staring at her.

"How do you know that?" Breanna asked, her thumbs poised above the numbers of her phone.

"Everyone knows that 999 was the first emergency phone number system and that it was started in London back in 1937," she paused, squinting one eye as she tried to recall the information. "Or was it 1938? I can't remember."

Breanna continued to stare at her.

"What?" Sadie asked, then looked at the phone. "Aren't you going to call?"

"Oh, right," Breanna said, shaking herself slightly. She punched in the numbers and put the phone to her ear. "I can't believe you know all that."

"Don't you ever watch the Discovery Channel other than for Shark Week?" Sadie asked.

Breanna opened her mouth to answer, then put up a finger and looked away from her mother. "Yes," she said. "My name is Breanna Hoffmiller. I'm visiting at Southgate estate and we found a dead body. . . . His name is John Henry. . . . It was in the sitting room, but it's gone now. . . . Well, I agree it's strange." She looked up at her mother and rolled her eyes. "No, we don't know who moved it . . . . I'm with my mother. . . . Southgate estate—I don't know the address—it belongs to the Earl of Garnett. . . . Um, about twenty miles out of Exeter. Can you just send someone . . . What?" She paused for several seconds. "I swear to you this is not a prank call. My mother and I found the body almost ten minutes ago. . . . We didn't call before because we thought the cook was going to take care of it but now we can't find her either. Look, can you just send someone?" She started tapping her foot and Sadie slowly crossed to the back of the room, looking at the now empty portion of wall that had once held John Henry. Her eyes were drawn to the thick rug set in the middle of the hardwood floor. Breanna continued to argue with the dispatcher while Sadie took a step back, toward the edge of the room. There were drag marks on the carpet, which meant—

"Unbelievable," Breanna huffed. Sadie looked over her shoulder to see that Breanna had hung up the phone. "They think I'm some college kid from America on holiday making a prank call."

"Well, other than the prank call, they're right—you are a college kid from America on holiday." She didn't wait for Breanna to answer before putting her hand up in a stopping motion. "Don't come any closer." Sadie pointed at the carpet. "Drag marks," she said. "We already messed them up a little bit."

Breanna had followed her finger and was now inspecting the

carpet. "Are you sure they're drag marks?" she asked, squinting toward them and leaning forward.

"Carpet never lies." Sadie motioned Breanna to come toward her using the very edges of the room. Once Breanna reached her, they both squatted down to get a better angle.

"I think you're right," Breanna breathed as she looked at the two parallel curving lines heading for the door—heel marks. She immediately lifted her phone.

Sadie was about to ask her what she was doing when she realized Breanna was taking a picture. She leaned toward her daughter, her quads burning from the squatting position she was in, and waited until the picture showed up on the screen of Breanna's phone. "It's hard to see them in the picture," Sadie said, looking between the carpet and the phone.

"I'll take a few more," Breanna said, turning the phone and holding it closer to the carpet. "They're sending an inspector out," she continued in an annoyed tone while snapping another photo. She looked at it, then held it toward Sadie. "This one's better, don't you think?"

Sadie nodded—the drag lines were a lot more distinct. "Did they say how long until the inspector arrives?"

Breanna shook her head and finally stood. She made it look so easy. Sadie nearly groaned out loud as she righted herself. Phew. She wasn't used to being so close to the ground and had become so busy with Christmas stuff that she'd missed a few of her weekly yoga classes. She made a note not to miss any more in the future—she could definitely feel the difference.

"We need to find Liam," Breanna said as they made their way toward the door. But she came to a stop when they reached the sitting area set up across from the fireplace. Sadie followed her eyes, and they both stared at the wrought-iron fireplace stand. Even from this distance Sadie could see that the handles of the hearth tools didn't match the handle of the poker they'd seen protruding from John Henry's heart—these were a filigree design, black. She took a couple steps forward to confirm that the poker for the set was still there. "Whoever killed John Henry came into this room armed."

Breanna nodded. "We need to find Liam—now."

They held each other's eyes and Sadie understood Breanna's urgency—they hadn't seen anyone but Mrs. Land and the runaway cook since their initial discovery of the body. What if there was something even bigger going on? What if the reason they hadn't heard from Liam was because he was unable to communicate?

Thoughts of terrorists, chain saw murderers, and bank robbers filled Sadie's mind and her heart rate increased accordingly. "You're right," she said, heading for the door. When they reached the doorway, they shared a nervous glance. Sadie felt safer here—well, now that the body was gone. Taking a deep breath, she grabbed the doorknob and began turning it, just as someone did the same thing on the other side of the door.

With a sharp intake of breath, she let go, startling Breanna as the door whooshed open, nearly knocking Sadie over in the process.

CHAPTER 5

"Liam!" Breanna said in surprise as Sadie stumbled backward. Liam stood rooted in place, as if not expecting to see them there.

"Bre," he said, looking at Breanna. "Sadie," he continued, taking her in as well. His already longish, sandy blond hair was a little more wild than usual as he looked back and forth between the two of them. "Are you okay?"

Sadie and Breanna shared a look as if waiting for the other person to start, then they both took a breath and began talking at once.

"John Henry—"

"A fireplace poker—"

"Told Mrs. Land—"

"The body is gone—"

"I texted you *four* times!"

"What?" Liam said, interrupting them and looking sufficiently confused.

Breanna hurried to tell him a very abbreviated version of how the events had played out. Liam listened, his expression becoming more and more troubled the further into the story she went. When she finished, Liam blinked at them.

"Why didn't you return my calls?" Breanna asked.

"I, uh, had my phone turned off," he said, looking past her into the room with trepidation. "The body's gone?"

They both nodded like a pair of bobbleheads. "See for yourself," Breanna said, leading the way toward the back window, pointing out the drag marks. Sadie held the curtain back while Liam inspected the missing chunk of plaster. He reached toward it as if to feel the plaster, but Sadie grabbed his hand. "We already called the police," she said. "We better not touch anything else."

"You called the police?" Liam said, looking at Breanna.

"Of course," she said. "I tried calling you; we didn't know what else to do."

"Did you see anyone?"

They shook their heads. "We were waiting for Mrs. Land to come back to the kitchen," Breanna said.

"But you didn't see anything or hear anything?"

"No," Breanna replied, but she sounded annoyed by the fact that he kept repeating himself.

Liam nodded, staring at the wall for a few more seconds. Sadie was just about to ask him if he was okay when he reached out and grabbed Breanna's wrist. She startled, as did Sadie.

"I want you both to go back up to your room," he said. He turned and began pulling Breanna toward the door.

"Wait a minute," she said, trying to twist her arm free of his grasp. He didn't let her go and Sadie had no choice but to follow. "Liam," Breanna continued, "you're hurting me!"

He let go of her then, but he didn't apologize and he didn't slow his steps. "Right now," he said. "Go up there, lock the door and wait for me."

"But," Breanna said, "we—"

"Bre," he cut her off. "Please, upstairs now."

Sadie watched the exchange, too shocked by Liam's reaction to be of much help in either side of the battle. Liam was always so soft-spoken and meek, to see him jump into action was . . . impressive, but a little unnerving as well. Breanna opened her mouth to protest again, but Liam took a step toward her, bringing himself intimately close to her face. "Please, Breanna," he said in a fierce whisper, almost a growl. "I'll call you when it's safe, but until we figure this out, I want to make sure *you're* safe."

Breanna looked like she wanted to argue, but she didn't. "Come on, Mom," she said, heading for the stairs. Sadie paused, looking between a retreating Breanna and Liam who stood in front of the sitting room door, watching Breanna. The last place Sadie wanted to be right now was in her room, twiddling her thumbs. There was a body to find, a murderer to pin it on, and clues to sniff out in order for those two ends to be realized; and she was going to wait around in her room? She'd already assisted in the capture of one murderer. Liam should probably go to his room and let Sadie take charge.

Breanna was three steps up the marble staircase when she turned. "Mom," she said. "Come on."

"But—" Sadie looked at Liam, trying to send him a telepathic message to insist she stay behind. He needed her; she knew he did.

"Please go with her, Sadie," he said quietly, so Breanna couldn't hear. "I don't want her to be alone. It's not safe."

His receptors for telepathy were horribly out of service. However, she couldn't argue with his reasoning and so she turned and followed Breanna, all the time letting the questions run through her head like the ticker tape at the bottom of a news program. She remembered the assistant cook running out of the kitchen. Should she tell Liam that?

At the top of the stairs, Sadie and Breanna headed toward the west wing, where their room was located. They'd been offered separate rooms, but preferred staying together, even if it seemed to offend the staff a little bit. As soon as the door closed behind them, Sadie inspected the room closer than she ever had before. It was a beautiful room, to be sure, and both she and Breanna had oohed and aahed when they arrived and then tried to determine the cost of furnishing this room. A huge four-poster bed, draped with a satin bedcover, was centered on the wall opposite the door. At the foot of the bed was a bench upholstered in the same fabric as the drapes and several of the accent pillows on the bed. The walls were covered with a light green wallpaper, the tone picked up from a contrasting fabric used to trim the pillow shams and the ruffle on the bench. But this time Sadie wasn't looking for the sake of admiration. This time she had a purpose.

Breanna sat on the bed while Sadie began running her fingers along the wall.

"What are you doing?" Breanna asked.

"Just looking around," Sadie said innocently. She encountered a seam in the wallpaper and ran her fingers down it all the way to the baseboard, then felt up as high as she could go. "Does it seem weird to you that they have a wallpaper seam this close to the door? Usually wallpaper is begun around doors and windows so the longer portions are closer to the focal points in the room."

"It's not the edge of a secret passageway," Breanna said dryly.

"You don't know that for sure," Sadie said. Unfortunately, after closer inspection she surmised it really was just the wallpaper seam. Bummer. "Where there is one mystery, there is often another, and these old estates are full of secret passageways and things."

"Please don't do this, Mom."

Sadie stopped and turned to look at her daughter. She softened her expression in hopes of looking innocent. "Do what?"

"Go all Scooby-Doo on me," Breanna said, sounding annoyed. "I can see it in your face, Mom, it's like you're infected."

Sadie put her hands on her hips. "Infected?" she repeated.

"Yes, it's like you have some disease—Detectivitis."

"You act like it's a bad thing," Sadie replied, frowning.

"It *is* a bad thing," Breanna countered. "Remember Sister Ferret's root beer at the church Christmas party? You thought it was poisoned."

Sadie cringed just a little bit. That incident had been rather unfortunate, but Sadie still stood beside her investigative skills that drove her to the conclusion. "No one brings root beer to a party in December," Sadie said. "And it smelled weird."

"So you *accidentally* knocked it on the floor," Breanna summed up.

"It was never tested," Sadie added. "You don't know that I'm not responsible for saving a hundred lives that night."

"And what about that Christmas card you opened with latex gloves?"

"There was definitely something white and powdery on the outside of the envelope," Sadie said. "And your father's aunt Beulah has never liked me very much. I've always found it strange that she keeps sending me Christmas cards."

"And so you thought she'd got a hold of some anthrax and sent it to you in a Christmas card?"

Okay, it did sound a little silly when Breanna said it like that. But at the time, it made a lot of sense. "Better safe than sorry," Sadie said.

"Then we should stay in our room and keep our noses out of all of this because that would be *much* safer." She paused and her expression softened with exhaustion. "Please, Mom, I can't take it right now. Promise me you won't put your nose anywhere it doesn't belong."

Sadie thought back to Breanna's reaction at finding John Henry, and to the reserved mood she'd had all day—did Sadie really want to add to her daughter's stress? No. But neither did she want to sit here and do nothing. Still, she noted that the phrase "won't put your nose anywhere it doesn't belong" was pretty open-ended. Who determined where Sadie's nose did or did not belong?

"Promise me you won't play detective," Breanna insisted.

"Okay," Sadie said, feeling and sounding very dejected. "I promise I won't play detective," she repeated, though it wasn't playing if she were doing something that was truly effective. She sat down on the bed next to Breanna, symbolizing that they were together in their approach—for now. "So, we just wait for Liam to call us?" she asked.

Breanna nodded, so they sat there for a few seconds. Then she furrowed her brow. "Why wouldn't he have his phone on?" Breanna asked.

Excellent question, however Sadie was under orders. "Don't think about it."

"But it doesn't make sense," Breanna said. "He always has his phone on."

"You don't want to be putting your nose where it doesn't belong," Sadie said in mock reprimand. "You don't want it to get all infected."

"My wondering why Liam didn't have his phone on is not the same as trying to solve a murder." Breanna threw herself back on the bed and covered her eyes with one arm while letting out a breath. "I just want to go home."

Sadie reached out a hand and rubbed Breanna's arm, filled with sympathy. "The sooner this is solved, the sooner we can do that."

Jungle sounds coming from the vicinity of Breanna's front pocket signaled that she'd received a text message and she sat up in order to retrieve her phone and read the message.

"Now he's got his phone on," she said grumbling. "Liam wants us to come to the library." She turned so that her legs were off the bed. "He's assembling the staff to see if anyone has any information."

"Oh, well, maybe we shouldn't go, it's not really any of our business," Sadie replied, folding her hands demurely in her lap as if she weren't using all her powers of restraint to keep from running downstairs right that second.

Breanna gave her a withering look. "You're impossible, do you know that?"

Sadie smiled. "At least I admit to my curiosity," she said, getting off the bed and straightening the blue pinstriped button-up shirt she'd worn today thinking it would be comfortable for the flight home. "You're trying to deny it but you're just as intrigued as I am."

"Not true," Breanna said as they headed toward the door.

"Whatever you say, dear," Sadie said with another knowing smile. She didn't believe Breanna was any less curious than she was. However, she did agree that other feelings were likely overwhelming Breanna's questions. She opened the door and held it so Breanna could exit first.

"To the library," Sadie said, unable to hide her excitement.

Breanna's response was as dry as Sadie's had been upbeat. "To the library," she repeated. "May the inspectors hurry and get here so we can go home."

CHAPTER 6

Sadie looked around at the faces of the people in the room, noting that most of them were also taking inventory of who was here. Curiosity was thick in the air as everyone waited to find out the reason for the meeting. Only a few faces seemed tense—specifically Mrs. Land, who'd been located back in the kitchen. She claimed she hadn't seen the body and so she'd just gone back to the kitchen. Sadie wanted to ask how that was possible, since she and Breanna had been waiting for her return, but she hadn't had the chance yet.

There were thirteen staff members, many of whom she'd never seen before this moment. It was creepy to think they had been doing their jobs without her seeing them even once over the last two days. Some were obviously groundskeepers, as they wore work boots and scruffy jeans. They seemed ill at ease in the ornate room and chose to stand clustered together on one side, while the house staff had taken chairs set about the room and pulled them forward. Grant stood at the double doors that led into the hallway. Sadie looked closely at each face, trying to discern the one belonging to the murderer, but none of them were giving up their secrets. Not yet, anyway.

Liam nodded at Grant, who then shut the doors. Liam made his way to the front of the room, passing twelve-foot bookcases, not to mention the floor to ceiling bookshelves built into the walls. The room was immense and beautiful, making Sadie wish she had another day to just read in this room. There were several sitting areas around the room as well as a large executive desk set by the windows that looked out over the front gardens of the house.

Mrs. Land had brought some wonderful, delicate little lemon cookies with an even yummier lemon glaze. No one else seemed in the mood to snack, but Sadie had already eaten five of them—she blamed it on her nerves. It didn't hurt that the cookies were wonderfully delicious either.

Liam turned to face his audience once he reached the desk and he pulled at the sleeve of his Denver Broncos sweatshirt—Breanna had given it to him for Christmas. He cleared his throat and shifted his weight. His discomfort made Sadie squirm and she couldn't help but wonder how he would ever be earl when he was so uncomfortable with authority.

"Um, well, we find ourselves in quite a predicament," he began. He glanced quickly at Breanna, who, with Sadie, stood behind the staff, directly across from him. "Um, maybe Sadie—uh, Mrs. Hoffmiller—could come up and tell everyone what you and Breanna saw." He hurried to move to the side before Sadie even had a chance to answer, and he tripped on the edge of the rug, causing him to stumble forward and catch himself. Sadie looked around and realized he hadn't left her much of a choice, not that she minded so much.

As she made her way to the front, one of the groundskeepers nudged another one and they both lifted an eyebrow before looking at the floor, hiding smiles. Their lack of respect for Liam was obvious. Sadie wondered how many of the other staff members had similar thoughts.

"Um, well, I'm Sadie Hoffmiller," she said by way of introduction, assuming that since she didn't know everyone, they didn't know her either. She took a breath and began telling them what she and Breanna had seen. She was at the part where they left the sitting room in search of help, when one of the doors to the library opened. Everyone turned to look toward the door, and then seemed to sit or stand straighter. Grant hurried to hold the door as a man entered the room and leaned against the back wall with his arms crossed. Grant closed the door, bowed slightly toward the newcomer, and then returned to his place, his hands behind his back and his posture ramrod straight. The man who had entered had dark curly hair and was dressed in what Sadie would call business casual: a button-up shirt, high-quality slacks, and highly polished shoes. He looked about Liam's age—late twenties—maybe a little younger. It was obvious by the way he carried himself that he wasn't a staff member.

"Austin," Liam said, nodding a greeting toward the other man. His tone seemed a little tight, but Sadie was busy scanning her memory banks for the name Austin. She couldn't find a match.

The man nodded in return, then shooed his hand toward Sadie as if telling her to continue. She took a breath and picked up the story despite her curiosity as to who this man was and why everyone, including Liam, seemed to be standing at attention now that he was here. No one said a word as Sadie continued with her story. Mrs. Land fidgeted more than ever with the hem of her smock and Sadie couldn't help but keep looking in her direction. "And so then we called 999 and . . . uh, found Liam." She knew she'd rushed through the end of the story, but the interruption had thrown her off.

"Where was Liam when all this was happening?" Austin asked from the back of the room.

It took a few seconds for Liam to realize he was supposed to answer. "I . . . I was upstairs with my father," he said, looking at the floor—completely cowed. "I was saying good-bye."

Austin nodded his acceptance of this explanation, and looked around at the staff as he pushed away from the wall. "And what did you find in the sitting room, Mrs. Land?" Austin walked toward the front of the room, every eye watching him. In a matter of seconds, he'd managed to take total control of the meeting despite the fact that he'd missed half of the story.

"Well, I saw . . . nothing," Mrs. Land said, the nervousness in her voice ringing like a bell as Austin reached the front of the room and turned to face her. "There was nothing there when I arrived in the sitting room."

"Really?" Austin said with condescension. "These two women would have reached the kitchen in a minute or less after leaving the sitting room, and the body managed to disappear before you arrived?"

"I suppose so, sir," Mrs. Land said. She swallowed. "Or else it was never really there." She looked at the floor as she said it, but her words hit Sadie like a slap. Why would she and Breanna lie about something like that? How could anyone think that of them?

Austin turned to Sadie, eyes narrowing slightly. "You say he was stabbed through the heart with a fireplace poker?"

His antagonistic approach struck a nerve and she decided that if he could talk to Liam that way in front of his staff, she could return the same attitude. "And how did you hear that?" she asked, cocking her head slightly and resisting the urge to put her hands on her hips. "I don't know who you are or why you're here, but I'm wondering how you know so many details when you've only just arrived."

Whether she actually heard a gasp, or simply felt a collective pause from the people in the room, she wasn't sure, but she felt as though she'd managed to shock every one of them by talking to this man the way she had. She looked into the startled faces of the staff around her as Liam cleared his throat and leaned toward Sadie. "This is Austin Melcalfe, my cousin of sorts—his grandmother is my Aunt Hattie—or I guess you would call her Lady Hane—and his father is the physician tending to my father. Austin's been the trustee managing the affairs of the estate since Dad's stroke."

Sadie's first thought was why hadn't he told her about Austin before now. Liam had avoided talking about his father most of the trip, and Sadie had chalked it up to the fact that it was difficult for him, due to his father's condition. Now she wished she'd asked more questions.

When Liam finished the introduction, Austin lifted one eyebrow as if triumphant in having Sadie put in her place. What place that was, Sadie didn't know because she wasn't all that impressed with Austin.

"I'd still like to know how he knows so much about what happened to John Henry," Sadie said. Saying John Henry's name seemed to cast a further pall over the room. Mrs. Land closed her eyes and shook her head slightly. Grant, on the other hand, stood even straighter next to the door—he'd refused to sit when Liam had brought the rest of the staff in. No one met Sadie's eye as she scanned the room. None of them could ignore that though this room was supposed to have every staff member in it, John Henry was absent.

"Grant called me. I was in Exeter and came right out," Austin explained.

"How did Grant know?" she challenged. "Fifteen minutes ago Liam had only just arrived at the sitting room—Grant was nowhere in sight."

Liam took a few steps to the side as if relinquishing the floor to Austin and not wanting to be involved in their exchange. Sadie was not impressed with his backing down and refused to move even though Austin was only a foot or so away from her. She could smell the woodsy scent of his cologne, but noticed that he had sweat rings under his arms. Ewww. It wasn't overly warm, which made Sadie wonder if, despite his dominating manner, he was nervous about something.

"Where were you, Grant?" Austin asked, looking at the butler.

"I was speaking with Kevin, sir."

"You are to be on hand at all times, especially when we have guests, are you not?"

"Yes, sir," Grant said. "I was waiting outside to assist the ladies into the car once they finished their tea. I'm very sorry, sir."

Austin accepted this explanation with a nod.

Sadie didn't. "You didn't hear us scream for help?" she asked.

"No, madam," he said.

Sadie watched him carefully. She'd yelled for help when they first came out of the room, and then again when they'd come up from the kitchen. There had been almost ten minutes between the two occurrences. And Grant had been outside the *whole* time?

He cleared his throat. "I enjoy a cigarette once or twice a day." He glanced at Austin, who scowled even deeper—which was a feat. "I moved away from the house so as not to disturb anyone. It was a poor choice to make at that time and I apologize." Though Sadie didn't fully accept his explanation, he sounded quite sincere in his regret.

Austin continued. "Mrs. Hoffmiller would like to know how you found out what had happened and when you called me."

Grant nodded. "Master Liam came outside to tell me what had happened. He said the Hoffmillers had gone to their room and he needed my help in gathering up the staff. I called you from the kitchen. You knew within seconds of my own awareness, my lord."

Sadie scowled at the title. Though she knew it was common in England, it just rubbed her wrong. In her Christian mind there was only one person fit to be called Lord, and it certainly wasn't Austin Melcalfe.

"Is this true, Liam? Did you find Grant outside?"

"Yes," Liam said. Sadie half-expected him to tack "sir" on the end of his answer.

"Mrs. Land," Austin said, waiting until she looked up and met his eyes. "When you came upstairs did you see anyone else?"

She paused for a good three seconds, making her answer that much more unbelievable. "No, sir," she finally said. "I didn't."

Austin nodded as if satisfied with her response—something Sadie certainly wasn't—before scanning the rest of the staff. "And who was the last person to see John Henry today?"

No one answered and Sadie shifted her weight. How could they answer such an impossible question? None of them knew if they were the *last* person to see John Henry. Well, except whoever murdered him, but she didn't think Austin was being clever.

"What he means," Sadie interrupted, unable to hold back, "is who saw John Henry *today*." She looked up at Austin who was scowling at her. She scowled right back. He reminded her of Detective Madsen, one of the detectives on her neighbor's murder case who had rubbed Sadie wrong from the very beginning. In hindsight she wished she'd stood up to Madsen a little more in the beginning and she did not want to repeat the mistake. Giving in to Austin would only feed his already inflated ego.

Still no one spoke, but Sadie caught Mrs. Land glancing up at Liam nervously. Sadie didn't understand how the woman could be intimidated by Liam, who looked pale and rigid despite his position of authority. After another moment, Mrs. Land looked back into her lap.

"He rang for breakfast this morning," Grant finally said. "Around seven. I had Charlotte take it up to him. He then called for lunch around eleven—earlier than usual. Charlotte took it up as well." He looked at Liam once he stopped speaking. Liam was looking intently at nothing and no one—seemingly content to turn over the entire situation to Austin while he lost himself in his own thoughts.

"So you didn't actually see John Henry at all today?" Austin clarified.

Grant shook his head. "Charlotte retrieved the lunch tray around two o'clock."

Austin turned toward a redheaded maid—Charlotte, Sadie assumed—who seemed to both shrink and straighten under his gaze. "Did you see John Henry when you picked up the tray?" Austin asked.

"No, sir," Charlotte said, glancing up slightly, then looking back down at her knees again. "The tray was in the hall."

Austin nodded, and Charlotte relaxed. "Did anyone else see John Henry today?" Austin asked, scanning the faces once again.

Everyone shook their heads.

"John Henry kept mostly to the earl's room—even took his meals there," Grant said. "We saw very little of him about the house. I took a tea tray up to Master Liam in the earl's room after serving Mrs. Hoffmiller and her daughter this afternoon—John Henry wasn't there."

"When you were with your father," Austin said, turning to Liam, "was John Henry there as well?"

"Yes," Liam said. "He was there when I arrived in my father's room this morning. I asked to be alone with my father until it was time to leave."

"Did John Henry indicate where he was going while you stayed with the earl?"

Liam shook his head, pushing his hands into his pockets as if he were being reprimanded. "No." Everyone looked at him, and Sadie expected him to expound on his answer, but he didn't.

"But he had to have come down from the earl's room at some point," Sadie said, realizing as she said it that John Henry must have also been in the sitting room when he was attacked . . . in fact, his shoes had been flush to the floor as though he'd been standing. She thought about the expression on his face—shock. For an instant she pictured what it could have looked like for John Henry standing behind the curtains, in the dark, waiting for . . . something, and then the curtain was whipped back. Before John Henry could even process what was happening, the poker was shoved through his heart. Sadie shivered at the visualization and though she hoped she was wrong, it was an incredibly clear image and all the details fit—except why he would be hiding behind the curtain in the first place? Wouldn't he have screamed? Would the poker have killed him instantly, or would his death have taken a few minutes? Sixteen sets of eyes staring at her brought her back to the present.

"No one saw him come down?" She looked specifically at Grant who was supposed to be "on hand at all times" according to Austin. But he hadn't seen John Henry come down and he hadn't been there when Sadie and Breanna found the body and he hadn't heard their screams for help.

The staff either shook their heads or made no expression at all—except for Mrs. Land who continued fidgeting with her smock and staring at the floor. Why wasn't she telling the truth? Could *she* have moved the body? Mrs. Land's thin arms and sloped shoulders made that thought ludicrous. The woman might be able to lift a turkey in and out of the oven—if it was a small one. No way could she drag a grown man, let alone pull him off the wall he'd been pinned to. But she knew something, and gauging from her behavior so far, it likely wouldn't be an easy thing to get out of her. Someone had cleaned up the bloodstain on the wall—where were the cleaning products kept? Were they accessible for anyone who needed them, or would someone need keys to a janitorial closet?

"I assume the police said they're on their way?" Austin asked, turning toward Liam, who looked at Breanna for the answer.

"Yes," Breanna offered from where she stood at the back of the room. She looked at her chunky watch. "They should be here any minute."

"Then let's do a thorough search of the house before they get here," Austin said.

"I think we should wait for Scotland Yard," Sadie said. "This is a crime scene."

Austin looked at her as if he'd love nothing more than to duct tape her mouth shut. "Scotland Yard operates out of London. We deal with the Police Authority here." He turned back to the staff. "We'll search the estate. The police don't need this kind of nonsense filling up their afternoon."

Sadie tried not to glare at the man, but it was very hard. Austin called each of the staff members by name, assigning them portions of the house and grounds to search. Sadie realized that Austin must manage the estate in addition to the earl's holdings. He was certainly comfortable with being in charge. Liam continued to hang back, hands in his pockets.

"We'll meet back in twenty minutes," he said as the staff began to mill about. "I'm sure John Henry is taking a break somewhere, so let's find him."

Sadie watched the staff leave the room. Austin had sent most of them out in pairs, but Sadie found that a far from optimal arrangement. "They aren't going to find a man taking a smoke break," she said to Austin as the last two staff members passed through the door. "They're going to find a corpse. Don't you think they ought to have been prepared for that?"

Austin shrugged, and turned to look at Sadie. "I mustn't believe they are going to find a corpse then, must I?" His hazel eyes were hard, relentless as they stared her down, telling her in no uncertain terms that he was not a man used to being questioned about anything.

"Do you really think we would make this up?" Sadie asked him, feeling a bit more bold than she had when the staff had been there. "Why would we do that?"

"Why would someone kill the earl's nurse in the first place?" Austin questioned, crossing his arms. "If someone did kill him, why use a fireplace poker in the sitting room? And if someone *did* kill the earl's nurse with a fireplace poker in the sitting room, why move the body? Do you really think those questions have an easier answer than why two American women, one of whom will become a countess if things work out just right, wouldn't make up a story that ensures they miss their plane so as to stay at the earl's estate a few more days? Every minute helps build a bridge, right, Mrs. Hoffmiller?"

High Tea Lemon Cookies

*Shawn will eat half the cookies—hide some of them!

Cookies
2 cups butter (room temperature)
2/3 cup powdered sugar
1 teaspoon grated lemon zest
1/2 teaspoon vanilla
1 3/4 cups flour
1 1/2 cups cornstarch (this is not a typo ☺)

Preheat oven to 350 degrees. Beat butter until creamy. Add powdered sugar and mix until light and fluffy. Add lemon zest and vanilla. Beat well. Add flour and cornstarch and beat until well combined. Do NOT refrigerate.

Roll by hand into 1-inch balls or use a well-packed scoop, placing cookies about an inch apart as they do not spread much while baking.

Bake 15 minutes on ungreased cookie sheets until bottom edges are light brown. Cool on wire racks before frosting with lemon glaze (below).

Makes about 5 dozen small delicate cookies.

Lemon Glaze
4 tablespoons butter
3/4 teaspoon grated lemon zest (get zest from lemon before juicing)
1/4 to 1/3 cup lemon juice*
2 1/2 cups powdered sugar

In a medium bowl combine butter, zest, juice, and sugar. Stir until well mixed. Place a piece of wax paper beneath the wire racks where the cookies have been cooling and drizzle glaze over cookies.

*For best results when using lemons, choose the largest lemon you can find and roll it on the counter for about a minute before juicing in order to get as much juice as possible. Zest only the yellow part of the lemon peel; the white portion leaves a bitter taste.

CHAPTER 7

Sadie was absolutely stunned by Austin's accusation that they would lie about a dead body as part of some gold-digging scheme. Her head and chest prickled with shocked rage and indignation. "I—I can't believe you just said that! You think we'd make this up for a . . . a title?" It was so completely ridiculous that she could barely say it out loud. She looked at Breanna who looked as shocked as Sadie felt, and then at Liam, who was also stunned into silence.

"Oh, don't take it so personally," Austin said, every word dripping with patronizing arrogance. "It happens all the time. My point was simply that there are a lot of questions in the world, woman, and what we need now are answers—which no one seems to have."

Woman?

Sadie counted to ten very slowly in her head to keep from exploding. She looked to Liam to step in, to defend Breanna, but he was looking at the floor as if deep in thought, his hands still in his pockets. Breanna's face had turned red as she too looked at Liam for rescue.

Sadie was just opening her mouth to say something to defend Breanna's motives when Liam finally spoke.

"You're wrong, Austin," he said, his voice surprisingly calm. "Breanna doesn't want my title."

Sadie felt his defense was a bit deflated. Austin seemed to think the same thing. He shook his head. "You've been gone too long, cousin. You've forgotten how it works."

Liam let his eyes rest on Breanna before meeting those of his cousin. "Trust me on this, Austin. I know how it works, but not everyone plays the same game. Breanna isn't after my title, and neither of them would make this up. If they said they saw him, they saw him."

Austin didn't seem impressed by Liam's explanation, and he shrugged slightly as if the argument wasn't worth his efforts. Sadie was as steamed as an English teapot, and not willing to just let this go. She glanced quickly at Breanna, ready to fire at Austin with all guns blazing, until she saw Breanna shake her head slightly. Sadie clamped her teeth together so hard her jaw hurt. Restraining herself took so much of her focus that she missed the first few words of what Liam was saying to Breanna.

" . . . okay here while I check on my father?"

"I'll oversee the search," Austin said as he turned and headed out of the room.

That's it? Sadie thought. Austin could come in and say those kinds of things and both Breanna and Liam were okay with just letting it go? Sadie's blood was still sizzling in her veins.

"We're fine," Breanna said in answer to Liam's question. Sadie hadn't dared answer, afraid she'd breathe fire if she opened her mouth. "We'll wait here—is your phone on?"

Liam nodded, looking a bit sheepish, and then left the room, closing the double doors behind him.

As soon as they were alone, Sadie dropped her arms, balled her hands into fists and let fly the things she'd been holding back. "Of all the arrogant, patronizing, pigheaded, arrogant—"

"You said arrogant already," Breanna cut in. She walked over to one of the padded chairs the staff had occupied a few minutes earlier and plopped down.

"I can't believe he said that," Sadie finished, though Breanna's interruption had thrown her off her rant. Shouldn't Breanna be offended by the insinuations Austin had made? "Am I the only one who thinks he's out of line? No matter who he is or what he's done to help the earl he has no right to say things like that." She watched Breanna for a nod or some other gesture to indicate she agreed with her mother, but Breanna just looked thoughtful.

"Who has the energy to be offended?" Breanna said.

"I do!" Sadie responded automatically, rapping her knuckles on the large desk next to her.

Breanna let out a breath and met Sadie's eyes. "The reason Liam said what he said—about my not wanting the title—is because last night I told him I don't think we should see each other after we get back to the U.S. I didn't want to tell you about it until we got home." She crossed her arms over her chest as if trying to comfort herself, or shield herself from Sadie's reaction.

"What?" Sadie was stunned. Both at Breanna ending the relationship as well as her keeping it a secret. Sadie hated being out of the loop in regard to . . . well, anything.

Sadie really liked Liam. He was the first serious boyfriend Breanna had ever had and, despite the strange circumstances of his life, Sadie felt they were a good match, which was the first step in overcoming any difficulty in a relationship—well, except maybe this one.

Breanna continued, "It's been a difficult decision to make, Mom, but as much as I care about him, I know I can't live this way. And pretending that maybe I can isn't going to make it any better. It didn't work for his parents and I'd rather learn from their mistakes than make the same ones."

"And you told him this last night?" Sadie asked, imagining what it had been like for Liam to hear that. Poor Liam.

Breanna nodded. "It's been hanging between us this whole trip—whether we were working toward marriage somewhere down the road or not," she admitted. "And although we've both tried to ignore that it was the whole reason for this trip, he finally asked me outright what I expected would happen between us now that I'd seen this part of his life. I couldn't lie to him, Mom—even if it would have made the last bit of the trip easier. He deserved to know the truth."

"That you can't live this way?" Sadie offered, wanting to be absolutely clear on what had been said.

"That I *won't* live this way," Breanna clarified. "I didn't ask him to give it up for me or anything, but you've always told me that my future is based on my choices. It would be foolish for me to expect that my feelings for Liam will always be enough to overshadow the fact that I don't fit in here and I don't want this lifestyle. I don't want to run a household and manage servants. I don't want to spend my life in a foreign country away from my family, friends, and career. And pretending to agree with social systems I just don't feel are right would be giving up who I am. I won't do that to me or to Liam. He deserves to find someone more worthy of his . . . station, or at least someone ready to try. I'm not that girl."

Sadie was filled with pride mixed with sorrow at what this realization was costing her daughter. Love would not make all those other things disappear, but Sadie also knew that Breanna's feelings for Liam wouldn't go away because of her decision. What a heartbreaking reality. Poor Breanna. Poor Liam. "And what did Liam say when you told him this?" Sadie asked.

"He's been raised for this, Mom," she said, waving her hand at the opulent library. "He came to the States when he was young but he was still the son of an earl. Even when the people around him didn't know, he knew. He'd always planned to return to England when he needed to fulfill that responsibility—that's why he never became an American citizen, remaining true to the Crown, I guess. His duty and responsibilities were something he and his father talked about a lot, but he didn't expect to come into the title for a long time—Liam's grandfather lived to be eight-six years old and had been the earl for over forty years. His father has only been an earl for eighteen. To have it happen this soon changes everything."

"Everything?" Sadie asked.

Breanna dug into her pocket, producing a hair band. She pulled her hair into a ponytail at the base of her neck. It was her usual hairstyle at home, but she'd worn her hair down most of the week. Sadie knew that Liam loved Breanna's long dark hair, especially when she wore it so that it cascaded over her shoulders and down her back. "Liam called Portland his first life. It was his chosen life and he expected to enjoy it to its fullest before the earldom reached out for him—just as his father had. Becoming the tenth Earl of Garnett would one day become his second life."

Breanna kicked off her brown leather clogs and flexed her toes encased in brown-and-white striped socks. She seemed to be making a point, proving that she was not a countess. It hadn't crossed Sadie's mind that Breanna had been trying to act any part this week, but she had worn her nicer jeans and kept her hair down. For Breanna that was perhaps as much role-playing as she could stomach. She was done now—the pretenses were over. The thought made Sadie a little bit sad.

"It reached out to him sooner than he expected," Sadie summed up when it felt as though Breanna might not continue.

"And he's chosen to take its hand," Breanna said with just a touch of annoyance. She picked up one of the lemon cookies still sitting on the tray and shoved the whole thing in her mouth.

"But, really, does he have a choice? He's the heir," Sadie admonished while Breanna's cheeks bulged out like a chipmunk. She came around the front of the desk and leaned back against it—telling herself that having another cookie was a bad idea even if Breanna had had one. It was always hard to focus when there was food around, and she'd been doing so well up until now.

Breanna looked up at her mother and met her eyes directly. "You're the one who says we always have choices."

Sadie hated it when her children used her own words against her. "This might be a little different," Sadie said. "Can he turn it down?" She finally picked up a cookie, but tried to do the ladylike thing and just nibbled the edges.

"Why not?" Breanna asked. She waved a hand toward the double doors. "You met Austin—or *Lord* Melcalfe," she added with derision. "That's the kind of man Liam needs to be. Liam can barely talk to the staff let alone hire, fire, direct, or chastise them. For all his saying he was raised for this, he's not ready for this kind of responsibility and if he truly cares about the earldom he would want it to go to someone who could preserve its heritage—its *English* heritage." Breanna sighed. "Liam has lived in the U.S. for almost sixteen years and his memories of England revolve around boarding school and summer vacations spent with a governess. He doesn't have what it takes to manage the holdings of the earldom. As much as I love the man, even I can see that. He's a zoologist, and a good one at that. He doesn't belong here any more than I do, but I can see it and he can't."

"You love him?" Sadie asked, lifting her eyebrows and putting the cookie down on the tray. Her thoughts had been adequately hijacked. She'd assumed as much, but hadn't heard Breanna say it outright.

Breanna paused and seemed to sink into the chair a little bit. Her eyes filled with tears, causing Sadie to hurry across the room and sit on the arm of the chair. Breanna turned her head into Sadie's shoulder. "Oh, why couldn't he have just been a zoologist in Portland?" she asked in a quiet voice. "And have annoying parents who traveled the country in a Winnebago with a yappy little dog? I'd have even settled for half a dozen siblings who made holidays a nightmare so that we always fought about having to visit them." She sniffed and Sadie stroked her head as she cried. "Why did he have to be the son of an earl? Of all the rotten luck."

Sadie wasn't sure there were any answers to Breanna's questions, so she said nothing—something she didn't do very often. For nearly two minutes they stayed that way, then Breanna pulled away, wiping at her eyes that were only slightly red. It was as much of a breakdown as she'd allow herself. Breanna stood up and took a deep breath, working hard to get over her emotions.

"I'm sorry," Sadie said as Breanna walked to the windows behind the desk. Breanna folded her arms and looked out over the manicured gardens that could have been hers. She was beautiful, framed against the window, her strong cheekbones and full lips lit by the cloud-filtered amber light of evening. Sadie watched her from the arm of the chair. "I'm really sorry for both of you."

"Thanks, Mom," Breanna said with a grateful smile, glancing over her shoulder before looking back at the English sunset. "I'm so glad you came with me. I'd have been lost without you this week."

"I didn't do much." Sadie shrugged her shoulders, though she always liked a sincere compliment.

"You were my buffer," Breanna said, turning to face her. "And you let me enjoy this trip and keep my head on straight. Had it just been Liam and me—well, I might not have been able to be quite so objective and that would have made everything worse. It's better that this is over now rather than later when we've both let our expectations grow."

Sadie knew she wouldn't want Breanna to be anything less than honest with Liam, but that thought caused her to wonder about something. "Have you told Liam you love him?" she asked.

Breanna paused, then shook her head. "We've both said . . . things, but not that exact word." She looked at her mother strongly, staring down her nose slightly. "And you do not have my permission to tell him in my place."

"Of course not," Sadie said, offended that Breanna would think Sadie would share her personal thoughts. She'd only do something like that if she felt she had to. "I just wondered if he knew."

"I wasn't sure I knew until this trip. How ironic is that? I come here and simultaneously determine I am in love with a man I can't share a life with."

Sadie felt her own throat thicken with emotion to hear Breanna say such things, but she knew her emotion would only make it harder for Breanna. She thought back to the earlier comment Breanna had made about being glad Sadie had come so as to spare them both the ongoing pain of facing such a sad turn of events.

"Well, I'd have never forgiven you if you'd have left me behind," Sadie teased, trying to lighten the mood. "And though I'm sad things didn't work out differently between you and Liam, I'm glad we came. I mean, the English trifle alone was worth the trip. Do you think I could sweet-talk Mrs. Land into making it for us again? There ought to be some perks to staying a couple more days, right?"

"English trifle," Breanna repeated, not taking the opportunity to change the subject as she looked back at the window. "Maybe that's all this has been for me—trifling with something foreign."

Sadie didn't like any negativity associated with English trifle—it was too delicious for that—so she threw in her own symbolism. "But just like trifle, life comes in layers. This happens to be one of yours and so long as you learn the important things that ensure the next layer is just a little sweeter—well, then it's not wasted."

Breanna gave her a look that showed she wasn't buying it, but then she let out a breath. "Well, this *layer* has us caught in the middle of a murder mystery without a body."

"Which no one believes we really saw," Sadie added, disappointed that Breanna didn't appreciate her analogy.

"And without a Big Mac in sight to help us cope."

Sadie was poised to offer up another lecture on the wonderful aspects of English cuisine when the door to the library opened. Austin entered with a thin, gangly looking teenager following behind him. The young man looked as though he were wearing his father's clothes, as they all appeared too big for him. Sadie was trying to determine who he could possibly be when Austin introduced them to him.

"Breanna and Sadie Hoffmiller," he said formally. His eyes rested on Breanna for a moment and he looked concerned, something Sadie wouldn't have expected he was capable of. Sadie wondered if he could tell she'd been crying. Breanna's whole face didn't get blotchy like Sadie's did, but her eyes were still a little red. Breanna looked away from his gaze and after a moment, Austin continued. "This is Inspector Colin Dilree with the Police Authority of Exeter. He's here to take your statements."

CHAPTER 8

Inspector Dilree? Sadie thought, looking over the man in hopes of finding even the smallest sign of authority she expected from a homicide inspector. She saw none. Instead, he looked as though he'd dressed up as a detective for Halloween.

The inspector smiled, showing a slight gap between his two front teeth which made him look even younger. He hurried forward and held out his soft little hand. He wasn't much taller than Sadie, which meant Breanna had several inches on the man. "Pleased to meet you," he said, shaking Sadie's hand quickly before letting go. He seemed very excited to be here, which worried Sadie at least as much as his adolescent appearance. "Pleased to meet you," he repeated as he shook Breanna's hand as well.

He held a briefcase in his other hand and as soon as he finished his greetings, he moved around the desk and set his case on the floor. He began clearing everything to the upper left-hand corner of the desktop. Sadie watched as he stacked papers perfectly, squaring up the corners after each addition, then placed all the other little accessories on top of the stack, and more accessories on top of those. The result was a well-engineered pyramid that fit perfectly on the desk. Once finished with his creation, he moved his briefcase to the cleared area of wood and opened it, removing a couple of folders, a box of paper clips, a small stapler, and a collection of his own pens, placing them all on the desk in such a way as to make the desk look as though it was his very own. Sadie half-expected him to produce a family picture as well, but he didn't. Probably because he wasn't old enough to date, let alone have a family of his own. Was he really an inspector?

When he finally sat down, the huge desk came nearly to his chest—he didn't seem to notice. He smiled at them and asked, "Who shall I speak with first?"

Breanna and Sadie shared a look, but the inspector didn't give them a chance to answer his question.

"Miss Hoffmiller," he said, smiling at Breanna. "Let's start with you." He turned his eyes to Sadie. "If you'll be so good as to wait in the hall, then."

"Sure," Sadie said, still trying to process that this little man was the inspector assigned to the case. If his presence was any indication of the regard his entire department was giving to their report . . . well, then, Sadie wasn't holding out much hope. She followed Austin out of the library while reviewing the promise she'd made to Breanna about keeping out of the investigation. There had to be a loophole in their agreement to take into account the fact that someone had sent their son to take notes.

The staff was lined up in the hallway when she came out of the library—indoor staff on the right and outdoor staff on the left. They all looked various shades of glum, irritable, and downright nervous—the nervousness award going to Mrs. Land who still wouldn't meet Sadie's eyes. Liam wasn't there. Neither was Grant.

Austin took his place against the wall across from the library door, apart from the staff. He crossed his arms over his chest and he watched her like he had when they'd first met. The only way Sadie could think to describe his gaze was piercing. It was difficult not to straighten her shirt or tuck her hair behind her ear under his scrutiny.

"Liam's with the earl," he said, tempting Sadie to tell him that she knew that already. "I had your bags taken back to your room. Liam didn't feel it wise to head for London tonight."

Sadie probably should have thanked Austin for the information, but she had too much pride, especially where he was concerned. Besides, she felt he still owed her an apology for saying what he'd said about Breanna. Unfortunately, she also had questions that needed answers and he was the only one she thought would talk to her right now. After a few seconds, he pulled his phone out of his pocket, frowned, and then typed out a text message before returning it to his pocket and looking at Sadie again.

"Where's Grant?" Sadie questioned, finding a blank space next to the library doors where she could lean against the wall like everyone else.

"The inspector gave him an assignment," Austin said simply.

He didn't offer anything else and Sadie scanned the faces of the staff, hoping to glean whether they had found anything during their search. She hated directing all her questions to Austin, feeling that he took great satisfaction in her ignorance each time she showed it, but finally had no choice. Even though she was pretty sure she knew the answer, someone had to say it out loud. "Did anyone find John Henry?" she asked.

"If we did, he'd be standing here," Austin answered, as patronizing as ever. "Or I suppose lying here with a poker in his chest for all of us to see. However, you'll notice there is no body on the rug."

The man was insufferable.

"Are there more inspectors looking through the house now?"

Sadie asked. The body had to be here; if the staff didn't find it, surely the police would.

"There is one inspector," Austin said. "And he is talking to your daughter. I showed him through the sitting room and he took some pictures and samples."

"He came alone?" Sadie said, dejected by the proof that the police really hadn't taken Breanna's call seriously.

"Tomorrow is New Year's Eve," Austin said. "Exeter is hosting a Hogmanay celebration and the Police Authority is in charge of supervising the road closures and such. They are apparently unable, or unwilling, to spare many of their men."

"Hogmanay?" Sadie said, trying to pronounce it like he did, stressing the last syllable.

"It's the Scottish version of New Year's Eve," Austin said as though she should already know this. "A loud, obnoxious festival with lots of fire and shouting and basic cacophony."

"So a big ol' party trumps a murder at the earl's estate? I thought you people were important."

The staff looked at her in shock; Austin gave her a slight smile in response. She couldn't tell if he was being arrogant or if part of him liked that someone was standing up to him. Sadie put her hands behind her back and looked at the floor, preparing herself for a long and awkward wait until it was her turn to talk with the inspector. She'd rather not spend that wait talking with Austin who seemed incapable of saying anything without attaching an insult to it. Expecting several minutes before it would be her turn, she was surprised when the library door opened.

"Your turn," Breanna said dryly, giving her mother a look that seemed to warn her not to expect much. Fabulous.

Sadie entered the library, and watched as Inspector Dilree

repositioned a chair. He moved it a few inches to the left, pulled back to observe it, then moved it a few more inches to the left before observing it again. Then he moved it several inches to the right instead. Sadie stopped a few feet away, trying not to sigh in irritation as he repositioned the chair three more times before he finally accepted it was in its optimal location.

"Please have a seat, Mrs. Hoffmiller," he said, indicating the chair before scurrying to the other side of the desk and taking his own seat.

"So, Mrs. Hoffmiller," he said, picking up a pen and removing a piece of paper from the top file. "Please tell me, in your own words, what you encountered in the sitting room."

Sadie wasn't sure whose words he expected she might use instead of her own, but she complied, spending a few minutes to give him a detailed report of exactly what had happened in the sitting room. Inspector Dilree scribbled madly on the paper as she spoke, his shoulders curving inward as if protecting the paper from a strong breeze despite the fact that he was in a library.

"Right," the inspector said, quickly reviewing his notes. "Did you see any blood or tissue?"

The word *tissue* made Sadie grimace and she shook her head. He lifted his head enough to peer at her. "Is that a no?"

"No," Sadie said. "I mean yes, it's a no, but no I didn't see any blood or . . . or stuff—well, other than the bloodstain on his shirt and I assume there would have been blood on the wall—but the body was in the way, of course."

Dilree nodded. "Did you smell anything?"

She tried to remember, then shook her head. "No."

"Did you hear anything?"

Like what? she wondered. *Dead body sounds?* "No, I didn't hear anything."

"Very good," the inspector said, sitting up straight. "That will be all."

"That's it?" Sadie asked.

"Yes," Dilree said, looking quite pleased with himself. "That's it."

Sadie watched him for a few moments, comparing everything she knew about detectives and inspectors and investigations. Not one of them fit this man. "Did you see the sitting room wall, the missing plaster?"

"Yes, madam," he said. "It's been suggested that the plaster has been damaged there for a period of time, something about new window treatments a few months back that resulted in the injury to the wall."

"Who suggested that?" Sadie asked.

The inspector just smiled and tapped his paper. "It's in my report; no need to worry yourself about it."

"Are you a homicide detective, Inspector?"

His expression didn't flinch in the slightest. "I'm a recorder," he said, grinning broadly. "It's a unique position where I document certain cases and reports."

"Document?" Sadie repeated.

Dilree nodded. "Yes, I take statements, organize reports, manage case files—that kind of thing."

"And you were sent here to document this case—not investigate it?"

Dilree nodded sharply. "Yes, exactly."

Sadie let out a breath. "Will they be sending a real inspector?"

Now Dilree's face fell a bit. "I *am* a real inspector, madam," he said. "A recorder."

"I didn't mean to offend you," Sadie said, trying to offer a smile she didn't feel. "I just meant would they be sending a *homicide* inspector. In America these kind of things are investigated with the assumption that people don't make up a murder."

It was the wrong thing to say. Inspector Dilree's face hardened. "In England," he said, "we proceed with a bit more caution, especially when told that those reporting certain circumstances are unreliable. We are proceeding as we see fit."

"Someone told you we were unreliable?" Sadie asked. "Who?"

"That is not information I can share," he said. "Let's just say that we do not take such claims lightly—unless given reason to do so."

"And has it crossed your mind that perhaps whoever said we weren't reliable could be the very person who is responsible for this crime? Was it the same person who suggested the damage to the plaster was a result of new curtains?"

That stumped him, but only for a moment. "If in fact my documents show good cause for there to have been a homicide, a homicide detective will be sent out. It will be determined upon the completion of my investigation. I've already taken pictures and samples of the area where you say there was a body. We'll have those results in a few days."

Days? she repeated in her mind. "I see."

"Please send in . . ." He looked over the paper in front of him until he found the name he was looking for. "Mrs. Land, please."

Sadie stood to leave the room, but had just turned when the door opened. Grant came in holding a large metal bucket, similar to a garbage can. At first, Sadie couldn't see what was in it. Then Grant reached in and pulled out a fireplace poker, causing Sadie to startle.

"Pokers?" she said out loud, shocked by the sight before her as she turned back to look at the inspector. "You had him gather all the pokers?"

CHAPTER 9

Dilree came around the front of the desk, looking quite pleased with himself. "Please lay them out on the floor," he said to Grant who complied, though he didn't seem to like being ordered around by this man. Sadie watched, shocked, as Grant laid out all the pokers. A total of seven were soon lined up on the library floor.

"Some of the fireplaces have been converted to natural gas," Grant explained. "And others have fireplace stands only as decoration, but I brought all of them."

Sadie continued to stare at the display he'd set out on the floor. There were three different styles of both handle and the end hook—some had a double hook on the end, others just one—but Sadie's eyes were immediately drawn to two pokers with brass handles that looked exactly like the handle she'd seen sticking out of John Henry's chest. She looked carefully at the one closest to her—it had a thin shaft, thinner than the others, and though it did have a small hook on the end, the point was sharper and finer than the others. The longer she looked at it the more it looked like an actual weapon—almost like those thin swords used for fencing, only with a hook—or barb—on the end. Despite herself, Sadie pictured how perfectly it would fit between the intercostal spaces of John Henry's chest. The vision was very *CSI*-ish and she could imagine the metal pushing through John Henry, where the delicate—but deadly—hook then grabbed the plaster, holding John Henry to the wall. She swallowed at the image of it. What a horrible way to go—and yet no one seemed to believe it had actually happened.

"Do any of these look familiar to you, Mrs. Hoffmiller?" Dilree asked.

"The ones with the brass handles," she said, pointing at the one that had brought on such a dark vision of John Henry's death. She looked up at Grant. "There's one missing, isn't there?"

The butler looked uncomfortable and didn't answer, but he seemed to be thinking about it. The inspector came to stand in front of the pokers, rubbing his smooth face with his hand as if he had a beard, which Sadie felt sure he couldn't grow even if he wanted to.

"How many rooms have brass sets?" she asked, then immediately looked toward the large stone fireplace in the library. A wrought-iron stand was placed just to the left of the hearth—two brass handles, one for the broom and one for the shovel, reflected the final rays of sunset filtering through the windows. Of course the poker was missing from the stand because—wait. "Did you gather the poker from this room?" she asked. When Grant still didn't answer, Inspector Dilree looked up at the butler.

"Grant!" she nearly yelled, completely losing her cool. "Answer me!"

Grant stiffened and the inspector looked at her in surprise. An awkward silence descended between the three of them, causing Sadie's cheeks to heat up with embarrassment.

"That will be all," the inspector said to her.

"No, wait," Sadie said, putting up her hands as if she could wave away her reaction. "I'm sorry, Grant, I didn't mean to yell." She took a breath to calm herself. "Did you gather the poker from this room?"

There was silence for a few moments as Sadie waited. Thankfully Grant spoke before Dilree had the chance to tell her to leave again. "No, madam," he said. "I did not gather the poker from this room. Besides the brass set in the library, there are two other brass sets in the house—one in the earl's sitting room and one in the billiard room."

"And they were both in place?" the inspector asked.

"Yes, sir," Grant said, nodding.

A wind seem to rush through Sadie's chest. That there was a missing poker lent credibility to Sadie's story. That the missing poker had a brass handle and was just a couple rooms away from the sitting room said even more. She tried not to appear smug as she looked back at Inspector Dilree, assuming he'd want to ask her more detailed questions now.

However, he didn't. "That will be all, Mrs. Hoffmiller," he said, turning back to the desk. "And thank you, Grant, for your help. Please see that Mrs. Land is shown in."

"But, don't you want to—"

"That will be all," Dilree said, sitting down. He picked up his pen and made some notes.

Sadie couldn't believe he wanted her to leave. "But—"

"Mrs. Hoffmiller," he said in a booming voice she wouldn't have thought him capable of. "Please send in Mrs. Land. If I have any more questions for you I assure you I will ask."

Sadie pressed her lips together and pivoted on her heel, practically stomping her way to the door. Grant was already there and held the door open for her, his expression impassive.

As soon as she saw Austin, Sadie knew who had told the police that the report they'd received was unreliable. She could see it now—him hanging up with Grant and immediately calling the police and explaining that they had a couple American houseguests with Agatha Christie complexes. That the police sent anyone at all was perhaps a point in their favor, but she looked at Austin now with more than just anger and annoyance.

"The inspector would like to speak with you, Mrs. Land," Grant said, still holding the door open. Mrs. Land turned a shade paler, but didn't look at anyone in particular as she headed for the library. The door shut behind her and Grant took up his post beside the door as if it were an everyday occurrence to be assisting an inspector with interviews.

Sadie's thoughts remained squarely on Austin, who stood against the wall with everyone else, though they gave him ample room on either side. "Why were you in Exeter today?" Sadie asked him, standing next to Breanna and across from Austin.

"Business," he said simply. "I had a meeting with the manager of one of the earl's shops."

"Where do you live?" she asked. "You haven't been here since we arrived."

"Haven't I?" Austin asked, raising one eyebrow. "Perhaps I have been here the whole time, but simply chose to keep to myself. It's a large house, Mrs. Hoffmiller. All kinds of things can happen without the other occupants being aware of it."

His insinuation that he could have been here these two days without any of them knowing about it gave Sadie a shiver. What was he trying to say anyway? Why tell her that at all?

"I left Southgate early this morning. When Grant called, I

cut short my meeting to return. I can give you the shop manager's information if you'd like to check up on me."

Sadie narrowed her eyes a little more and didn't reply.

"Liam said he would work on finding new flights for you," Austin continued, changing the subject. "Mrs. Land has assured me that dinner will be ready at eight. You're welcome to retire to your room until then."

Sadie didn't know how that was possible, since there didn't seem to be any dinner preparations underway when she'd been in the kitchen, and Mrs. Land had spent the last hour up here, not cooking in the kitchen.

"Does she need any help with the meal?" Breanna offered, apparently mirroring Sadie's own thoughts.

Sadie thought that was a great idea and hurried to help explain the offer. "Breanna and I are pretty handy in the kitchen and obviously don't have anything . . . to . . . do." Her voice trailed off in reaction to the looks she and Breanna received from Austin and the staff. They looked at them as if they'd suggested everyone build birdcages out of popsicle sticks while they waited.

"Dinner will be at eight," Austin repeated, his tones clipped. "And you will both remain *out* of the kitchen. You are guests, not part of the staff."

She wondered if he treated all guests so rudely. "I only meant that seeing as how Mrs. Land is shorthanded and this afternoon has taken a time-consuming turn that we could—"

"No," Austin said sharply. "It's simply not done. Guests do not help run the household. Mrs. Land has ample assistance."

Sadie clenched her teeth. "Fine," she said in surrender. "I guess we'll be in our room. If you have some needlepoint we could work on, we'd be ever so grateful for the distraction." The ladies were always doing needlepoint in the Regency romance novels. She hoped Austin understood her insinuation, but didn't wait to see if he'd come up with an equally quippy comeback. Instead she turned to Breanna, who nodded her agreement. They fell in step with one another, heading for the staircase.

"He's watching us," Breanna said, glancing quickly over her shoulder when they reached the bottom of the stairs.

Sadie nodded. She swore she could feel his eyes on her back.

"Something really weird is happening here," Breanna continued.

"You mean other than bodies stabbed with fireplace pokers?" Sadie asked sarcastically.

"That then mysteriously disappear so that no one believes us," Breanna added with a frown. "I showed the inspector the pictures on my cell phone—but he didn't even ask for a copy; just told me to hold on to them."

"The poker came from the library," Sadie told her, since they were sharing information. "There are two other sets like it in the house, but the poker from the library was missing from its stand. Whoever went into that sitting room had to bring the poker with them."

"Premeditation," Breanna said, shaking her head. "And they still act like we're making this up."

"You know," Sadie said carefully as they reached the top of the stairs. "There's really only one way to convince them we're telling the truth."

"Find John Henry?" Breanna suggested. "He's got to be around here somewhere, right?"

Sadie's heart leapt with hope that Breanna was beginning to see things her way—that, like it or not, they *were* involved and that they could very well be the solution. "Or find out who killed him and why everyone seems to be working together to keep it a secret."

They reached their door and Breanna turned to her mother. "Do you think that's it? Some kind of conspiracy?"

Sadie shrugged. "It has certainly crossed my mind. And I've got a feeling that we're going to be shipped to London first thing tomorrow. I had thought maybe having an investigation would mean we'd be ordered to stay—but since they sent a secretary to document everything instead of investigate, I think we're out of luck. "

Breanna bit her bottom lip for a moment, then let it go and nodded. "I agree. You can count me in," she said with a nod before pulling open the door. "And consider yourself released from your promise. You are now free to put your nose into absolutely anything you like."

CHAPTER 10

Sadie raised her eyebrows once they were in their room and the door was shut. "Released? Really?" She crossed her arms over her chest. "Now, you're not going to go back on that, are you? Get my hopes up and then tell me that I'm diseased again?"

"Diseased?" Breanna asked, looking confused.

"You called it Detectivitis," Sadie said.

"Are we really going to get caught up in semantics, Mom?"

Sadie glared at her, but Breanna managed a small smile. She held out her hand, as if inviting Sadie to shake on it. "I give you permission to put your nose in things," Breanna said.

Sadie grinned, basking in the feeling of power only produced when a grown woman gets her way. She took Breanna's hand. "Deal."

They smiled at each other—sealing the agreement.

"So, what do we know so far?" Breanna asked, heading to her framed backpack she'd brought as luggage. "Did you bring a pad of paper?"

"Of course." Sadie always packed well. She opened her bag and shuffled through her sewing kit, address book, recipe book, lint roller, and collection of Ziploc bags that contained a myriad of lotions, cleansers, and other hygiene essentials like shaving cream and Preparation H—for bags under her eyes, of course. Finally she found both pads of paper she'd brought with her. "Full or half-sheet?"

"Either one," Breanna said. She was going through her carry-on. "I can't find my pen."

"Oh, I've got pens," Sadie said. "Or do you want a pencil?"

"Doesn't matter," Breanna said, still digging. Finally she let out an exasperated breath and stopped looking. "Pen."

"Ballpoint, felt-tip, or gel? I've got a couple of Sharpies too, but they'll bleed through the paper."

"O-kay," Breanna said, eyeing her mother strangely as she climbed up onto the bed and crossed her legs. "Ballpoint."

"What color?"

"For heaven's sake, Mom, are you really this neurotic?"

"Don't you mean 'are you really this organized'?"

"At some level it becomes the same thing."

Sadie cocked her head to the side. "Do you or do you not want one of my pens? Because if you *do* want one of my pens I think you owe me an apology."

Breanna took a breath and put out her hand, palm up. "Yes, I want your pen. I'm sorry."

Sadie leaned toward her and cupped her hand around her ear. "What was that?"

"I'm sorry with cream, sugar, and chocolate ganache on top?"

Sadie smiled at the saying she'd taught them as children. Shawn was the only kid in the fourth-grade spelling bee who could spell both *ganache* and *frittata*. That had been a proud day.

Sadie placed the pen in Breanna's hand. "Apology accepted,"

she said with a nod, returning the rest of her writing instruments to her bag.

"Okay, so, other than seeing John Henry and his unexplained disappearance, what do we know?" Breanna asked again.

Sadie opened her mouth to answer, but paused, scowling. What *did* they know? A lot of very strange things had happened, but did they *know* anything for sure? Breanna seemed to be thinking the same thing. "Well, we know Mrs. Land is hiding something."

Breanna hurried to write it down. "Right—what else?"

"The staff was gone both when we found John Henry the first time and when we discovered the body had been moved," Sadie offered.

"What if they were hiding from us?" Breanna asked. Sadie pictured them all secreted away in nooks or crannies watching her and Breanna run out of the sitting room and then into the kitchen. The idea made her shiver.

Breanna wrote down a note about the missing staff.

"The other cook ran off," Sadie said, pointing at the paper so that Breanna would be sure to write that down.

Breanna looked up at her mother, her eyebrows puckered. "I don't think you told the staff about her running off when you recounted everything in the library."

"I didn't?" Sadie asked, reviewing her own words. "Austin interrupted right about then, didn't he? He threw me off." One more thing to hold against the man.

"I wonder what Mrs. Land would think of that," Breanna offered.

Sadie shrugged, wishing she'd included the information so that she could have seen Mrs. Land's expression. Too late now, but perhaps she'd have another chance to watch Mrs. Land's reaction to the news. "We also know from the heel marks in the rug that someone dragged the body—"

"Which means it was probably just one person," Breanna interjected, writing as she spoke. "Two people would have just lifted him and avoided creating any evidence, don't ya think?"

They continued sharing suspicions for another fifteen minutes before running out of ideas. As Sadie had feared in the beginning, they didn't know many specifics.

"Maybe the butler did it?" Breanna said, with a wry smile. "Isn't that how it usually works in those mystery novels?"

"Actually," Sadie said, wriggling a little bit—she loved knowing details other people didn't—"the butler doesn't do it—it's cliché. The butler makes an ideal suspect due to his intimate knowledge of the house, but very rarely is he actually guilty—mostly because he has no motive. Being a butler is a highly respected position in a household, and they have to be absolutely trustworthy in order to hold so much power."

Breanna looked at her incredulously. "O-kay," she said with sarcastic emphasis. "I'm totally creeped out that you know that, but there isn't much that points to Grant anyway, other than him being conveniently missing during the time we needed help—but everyone was conveniently missing during that time anyway."

"Exactly," Sadie said. "That's not to say that he doesn't deserve the same scrutiny anyone else gets—but I'm just saying."

"Duly noted," Breanna said. She glanced toward the door. They hadn't been there too long, but knowing that important things were taking place downstairs made the time seem longer.

"Do you think the inspector is finished yet?" Sadie asked, then hurried to add, "Or perhaps I should just call him a *recorder* since that's his official title." She shook her head, then peered over the pad of paper. "Did you write about someone telling him that we couldn't be trusted?"

"Yes," Breanna said, nodding as she placed the tip of her pen on the line where she'd written about it. "So, now what?"

"I think we need to talk to Mrs. Land," Sadie said. "She's lying."

"But do you think she'll tell us anything just because we ask?"

Sadie nodded as she went back to her bag and looked for her recipe journal. It took only a few seconds and she held it up triumphantly. "She'll have no choice."

Breanna looked at the book with a doubtful expression on her face. "Because you're armed with your recipe book?"

"No, because the woman lost her kitchen help and has a house-ful of people—some she expected would be gone today—that she still has to cook for. Not to mention the fact that she's spent the last hour and a half dealing with all this. It's after six, so there is no way she has time to get dinner on the table by eight if she's doing it all by herself, which means she's likely to be running around crazy about now."

"Austin said you weren't allowed in the kitchen," Breanna re-minded her. Sadie could see her hesitation. It was one thing to make a list, quite another for Breanna to break the rules—a drawback for being such a good girl, Sadie supposed. She hoped Breanna could make some exceptions to her internal codes of right and wrong—it had been her idea to start looking into things, after all.

"Austin not wanting us in the kitchen is just one more reason why that's exactly where we need to be." She looked at Breanna strongly before she bent over to take off her shoes. Once her shoes were off, she padded to her suitcase and removed her orange Crocs—they were so comfy and since she expected to be on her feet for the next couple of hours, they were exactly what she needed. She slipped her feet into the spongy goodness and made eye contact with Breanna again. "Of everyone we have met, talked to, and dealt with, who is it that stands out in your mind as the most suspicious?"

"Mrs. Land," Breanna said, giving Sadie a half smile that indicated she knew very well that wasn't the answer Sadie was looking for.

"Okay, other than Mrs. Land," Sadie prodded.

"Fine," Breanna said with resignation. "Austin."

"Exactly," Sadie said with a triumphant nod of approval, going back to her suitcase for a few more necessities: her favorite apron, some lip balm, and her jogging whistle—just in case. On second thought, she put the apron back, not wanting to alert anyone to her destination before she arrived. The lip balm and whistle, however, went into her pocket while she continued explaining herself. "He shows up halfway through the explanation but knows everything that's happened, he's ordering people around, doubts your intentions with Liam, and is as hard and gloomy as a man ever was. Someone told the inspector we were lying and he's just the person who could influence the staff to go along with his deceit, not to mention he's the one who showed the inspector around the sitting room and could have given him an earful. I know he's Liam's cousin or whatever, but he's hiding something and he doesn't want us anywhere near it."

"Well, it's hard to argue with that," Breanna said, though she still seemed hesitant. She glanced at her watch. "We better hurry if we're really hoping to help with dinner," she said.

Sadie smiled, and waved Breanna toward the door. "After you."

CHAPTER 11

"I don't think we need to be quite so covert," Breanna said while Sadie pressed herself against the wall as they made their way toward the top of the stairs. Breanna walked a few feet behind her mother in the center of the hallway, not using any stealth at all.

"If Austin finds us, we're done for," Sadie said, moving slow enough to adequately see ahead but quick enough to make good progress.

"If Austin finds us, we come up with an excuse for being where we are—we can tell him we're hungry and want some more scones or something. If he finds us hugging the walls, he might suspect we're up to something."

Sometimes Breanna had no sense of adventure. "No matter what excuse we use, he'll stop us. We can't afford that to happen."

"Aren't there other staircases and servant entrances?" Breanna asked. "English movies always show a billion of 'em. Maybe we can find one and not have to go down the main stairs."

It's a valid thought, Sadie admitted to herself. But she knew exactly where the kitchen entrance was under the stairs and couldn't help but think that was the fastest way down—plus, Mrs. Land might suspect Sadie's motives if she showed up from another direction. Mostly, however, Sadie didn't want to waste time looking around and chancing getting lost. "This will be faster," she explained, scanning the way before them as they approached the stairs.

"Do you really think she'll tell us anything?" Breanna asked.

Sadie crouched lower so as to be better hidden by the seating area at the top of the stairs. "Well, the trick to getting her to talk is that we're not going to ask about John Henry at all," Sadie explained. "If we come right out and ask about him, she'll clam up—I'm sure of it. But there are plenty of other questions that need asking. People give themselves away even when talking about something else."

"I really think we should stay in our room like Austin asked," Breanna said. "Or maybe we should talk to Liam about all this first."

Sadie gave her daughter a withering look. If she didn't know Breanna was adopted, she'd have certainly guessed it now. Still, having been raised by Sadie, one would think the girl would have developed a little more appetite for adventure. "I thought you wanted to figure things out?" Sadie asked, exasperated by her daughter's changing moods. She respected the fact that Breanna was under a lot of pressure, but having such an apprehensive sidekick wasn't easy.

"I do want to figure things out," Breanna said with a slight shrug. "By putting our heads together and then talking to Liam—I'm even okay with us grilling Mrs. Land. But I'm not such a fan of sneaking around the estate like cat burglars."

"We put our heads together already and didn't come up with much except for several 'people of interest.' The only way to learn more about what's happening here is to start asking questions. We'll learn nothing just sitting in the room." She straightened as an idea came to mind. She looked back down the hallway from the direction they'd come. "I just had a thought: what if they bugged our room? We should have checked—they could be on to us."

Breanna closed her eyes for a moment and took a breath. Then she opened them and gave her mother a hard look. "Why would they bug our room?"

"Why would they move the body?" Sadie challenged.

"Um, maybe so no one would find it and they could tell the cops we had both lost our minds so no one would wonder 'whodunit'?"

Sadie placed her hand on Breanna's arm and smiled. "Exactly." She turned away from her daughter's expression, peering ahead and staying close to the wall. "If you want to stay in the room, that's fine," she said, using reverse psychology—at least she thought that was what she was doing, she wasn't sure if she really understood the term. "But if the deranged murderer comes by and stabs you through the heart with another poker because we didn't do everything we could to get to the bottom of this, don't come crying to me."

"I guess I couldn't come crying to you, seeing as how I'd be dead and all. But I'm glad to know that my murder would at least give you the satisfaction of being able to say you were right."

She made it sound so heartless when she said it like that. Sadie was trying to think of a way to soften her statement when she heard voices. She reached out and grabbed Breanna's hand, pulling her to the wall where she crouched down behind a chair set in an alcove at the top of the stairs. They had reached the landing of the staircase where the two wings connected, and could easily be spotted now that they were out of the shadows of the west wing. Luckily Breanna gave up the role of difficult daughter long enough to squeeze in behind Sadie. It took a little maneuvering, but Sadie was able to position herself so that she could see down the hall of the west wing, toward where the family rooms were housed. The voices came toward them, becoming clearer as they got closer.

" . . . doesn't make any sense why he's not here," the voice said. Sadie didn't know who it belonged to.

"He simply ran an errand, of course," the answering voice said. This one Sadie thought sounded like Grant.

"And left the earl unattended? He's never done that before. Not without telling someone. The man hasn't taken a day off in weeks."

Grant came into view, and when the other man appeared a moment later, Sadie recognized him as Kevin—the driver that was supposed to take Breanna and her to the airport. He'd been in the library when Liam had tried to question the staff.

Grant turned at the top of the stairs to face the driver. "You honestly believe that someone stabbed him with a poker in the sitting room? Really, Kevin, I'd be less surprised if the Queen herself asked me to take her skydiving." He began making his way down the stairs; Kevin hesitated. "Austin wants the Hoffmillers taken to London tomorrow morning," Grant continued. "Probably around nine o'clock. Can you be back by then?"

"Well, sure," Kevin said, though he didn't sound as if he were content with the answers he'd received. "But I still can't figure out . . ."

Whatever else was said was lost as Kevin hurried forward and the two men disappeared down the stairs. After assuring herself that the coast was clear, Sadie straightened and moved forward again, taking careful steps with Breanna right behind her. At the top of the stairs, Sadie ducked to look through the rungs of the stairway banister, scanning the foyer below. Grant and Kevin disappeared through the front door. She didn't see anyone else, but didn't want to be hasty. Too bad she didn't have a Marauder's Map like Harry

Potter. It would definitely come in handy to know where everyone in the household was right now. Then she'd know when the coast was truly clear. An invisibility cloak would be nice too, but she didn't want to seem greedy by wishing for both.

"Breanna? Sadie? What are you doing?"

Sadie sprung up and back, almost knocking over a table; she grabbed it in hopes of steadying herself as she looked around. Liam stood a few feet away, as if he'd just exited the east wing himself. Sadie chastised herself for doing what every idiot detective did in those tongue-in-cheek mysteries: only looking ahead, never checking the rear. Pathetic.

Breanna, who hadn't been crouching at all, didn't immediately move toward Liam, reminding Sadie that they weren't "together" anymore.

"Austin said you were staying in your room until dinner," he said, looking between them. Did she detect a bit of a reprimand in his look?

Sadie glanced at Breanna. She couldn't remember the excuse they'd come up with. After a couple of seconds, Breanna spoke up. "Um, well, Mom wanted to go to the kitchen to—"

"Have a scone," Sadie said, pronouncing it correctly and giving Breanna a strong look to communicate that she was not to abandon the game plan. She didn't know for sure if Breanna was about to give up, but didn't want to chance it. She had little doubt that Liam would be less than excited about their wanting to talk to Mrs. Land. "I'm simply starving and thought I could sneak in there for a bite or two. I'm not used to such late dinners." Of course they had high tea in the afternoon that helped with that, and Sadie had eaten three scones a couple hours ago, not to mention the cookies in the library, but she still needed an excuse to go to the kitchen.

"Let me ring for Grant, then, he'll bring up a tray."

"No, no, no," Sadie said. Realizing she'd come across far more indignant than she ought to, she forced a smile. "I mean, it's been such a trying afternoon for everyone, I hate to bother them. I'll just run down quickly and then return to my room. No need to bother anyone."

That pained expression returned to Liam's face. She could sense that he was only a few internal arguments away from saying, "Well, it doesn't exactly work that way around here." But she beat him to it.

"I know, I know, it's out of the ordinary—but it will be okay." She glanced quickly at Breanna's stiff expression. "Besides, don't you and Breanna have some things to discuss? Something about flights and going to London and things like that?" What a terrible mother, using her daughter for bait. And yet, it worked so well. Liam's face instantly lit up, although his expression didn't necessarily change; Breanna clenched her jaw.

He looked at her, "Actually, that's what I was doing—coming to see if you and I could talk for a few minutes."

Breanna hesitated long enough that Sadie felt the need to help her out. "That would be great," Sadie said in a mother-knows-best kind of voice. "I'll just head down to the kitchen so you two can talk in private. Breanna can fill me in later with whatever I need to know."

Unfortunately, it seemed that mentioning the kitchen was the wrong thing to say. "I still don't think that's such a good idea," Liam said. "We called a security company to stay here tonight, but they won't be here for another hour."

"So, you believe us?" Breanna asked, watching Liam carefully.

Liam paused a little too long before he answered. "Of course I believe you," he said.

"That's why you called in security?" Breanna pushed.

"Well, actually Austin thought it would be a good idea, to assure the staff that everything's okay—oh, and you guys too. We want you to feel safe here, and it's too late to head for London tonight."

"Austin doesn't believe us, does he?" Sadie asked.

Liam shrugged. "It doesn't matter what Austin thinks." His voice was gruff, almost angry when he said it. He looked at Breanna and waited for her to return his gaze. "Can we talk?" When she didn't answer right away, he added in a softer voice. "Please, Bre."

The pleading tone in his voice undid Sadie—and she wasn't even the one who had been dating the man. One look at Breanna showed it had had a similar effect on her. She lost her defensive stance. "Sure," she said, managing a small smile. But then she turned to her mother. "Do you want to wait for me?" Her strong look said she very much wanted Sadie to wait; it would likely force her conversation with Liam to be a short one.

Sadie pretended she wasn't such an expert at deciphering facial expressions. "No," she said, perhaps too fast. "I'll be fine."

"Alone?" Liam questioned.

Sadie smiled triumphantly and dug her jogging whistle out of her pocket. "Believe me," she said. "Anyone who messes with me will long regret it—this baby can cause permanent hearing damage. And if that's not enough, I've got my kung fu skills to fall back on." She crouched slightly and put her hands into a defensive Tae Kwon Do stance. Liam and Breanna both watched her with troubled expressions as she held the position for a few seconds. Surely they could see how good her form was.

"Mom took a self-defense class a few years ago," Breanna said. "We call her 'Sadie Lee' sometimes just to remind ourselves of what a danger she really is." Sadie thought Breanna's tone was a little flat for the level of important information she was giving out, but she didn't want to engage her daughter in yet another discussion-veiled argument. She was also glad Breanna was participating in a conversation with Liam. Sadie said good-bye before either of them came up with another way to hold her back, and walked down the stairs like any normal person would.

Once she reached the bottom however, she looked up to ensure that Breanna and Liam were out of sight, and then jumped behind a ficus, returning to her role as invisible detective. If only she'd thought to bring a black stocking cap on this trip. She'd brought a pink one—it matched her gloves, just in case everyone had lied about the weather in Devonshire this time of year—but pink wasn't nearly as inconspicuous as black would have been. She made a mental note to not be so lax in her packing next time. Luckily, she *had* brought her green Colorado State jacket and it was dark enough to make her feel like she blended into the walls better. She took a moment to zip it up to her chin and pull the hood up now that Breanna wasn't here to make fun of her for it.

Sadie made her way to the other side of the stairs and then crisscrossed the room toward the baize door, using the furniture as shields. Thank goodness for prolific interior decorating. With darting glances in every direction, even behind her this time, she finally made a run across the last dozen feet, pulled open the door and then pulled it closed behind her, slowing at the very last second so as not to slam the door.

She'd made it! With ebullient self-praise, she complimented her skills and tiptoed down the stairs. No need to give Mrs. Land too much warning. With a steady hand she slowly pushed open one of the double doors, slipped inside the dish room, and closed the door just as quietly before stealthily crossing the floor. She flattened herself against one side of the doorway and then turned her head enough to peek into the kitchen. Aha! Mrs. Land was washing dishes. Sadie tried to rack her brain for a reason why that activity would be suspicious, and although she couldn't come up with anything, she did not let it deter her. She'd be patient, knowing that sooner or later Mrs. Land would betray the secrets she was hiding. Maybe Mrs. Land would make a phone call, or have a whispered conversation with another staff member—though Sadie hoped any incoming staff wouldn't use these same doors. She quickly scanned the dish room and determined that if anyone came, she could hide under the desk in the corner and hope they didn't look at it as they passed by. It would be tight, but she'd been in tighter spaces before. And what were a few sore muscles compared to the pursuit of justice?

Five minutes passed. Then ten. Sadie was being patient. She was waiting for something to happen, but she quickly grew bored and wondered exactly what she'd expected. Mrs. Land had finished the dishes, wiped down the countertops, and swept the floor. The woman hadn't prepared or cooked any food. Sadie smelled chocolate—a very good sign—but nothing else. Dinner was supposed to be served in little over an hour and all she could smell was dessert? The waiting was horrendous and though she'd started her stakeout pressed against the inside wall of the dish room, she eventually sat down and after awhile found herself counting all the different sets of dishes displayed in the glass-fronted cabinets in the room. Thirty-six. One was obviously Christmas-themed, and another was bright gold, while still another set was very delicate looking with tiny pink flowers around the edge. Each set was complete with gravy boats and butter platters in addition to all the varying sizes of plates and bowls. Sadie imagined that if there were ever an earthquake, this room alone would be responsible for a great deal of heartache. It wasn't until she heard a buzzer in the kitchen that she realized how far her mind had wandered. She hurried to her feet and peered around the doorway. Mrs. Land was gone.

Blast!

Carefully she stepped into the kitchen, scanning the corners to see where her quarry had gone. She noticed a bakery box open on the big butcher-block table, half-full of those lemon cookies from the library—store-bought cookies?

She looked up to spot Mrs. Land standing at the outside door the assistant cook had disappeared through a couple hours ago. She was talking to a young man as she took several large white bags from him, then turned and let the door shut behind her.

"Oh," she said in surprise when she saw Sadie standing there. Then her face went red and although Sadie wasn't sure what she was seeing exactly, she knew it was something Mrs. Land had hoped to keep from her. Sadie looked at the bags, trying to discern what they held in them—and then she smelled new aromas she hadn't noticed until now. It took a moment to add up the equation.

"Takeout?" Sadie accused. Instantly she tried to justify it, reminding herself that under the circumstances it made sense that Mrs. Land wouldn't have time to cook. Then she thought back to the garbage can brimming with paper and Styrofoam containers when she and Breanna had been in there earlier today, the fact that no dinner preparations had been underway even then, and the immaculate state of the kitchen. Besides all that, why would one take-out meal embarrass the cook so much?

CHAPTER 12

The bags in Mrs. Land's hands read *The Cliff—Fine Dining in Devon*. Sadie lifted her eyes to meet those of the embarrassed cook as all the meals served at Southgate came to mind. She had noticed they seemed a little commercial—a little . . . non-homemade—but had assumed it was just the fact that she'd never eaten at an English estate before.

"That's what we've been eating all week, isn't it?" Sadie asked, barely able to fathom it. "Takeout."

Mrs. Land swallowed and then hung her head. "I told them you'd figure it out," she said, putting the bags on the large butcher-block table. "When you kept asking after the recipe for those scones I knew we was in trouble."

Sadie was pleased to hear that she'd been recognized as a serious cook, though she'd like to know who "them" was. However, she found herself at a crossroads. She could verbalize her disappointment that the wonderful English meals she'd enjoyed were a farce. But doing so would not get her the information she so desperately wanted. The other option was to take the bosom friend approach. It helped that, for whatever reason, people generally wanted to like Sadie, trust her, help her. She must have one of those faces that communicated to people she was harmless. She only hoped it worked as well here in England as it did back home in Garrison. Sadie smiled widely. "I wondered if you needed any help," she said in as sweet a voice as she could muster. "Seeing as how you weren't counting on extra people to be here tonight." She held up her recipe book. "I take this with me everywhere I go, just in case."

Mrs. Land squinted at the book, clearly not understanding its significance.

"It's my recipe journal," Sadie said, placing it on the table and shrugging out of her jacket—it was warmer down here than it had been upstairs. While she talked, she walked over to a row of hooks on the wall and hung up her jacket. "All of the recipes are tried and tested and determinedly perfect, if I do say so myself. I've got a great recipe for Rosemary Roasted Vegetables, or ninety-minute rolls if you need a little something to round out the meal."

Mrs. Land's eyes darted to the side, then back to meet Sadie's. "We have plenty."

"Wonderful," Sadie replied, trying to hide her disappointment. She took a few steps and put her recipe book down on the counter. "I'll just help you dish it out then."

"Well, see," Mrs. Land stammered, shifting her weight from one foot to the other as she continued to hold the bags. "Only staff is supposed to be in the underside." She glanced toward the dish room as if afraid someone was watching them.

"Then I'll make Liam pay me for my time," Sadie said with a chuckle. She moved forward and took one of the bags from Mrs. Land's hands. She would need to be assertive or she'd never get any-where. Mrs. Land seemed unsure whether to stop her and resorted to just watching with a somewhat horrified expression. She glanced toward the dish room again.

"Now, what's on the menu?" Sadie asked, putting the bags on the butcher-block table.

Mrs. Land paused for a moment, then walked slowly toward Sadie who was unpacking the Styrofoam containers from the bag. She paused another moment before putting the bag she still held on the table. "Well, I ordered roasted pigeon this time."

Sadie's hand stopped and an immediate replay of the discussion she'd had with Breanna that afternoon came to mind. She turned to face Mrs. Land, wondering how she'd live it down when Breanna figured it out. "Pigeons?" she asked, trying not to grimace at the thought.

"It's very posh nosh," Mrs. Land said, looking worried that she'd done something wrong.

"Posh nosh?" Sadie asked, completely confused.

Mrs. Land returned the look. "You know, fancy food. I've never had pigeon, meself, but I hear they are delicious."

"Oh," Sadie said, adding *posh nosh* to her mental vocabulary book. She smiled even wider, though her cheeks were beginning to hurt. "I'm sure it's delicious and I'm always up for trying new things." She'd fully planned on complimenting Mrs. Land's cooking up and down in order to earn the woman's trust, but now found herself in a bit of a pickle. Complimenting the woman's skills at ordering takeout was a much trickier approach. However, it was all that Sadie had to go on. "This smells wonderful," she said as she removed the final container from the paper bag. "It was an excellent choice and I'm impressed with the variety you've supplied us with all week."

"I've been careful to order something we hadn't served," Mrs.

Land said, sounding a bit more comfortable, but still hanging back. "If you'd like to return upstairs now I'll—"

"I'm sure we'll love it," Sadie interrupted as she opened the first Styrofoam container. It was full of red potatoes. "Oh, roasted potatoes." She smiled at the other woman. "Yum." She nearly told Mrs. Land about her own recipe she used at home, but then realized that would not help strengthen their relationship.

Mrs. Land didn't seem to know how to react. Sadie glanced up at the clock. It was nearly seven. "What time is dinner?" she asked for want of something to say, even though she knew the answer.

"Eight o'clock," Mrs. Land said, taking a small step closer to Sadie. "But I can take care of it myself, ma'am. You're a guest."

We're back to that already, Sadie thought. She decided to ignore it. "Is there anything else we need to put together? Bread to slice, sauces to make?" Yet even as she said it, she looked at the Styrofoam cups full of what looked like gravy for the pigeon. Pigeon gravy. Oh, Breanna would never let her live this down. "Dessert?"

Mrs. Land's eyes darted toward the oven. "Well, I've got a chocolate torte baking," she said.

Sadie smiled, relieved to know the woman did cook some things after all. "Oh, you made it?"

Mrs. Land shook her head slightly. "It was frozen," she said. "I can't cook much."

So why on earth was she in charge of the meals at Southgate estate? Sadie couldn't figure out how to ask without sounding offensive so she moved on. "Do we use special plates?"

"No," Mrs. Land said. "Just the everyday china." She watched Sadie open the different containers for a moment, then seemed to give in. She moved past Sadie to a stack of dishes on the sideboard next to a commercial dishwasher. Sadie had always wanted one of those—they washed dishes in just three minutes. But she didn't cook for enough people to make it a worthwhile expense, and it wouldn't fit in her kitchen very well anyway.

"Do we serve it up now?" Sadie asked, turning so she could grab a slotted spoon out of a ceramic crock brimming with serving utensils.

"Well, I make up the plates and then put them in the warming oven until it's time to serve so I can get all the other things ready—butter, sauces, that kind of thing."

"Oh, that's a good idea," Sadie said brightly. Mrs. Land returned with the plates in hand and hesitantly set them down on the table. Sadie grabbed the top one off the stack and put a spoonful of potatoes on it before placing it on the table and picking up another plate while Mrs. Land seemed to be considering how she could stop it. Sadie pretended not to notice. "What about the staff?" Sadie asked, realizing there were a lot of potatoes. "Do they eat this too?"

Mrs. Land hesitated a moment before speaking. "No, ma'am, Saturday is always curry night for the staff. I've already sent out for it."

"Curry night?" Sadie said, looking up at the other woman. "Really?"

"Curry dishes are very popular in the UK," Mrs. Land said, sounding a bit more comfortable.

Sadie was thrilled that Mrs. Land had given more than a basic answer to her question. "I'd noticed you have a lot of Indian restaurants."

Sadie had learned several years ago, when a family from Persia had moved into the neighborhood, that curry was a type of cooking rather than just one dish. She hoped her knowledge would help forge a bond with Mrs. Land and tried to think of what she could say to extend the conversation. "I make a wonderful Chicken Tikka Masala—have you ever had that?"

Mrs. Land's eyes went wide. "I love masala," she said, smiling for the first time. "You make it?"

Sadie nodded, "Back in the States I run my own household top to bottom—though it's just an ordinary house, nothing like this. I cook, I clean, I drive, I do the shopping—the whole bit. Masala is one of my favorite meals to make in the winter. All those spices in the creamy sauce . . ." She shook her head as her stomach rumbled. "Delicious. And it wasn't nearly as hard to make as I thought it might be when I first had it at a restaurant." She nearly offered to share her recipe before remembering that Mrs. Land didn't cook.

"Perhaps I should have ordered curry for you," Mrs. Land said, daring a smile.

Sadie laughed. "I'd have loved it, but this looks delicious too. I'm sure I won't be disappointed." Sadie had dished up the plates with potatoes and opened another container only to find more. "What should I do with all the extra potatoes?"

Mrs. Land picked up another container and flipped the lid back to reveal fresh green beans. Sadie thought she smelled dill. "Just put them in the fridge—Lacy's in charge of breakfast in the mornings and she's good at whipping up things for the staff from what we have left over. She'll be a right good cook one day—not that she needs to worry about that."

"Lacy?" Sadie asked. "Is she the young woman who was in the kitchen with you earlier?"

It was the wrong thing to say. Mrs. Land clamped her mouth shut and stiffened. Sadie waited, trying to keep her expression inviting, but it didn't seem to have any effect on Mrs. Land this time. Sadie decided this might be the best opportunity she'd have.

"I've been meaning to tell you what happened after you left us in the kitchen," Sadie began, keeping her voice soft and leaning toward the other woman as though sharing a secret. "I'm so sorry, I know you wanted me to keep her here, but as soon as you were gone, she ran for the door." She pointed over her shoulder toward the door Lacy had escaped through; Sadie considered how much more to tell Mrs. Land. Did she dare admit she'd *let* the girl go? And why did Mrs. Land want the girl to stay behind anyway?

Mrs. Land looked just as anxious, but there was a curiosity in her eyes as well, proof that she wanted to know what Sadie was building up to. Sadie decided to go for it, and let the chips fall where they may.

"I managed to grab her arm, but she was so upset, Mrs. Land. She said *he'd* told her if something happened to him that she had to leave. Was she talking about John Henry? Could he have known someone wanted to kill him?"

Mrs. Land's mouth opened slightly. "John Henry," she repeated, her shoulders slumping as she looked at the floor, seeming to be deep in thought and not the least bit interested in explaining what those thoughts were.

Sadie's stomach was tight as she waited for Mrs. Land to continue. But instead, Mrs. Land began scooping the beans onto the plates, all her focus on the task at hand. Sadie wasn't sure what to do, so she opened another container which held four browned birds, smaller than the Cornish hens they'd had in York, but fairly similar. They smelled wonderful.

"Mrs. Land," she finally said when she couldn't stand the silence any longer. "Do you think that's what Lacy meant? That John Henry had warned her?"

"I don't know," Mrs. Land said, her hand slowing. "It's just that—" She turned to face Sadie with a look of wanting to tell her something.

Oh, please, Sadie prayed in her mind. *Please tell me something.* "It's just that—what?"

Mrs. Land's shell was cracking, Sadie could feel it, see it in the other woman's expression, but she feared at any moment Mrs. Land would realize how much she was giving away and retreat. Or someone would interrupt them. Sadie scrambled for a way, any way, she could gain this woman's confidence and knock her off the fence she seemed to be sitting on and directly onto Sadie's side. She took a step toward the other woman as an idea entered her mind. She wasn't sure it would work, but it was worth a try. She'd used it with her kids when they were young, and it worked beautifully. If she pretended she knew more than she really did, then they didn't feel like they were confessing, just confirming what Sadie already knew.

"I promise you that I don't want you or Lacy or anyone to get into trouble," Sadie said, smiling sympathetically. "But I'm worried, now that the police are involved. If they find out what's been going on here, we could all find ourselves in a mess."

Mrs. Land was horrible at hiding her feelings and a variety of thoughts passed over her face, ranging from surprise to relief. "That's what I'm so very afraid of," she whispered. "What if, after everything, I end up in jail for my part in this? What will Rupert do without me?"

Chicken Tikka Masala

Chicken
1 cup plain yogurt
2 tablespoons lemon juice
2 teaspoons cumin
2 teaspoons cayenne pepper (1 teaspoon for a milder flavor)
2 teaspoons black pepper
1 teaspoon cinnamon
1 teaspoon salt
1 teaspoon ground ginger (or $\frac{1}{2}$-inch piece of ginger root)
$1\frac{1}{2}$ pounds boneless chicken breasts or thighs, cut into bite-size pieces (thighs are a more tender meat—worth a visit to the meat department)

After combining all ingredients in a gallon-size Ziploc bag, seal bag and knead the mixture together by hand. Allow chicken to marinate at least 1 hour in refrigerator. (Can marinate all day or overnight.)

After marinating, remove chicken from bag. Grill or broil chicken until cooked through. Marinade will be thick and will cook off. You do not need to save the drippings.

Sauce
1 tablespoon butter or margarine
2 garlic cloves, minced
1 jalapeño, minced (Breanna doesn't like a spicy sauce—leave out the jalapeño, it'll still have the kick of the cayenne)
2 teaspoons ground coriander
1 teaspoon cumin
1 teaspoon paprika
1 teaspoon garam masala (optional)*
$\frac{1}{2}$ teaspoon salt
1 (8-ounce) can tomato sauce
1 cup whipping cream

Basmati rice, cooked
Cilantro (for garnish)

Melt butter in a large skillet, add garlic and jalapeño. Cook 1 minute. Add coriander, cumin, paprika, garam masala, and salt. Add tomato sauce and cover skillet. Simmer 15 minutes. Add cream and simmer until sauce thickens, about 5 minutes. Add cooked chicken to sauce; simmer an additional 5 minutes. Serve over basmati rice. Garnish with cilantro.

Serves 6.

*Garam masala adds to the traditional flavor of the dish but it isn't absolutely necessary if it's difficult to find at your local grocery store. However, the dish is better with it than without it. Garam masala is made up of a combination of different spices and can be mixed at home.

CHAPTER 13

Sadie's heart began to pound in her chest. Even though she'd known Mrs. Land was hiding something, to have her admit it was a huge validation. It was all she could do not to shake more answers out of the woman. She was so close but knew that pushing would only force the woman's defenses back up. In an instant she reviewed what Mrs. Land had said. Rupert. Was he a husband? A boyfriend? Was Mrs. Land protecting him somehow?

"Is that why you went along with this?" Sadie asked. "For Rupert?"

Mrs. Land's eyes filled with tears. "I had to do it for my boy."

Her boy, Sadie repeated. Her son. "I know," she said with a sympathetic nod. "We'll do anything for our children, won't we?"

"There's just so much I can't do for him," Mrs. Land explained. "It's not easy, raising a boy without a man around—but they promised me he'd be okay if I just did my part—that they'd get him a good lawyer. But you can't imagine how hard it's been. I'm not a liar, Mrs. Hoffmiller. It's been tearing me up something awful. And Lacy, oh, that poor girl, she just didn't know what she was getting herself into when she came here. I'd hoped she'd come back for dinner, but if she left like you said, oh my, I just don't know what to do."

Sadie nodded encouragingly even while shouting in her mind for Mrs. Land to get on with it. What was Mrs. Land's part? What did Lacy not know? Who were *they*?

"I have to know," Sadie said, trying hard to be patient so as not to scare off Mrs. Land from talking to her even though it was so hard to know where to start with her questions. "Was John Henry in the sitting room when you went up there?"

After a moment, Mrs. Land nodded, triggering a hallelujah chorus in Sadie's mind.

"You cleaned up the wall, didn't you?" Sadie offered. Mrs. Land was the only one Sadie could think of who would do it.

Again Mrs. Land nodded. "The maids keep a few rags and some cleaner in every room to clean up spills and things. I was so relieved that it cleaned the wall so well, even though I felt sick the whole time. This wasn't supposed to happen—nothing like this. I don't understand what went wrong."

Sadie couldn't help but ask herself one more time if Mrs. Land could have killed John Henry. But she'd seemed too genuinely surprised when Sadie had burst into the kitchen this afternoon to have known he was already dead, and Sadie had already determined that Mrs. Land wasn't strong enough to move the body—let alone stab a poker through his chest; an action such as that would take a good deal of strength to pull off. No, the murderer had to be strong, and able to sneak up on a man hiding behind the curtains. She believed that Mrs. Land was telling the truth—but she'd cleaned up the blood, so she must have been aware that someone had moved the body. Sadie was lining up her next question when Mrs. Land continued.

"I feel right awful about it. It ain't right and no one told me anyone would be killed or that the police would be involved or nothing like that."

"I don't know how you've held up for so long, Mrs. Land," Sadie soothed. "Can you please tell me who moved the body?"

A male voice startled her from behind. "Mrs. Hoffmiller?"

Sadie spun around to see Grant standing a few steps away. With her focus so intent on Mrs. Land and what she was about to divulge, Sadie hadn't heard his approach. She would have bopped him on the head for his ill-timed interruption if she'd had the chance.

Grant was watching them closely and although he looked perfectly professional, Sadie could read the irritation in his posture and the set of his brow. He held Mrs. Land's eyes for a moment, which seemed to communicate something Sadie wasn't supposed to understand. But then he didn't know Sadie very well. She wondered how much he'd overheard and her stomach sank. Mrs. Land had hinted she wasn't alone in whatever deception was going on; it wasn't hard to imagine that Grant—the butler who wasn't there when they found the body—would be in on it too. He practically ran the household. Sadie would need to be careful around him.

He turned his eyes back to Sadie. "May I please escort you back upstairs?"

Whether it was the tone in his voice or the fact that she might make things worse for Mrs. Land if she stayed, Sadie felt she had no choice but to agree. She'd have to find a few minutes with Mrs. Land later somehow. A quick glance at the table showed that her recipe book was still there, giving her a perfect reason to return to the kitchen and this conversation. In fact, the time between now and then might very well soften the woman up and give Sadie time to plan the best approach and process everything she'd learned. She looked back at the reluctant cook. "Thank you for the snack," she said, trying to cover up the real reason she had been there. "Dinner smells delicious."

Mrs. Land gave Sadie a tremulous smile. Sadie followed Grant back through the dish room, glancing at her jacket still hanging on the hook as she did so. She decided to leave it there as well; now she had two excuses to return later. She followed Grant back to the main floor. He opened the door for her, but then hesitated. Sadie could hear Austin's voice and a quick look at Grant clued her in to the fact that he didn't want Austin to know she'd been down there.

"Go back downstairs," Sadie said quietly. "I don't want you to get in trouble."

He regarded her for a moment, then shook his head. "I have no reason to hide from my employer, madam. I keep no secrets from him." He watched her carefully as he continued in the same whisper, "None of us do."

CHAPTER 14

Sadie held his eyes for a few seconds, wondering what exactly he meant by that. "But Liam is more your employer than Austin—"

"*Lord* Melcalfe," Grant corrected her. "And Master Liam."

Sadie bit back an argument about the ridiculous nature of the title. Lord and Master—how arrogant did you have to be to come up with that kind of thing? But she didn't want to put the butler off. "Sorry, what I mean is that Master Liam is more your employer than Lord Melcalfe is, and it's obvious that the staff is keeping things from him."

"I'm sure I don't know what you're talking about," Grant said, pulling himself up even straighter.

"Why does Mrs. Land's son need a lawyer? Who's blackmailing her? What's being covered up?"

He looked at her quickly and she realized that she'd gone about it all wrong. He certainly wouldn't give up such information that easily. "I'm sure I wouldn't know," he said quickly, then turned away from her, took a breath, and stepped around the tree. Sadie scowled at him, but followed all the same. She saw his shoulders relax slightly when he realized that both Liam and Austin had their backs toward them. He would not be reprimanded for having let Sadie get into the kitchen.

Liam and Breanna were half a step behind Austin who was talking to three men dressed in suits. They must be the security guards Liam had mentioned—they looked a little like the Secret Service in their dark suits. Or maybe more like Men in Black.

She tried to catch Breanna's eye for a hint of what was going on, but Breanna didn't look her way. She was probably still mad that Sadie had set her up to talk to Liam. Sadie hoped Breanna would accept her apology once she realized how much Sadie had learned from Mrs. Land. She itched for her notebook so she could write down all of the details before she forgot.

"It would be helpful for us to have a list of everyone on the premises," one of the three men said. He had a dark complexion, Middle Eastern, Sadie assumed, but spoke with a British accent. His eyes watched Sadie as she approached the group and she wondered if she should continue up the stairs to her room.

"Grant will assemble that list for you," Austin said, looking over his shoulder to where Grant stood. The butler inclined his head. "He'll also assemble the staff below so that the security detail can meet them."

"Would it be possible to wait until after dinner, sir?" Grant asked in his formal tones. "Many of the staff members are required to execute the meal."

Sadie thought it ridiculous that so many staff members were needed in order for the four of them to eat. Equally ridiculous was the idea that dinner couldn't be moved back half an hour to accommodate the security team's meeting with the staff members. One more example of the low priority everyone gave to John Henry's death. Sadie was amazed security was there at all.

Sadie looked at Austin, wondering why he'd suggested the security team in the first place. He'd been plenty clear about the fact that he didn't believe John Henry had been murdered. However, he apparently still wanted to put on a good show of covering his bases. She reflected back on what he'd said about having stayed at the house all this time, purposely not being seen. Even with his being a snob, she couldn't figure out why he wouldn't at least have introduced himself to them. He *was* Liam's cousin and managing the holdings that Liam would soon be taking over. Then again, he also thought Breanna was a gold-digging American willing to tell outrageous stories in hopes of weaseling her way into the family tree. Hmmm.

"This is the final houseguest," Austin said, pulling Sadie out of her ponderings as he waved toward her. "Mrs. Sadie Hoffmiller."

She stepped forward and shook hands with each security guard. "You can call me Sadie," she said warmly. "Everyone does."

They all nodded and smiled and made polite noises at each other.

Austin cleared his throat, drawing the attention back to himself. He looked at the security guards. "Would you like a tour of the estate before dinner?"

The men agreed, and headed toward the west wing of the main level to begin the tour; Liam, a couple steps behind the rest of them, looked like a little brother tagging along. As they walked away, Liam looked at Breanna, a scared, sad, but hopeful look on his face. Sadie was embarrassed for him and wondered if part of Breanna's decision to break things off was because he wasn't very assertive. She'd pegged him as quiet and easygoing from the first time they'd met, but over these last few hours, she felt like she was seeing those qualities in a different light. Only dominating women wanted weak men. Breanna wanted a partner, and seeing Liam in this setting did not reflect well on that potential.

"I'll, uh, see you at dinner," Liam said. Breanna nodded and watched him go.

Sadie and Breanna returned to their rooms where Sadie retrieved her notebook and began filling it full of every innuendo and detail Mrs. Land had shared with her.

"So how did it go with Liam?" Sadie asked when she finished.

"How do you think it went, Mom?" Breanna said, flopping onto the bed. "We've broken up. I can't believe you set me up like that."

"I'm sorry," Sadie said, giving her best repentant expression. "But I could tell he was intent on keeping us out of the kitchen. You were the only reason he'd give in. Was it horrible?"

Breanna let out a breath. "No," she said. "He wanted to tell me some . . . things." She looked away, making Sadie wonder what Liam had said that Breanna didn't want to tell her. "He found flights for Monday morning, but he's not coming back with us."

Sadie was surprised to hear that. "He's not?"

Breanna shook her head. "He's afraid if he leaves he won't get back before his father passes away. He wants to take over the trustee position and manage his father's affairs."

"What about his job in Portland?" Sadie asked. She simply couldn't imagine Liam doing what Austin did. Were his father conscious, she felt sure he'd feel the same way.

"Liam left a message for his boss to call him," Breanna said, making a face. "It's going to be ugly. Honestly, even under these circumstances I can't believe he's just walking away. I told him I thought he was acting rashly—but he's determined."

"Wow," Sadie said, imagining what a difficult decision that must have been for him to make.

"How did it go with Mrs. Land?" Breanna asked, changing the subject and looking at the notebook Sadie held. "Did she tell you anything?"

Eager to discuss her findings, Sadie took about two minutes to share everything she'd learned from Mrs. Land.

"Oh, my gosh," Breanna said when Sadie finished relaying Grant's untimely interruption. She'd propped herself up on her elbows during Sadie's recital. She looked decidedly shaken by what Sadie had told her, making Sadie wonder if she shouldn't be telling her daughter so much. As the day had continued on, Breanna seemed to become more and more fragile around the edges. "Five more seconds and you would know who'd moved him." Rather than sounding excited by this, she sounded scared.

Sometimes Sadie had to remind herself that not everyone was as well equipped for a crisis as she was. Not everyone had lost so many people they loved—picked off one by one by twists of fate, circumstance, and just plain mortal tribulation. Then again, at Breanna's age, Sadie hadn't lost anyone yet. Within ten years she was a widow and motherless—Neil having died of a massive heart attack and Sadie's mother killed in a car accident. Just over a year ago, Sadie's dad had died after a long battle with colon cancer. Understanding that loss was a part of life was as ingrained in Sadie as was the recipe for the Everyday Ganache she required to be specified in her children's apologies.

"I was so close," Sadie reiterated, shaking her head in disbelief. Then she stopped and sat up straighter. "I bet Grant is busy getting the dining room set up about now. I wonder if I could catch Mrs.

Land before dinner starts. I left my recipe book down there so I'd have an excuse to go back."

"I don't know," Breanna said, her smooth forehead puckered with concern. "Maybe you ought to leave it alone."

"You told me I could look into things," Sadie reminded her.

Breanna shrugged. "I've had time to think about it since then, and I think it was a mistake."

"Did something happen when you and Liam talked?" Sadie asked, annoyed at the flip-flopping behavior. "It's almost as if you're doubting that we saw a dead body at all."

"I'm not doubting anything," Breanna said. "I know what we saw—but I guess maybe I've realized how serious this really is. I don't want us getting too involved or causing any problems. Liam's going to send us to London in the morning."

"London?" Sadie repeated, then immediately shook her head, reminded that they'd overheard Grant saying the same thing. "No way, we can't just leave. We know what's happened here—what really happened." She paused and looked hard at her daughter, wishing for the millionth time that Breanna's face was more reflective of her thoughts and feelings. Shawn, Sadie's son, was an open book. Every lie about why he was late for curfew, every denial that he'd eaten the last of the chocolate chip cookies, every assurance that the girl was "just a friend" was betrayed by his eyes, the set of his jaw, the way he clenched his fists. Poor boy couldn't get away with a thing—Sadie hoped that wasn't why he decided to go to school at Michigan State. Hmmm, something to think about later.

Right now, however, she was up against Breanna, who kept most of her thoughts and feelings locked up tight, only offering general moods or emotions up for examination. Right now, she was holding something back, but it was impossible to tell if it was just the stress of everything going on or if it was something else. "What did Liam say to you that's made you pull back from all this?"

Breanna made a sound between a growl and a groan as she stood up from the bed and smoothed back her hair. "Fine," she said with frustration. "Let's go see Mrs. Land."

Sadie couldn't keep up with the rate at which Breanna changed her mind but she liked this new direction so she went with it. "Good," she said.

The notebook was too big to fit in her pocket and it made her look like some kind of auditor, so she put it in the nightstand drawer next to the bed before she and Breanna headed for the kitchen again. This time she didn't bother with stealth, though they hung back at the top of the stairs while Liam, Austin, and the security team entered the sitting room. Sadie hoped the security guards were ex-cops and would realize the faulty investigation going on. Maybe they could step in. As soon as they were all in the room, she and Breanna hurried down the stairs, around the Christmas tree, and through the doors that led to the kitchen below.

They slowed their steps as they entered the dish room, then stopped completely when they saw Grant pace into view in the doorway leading to the kitchen. He had the wall phone to his ear, and Sadie and Breanna froze, catching snippets of his conversation. "Yes, please call me as soon as you know their availability. . . . I understand the holiday makes it difficult, but we still need a cook. I've a houseful of people. . . . Right. Until then."

As soon as he hung up, he turned and noticed them standing there; he straightened immediately when he realized he'd been overheard.

"I left my recipe book here," Sadie said. She moved toward the recipe book she could see on the far counter, wondering why Grant was looking for a new cook. She picked up the book and held it to her chest, scanning the kitchen. Grant and Breanna still stood near the doorway to the dish room; other than that, no one else was there. "Is Mrs. Land here?" she finally asked when she saw no sign of the woman. "I've been after her all week for that scone recipe and she said she'd think about it. I'm hoping she's taken pity on me."

"She's gathering her things," Grant said, as professionally as ever.

Sadie tried to keep her surprise to herself. "Her things?"

Just then Mrs. Land emerged from the servant side of the kitchen and all eyes went to her. She had a large duffel bag over her shoulder. No one seemed to know what to say for a moment. Finally, Grant cleared his throat. "The car is ready to take you to the train station," he said to Mrs. Land. "Have a nice holiday."

"Holiday?" Sadie couldn't take her eyes off of Mrs. Land, who managed a smile that seemed legitimate even if it was nervous. "Grant is allowing me to go to London early," she said. "To see my boy for the New Year." Her face lit up when she talked about her son, solidifying what she'd said about her commitment to Rupert. However, Sadie didn't miss how convenient it was that she would not be here for the duration of Sadie and Breanna's stay. Had Grant pinned Mrs. Land as a weak link?

"Early?" Sadie asked.

"The staff takes two days off at New Year's," Grant explained. "Mrs. Land is simply leaving early."

Sadie looked at the man, trying not to glare. Had *he* killed John Henry? He was probably strong enough to both stab the smaller man with a poker and drag his body away once she and Breanna had left the room. Is that what Mrs. Land had been about to unveil? And now Grant was sending her away before she'd have the chance to tell Sadie the truth. Sadie should never have asked Grant about Mrs. Land's son. She'd given away their conversation and now Mrs. Land was leaving.

All these thoughts rushed through her mind but she only spoke one out loud, mostly in hopes of masking the direction of her thoughts; she didn't want him to know what she was really thinking. "But who will do the cooking? Did Lacy come back?"

She caught Grant shoot a questioning glance at Mrs. Land, but Mrs. Land didn't seem to notice. Had Mrs. Land told Grant about Lacy running out? Sadie didn't think so, judging from his reaction.

"I don't know where she is," he said. "But since she usually does breakfast I'm hoping she'll be back in the morning. It's been a trying day for all of us."

Sadie mentally kicked herself again for letting Lacy leave. She wished she could ask Mrs. Land more about Lacy and what would keep her from returning to Southgate. She still didn't know who had warned Lacy to leave or why Mrs. Land had seemed protective of the girl.

"The kitchen is none of your concern," Grant said. He smiled, but it seemed forced. "Dinner will be served shortly. Please return upstairs. As I told you before, only *staff* is allowed in this part of the house."

Sadie ignored his emphasis. "I'd be happy to help out until you find someone else," Sadie said, imagining how perfect that would be. They had a cook who didn't cook, certainly having a guest who did cook wouldn't violate any of their silly rules more than that. It would only be for a meal or two anyway, and it would give her something to do. Plus, she'd have this beautiful kitchen all to herself, and she had no doubt that if she were part of the inner workings of this house, she'd be privy to all the innermost knowledge as well.

"That won't be necessary," Grant said.

"Oh, it really wouldn't be a problem," Sadie assured him, wondering why no one would even consider it. She was always happy for help in her kitchen at home. Why was this so different? "I love to cook and am quite comfortable in any kitchen."

"It just isn't done, Mrs. Hoffmiller," he said by way of explanation, though he sounded more sympathetic than frustrated, which made her question his position as potential suspect in her mind. Would a murderer be sympathetic toward her in regards to anything? He didn't seem defensive, just trying to do his job. She wondered if Austin had committed him to making sure Sadie didn't take on any responsibilities. "Please return upstairs." There was a pleading tone to his voice that ignited her concerns even more. Yet it would be foolish to discount him all together. She made a note to watch him carefully, one way or the other.

Sadie looked between him and Mrs. Land, and felt she had no choice but to give in again. She did not want to suffer Grant's poor favor any more than she already had, especially if Mrs. Land wasn't going to be around to give her any more information. It killed her that Mrs. Land was leaving; she should have pushed harder when she'd had the chance.

"Have a wonderful visit with your son," she said, trying to hide her disappointment even while scouring her mind for a way she could steal just a few more minutes with this woman. "He's lucky to have a mother who loves him as much as you do." She wondered again what the lawyer was for. Just how much trouble was Rupert in? And who was paying for the lawyer—Austin?

"Thank you," Mrs. Land said with a slight incline of her head. "I'm anxious to see him, that's for sure." Her eyes moved to the recipe book Sadie had forgotten she was holding. "Oh, good, you found your book."

"Yes," Sadie said with a distracted nod.

"I asked Grant to make sure you got your book back," Mrs. Land said, looking at Sadie. "And your jacket."

"Thank you," Sadie replied, wishing Mrs. Land hadn't said anything about the jacket. She might still need an excuse to visit the kitchen. She hurried to move past it. "Are you sure there's nothing we can do to help?"

"Yes," Grant said as Mrs. Land opened her mouth to answer. "Everything is taken care of." He lifted a hand toward Sadie's jacket. "Your—"

"So, you're taking the train?" Sadie asked, cutting him off. Oh, what she wouldn't do for even thirty seconds with Mrs. Land. "We took it when we went up to Northampton," she said. "The transportation here is nothing short of amazing."

"Yes," Mrs. Land said with a confused nod as to why they were discussing the train system.

"Do you have many stops between here and London? We took a car, so I'm not familiar with the route."

"Well—" Mrs. Land began.

"Please, Mrs. Hoffmiller," Grant said, taking a step forward. "You really must return upstairs."

"Alright, sorry to keep you," she offered, then turned and led the way, walking right past her jacket in the process. No one stopped her. Good. And Grant didn't follow her, which was even better.

Breanna reluctantly followed Sadie into the dish room. "Huh," she said quietly. "That was weird."

"I'd say," Sadie agreed. She kept her voice soft so as not to be overheard. "Why let the cook go to London when you have a house full of people? Do they really give the staff two days off?"

"I remember Liam saying something about that," Breanna said. "That's one of the reasons we were supposed to leave today—because the staff was leaving anyway. His dad does it every year—two days paid leave for the New Year."

Now that she thought about that, Sadie did remember Liam talking to Breanna about it during one of the meals they'd had in London. Sadie had been lost in her Beef Wellington and had only paid their conversation half the attention it deserved. "They come back on January second, right?"

"I think that's what he said," Breanna whispered as they made their way up the concrete steps toward the door that would connect to the foyer of the house. Sadie couldn't be sure, but Breanna seemed relieved to be out of the kitchen. Was it just because Breanna didn't like confrontation? Did Grant make her uncomfortable?

"So, to give Mrs. Land—the only person in the kitchen—an extra day off means that her *not* being here must be more important than her *being* here. Which must mean she knows something that would help us."

"Or hurt someone else," Breanna offered. Sadie looked to the side, smiling at her daughter. That was a good point. Perhaps the injustice of having Mrs. Land sent away had made an impact on Breanna—maybe she was catching the spirit. But the concerned look on her daughter's face didn't seem to reflect that at all. Rather, Breanna just looked worried. Sadie let out a breath, accepting that she might be in this alone after all.

They came out from the staff entrance and were coming around the Christmas tree when the sound of voices slowed their steps. They shared a look while Sadie stepped forward carefully, as close to the branches as possible without disturbing the needles of the tree. She crouched down enough to look through a space in the tree and could make out the profile of one of the chambermaids—Charlotte—standing to the side of the staircase, looking up into the face of someone Sadie couldn't see. However, she recognized the voice.

"What time was this?" Austin asked. Sadie was surprised by the fact that his voice was not hard and cynical as it usually was; rather, he seemed quite calm—the kind of tone that would invite someone's trust. Tricky.

"Around one-thirty," Charlotte answered. "I had taken Master Liam his lunch around noon and was going back to pick up the tray. It wasn't in the hall as I expected, and I was about to knock when I heard them through the door. Master Liam was very angry and told John Henry to leave."

Sadie lifted her eyebrows. Liam certainly hadn't said anything about *that*.

CHAPTER 15

H ow did the argument end?" Austin asked.

"John Henry came storming out of the room," Charlotte said. "I knew he'd be angry if he knew that I'd heard the argument, so I stepped into a doorway. Then Master Liam slammed the door. I waited another half an hour before I went and picked up the tray."

"Did you tell any of this to the investigator?" Austin asked after a moment.

Charlotte shook her head. "I felt that it would be best to tell you, and proceed as you saw fit. I only told him what I told everyone else—that I took the tray at noon and picked it up at two."

"I appreciate that, Charlotte," Austin said. "Have you told anyone else?"

"No, sir," Charlotte said. "Also, no one has seen Lacy—not since those ladies ran into the kitchen and Mrs. Land went upstairs."

The ensuing pause lasted a few seconds, causing Sadie to strain toward whatever he might say next.

"I'll look into it," Austin told Charlotte. "It's nearly time for dinner so you better go."

Sadie took a step back. She had little doubt that as soon as

Austin dismissed Charlotte she would head for the staff entrance. Sadie grabbed Breanna's arm and pulled her around to the other side of the tree—the side pushed up against the staircase. Breanna didn't resist—thank goodness—and they both crouched down, pressing into the branches as much as they dared. Sadie was glad that the tree also cast most of the corner in shadow, but she held her breath anyway, willing the maid not to see them. Moments later Charlotte appeared, and any fears Sadie had of being seen were extinguished by the fact that Charlotte was intent only on the door, a troubled look on her face. She moved quickly, making Sadie wonder if she'd been on her way downstairs when she'd run into Austin and took the opportunity to tell him the truth. It seemed a very dangerous protocol to approve of staff lying to the police in favor of their employers. Sadie and Breanna listened to Austin's steps on the stairs above them, shrinking down so that he couldn't see them through the highly-polished mahogany railing.

Charlotte pushed through the staff door; Sadie and Breanna waited a few seconds before standing up and moving around the tree, proceeding into the foyer carefully as they anticipated running into someone at any moment.

Once assured they were alone, Sadie turned to look at Breanna, fully expecting to discuss this new discovery. However, the guilty look on her face showed everything for once, causing the words to fizzle out on Sadie's tongue.

"Liam and John Henry had an argument," Breanna said.

Sadie glared at her. "Oh, really?" she asked sarcastically.

"I was going to tell you," Breanna added.

"No, you weren't," Sadie replied. "If you were going to tell me, you'd have told me already."

Breanna clenched her jaw slightly and when she spoke, her words had a bit of an edge to them. "Okay, maybe what I meant was that if I'd thought you wouldn't totally freak out about it and suppose all kinds of horrible things about Liam, I'd have told you."

"That's not fair," Sadie said, narrowing her eyes at her daughter. "I have a very open mind about things, but I can't make the proper determinations without all the information. I can't believe you would keep this from me. I've told you everything I've discovered. It never crossed my mind that you wouldn't do the same."

Breanna let out a breath, giving up the fight under the weight of Sadie's guilt trip. "I'm sorry," she said, the sharpness no longer in her tone. "It wasn't that big a deal—he and John Henry just disagreed with something in regard to the earl's care."

Sadie wasn't buying it. "Then why didn't you want to tell me?"

"Like I said, I worried you'd freak out."

"Did Liam tell the inspector about the argument?" Sadie asked.

Breanna shrugged and met her mother's eyes. "I don't know." She glanced up the stairs. "I need to tell Liam he was overheard by the staff, though—he thought it had been between him and John Henry."

"And then John Henry ended up dead," Sadie continued.

Breanna nodded. "Right, so you can see why he didn't want to make the argument public knowledge."

"What was the argument about?"

"The earl's care," Breanna said, her words slow and careful. "Liam has some concerns."

"So, then why was John Henry in the sitting room?"

Breanna shook her head. "I have no idea, and neither does Liam." She glanced up the stairs again. "I really need to talk to him." She looked back at her mother. "I know it makes him look bad, Mom, but will you please keep it to yourself for now?"

Sadie's hesitation must have shown on her face.

"You believe Liam's a good man, right?" Breanna asked imploringly. She waited expectantly for an answer.

"Yes," Sadie said. "Except that he—"

"And you know he's dealing with a lot right now, right?"

In spite of herself, Sadie reviewed everything that was sitting so heavy on Liam's shoulders right now: his father was sick, likely dying, his girlfriend had dumped him, he was facing a drastic change in circumstance and lifestyle whether he liked it or not, and the man he'd argued with that morning had wound up dead. "Yes, he is dealing with a lot, but—"

Breanna cut her off, looking relieved that Sadie was agreeing with her. "I promise you that he will tell the inspectors everything tomorrow, okay? But give him tonight to make some sense of everything and get up to date with his dad's care. The fact that someone killed John Henry has Liam terrified for his father—please help me give him the time he needs to come to terms with all of this."

"You're not telling me everything," Sadie said, narrowing her eyes slightly. "I can feel it."

Breanna let out a breath. "I'm telling you what I know, okay? Liam kind of downloaded on me earlier—and not all of it made sense, but I promised him I'd wait until tomorrow to tell the inspectors." She paused a moment before continuing. "That means you have one more night to figure out what you want to figure out too. I did give you permission, remember."

That's right, Sadie realized. It was wrong not to tell the inspectors everything, and yet security was in place, there was no body to convince anyone they were telling the truth, and Sadie still had far more questions than answers. She knew she was being manipulated, but if it helped her get what she wanted, maybe it was worthwhile.

Finally, she nodded under the pleading look of her daughter. Breanna noticeably relaxed. "Thank you, Mom," she said, smiling slightly. She put one foot on the stairs and glanced back at Sadie one last time. "I'll see you at dinner, okay?"

Sadie nodded again, and watched Breanna climb the stairs. Dinner was in twenty minutes, but that meant she had twenty minutes to get herself lost wherever she felt she had the best chance of getting more information. The question was where to start.

She was in the process of scanning the foyer, considering her options, when she heard a voice coming from the east hallway. Before even considering the reasons why she did it, she ducked behind the east Christmas tree—on the opposite side of the stairs that hid the door to the kitchen. She crouched down and held very still as the voice got closer.

"Yes, Charlotte took care of it, but I feel it would be better if you came down here—Liam kicked him out of the earl's room. . . . I had managed to stay out of their way until today. . . . He's been with the earl nearly every minute since then." She was pretty sure she recognized the voice, but moved so she could see through a gap in the branches. It was Austin, talking on the phone—currently listening to whoever was on the other end of the line. "No, things are not going to be okay," he said sharply as he reached the stairs and started taking them two at a time. "Liam agreed they should head to London tomorrow . . . around nine I think, but that's not going to solve this . . ." His voice tapered off as he walked out of range and she pursed her lips at the missed opportunity to eavesdrop a little longer. Who was he talking to? Then she remembered that his father was the earl's doctor. Maybe Austin was talking to him. If it was Dr. Melcalfe, he didn't seem like he wanted to come to Southgate even though the earl's nurse was missing. Maybe he had plans for the holiday. She made a mental note to write it all down when she got back to her room.

After a few seconds, when no one else came by for her to overhear, she casually stepped out from behind the tree, looking around to make sure no one was watching her even while making up the excuse of a lost earring in case anyone asked what she was doing behind the tree. She took one of the small, silver snowflake earrings out and put it in her pocket to lend credence to her story just in case. She glanced toward the hallway Austin had come out of—the one leading to the library as well as the smoking room, the trophy room, and the billiard room. She wondered why Southgate didn't have a TV room and a talk-on-the-phone room and a gift-wrapping room—those seemed a lot more practical, but who was Sadie to judge?

The first room she came to was the library, on the left side. The light was on and the door slightly open. Was this where Austin had been? Sadie pushed open the library door, looking carefully to see if anyone was inside. She continued her vigilance as she took a few steps into the room. If Austin hadn't been in this room before he received his phone call, someone else might be here and she'd had enough surprises for one day.

"Hello?" she asked quietly, though it sounded very loud in the cavernous room.

No one answered back, which helped her relax a little bit and move forward with a bit more courage. When she reached the middle of the room, she stopped and looked, overwhelmed by the sheer amount of information available. She found herself heading toward the nearest bookshelf and just scanning the titles of the books there. It only took a few minutes to realize they were categorized—with shelves and shelves of poetry, and other shelves full of several different editions of the Encyclopedia Britannica—just in case you wanted to see if the Spanish Inquisition changed between 1954 and 2008. Sadie browsed through history books, novels, philosophy, even a section dedicated to world religions, before turning to see that a rather large book had been opened on the desk—a book she hadn't seen there when they'd met with the staff a couple hours earlier. A tremor of excitement rushed through her as she considered that Austin could have been looking through that book before his phone call. Surely if the book had been here very long, a staff member would have reshelved it. She glanced at the door to make sure she'd closed it behind her, then fairly ran to the book.

CHAPTER 16

The first thing Sadie did was put one hand on the open page and turn the cover over in order to read the title: *Martin Book of Heraldry.*

What on earth did heraldry *mean?*

She ran her fingers over the gold-embossed leather cover. The book measured about ten by sixteen inches and wasn't traditionally bound, but rather had a removable spine that looked as though it allowed pages to be added to it—like a scrapbook or a Book of Remembrance. Was heraldry a fancy name for remembrance or heritage or something?

She flipped the book back open and scanned the page it had been opened to. It was a pedigree chart and, after fanning the pages, she realized it spanned almost four hundred years—longer than the earldom had even existed. Wow. Sadie's friend Gayle was big into genealogy, spending hours on it every week, and had managed to trace her family back to the 1700s. Sadie, on the other hand, had yet to develop much of a desire to study up on dead people. Living people were far more interesting—with the exception of the dead man pinned to the wall with a poker.

Flipping through the pages revealed that the book had three

distinct sections—the pedigree charts, a section that included written histories, and a section that had copies of actual documents belonging to those people included on the pedigrees. Gayle would lose her mind! There were copies of parish records three hundred years old, with an arrow to indicate which of the chicken-scratch names were being referenced, as well as birth, marriage, and death certificates for more recent members of the Martin clan. Even a non-genealogical mind such as Sadie's could appreciate the priceless nature of the book. She turned back to the page that had been open when she came in.

The pedigree chart followed the family line of the second Earl of Garnett, who had a whopping seven children, resulting in numerous other family lines laid out over the next fifteen pages. She tried to follow them, but gave up after a couple minutes when she found herself horribly lost. Instead she decided to look for Liam. She paged through the pedigrees—it hurt her brain trying to track where one generation ended and then picked up on the next page. Finally she just flipped to the very last page of the pedigree—which is where she assumed she'd find Liam's name. However, though his father, William, was listed as one of two children born to the eighth earl, and though there should have been a new page for William's own pedigree—like there had been for the other men in the Martin line—there wasn't. She found it ironic that the current heir apparent wasn't included, but perhaps the book simply hadn't been updated recently enough to include Liam or his mother. Maybe they didn't add the new generation until the current generation had passed away. It was smart to compile information in a format that could be added to as needed.

Using her finger, Sadie started with William, Liam's father, and followed the lines that linked each earl to his father—the line through which the title had passed. She had to turn several pages to do it but she finally found herself at the fifth Earl of Garnett before she lost the line. It took her a moment to realize that he'd inherited the earldom not from his father, but from his older brother. Sadie tried to remember the explanations Liam had given about how the peerage worked but couldn't remember the details. However, there were some reference numbers listed beneath the fifth earl's name, so she turned to the reference section and scanned what was nearly a page-long summary of his life. She started reading word for word when she got to the part about the untimely death of his older brother. She then looked up the older brother.

The fourth Earl of Garnett had contracted pneumonia after a fox hunt, and when he died, he had left behind two young daughters. No male heir. Being a widow herself, Sadie wondered what that had been like for his wife—the fourth countess. She lost her husband and the father of her children, which must have been horrible, but she also lost the earldom. When Neil died, Sadie had been grateful he'd taken life insurance so seriously. With good investments and provident living, Sadie had managed to do quite well financially— though she had gone back to teaching when Shawn started school. But if this woman had married an heir apparent to an earldom, she likely hadn't been raised to be very self-sufficient. Did losing her husband also mean losing her home? Her mode of income? It seemed like such a strange way to base prominence in a society—on birth order alone. In fact it seemed downright, well, un-American.

She returned to the pedigree chart. If the fifth earl hadn't become earl, Liam wouldn't be facing the title at all—it never would have come into his family line. If not for that one silly fox hunt, the fourth earl might have had a son later on who would have inherited the title. Liam and Breanna might very well be fighting over wedding colors like any other couple instead of matters of inheritance and titles. It was strange how fate worked sometimes. She traced the title back another genera-tion—to the third earl—wondering if he had an interesting story be-hind his inheritance as well, but he didn't. He was just the oldest son.

"What are you doing?"

Sadie spun around to see Liam standing ten feet away from her. His sudden appearance unnerved her—especially in light of what she'd learned about his argument with John Henry—but at least it wasn't Austin sneaking up on her. "It was just lying open on the desk," she explained, wondering if she should confront him about what Charlotte had said. But then, Breanna had already talked to him about the John Henry stuff and, more than an explanation, Sadie wanted Liam's trust so that if he had other secrets he wouldn't keep them to himself. "I'm sorry if it was private," she said when Liam took a step closer and looked at the book.

"It's not private," he said. Sadie stepped to the side to accom-modate him. He turned a few pages, then let out a breath and shut the book, running his fingers across the title as if contemplating the power the Martin family line had in his life. Some of his earlier anxi-ety seemed to have moved on and he was more like the Liam she knew—easygoing, mild-mannered, and confident—but there was still tension, and perhaps a little fear, in the set of his jaw.

"It's an impressive compilation," Sadie said. "I've never seen any-thing like it."

"Yeah," Liam agreed, picking up the book and taking it to a shelf located behind and to the side of the desk. "Lady Hane—my Aunt Hattie—had this put together several years ago as a gift to her father when he celebrated thirty-five years as earl."

"Aunt Hattie is Austin's grandmother?" Sadie asked for clarification.

Liam nodded. "Aunt Hattie is twelve years older than Dad. She had her children young, though. Dad met my mom when he was in his mid-thirties, making me the same generation as her grandkids—though Austin is the oldest and still a few years younger than I am."

"I see," Sadie said with a nod. "What does heraldry mean?" she asked.

"Titles were a kind of herald, a pronouncement of greatness or whatever, given by the king as a reward for some great act or friendship or something—I think the first Earl of Garnett discovered an assassination attempt on the prince or something like that. The Book of Heraldry follows the bloodline. I heard it took almost three years for Lady Hane to get it all put together."

"So she didn't do it herself?" Sadie asked, looking at the book now on the shelf.

"Oh, no," Liam said with a dry chuckle. "She hired professional genealogists."

He stood facing the bookshelf and Sadie moved up behind him, wondering what it was he was looking at when he fell silent. Next to where he'd put the pedigree were several nearly identical volumes—each dedicated to one of the eight previous Earls of Garnett.

"Are those all personal histories?" she asked.

"Yes," Liam said, looking at the books. "Each earl has his own, but they are about as boring as you can possibly imagine—they include things like agricultural yields, taxes paid, renovations done to different buildings. Dry as a pile of straw, if you ask me."

Sadie smiled, but wondered if he was contemplating that his father might soon have his own volume. And that one day Liam would have one too. It was a stark reminder that every day was writing Liam's life story, a story that would go down in history as the tenth Earl of Garnett. A story that wouldn't mention Breanna Hoffmiller. Would it mention a dead nurse named John Henry, she wondered?

Liam turned toward her. "You said it was open on the desk?"

"Yes," Sadie said. "I'd only been in here a few minutes before you arrived. I think I saw Austin leave the room though—maybe he got it out." She watched to see his reaction.

Liam scowled. "Hmmm," he said, looking at the book again.

That look showed a lot of consideration in Sadie's opinion. "Should Austin not be looking at it?" That seemed odd, since it was in a rather public area and Liam had said the book wasn't private.

"Not necessarily," Liam said. "It's just that—oh, I don't know."

"What?" Sadie pushed while trying not to sound pushy. It was a difficult balance.

"It's just that this book is a compiled history with documents and records, but there's another book with pedigree information— the Martin family Bible. And I can't seem to find it."

Sadie had heard of family Bibles where people recorded births and deaths and marriages. But did you need one when you had a compiled book like the one on the shelf? "Is it important that you find it?"

Liam shrugged. "My father mentioned it a few months back. It had been lost for a long time and he was excited to have it back— but it isn't here. I asked Austin about it and he said he didn't know anything about it being found at all."

And yet, Sadie mused, *Austin was looking through the Book of Heraldry.*

"But your father mentioned the Bible and you expected it to be here?" Sadie asked by way of clarification, keeping her thoughts of Austin to herself.

"He'd been studying the family line and felt he'd done a disservice by not respecting it more when he was younger."

"And so you thought that perhaps you ought to study the family Bible like your father had, grow some appreciation for it."

Liam smiled, but it was sad. "Something like that," he said, then he looked at Sadie with sad eyes that made her want to give him a hug. "Last August Dad e-mailed me and asked me to come back to England."

Sadie lifted her eyebrows. "As in, for good?"

Liam nodded and pushed his hands in his pockets, rocking back slightly on his heels as he looked between Sadie, the floor, and the bookshelves around the room, not letting his eyes stay in any one place for too long. "He said he regretted that he hadn't been more involved in the earldom before he inherited it. He said he wanted me to come out and help him manage things and learn the ropes."

"Isn't that what Austin does?"

Liam met her eye briefly and nodded. "Yeah," he said. "In fact that's what Dad said—that I should be the one doing what Austin was doing—that it would be better for everyone if I did."

"Was he angry when you said no?"

Liam shook his head. "No," he said. "I told him I wanted a few more years, that I wasn't done with my life yet. He seemed to understand, but I know he was disappointed all the same." He shrugged his shoulders but Sadie felt he was trying to convince himself it wasn't a big deal more than he was trying to convince Sadie. He'd had a chance to work side by side with his father and turned it down. Now his father was in a vegetative state. "We agreed that I would come out for a couple weeks at Christmastime in order to familiarize myself with the earldom a little bit."

"And here you are," Sadie said, commiserating.

Liam let out a breath. "Yep," he said, turning back to the shelves. "Here I am." He reached up and straightened a book on a higher shelf. "I've been through the whole library looking for that family Bible."

"You said it had been lost for a long time," Sadie said. "So, maybe Austin really didn't know your father had found it."

"Which in and of itself seems strange," Liam said. "They worked together very closely."

That is strange, she agreed silently. "Could it be somewhere else? Aren't family Bibles valuable? Maybe your dad kept it in a secure location."

Liam scratched his head. "Maybe." Then he looked at her. "But I don't want to make a big deal out of it—especially to Austin."

Sadie knew she was supposed to nod and agree, but she couldn't let this opening go unexplored. "Why?"

Liam paused and looked up toward the ceiling as if trying to think of how to say what he wanted to say. Sadie just smiled with a perfect expression of sympathetic interest on her face. After a few seconds, Liam looked down at Sadie. "Let's just say I have reason not to trust him as much as I would like to."

Well, that was certainly cryptic.

"And I don't want him thinking the family Bible is too important to me." He looked at the Book of Heraldry and Sadie could practically read his thoughts. If Austin was looking at the pedigree charts, maybe he already knew the Bible was important. But it also attested to the fact that he probably didn't have it—otherwise why would he need to look through the pedigree book at all?

The door to the library opened just as Sadie was about to push Liam for more information about his feelings. Austin stepped through the doorway with a long stride that he brought up short when he saw them there. He looked at both of them, and then at the empty desk where the book no longer sat open. They all stood watching each other in silence for a few moments before Austin spoke. "Dinner's waiting on you," he said, not looking pleased.

"Oh, right," Liam said, moving forward and pulling his hands out of his pockets. He turned to Sadie. "That's why I came looking for you in the first place—Breanna's probably wondering what happened to me."

He passed Austin with a slight nod that was more polite than friendly. Sadie followed, watching Austin as she approached him.

"Mrs. Hoffmiller," he said in a formal tone. "I believe I owe you an apology."

She stopped and met his eyes, unable to hide her surprise.

Austin continued before she had the chance to answer. "I was inappropriate in my behavior toward you this afternoon. I have a great deal of work to take care of before the holiday and I'm afraid I let my schedule"—he pronounced it *shedule*—"put me in a foul mood. It was not fair that I let my personal affairs get in the way of my manners and I apologize for allowing it to do so."

Sadie continued to stare at him. There was part of her that felt vindicated by his apology, but the absolute lack of sincerity was impossible to ignore. It sounded like the kind of apology a child gave when being threatened with punishment if he didn't say he was sorry. Then again, it could simply be that Austin wasn't used to making apologies and therefore didn't know how to do it.

Sadie forced a smile and nodded her acknowledgment, but couldn't make herself give him the satisfaction of a verbal response. He seemed to sense her exact thoughts, but didn't seem bothered. He'd done his part—apologized—and that's all he really cared about.

But Sadie cared about something else: Why was he reading the pedigree? And why did his staff go to him with information they kept from the police? She moved past him through the doorway and wished there was a book she could pick up to read all about him—he was the one she wanted more information on.

CHAPTER 17

The only sound in the dining room was the clinking of silverware and the movement of the staff's feet as they served the plates. Sadie had begun the meal saying thank you for every little thing any of the staff did for her, but finally gave up after feeling rather foolish when no one else was saying anything. Plus, the staff seemed uncomfortable with her gratitude. She put a bite of potatoes in her mouth as she looked around the table. It was a very different dinner tonight than it had been last night when it had just been Breanna, Sadie, and Liam. Last night, the three of them had talked about their trip, the places they'd seen, and things they'd done—a fitting conclusion since they believed they would be on a plane for home the next day. Breanna and Liam's discussion about their future hadn't taken place yet, Liam's argument with John Henry hadn't happened, and no dead bodies had turned up behind any curtain panels. Last night's dinner of roast beef, mashed potatoes, Yorkshire pudding, and vegetables was comfortable, easy, nice. They'd finished out the meal with that wonderful English trifle. Sadie now wondered who had made it, since it likely hadn't been the non-cook Mrs. Land. Maybe Lacy? Where had that woman gone? Would she come back like Mrs. Land had suggested? Sadie hoped so, but based on Lacy's parting words, she didn't think she'd be seeing Lacy again.

Liam dropped his knife, causing everyone to look at him. He ducked his head and muttered an apology while picking up his knife. Austin watched his cousin for several seconds before returning to his meal. Sadie was reminded that a lot could change in twenty-four hours and this new layer wasn't very sweet at all.

Despite having a lot of factors to choose from, Sadie felt sure that if not for Austin, the three of them would be discussing the situation rather than eating in silence as if there had been no murder at all. Austin and Liam sat at the ends of the table—Sadie didn't know which end was considered the head—while Breanna and Sadie sat directly across from one another in the center of the table, with no fewer than four empty seats on either side of them. The staff had to pass the different condiments and dishes around the table since none of the diners could reach one another. However, each setting had its own cute little miniature set of salt and pepper shakers. Sadie was tempted to smuggle a set of them home.

Sadie tried to watch Austin without being too overt about it. To his credit, he did seem a bit more relaxed than he'd been this afternoon, but was still quite broody. An unspoken agreement had settled around the table and no one brought up John Henry or Inspector Dilree.

"This is delicious," Sadie said after taking a bite of the pigeon and unable to stand the silence any longer. She looked toward the far end of the room where Grant stood at attention near the door—presumably in case there was some kind of dining emergency they couldn't resolve on their own. She met his eye and smiled. "Please give my compliments to Mrs. Land if she's still here," she said, hoping it would help assuage any suspicion he might have as to her motives and discoveries in the kitchen. Grant did not look pleased to be addressed, but after a moment he inclined his head slightly.

"Roasted pigeon," Breanna said, catching her mother's eye from across the table. "How about that?"

"It's a good thing no one in America knows how good this is," Sadie replied, hoping to start a conversation. "We'd never see another pigeon in the park again."

Austin looked up from his plate. "These aren't park pigeons," he said with derision. He took a long draw from his wineglass.

"I didn't mean to insinuate they were," Sadie said, smiling to hide her annoyance with his continued negativity. She went back to her meal, wondering why she even bothered trying to be sociable. The next few minutes continued without anyone speaking.

"Mom, did you lose an earring?"

Sadie's hand went to her naked earlobe and she felt her face heat up a little bit. "Oh, I guess so," she said, and busied herself with removing the other earring.

"I hope you find it, I love those earrings on you."

"Thank you, dear," Sadie said, feeling bad for perpetuating deceit. "I'm sure it will turn up." She put the second earring in her pocket with the first one and quickly took another bite of her dinner.

Silence returned to the table.

When Austin, of all people, spoke next, Sadie looked up in surprise. "And what have you thought of your trip?" he asked, putting down his knife and fork and looking between Breanna and Sadie.

Sadie and Breanna exchanged a look as well, asking each other with their eyes who wanted to answer. Sadie was chewing, so Breanna took the lead. "It's been very nice," she said. "Well, up until this afternoon."

Austin waved his hand as if this afternoon was of no concern and picked up his wineglass—Grant had refilled it twice already and Sadie wondered if that was why Austin was suddenly becoming a conversationalist. "What was your favorite portion?" he asked, looking straight at Sadie with those intense eyes that didn't seem the least bit interested in whether or not she'd enjoyed her trip. However, she believed that even the best meals could be ruined with tension of the kind that was hovering over the table so she was willing to do her part to salvage the dinner.

"Well, I loved every bit of it," Sadie said. "I loved the history and the culture and the food. Everything." Yes, she realized she might be sucking up just a little bit, but a little brownnosing never hurt anybody and if it worked in changing Austin's mood, it would be worth it.

Austin nodded as if to say she'd given an acceptable answer, then looked at Breanna. "And how about you, Miss Hoffmiller?"

"London," Breanna said easily, stabbing a potato with her fork. Sadie reminded herself to tell Breanna about Austin's apology as soon as she had the chance, but then was bothered by the fact that without knowing he *had* apologized, no one seemed bothered by his earlier insults. "I loved seeing all the things I'd heard so much about—Westminster Abbey, Tower Prison, Changing of the Guard, London Zoo—it was all fascinating."

"I should have guessed Liam would take you to the zoo while you were there," Austin said. His tone implied that he found it childish. Sadie watched Breanna straighten. She did not take kindly to cracks about her passion which would soon be her profession. Though there were many careers she could use her zoology degree toward, she'd always had her heart set on working at an actual zoo—a choice that was often seen as immature. But right now wouldn't be a good time to go off on Austin about that—even if he was asking for it.

"It wouldn't make much sense for me not to go," Breanna said, and Sadie held her breath. "I'll begin my career working at a zoo in Florida after I graduate in the spring."

Phew, Sadie exhaled in relief.

"And did you enjoy our zoo?" Austin asked, saying it in such a way as to make it sound like a challenge.

"Very much," Breanna said, returning his tone and his look with one equally condescending. Sadie was glad to see the spark in her daughter's eyes. "London is one of only a few zoos in the world to have successfully hatched a Rhynchophis boulengeri snake in captivity—we studied it in my assisted reproduction class last year. Such snakes are highly respected in the zoo communities."

Austin raised his eyebrow, watching Breanna in a way that almost looked as though he were impressed. "I'll take your word for it," he drawled. "I myself haven't been to the zoo since I was a child and I can't remember enjoying it all that much back then either. I guess I didn't know about the rare snake."

"Well, it was a rather recent development," Breanna said after taking another bite.

"It was fun to see the python exhibit they used in the Harry Potter movie," Sadie broke in, wanting to divide the tension she felt building again. "But I guess it really holds a black mamba snake, which is actually olive green."

"The inside of its mouth is black," Breanna explained. "And it's among the most deadly snakes in the world, hence the name black mamba."

"Yes, I suppose green mamba doesn't sound quite as frightening." Sadie turned back to Austin. "Although it's still a snake, which is scary enough as it is. Anyway, we also got to see the castle they used for the Harry Potter movies when we were in Northampton earlier this week. That was fun too."

"Ah, yes, the beloved Harry Potter. What trip to England—the birthplace of Shakespeare, Winston Churchill, and Jane Austen—would be complete without the unfailing fortitude of the Harry Potter tour?"

Sadie knew he was being insulting, but the thrill of hearing Harry Potter's name spoken with a real British accent was just too much fun. Sadie wasn't sure how to respond, so she settled for a rather deflated, "Yep, we loved it."

The silence returned for several seconds until Austin looked up and pointed at the half-finished plate in front of him. Grant fairly tripped over himself to retrieve it while Austin shook his head slightly as though disappointed that the butler hadn't read his mind and picked up the plate before being told to do so. Grant handed the plate to a footman who stood near the door, giving the young man almost the exact same look Austin had given the butler, before proceeding to clean up any crumbs Austin had left behind. Grant used a scraper-type tool he swished over the tablecloth in wide arcs, catching all the crumbs before scooting them into his hand. Efficient.

"I've been wondering," Sadie asked, determined to keep the conversation alive. "How old is Southgate estate? Is it as old as some of the other estates and castles we toured?"

"Not nearly," Austin said, hinting that it was a ridiculous question; certainly anyone could look at the architecture and design and know it couldn't possibly be as old as Hampton Court Palace, for instance, or Chatsworth. Austin continued, "The earldom, however, predates Southgate by almost a hundred years. The fifth Earl of Garnett had Southgate built in the late eighteen hundreds. He married the third daughter of the Duke of Gloucester and built the home for her when she bore him an heir. Of course the boy was nearly fourteen before it was finished."

"Oh, wow," Sadie said. "My husband only bought me a rocking chair when we brought Breanna home."

"Well, I wasn't the heir to an earldom," Breanna said.

"True," Sadie said, glad to see Breanna helping to lighten the mood. "But you were no less loved." She smiled at her daughter but directed her next comment to Austin. "Are all the titles determined by birth order?"

She took a bite of her pigeon while waiting for Austin's answer—the bird was pretty good, though not as tasty as the Cornish hens in York. This meat was denser, not as moist. Then again, perhaps being transported in Styrofoam and then kept warm in the warming ovens had made a difference, but she chose not to dwell on that. "The younger sons don't get anything?"

"No," Austin said. "The heir is the oldest male in the line and he not only gets the title, but most dukes and earls hold numerous lesser titles as well. The other sons often receive inheritances that allow them to find means of supporting themselves, but the heir gets everything tied to the earldom. In fact, the heir is usually referred to by his father's next highest title until he fully inherits." He looked across at Liam. "Don't they refer to you as a viscount or something?"

"Viscount of Darling," Liam said, though he didn't look up and did not seem the least bit in favor of this conversation. Breanna didn't seem all that comfortable with it either as she pushed her food around her plate. Sadie was reminded that it was all these titles and inheritances that had gotten in the way of their relationship. She wondered if Breanna had known about the viscount thing.

"Darling Viscount," Sadie said, smiling and hoping that at least one other person at the table would laugh at her joke. "That's cute."

"But it's never said like that," Austin said, not sounding pleased with Sadie's attempt at humor. "It's the Viscount of Darling."

Sadie cleared her throat as she squirmed beneath the reprimand. She hoped that bringing up the question of titles and pedigrees wouldn't make Austin or Liam uncomfortable—then again, maybe she didn't mind their discomfort. Especially Austin's. So far, however, he didn't seem to be bothered by her questions.

"I noticed that the fifth earl was the second son."

Austin nodded. "The spare," he said. "Backup. Isn't he the one who inherited because the previous earl, his brother, had only daughters?"

"Yes," Sadie said, surprised he knew the details so well.

"Exactly, so if the title holder has no son, then the title passes to a brother—the next male descendant from the previous title holder. If there is no living male through a brother, the title can revert entire generations until it finds a male heir in direct line of the original Peer."

"Sounds complicated," Sadie said before taking another bite. The meat was just getting drier. She dipped the next bite in some of the gravy that had spread out on the plate. Better.

"It can be," Austin said. He held out his glass to the side and Grant hurried to refill it again. Austin took a long swallow, draining half of the deep red liquid from his glass. Sadie wondered if he always drank this much or if he was unusually stressed out tonight in particular. "But it's taken quite seriously to be even a potential heir. Just having a direct link—meaning an exact direct male line—to an earl or a duke in your history can make all the difference to some people. Schooling, profession, even marriages have been decided on that kind of merit—entire lives forged simply because there is a distant chance that a title could fall on their shoulders at some point." He shook his head and smiled slightly, as if amused by the whole idea.

"I'm assuming that it doesn't matter so much to you," Sadie said, wondering if she had misinterpreted what he'd said.

Austin waved his hand, again dismissing the comment. "My paternal grandfather was an untitled Scotsman, but he married well and was able to use those connections to do well for himself and send my father to the best schools. Eventually, my father became a doctor—a position above the class he was born into. He then married my mother, the daughter of a baron and the granddaughter of an earl, and those connections helped him even more in his career. Things are changing in England," he said, though his face had fallen and he stared into his wine glass. "Many of my generation use the station afforded us through our parents, but are trying to find a way to chart our own course as well."

"Hmmm, well, it's very interesting," Sadie said benignly, watching him closely. It was difficult to judge his sincerity, but she sensed a personal note in his words. He wasn't simply talking about his generation, he was talking about himself—his own desire to chart his own course. And yet, he had become an apprentice to the earl and was currently acting as trustee. It seemed to Sadie that he was staying very close to his family ties—specifically to the person who had the most power to give him a leg up when he needed it. It smacked of hypocrisy in her opinion. Maybe he felt like he had no choice and resented it.

She glanced toward Liam to see his reaction to what Austin had said, but he was simply eating his meal, his expression tense. She couldn't help but admit that Breanna might be right: he did not seem cut out to be earl. In fact, Austin was the one sitting at the head of the table, leading the conversation as if this were his home and Liam were his guest, instead of the other way around. Regardless of what Sadie felt about the way the social systems worked in England, she was disappointed in the way Liam seemed to almost refuse to stand up for his position.

"So, if your grandfather was a baron, are you heir apparent for that?" Breanna asked Austin, interrupting Sadie's thoughts about Liam.

Austin looked over at her, seemingly pulled out of his own thoughts. It took a few moments for him to completely reconnect. "Grandmother had three daughters, but no male heirs. Grandfather was an only child. When he died a few years ago, the barony reverted two generations and passed to a cousin."

"So your grandmother has no title any more?" Sadie asked, remembering the thoughts she'd had about the widow of the fourth earl. Did a woman lose everything if her husband died and she hadn't provided a son who would ensure she was cared for?

Austin stiffened slightly, but seemed to notice and forced himself to relax. "Grandmother is the Dowager Lady Hane—though the Dowager part is only used when the current Lady Hane is present, otherwise she's still referred to as Lady Hane. She has rights to the Dowager cottage located in Norwich, though she prefers to stay in London."

"How does she support herself?" Sadie asked. "I mean, does the new baron have to pay her expenses and things?"

"Yes," Austin said simply. "She has an allowance."

"Well, good," Sadie said, wondering at his reticence in talking about his grandmother. But maybe he just didn't like to gossip.

"So, then you have no title?" Breanna asked. Sadie could tell from her daughter's expression that she was trying as hard as Sadie was to follow all the intricacies.

Austin shook his head, not seeming to be at all offended. "I am simply Mr. Melcalfe."

"But the staff calls you *Lord* Melcalfe," Sadie pointed out.

Austin glanced at the butler standing at the door. "Grant does," he said succinctly. "It's simply in respect to my position as William's manager. The other staff have followed suit, but it's not an official title."

"Oh," Breanna said. "I—I'm sorry."

"Don't be," Austin said with surprising sincerity. "There is much to be said for choosing your own future."

And is this the future he wants? Sadie wondered. *To act in behalf of the earl?* Even though it rubbed her wrong in many ways, Sadie had to admit Austin had good leadership skills, though it was hard to equate that with the fact that he preferred working for his great-uncle rather than being his own man. But, perhaps that *was* his dream. Who was she to judge how anyone wanted to spend their life?

"Yes," Breanna said, her tone low and thoughtful as she looked at her plate. "There is something to be said for following your own dreams."

Austin, like Sadie, looked from Breanna to Liam as the comment dropped like a rock into the middle of the table.

Liam looked at Breanna with something between disappointment and anger before he let out a breath and stood slowly. "I'm going to sit with my father," he said in a guarded tone. "Charlotte has been with him for quite some time." He looked quickly at Breanna again, then shifted to catch Sadie's eye as well. He looked so tormented that Sadie's heart went out to him. "Call me if you need anything," he said before putting his napkin on the table. Grant hurried to open the door for him, then returned to his post. Sadie wondered if the family ever got tired of having staff members standing around all the time. Did they miss their privacy?

"So he's a bat keeper in California, then?" Austin asked once the door had shut behind Liam.

"He's a supervising zoologist in Oregon," Breanna clarified.

"He's very well-respected in his field and has been a great asset to the Washington Park Zoo. He'll be greatly missed."

Sadie liked that despite the changes in their relationship, Breanna was still defensive of Liam.

"Missed?" Austin questioned.

Breanna paused and Sadie could practically read her thoughts. Did Austin know Liam was planning to stay in England? If not, Sadie didn't think they should be the ones to spill the beans.

"When he becomes earl," Sadie quickly answered. "He's done a lot for the exhibit; he'll be hard to replace."

"Oh, yes, I've no doubt he's invaluable," Austin said with thinly veiled sarcasm. He took another sip of wine, seeming to relax a little bit. As he swallowed Sadie imagined that his mood could switch back and forth just as easily as the wine was draining from his glass. She wanted to take full advantage of it as long as she could—even if his attitude couldn't always be trusted.

"Did you and Liam know one another as children?" Sadie asked, hoping to get more information. "You're close to the same age."

"He's a few years older," Austin confirmed. "But we spent time together when he lived in London—at least before we went to school. I went to Harrow in Middlesex; Liam attended Gordonstoun until he went to the States."

Sadie nodded, although she would never understand how parents could send their children away for school. There were so many facets of English life—at least among the nobility—that Sadie simply couldn't make sense of. "So then you knew Liam's mother?" Sadie asked.

Sadie thought she noticed a slight stiffening in Austin's shoulders, but couldn't be sure. He was so hard to read.

"As much as any boy knows the mother of a playmate," Austin said. "I remember she talked strangely." He half-smiled at the memory, then seemed to drop it as soon as he realized what he was doing. "And she wouldn't dress for dinner—I'm not sure why I remember that but it stands out in my mind, her wearing jeans to a dinner where everyone else was dressed up."

"She didn't like it here very much, did she?" Breanna asked. "In England, I mean, not necessarily Southgate." She pushed the last of her beans up against the remaining potatoes and then mashed them all with the back of her fork, not looking at Austin at all.

Austin, on the other hand, watched her closely. "I don't believe they ever lived at Southgate," he said. "William took over his father's seat in the House of Lords and they lived in London. As to whether she liked it in England or not, I'm not sure I can say. I believe she didn't understand the kind of future she'd chosen when she married William." He picked up his glass again and swirled the dark liquid around in the glass.

"How did she and William meet, anyway?" Sadie asked. Liam had never been very forthcoming about his parents' relationship, and Breanna had said the divorce was very difficult for him, so Sadie hadn't pressed Liam for the story. Austin, though, seemed perfectly willing to talk about it.

"Well, as I've heard it, William's father was devoted to the earldom, which naturally spurred William to distance himself from it. William, like most heirs, was reared almost as if he were the earl already—educated, tutored, raised up in the expectations of his role. William took it all with a grain of salt. He defied his father and went to Yale instead of Oxford. William had a generous allowance, so after his schooling, he traveled a good deal, coming back to England once or twice a year, and having no desire to help run the earldom which his father had immersed himself in after the countess died. William loved America and eventually met Liam's mother there, married her without telling his family, and had a son. It was quite the scandal, according to my grandmother."

"When did the earl die?"

Austin's head snapped up. "What?"

"The earl," Sadie reiterated—maybe he'd had more wine than she thought. "William and your grandmother's father—when did he die?" Maybe she was sounding indelicate. "I mean, when did William become earl?"

Austin nodded his understanding and relaxed again. "I think Liam was four or five years old when they moved back to London."

"The earl had had a stroke, right?" Sadie asked.

Austin nodded and swirled the wine in his glass. "William returned and assumed the role of earl. A few months later, his father died and William became the ninth Earl of Garnett."

"It seems like that would have been hard for William," Breanna suggested. "To leave the life he had and suddenly be an earl."

"I'm sure it was difficult, but he's fulfilled his role quite well for having taken so many tangent courses before then." He took a long drink of his wine.

"I've wondered," Sadie asked carefully, "could he have refused it?"

"Refused the title?" Austin asked, somewhat surprised at her question but trying not to show it.

Sadie nodded. "Yes, I mean he traveled the world, married an American—it seems like he wasn't all that interested, even if he did accept it when the time came for him to do so. But does an heir *have* to take the title?"

"I suppose not," Austin said, his tone thoughtful. "The Peerage Act was passed through Parliament in the 60s and made it possible for people to renounce their title if they wanted to. But as far as I know the only people who have denounced it are those who, for political reasons, did not want the title which would keep them out of certain political offices. Renouncing did not affect their heirs and the title simply waited for the next generation to reclaim it. However, there is still the matter of holdings, land, estates, business interests, investments, and non-profit organizations that come with most titles. Even if a title is disclaimed, someone needs to take responsibility for the holdings and, although there is always the option of appointing trustees to do the work, I haven't yet heard of anyone, regardless of how much they don't want a title, not being happy to take over the money." He smiled. "So I suppose the answer to your question is, yes, William could have disclaimed his title. But why would he? Despite his wandering soul, William was an Englishman. He'd been raised to his station, and when it called for him, he fulfilled his duty."

Breanna had listened intently, but now she laid her fork on her plate. "I think I'll go up to bed," she said, giving a fake smile to Sadie and Austin as she pushed away from the table. Grant moved to the door to show her out. Sadie wondered if Breanna's last hope—that Liam could simply say "no" if he chose to—had been shot down.

"I'll be there in a few minutes," Sadie said, already turning back to Austin. As much as she wanted to offer comfort and sympathy to her daughter, Austin's honesty was surprising and she meant to take full advantage of it while she could. He might not get drunk tomorrow and afford her such a good opportunity again. However, he pushed away from the table as well, teetering just a little bit as he gained his feet.

"England is playing West Germany tonight," he said briskly. "I'd like to catch the second half. Have an enjoyable evening."

CHAPTER 18

Sadie scowled as he left the room, leaving Sadie alone with Grant. But perhaps that was yet another opportunity. "Grant," she asked after taking the last couple of bites of her dinner.

"Yes, madam," he said in his nasally butler-voice. Sadie wondered if they were taught that tone in butler school—right after how to stand for an hour without slouching while people ate.

"Mrs. Land was cooking a chocolate torte—do we still get it for dessert?" She worried she was being rude, and yet Austin had been ruder and it hadn't seemed to affect any of the staff.

"I'll go see," he said. He left the room and Sadie looked around the expansive dining room. If she knew more about design she was sure she'd be impressed and know what to call the carved ceiling design and color palate of light green and blue. As it was she found it very pretty, for lack of a better word, but cold.

Grant returned and set a plate of chocolate torte in front of her. She smiled up at him even though the torte was tipped on its side. Apparently, without Mrs. Land around to ensure proper presentation, no one else thought about it. She wondered if he'd had to cut and serve it himself.

"Thank you," she said sincerely before picking up her fork. "Breanna, Liam, and Austin will be mad they left so soon."

She cut her first bite and chewed it slowly. For having been frozen a few hours earlier, it was alright, but it wasn't wonderful. In fact she wasn't sure she'd eat it if she hadn't requested it, necessitating that Grant go all the way downstairs to get it for her. Grant remained at the door and after a few bites, she decided to try to strike up a conversation with the man. With Mrs. Land gone she needed another resource for information. She hoped he might be a bit more open to it than he'd been earlier. Maybe she was getting tired, but it seemed worth a shot. She'd be careful not to ask anything specific about John Henry or Mrs. Land so as not to earn his ire.

"So, Grant," she began, turning slightly in her chair so she could make eye contact, though he avoided it and stared intently at the wall across the room from where he stood. "How long have you worked here?"

He seemed to argue with himself before answering, finally saying. "I have worked for Lord Martin nearly fifteen years."

"Oh, wow," Sadie said, raising her eyebrows. "That's a long time. He must be a good boss, er, employer."

"Yes, madam," he said.

"And how long has the other staff worked here?"

He didn't answer for several seconds, during which time Sadie watched him expectantly. "Madam, it is improper for me to have such a conversation with you in regard to staff members." He made eye contact then, but only briefly. He didn't look happy.

"Oh, I didn't mean to be rude or do anything improper," Sadie said, smiling sweetly and hoping perhaps it would break through his crusty exterior. "I was just making conversation. I guess I don't know the rules very well."

Grant paused for several seconds before he finally spoke—giving Sadie the impression that he'd used that pause to consider whether or not to speak at all. "If I may say so, madam, the only rule you need to be aware of is that the staff and the family, along with their guests, are not *friends* with one another. The staff is here to serve, and the family provides that opportunity. The guests are simply partakers of the hospitality offered by both. When a staff member steps outside of those boundaries, allowing a guest of the household to assist in the preparations of a meal, for instance, they face the prospect of being removed from their position entirely, which then affects the livelihood not only of themselves, but also of anyone they are supporting. The family also suffers as they are forced to find a replacement for the staff member who has shown that, regardless of their dedication to the work they do, they do not respect the boundaries. Therefore, it is in the best interest of all parties for the family and the guests to function within the parameters of their circumstance and allow the staff members to do the same."

Well, Sadie felt sufficiently browbeaten and was without words on how to respond to the lashing she'd just been given with a most proper British tongue. "I-I'm very sorry," Sadie said, feeling repentant. "I didn't mean to get Mrs. Land in trouble." She looked up at Grant who remained stoic by the door, though she sensed a measure of satisfaction in his countenance. "Was Mrs. Land fired on account of me?"

"No, madam, Mrs. Land was not fired. Her son had a bit of trouble with the law and was unable to come to see her. She went to spend the holiday with him instead. The situation I used as an example was simply hypothetical. However, if Lord Melcalfe had discovered you and Mrs. Land in the kitchen, she very well could have been out of a job. Indiscreet staff members do not last long in this line of work, and while I came up with a solution to this particular situation, if not for the standard two-day holiday, it would not have worked. In a word, we were all very lucky."

Sadie looked at the remaining torte on her plate, but what had been somewhat appetizing a minute earlier was not at all appetizing now that she realized the risk she'd caused for Mrs. Land. She pushed away from the table. "Thank you, Grant. I understand."

"Of course," he said, bowing slightly as she passed him in the doorway.

At the top of the stairs she ran into the dark-skinned security guard, who stood as she approached. She smiled politely and took the hand he offered to her.

"Good evening, Mrs. Hoffmiller," he said.

"Sadie," she corrected him. "'Mrs. Hoffmiller' makes me feel old. I'm afraid I don't remember your name."

"Manny Heshad," he said. He smiled, revealing white teeth that looked even whiter against the cinnamon tone of his skin. "If you need anything, I'll be here."

Sadie thanked him and continued on her way to the room she and Breanna shared. When she entered the room, Breanna was digging through her backpack, emptying most of the contents onto the bed in the process of looking for whatever it was she was looking for.

"Is everything all right?" Sadie asked as she shut the door behind her. For good measure she locked it as well.

"Everything's fine, Mom," Breanna said without looking up.

"You just seem, um—"

"Overwhelmed?" Breanna offered sarcastically. "Tired? Stressed out? Worried about not getting back to school in time for the first day of my final semester?" She let out a huff at the end of her comments and clenched her jaw, still digging through her backpack.

"Confused over your feelings toward Liam?"

Breanna's hands slowed. "I don't want to talk about it," she said, finally pulling out her pajamas that had been expertly packed by being scrunched into a wad. Breanna shook them out but it did little to help the wrinkles.

"I know," Sadie said. "So I'll leave it alone, but you know you can talk to me about anything, right?" She wanted to bring up the argument between Liam and John Henry that Breanna had kept to herself, and yet it felt a little like beating a dead horse at this point. Breanna knew Sadie was unhappy about that and she'd apologized.

Breanna closed her eyes as if considering that. "Sure," she said. Without making eye contact she turned toward the bathroom, "I'll keep that in mind."

While Breanna changed, Sadie positioned, opened, and sorted through her luggage in order to find her facial kit, hand lotion, slippers, socks, and pajamas—purple flannels she'd made herself. She liked a larger top and smaller bottom, which meant she'd have to buy two pair of store-bought pajamas to be truly comfortable. Instead she made her own. They were nicely folded so as not to get wrinkled like Breanna's were. She rearranged her things while considering how best to start the day tomorrow. She wanted to make the most of her time before they were sent to London.

When Breanna came back into the room, Sadie announced her plan to make breakfast in the morning.

"Did Austin say you could be in the kitchen?" Breanna asked, looking up at Sadie as she pulled back the covers from the bed.

"Well, I figure I'll wake up early and just get to work. What is he going to do, kick me out?" She considered telling Breanna about her conversation with Grant but chose against it for fear that Breanna would agree with the butler. "Think about it, Bre, this is my chance to cook in a real English kitchen—I'm going to make crumpets." She smiled widely at the idea.

"Maybe you should at least talk to Liam first," Breanna said with none of the enthusiasm Sadie felt her announcement deserved. Breanna climbed into the bed and threw most of the two dozen pillows onto the floor. Sadie hoped the cases weren't real silk. "Austin already told you no."

"I know," Sadie said with a single shoulder shrug. "But it's not his house. I'd just like to surprise everyone and save them from takeout for breakfast."

Breanna burrowed down into the covers. "I still think you ought to get permission. And besides, you shouldn't be sneaking around by yourself."

"Sometimes repentance is better than permission," Sadie replied, stepping out of her shoes. "And I don't want to get anyone in trouble by asking. Besides, they've got security guards posted all over the place—you met Manny, right? *And,* I thought I'd make my Wake 'Em Up Breakfast Casserole—how does that sound?"

Breanna's eyes brightened, but only slightly. "Real food," she said with a sigh. "I'm not sure I know what it tastes like anymore. What time are you planning to get started?" She reached for her phone on the nightstand and flipped it open.

"Early," Sadie said as Breanna began texting. "Before anyone gets up who can tell me not to do it."

"Don't you mean us? Before anyone gets up who can tell *us* not to do it?" Breanna asked, looking up from her phone. "I'm going with you."

Sadie hedged. "Well, I know it's been a hard day for you, and it's not healthy to handle so much stress on less than adequate sleep. There've been studies, you know."

"Nice try." Breanna put her phone in her lap and picked up her watch that she'd set on the bedside table. "What time?"

"Five," Sadie said.

Breanna nodded and spent nearly a minute programming the watch before putting it back on the nightstand and picking up her phone again. "Be sure and wake me up, okay?"

"Sure," Sadie said on her way to the bathroom to get changed, picking up the notebook on her way. *Sure* was a great word, a wonderful way to give a positive but noncommittal answer. She closed the door behind her while coming up with the justification she'd use for not waking up Breanna in the morning. In addition to the fact that Breanna seemed intent on reining Sadie in, there were just times when she preferred to cook alone.

CHAPTER 19

Sadie grabbed Breanna's watch after the first beep—she'd moved it to her bedside table after Breanna had fallen asleep. After pushing buttons until it shut up, she got out of bed and slid the note she'd written in the bathroom last night from underneath her notebook. She didn't want Breanna to worry when she woke up and found her mother gone.

Sadie padded across the floor to the chair where she'd laid out her clothing for the day—her favorite Gap curvy jeans—a must for her voluptuous hips—and a black T-shirt with "Rock Star" written across it in rhinestones. Her friend Gayle had bought the same shirt and they loved wearing them out in public together and making people stare. Though Sadie wouldn't call herself old, and she certainly didn't think she looked like she was closer to sixty than fifty, it still confused people to see a *mature* woman dressed in silly clothes. Lastly, she slid her feet into her orange Crocs.

Mrs. Land and Lacy had worn a black uniform similar to hospital scrubs, but of course Sadie didn't have anything like that so she'd gotten as close as she could. She picked up the clothes and tiptoed to the bathroom where she took a quick shower. After drying off, she added a little gel to her hair and attacked it with the blow dryer, sending wet hair in every direction until it was mostly dry and stuck out like an electrocuted turkey. Then all she had to do was strategically add some sculpting putty and mold it into place—ingenious invention, sculpting putty. Once her hair tucked and curled and behaved itself nicely, she attended to her makeup, pronounced herself lovely—if she did say so herself—and tiptoed back through the bedroom, grabbing her recipe book, whistle, and ChapStick before slipping out the door into the dimly lit hallway. She wished she had her jacket since the house was rather cold. It was made of stone after all: what did she expect?

For the briefest moment she questioned her own judgment of being alone in a house where a murder had taken place. Or of leaving Breanna alone as well, but whether it was because of the security guards posted around the house or because she just really, really, really wanted to cook, Sadie wasn't nearly as freaked out as perhaps she should be. She had her trusty jogging whistle in her pocket for protection and besides, *someone* had to make breakfast. She went back and locked the bedroom door from the inside, testing the knob to assure Breanna was safe, and then headed toward the stairs.

Manny was sitting at the top of the stairs and rose to his feet when she reached him. His dark skin seemed even darker in the dimmed light of early morning.

"Mrs. Hoffmiller," he said, his lilting accent making her name sound so musical. "What are you doing up and about?"

She smiled. "Making breakfast," she said as if sharing a secret.

Manny began shaking his head but Sadie put a hand on his arm. "Manny," she said, looking him full in the face. "I have spent a week touring this beautiful country, seeing the sights, living the life of gentry, and yet right now all I want to do is get my hands in some flour and put together a breakfast that will last you all day." She swished her hand through the air. "Now, doesn't it seem ridiculous that some silly rules about who can and can't be allowed in the kitchen would get in the way of my doing this service?"

Manny chuckled. "Ah, Mrs. Hoffmiller, you're trying to manipulate me," he said. "But I'm not to be—"

"Oatmeal raisin," Sadie interrupted, lifting one eyebrow. "Is that your price? A fresh plate of oatmeal raisin cookies."

"I'm hired help for the estate, Mrs. Hoffmiller, I can't go against the instructions."

"Chocolate chip cookies," she cut in. "Fresh, gooey, oozy chocolate chip cookies. And no one told you specifically not to allow me to make breakfast, did they?"

He shook his head. "Mrs. Hoffmiller," he said again, placing his hand on his chest. "Regardless of whether I was specifically instructed or not, I was told that guests are to remain in the common areas of the estate."

Sadie narrowed her eyes, looking him over appraisingly as she tried to properly determine what would woo him to her side of this argument. Finally she leaned toward him. "Coconut macaroons," she said with confidence. How could she have forgotten how popular they were in England?

Manny's back straightened, and then he leaned forward. "Dipped in chocolate?" he asked.

Bingo.

"Oh, yes, each bite is a perfect combination of smooth, rich chocolate and sweet coconut. Together, they are food of the gods."

Manny, for all his brute strength, was putty in her hands. He reached down and unclipped a radio from his belt. "Mrs. Hoffmiller will be in the kitchen," he said into it. "I'm escorting her there now and will check on her intermittently." She dug in her pocket to show her whistle while he still held the walkie-talkie close to his mouth. She wanted to make sure they realized she was prepared. Manny furrowed his brows for a moment but nodded when she shook the whistle and smiled broadly. "She has, uh, a whistle."

"In case I need help," Sadie whispered.

"In case she needs help," Manny repeated.

Static-filled voices confirmed they'd heard his transmission and then Manny waved her forward, following her down the stairs. The house was mostly dark, lit by lamps here and there that cast pools of dim light. It was like something out of a romantic movie the way the furniture and walls blended into each other and the ambiance made Sadie think of Detective Pete Cunningham. They'd been dating for about two months, but things were going slowly. Pete hadn't quite come to terms with his wife's death two years ago and had yet to even kiss Sadie goodnight after one of their bi-weekly dinner dates. But here in the darkened estate, Sadie was quite sure that if she had the chance, this was exactly the type of setting she'd like to be in with Pete. Maybe she'd see if she could recreate the mood when she got home. It was good to remember that she missed him. She hoped he felt the same.

"What time are you off?" she asked Manny when they reached the double doors of the kitchen.

"Seven," Manny said.

Sadie nodded. "I'll do my best to have them ready for you, but I might be cutting it close."

"I believe I'll be back this evening, so you have plenty of time."

"Even better!" Sadie said with a grin. "I'll have the macaroons ready for you when you come back on shift." Sadie pushed through the doors into the dish room, but Manny put a hand out to stop her from going any further.

"Let me look around first," he said.

She nodded and waited while he entered the kitchen, turned on the lights, and made his way around the room.

"All clear," Manny said when he returned after nearly a minute. "Carl is posted outside that door." She followed his finger to the outside door of the kitchen that Lacy had disappeared through yesterday. "And I'll continue to check on you, alright?"

"And I've got my whistle," Sadie reminded him, patting her pocket.

One side of Manny's mouth went up into a smile. "Right."

Chocolate-Dipped Coconut Macaroons

$1^2/_3$ cups flaked sweetened coconut* (don't pack into measuring cup)
$^1/_3$ cup sugar
3 tablespoons flour
$^1/_4$ teaspoon salt
3 egg whites
$^1/_4$ teaspoon vanilla extract
$^1/_4$ teaspoon almond extract
   chocolate for dipping

Mix coconut, sugar, flour, and salt together in a small bowl. Set aside. Beat egg whites in a medium-sized bowl until frothy—about 30 seconds. Add extracts and mix until combined. Add coconut mixture and stir until combined. Drop by rounded teaspoonfuls onto well-greased baking sheets, parchment paper, or silicone baking sheet (macaroons are notorious for sticking to the pan). Shape with fingers so they are nice and round. Bake at 325 degrees for 18 to 20 minutes or until golden brown around the bottom edges. Let cool completely before removing from pan to prevent sticking. Dip bottom half of cookie into a bowl of melted chocolate.

Cool completely. Store in an airtight container.

Makes about 2 dozen cookies.

*For a tasty option, toast half the coconut by spreading coconut in single layer on a baking sheet. Bake at 350 degrees for about 15 minutes or until coconut is light brown. You can also put coconut in toaster oven on "dark" cycle. Check frequently to avoid burning.

CHAPTER 20

Manny left and Sadie walked into the kitchen, smiling with deep satisfaction at the expansive countertops, twelve-range stove, and triple ovens that, for today at least, were hers and hers alone. Mrs. Land might not know chicken stock from bouillon but she kept a very nice kitchen.

Sadie took a moment to familiarize herself with the room—it was pretty straightforward—but not well stocked. Lacy may have cooked, but she likely only did things here and there to fill out the meal. Sadie found several black aprons hanging on a hook next to her jacket and picked out the cleanest one.

Someone had done some shopping as there were the basics in the glass-fronted refrigerator. The freezer also had a few items—including frozen scones with instructions on how to properly thaw and reheat them. Sadie was downright offended, but managed to push her way past it in order to focus on breakfast. There were potatoes left over from last night, plenty of eggs, cheese, and some ham and even a little broccoli. Unfortunately, she only found an old bag of coconut, and it didn't have nearly enough for the macaroons. Plus, there wasn't any chocolate to dip the macaroons into. She'd have to find a way to get what she needed for the cookies—in fact, she'd definitely need a store run if she were going to cook all the meals today. However, she didn't let the missing ingredients overwhelm her excitement about the one English staple she'd been dying to make—crumpets.

Sadie had looked forward to tea and crumpets since she and Breanna first decided to take this trip, and she hadn't been disappointed. They were a savory, non-sweet tea treat, and Sadie had first tried them at a little tea shop in Northampton. From the first bite she'd known she wanted to learn how to make crumpets on her own. She was encouraged by a good selection of baking items in the cupboards. All she needed was a recipe.

At the far end of the kitchen she located a shelf full of cookbooks, and with eager excitement, she set out to find a crumpet recipe. Finding a crumpet recipe in an English cookbook was easy; however, once she read through the recipe, she realized crumpets were very different from anything she'd ever made. Before actually eating her first crumpet, Sadie had thought they were like a crepe, but they turned out to be more like a muffin—sorta—but not really. They were similar in size and shape to the English muffins Sadie bought at the grocery store, but they weren't the same thing. According to the recipe, they were cooked on top of the stove using something called crumpet rings to hold the shape. She'd never heard of crumpet rings. She'd never heard of baking muffins on a stove either.

The recipe called for yeast and rising time so she needed to verify that there was yeast somewhere in this kitchen before she got started. Luckily, a quick inspection turned up a couple packages of yeast in the refrigerator. She took it as a sign that she was meant to make crumpets since, despite the poor stock of the kitchen, she had everything she needed for the recipe.

She set the yeast to proof while combining the other ingredients—only wishing she had instant yeast to speed up the process. She soon wished that she also knew how to use metric measurements. It took a good deal of time to figure out all that math, but she eventually added the yeast and stirred until her arm felt ready to fall off. Once everything was thoroughly mixed, she covered the bowl with a damp flour-sack towel, preheated one of the ovens to 150 degrees, and put the bowl inside to speed up the rising process, which, according to the recipe, could take as long as an hour. Then she went on a hunt for crumpet rings.

She had to return to the recipe again in order to get a good mental image of what a crumpet ring really was. She assumed it must be round, at least an inch tall, perhaps with a handle to make it easy to remove once the crumpets set up. Then again, the recipe said to use tongs to remove the rings once the crumpets were ready to turn, so maybe there was no handle. It did say that crumpets made without rings were called pikelets. Sadie filed that bit of trivia away, but was determined to find crumpet rings if she could.

She was peering into the very back of a drawer she'd nearly emptied when the sound of footsteps made her stiffen. Whipping around with her heart in her throat, she half expected to encounter the murderer wielding another fireplace poker. Instead, Austin Melcalfe stopped in his tracks just inside the doorway of the kitchen that led to the staff dining room. For a moment his brooding expression was replaced with surprise, and then he quickly shut it down, opting for the disappointed frustration that was so at home on his face.

"What are you doing in here?" he asked briskly. "I told you specifically to stay out of the kitchen."

Sadie cleared her throat and pushed her hair from her eyes while standing up straight. "I assumed that only meant yesterday," she said innocently. "And we needed a cook; Grant wasn't able to find a re-placement for Mrs. Land."

"Grant said you could take her place?" Austin asked sharply, his eyes and face issuing her a challenge. He was dressed in rather trendy jeans, faded across the thigh, brown leather shoes, and a button-up shirt that he left untucked, the sleeves rolled up to his elbows. A rather casual country estate ensemble, Sadie thought, but nice.

"Grant didn't give me permission," Sadie said, not wanting to get the butler in trouble—even if he had put her in her place last night. She'd been careful not to put any staff members at risk with this venture; she'd feel horrible if anyone got in trouble. For that reason, she was glad Austin had discovered her before Grant had. "But Mrs. Land *is* gone," Sadie continued with a shrug. "And I like to cook. Everyone needs to eat and I'm just doing what I can to help."

Austin was silent as if it took a lot of concentration to process that thought. He looked at the drawer she had been rummaging through. "What are you looking for?"

"Um, crumpet rings," Sadie answered carefully. Why did he care what she was looking for? And what was he doing here anyway?

He lifted his eyebrows while still managing to show his disdain. "You're *making* crumpets?"

"Well, I considered praying for them instead, but I'm afraid my faith isn't quite that strong." She smiled at her own joke.

He didn't crack a smile. "No one makes crumpets anymore."

Sadie, still smiling as if he weren't being boorishly rude, shook her head. "If people still eat them, then someone must still make them."

His eyes narrowed and he walked further into the room. "I mean that households don't make their own. We buy them."

Sadie was not surprised and considered commenting on the fact that not having a real cook might have something to do with the fact that he assumed all crumpets were store-bought. However, she resisted saying so, choosing instead to turn the spotlight back on him. "And how would you know that? I don't imagine you're all that intrinsically involved in kitchen work."

"Everyone knows you buy crumpets," he countered.

"Well, I found a recipe," she said, dropping her hand from her hip and turning back to the recipe. "And I plan to make them, but I can't find crumpet rings."

"Because no one makes their own crumpets anymore."

"So you said," Sadie replied. After a few moments she looked up to see he was still watching her. She didn't mind so much so long as his watching didn't lead to him kicking her out of the kitchen. "Can I help you with something?"

"Help me?" he repeated as if not understanding the question.

"Well, are you hungry? Is that why you're here? I've got the crumpet batter rising and I'll be starting a breakfast casserole in a few minutes. I found some cute ceramic dishes that I think will work perfectly for individual casseroles."

"You shouldn't be up and about on your own," he said, completely ignoring what she'd said.

"Manny escorted me," Sadie informed him. "Didn't he tell you that? He's posted at the staircase." As soon as she said it, she cringed slightly, hoping she hadn't just gotten Manny in trouble. Grant had been talking about staff when he said they could get in trouble for talking to her; Manny didn't count as staff, did he?

"I came down another way," Austin said.

Sadie made a note of that. She loved the idea of secret passageways—well, she loved the idea of knowing where they were for herself. It wasn't nearly as much fun just to know they were there. That was actually kind of creepy.

"And why are you here?" Sadie pushed.

He paused and she imagined that he was trying to come up with a reason. "I heard noises," he said. "And I've always been an early riser."

"Apparently," Sadie said, glancing at the clock—it was a quarter to six. She gave up on the drawer she was rifling through and stood, looking around for any other place she might find the rings. They had to be here. This was an English kitchen and despite Austin's insistence that no one made their own crumpets, Sadie was not giving up. "Security knows I'm here and they said they'll be checking on me now and again." She considered telling him about the whistle, but no one seemed to respect it like she did so she let it go this time. He continued to stand there while she moved on to another drawer. "So, since security knows I'm here and you've solved your little mystery of noises in the kitchen . . ." He didn't make any move to leave so she continued. "Is there something else you needed?"

"Actually, I am hungry," he said, but made no move to get himself anything. Sadie gave up her crumpet ring hunt for the moment and headed for the fridge. He might not like that a guest was working in the kitchen, but he had no qualms about having her wait on him. She kept waiting for him to tell her to leave, but so far it didn't seemed to have crossed his mind.

"Well, what's your pleasure? I was about to dice up some ham, would you like a slice of that? There's also milk in here and some fruit—would you like an apple?"

"An apple would be fine," he said, as if doing her a favor. She took one out of the fridge, rinsed it off, and handed it to him. He regarded it for a moment, turning it around in his hand and then took a small bite while she returned to searching the drawer. After that one bite he put the apple on the counter, which to Sadie said he wasn't here for food.

Austin let out a breath and looked around the kitchen, crossing his arms and planting his feet as if he were some kind of sentry. "Where is the kitchen help?"

Sadie threw her hands up and out, cocking her head coyly as if she'd just burst out of a birthday cake. "Ta-da," she said with a big grin. It went over like BLTs at a bar mitzvah. Austin didn't react in the slightest, except to glower even more.

Sadie dropped her hands and cleared her throat. "I haven't seen anyone this morning other than Manny, the security guard." However, the fact that Austin had asked after the kitchen help reminded Sadie that Lacy was usually in charge of breakfast. And then Charlotte had informed Austin that Lacy was missing. Would Austin have come to see Lacy?

"So," Sadie said, trying to come up with something to keep him talking. "You spend a lot of time at Southgate, do you?"

Austin shrugged. "I've been living here since William became ill," he said dryly, not seeming to be in any hurry to leave but not thrilled to be talking to her either. She wondered if he had a headache from all the wine he'd drunk last night—but then he'd been like this when she first met him, so maybe it was just his overall personality.

"Where did you live before that?" she asked.

"I had a flat in Exeter, but still spent a great deal of time out here. Once I became trustee it was apparent I needed to be here full time."

"That's very generous of you," Sadie said, returning to the crumpets. She checked on the batter, but it wasn't quite doubled just yet.

There was still the problem of the crumpet rings. She wanted to explore the other parts of the kitchen, but felt funny doing so with Austin standing there. She decided to start the preparation for the breakfast casserole while she waited on the crumpet batter. She removed the ham and broccoli from the refrigerated case and set them on the butcher-block table. She diced the ham and began chopping the broccoli; Austin watched her with his eyebrows still pulled together.

Her thoughts went back to Lacy. "Do you make it a habit of watching the cooks when you're here?" Was that it? He had some kind of cooking fetish?

"No," he said simply, looking past her toward the staff dining room and, coincidentally, the door through which Lacy had disappeared yesterday. Sadie looked at him more closely, noting the tension in the set of his shoulders. Sadie finished the broccoli while Austin glanced at his watch and then looked up at her.

Sadie didn't respond; she just held his eyes for a few seconds, smiled, and headed toward a shelf stacked with various bowls, containers, steam trays, and other kitchen equipment. She had her eye on a large bowl on the top shelf, but had to stand on her tiptoes in order to barely brush it with her fingertips. She stretched even more and managed to scoot it off the shelf half an inch at a time before it finally dropped, allowing her to catch it. She felt it very poor manners on Austin's part that he didn't offer to help. Strike four . . . or twelve. She couldn't remember how many times he'd been rude to her in one way or another.

She put the bowl on the table, watching as his eyes went toward the door again. "Are you waiting for someone?" she asked easily.

"Why are you asking so many questions?" he snapped, glaring at her with what could only be classified as haughtiness. So much for his apology last night.

"I'm just trying to make conversation seeing as how you're intent on hanging out here with me, and, well, I'm a little curious about a woman that was here yesterday. I thought if you spent much time in the kitchen you might know her."

She was careful not to make eye contact while she said this, giving no impression she was leading him anywhere. The silence stretched itself tightly over several seconds, but Sadie forced herself to be patient. If she seemed too determined to get an answer, or too eager about what he would say, she might blow everything. She'd learned last night that Austin could reveal a great deal of information under the right circumstances. Too bad she hadn't offered him any wine this morning. That might have helped.

"What did she look like?" Austin asked after a moment, his words careful.

"Small," Sadie said, pulling open the refrigerated case to get the last of her ingredients—cheese, eggs, cottage cheese, and roasted potatoes. "She was wearing the same uniform as Mrs. Land, but she had a bandana tied over her hair."

"A bandana?" Austin asked crossly.

"Maybe you call it a kerchief here? A scarf-type thing tied over her head. And she had pretty brown eyes. I think she was part Asian."

"Why were you curious about her?" There was a new kind of urgency in his tone now.

"Well," Sadie said, trying to sound causal as she cracked the first egg into the bowl. "She was with Mrs. Land when Breanna and I came running in here after finding the body. Mrs. Land told me to keep her here while she went to see what had happened in the sitting room. I tried to do as she said, but the girl ran for the door as soon as Mrs. Land left."

Austin put his head down—Sadie would have thought he was praying if not for the fact that he didn't seem to be the type. But he said nothing. She cracked a few more eggs. Based on his interest in this girl, Sadie couldn't help but reflect on the dozens of romance novels she'd read over the last few months. After awhile they all started to sound the same, with similar themes and scenes and structure. For the moment, however, her mind grabbed hold of the infamous lord and maid relationship, where someone of title went below his or her class to have a relationship with a servant. The Regency era had been two hundred years ago, and yet looking at Austin made her wonder if some things never changed. "Do you know her?" Sadie asked.

Austin's head snapped up and his eyes narrowed. "Of course I don't know her," he said, his words clipped. "Why would I know her?"

Sadie put up her hands as if surrendering. The man was on a hair trigger this morning. "Okay, okay," she said before lowering her hands to return to the eggs. "I was just curious as to who she was, that's all. Mrs. Land said she usually did breakfast so I've been wondering if she'd come back this morning." He continued to glare at her, but she couldn't help pushing a little further. "But then she was quite upset when she ran out of here, so it doesn't surprise me that she didn't return." His shoulder twitched slightly but he said nothing. It was all the encouragement Sadie needed to continue. "I apologize for insinuating you might know her. She's just a staff member, right? And you're a gentleman—two different worlds. It was silly of me to think you would know anything about her at all. My bad."

She finished with the eggs—sixteen in all since she was doubling the recipe—and began mixing them with a whisk. When they looked well-beaten, she added the cottage cheese and began looking around for a cheese grater. It was much easier to find than the crumpet rings had proved to be. She sampled one of the white cheeses that looked like Swiss. In fact it was Swiss, but had a kind of smoky flavor to it. Yummy. She grated it all into the bowl, then tasted another cheese. This one had a Roquefort flavor and she cringed. That wouldn't work at all. The next cheese was just a plain old cheddar—perfect. She became so immersed in her cheeses that she nearly forgot Austin was there until he spoke.

"This girl, yesterday, did she say anything before she left?"

Aha. He'd taken the bait she'd nearly forgotten she'd put on the hook. She quickly put her mind back where she needed it to be and turned to face him, folding her arms across her chest and leaning one hip against the butcher-block table. It was her turn to be difficult. "In fact she did say something on her way out the door. I tried to stop her, but she was very determined, and very upset."

He seemed to be waiting for her to tell him what the girl had said. She was waiting for him to ask.

"Well, what did she say?" he barked after a few seconds.

"Why should I tell you?" Sadie countered, lifting her chin slightly. "Seeing as how you don't know her, why would it matter to you that some cook went running out of here crying?" With his manners she felt sure many a staff member had been brought to tears due to his comments.

His jaw clenched and he took a deep breath. "It would be helpful for me to know what she said."

"Why?"

He paused again and she could tell that he wasn't used to people challenging him. He looked at the ground as if trying to figure out what to say next.

"I'll make you a deal," Sadie said as he searched for a reply.

He looked up at her warily and she knew he thought she was going to ask about him and Lacy. The fear in his eyes, however, gave her all the answer she needed—Lacy *was* important to him, one way or another, but Sadie wasn't supposed to know that. It was a secret. It didn't take a rocket scientist to figure out why a cute young cook would matter to him, but Sadie didn't let her thoughts wander too far in that direction. Although it would be interesting to hear the details, Austin's relationship with Lacy wasn't the most pressing bit of information she was after. Plus, she didn't think he'd tell her the truth since he'd skirted every other question she'd asked about Lacy so far. "Tell me who John Henry was."

A look of confusion crossed Austin's face. "John Henry?"

Sadie nodded, her focus and her voice sharper now. "Who is he? How long has he worked here? Who would want to kill him?"

"Why do you want to know?" he asked. Sadie realized that until this moment she hadn't tipped her hand, hadn't done anything that hinted at the investigation side of herself—she'd just been a bit of a pain in the tush for Austin to deal with. She hoped she wasn't making a mistake by revealing her true intentions now.

"I asked you why *you* wanted to know what Lacy said and you refused to answer," Sadie countered, using Lacy's name out loud for the first time. Austin reacted to it just enough for Sadie to notice. "So, I'll ignore your motivation and you can ignore mine. But if you tell me about John Henry, I'll tell you what she said as she was running from the room, deal?"

Austin considered it a moment before nodding slightly. "Okay," he said, though his voice was still wary. "Deal."

Wake 'Em Up Breakfast Casserole

1 pound sage sausage or ham or crisp bacon
8 eggs
$\frac{1}{2}$ teaspoon dry mustard powder or 1 teaspoon prepared mustard
1 green pepper, diced
$\frac{1}{2}$ teaspoon salt
$\frac{1}{2}$ teaspoon black pepper
$1\frac{1}{2}$ cups small-curd cottage cheese
1 cup shredded Swiss cheese
1 cup shredded cheddar cheese (sharp is best)
4 cups frozen shredded hash browns
$\frac{1}{2}$ cup of your favorite vegetable (optional) (Breanna—steamed broccoli; Jack—lots of onions and mushrooms)

In a skillet, brown sausage or cook bacon until crispy; drain well. In a large bowl combine eggs, mustard, green pepper, salt, pepper, and cottage cheese. Mix until eggs are slightly beaten. Add cheeses and hash browns, mix well. Add meat and any optional veggies. Pour into a greased 9x13-inch baking dish. Bake uncovered at 350 degrees for 35 to 40 minutes or until center is well-set and edges are browned. Let sit for 10 minutes before cutting.

Serves 8.

*Casserole can be made the night before and kept in the fridge. Add an additional 10 to 15 minutes to the baking time. (Lifesaver for when Shawn was playing football.)

*Bake in muffin tins to make individual casseroles that are perfect for brunch. Decrease cooking time to 25 to 35 minutes.

CHAPTER 21

Sadie wished—for the hundredth time—that she had her note-book, and yet by the time Austin stopped talking, she wasn't sure he'd told her anything of substance. Dr. Melcalfe had hired John Henry as the earl's caretaker a day or so after the earl's stroke. He was very attentive to the earl and helped keep him as comfortable as possible. He had previous experience with caring for the infirm, but had been a valet at some point earlier in his career so he also understood the consideration of caring for a nobleman. Austin described him as a congenial man who got on well with the rest of the staff and had never caused any trouble, although he did keep to himself in the earl's quarters, going so far as to sleep on the sofa in the earl's sitting room.

"So he cares for the earl 24/7?" Sadie asked. That didn't seem healthy.

"Hiring a caretaker for an earl is not a decision to be made lightly," Austin explained. "John Henry was hired because he is very committed. He has a day off every week that he can take at his leisure; Grant arranges for a maid or a footman to step in when John Henry is not available."

Sadie felt downright ripped off when Austin reached the end of his information. She'd hoped for a past criminal record, or, at the very least, a tragic childhood that could explain the dramatic end to his existence. Only as these disappointed thoughts came to mind did Sadie realize that she assumed John Henry was a "bad guy." She was disappointed in herself for thinking such things, but considering that the victim in the last murder she'd helped solve had in fact made choices that led her to the end she met, Sadie had assumed that John Henry had also done something wrong enough to have gotten himself killed—not that it justified his grisly death.

"So, that's it?" Sadie said, trying not to sound dejected.

Austin nodded. "That's it. I don't know of any reason anyone would want to kill him—if that's what you were getting at—if in fact you really saw what you think you saw."

"Oh, I saw it," Sadie said, annoyed that he still questioned her honesty. "It's not something I'd get wrong." She paused for a moment, reviewing what Austin had just told her. "And if John Henry is that committed to the earl, doesn't his disappearance lend credibility to the fact that Breanna and I could be right about his murder?"

"We searched the estate, and the police took everyone's statements. There is simply no evidence of foul play."

"No one was looking for that kind of evidence," Sadie said, shaking her head. "And John Henry is still missing."

"Maybe not," Austin said with a shrug of his shoulders. "Maybe he's up with William right now."

"Have you checked to see if he's there?" Sadie asked, even though she knew he hadn't.

Austin let out a breath, his arms still folded across his chest. "I have answered enough of your questions, now tell me what happened with the girl you spoke to yesterday."

Sadie complied—there was no reason not to since Austin had upheld his part of the bargain. Austin listened with his usual scowling expression.

"That's exactly what she said? That *he* made her promise to disappear if something happened?"

Sadie nodded. "Yes."

"And she didn't say who *he* was?"

"No," Sadie said, shaking her head for emphasis. "She didn't say." She kept to herself the fact that she thought Lacy had been talking about John Henry.

"Hmmm," Austin said, looking past Sadie's shoulder. Without another word he turned and left.

Sadie narrowed her eyes. Privilege did not necessarily come with personality any more than poverty did.

With a shrug of her shoulders she went back to the work she'd neglected during her conversation with Austin and began chopping the potato wedges into smaller pieces. When she finished, she added them to the egg-and-cheese mixture along with the broccoli.

It was time to find the crumpet rings—the batter should be ready soon and she really wanted to serve crumpets with breakfast, not pikelets. She looked all through the kitchen and then stepped into a hallway where there were three walk-in freezer-type doors with signs that read "Freezer," "Cooler," and "Vegetable Pantry." Past these walk-ins was a narrow door—like a closet. She opened that door and flipped on the light, looking down the narrow room full of shelves on either side. The room was about twenty feet deep and smelled like dust and wood; she didn't imagine it was used very often, and probably not at all since Mrs. Land had taken over the kitchen. After a small hesitation, she stepped inside, looking up and down the shelves. There were old kitchen appliances, more cookbooks, platters, mismatched cups, and stacks of papers and notebooks. Several rolls of toilet paper were even scattered across the floor—in a word, the room was a mess. After a full five minutes of looking, Sadie began to prepare herself for the fact that there might not be any crumpet rings. She'd have to make pikelets after all. How discouraging.

She was in the process of turning back when she saw a box marked "Bottle Rings." She pulled the box toward her enough to see that it was full of what she would call canning rings—the metal rings screwed onto a Mason jar to hold the lid on tight while the jar cooled after processing. She'd put up several pints of applesauce just a few months earlier using rings exactly like these. She smiled, imagining that they would likely do quite nicely in place of actual crumpet rings.

She returned to the kitchen and sorted through the rings, choosing to use the larger ones made for wide-mouth jars. After throwing the rings in a sink full of hot soapy water to soak, she retrieved the individual casserole dishes she'd seen on the shelf by the dishwasher and finished mixing up the casserole. She was just about to start dishing out the mixture when she thought back to those three walk-ins. There hadn't been a green pepper in the refrigerated case in the kitchen, but might there be more items in the walk-in? Even an onion would help kick up the flavor factor. The clock said it was not quite 6:30—she still had plenty of time if she wanted to serve breakfast at 8:00, which was the time it had been served yesterday. It would only take a matter of minutes to check and see if there were peppers or onions available.

The third door down was the vegetable cooler and Sadie pulled up on the handle to open the heavy door. She shivered in the cool air as she stepped inside and reached up to pull on the chain connected to the single lightbulb. The storage room lit up, showing a less than impressive array of miscellaneous vegetables in open boxes along most of the shelves that ran the length of the room. A rank smell caused her to crinkle her nose—someone had left cabbage around for a little too long. More appropriately, they had likely left everything in here too long. A woman who didn't know how to cook wouldn't know how to rotate vegetables the right way either. Shame.

The door shut with a thud that made her jump and turn around. It was heavy, and likely on a spring hinge that would ensure the door closed on its own accord so the cool air stayed in. But she tested the handle to make sure it would open, which it did. Relieved that she wouldn't be stuck inside, she ran her hands up and down her arms in an attempt to erase the goose bumps that had popped up all over her skin. It wasn't exactly cold, not like a refrigerator, but compared to the kitchen, which was on the warm side, the vegetable pantry was a definite change in temperature.

Sadie scanned the shelves, noting that she would definitely need to add fresh produce to her ever-growing grocery list. Though she had a long repertoire of recipes, not one of them called for limp cabbage, rubbery celery, or mushy acorn squash. Mrs. Land must have just kept what they were going to use in the refrigerator, basically ignoring this walk-in all together. However, despite its limitations, on a shelf to her right she found onions and next to them a small open box holding several papery bulbs of garlic. As a whole they looked a bit frightening, but after picking through them, Sadie found some of both that would work just fine—though she'd want to be sure and have some fresher ones picked up before she fixed lunch. As she picked up the onion, her eyes moved to something wedged behind the box. Something long and black and non-vegetative.

She moved closer and then reached forward, almost touching

the object before a prickling of recognition made her pull her hand back and suck in a breath. The poker?

Immediately she told herself it couldn't be the poker, what would it be doing here? And yet in the next instant she was moving boxes until she could see the full length—brass handle and all. It *was* the poker—or at least *a* poker. But what poker other than the one used to hold John Henry to the wall would be hidden in the vegetable pantry? Hidden anywhere for that matter. Grant had presumably gathered all of them up yesterday—and yet one was right here, hidden behind the garlic.

The cold was forgotten as she let her eyes travel slowly down the three-foot length of metal. The handle was just as she remembered it sticking out of John Henry's chest, and the shaft ended in a deadly-looking point, with a barbed hook four inches from the end—exactly like the others Grant had laid out on the floor of the library. She tried to imagine how someone managed to rip that hook back out of John Henry's chest, but the thought made her sick so she pushed it aside as a rush of adrenaline heated her skin.

She had to call the police—they would have to take her seriously now. With the onion still in one hand, she backed toward the door. The history of disappearing objects and people in this house made her want to throw caution to the wind and lay hold of her evidence, but there might be fingerprints or DNA and she didn't want to tamper with it. Just before reaching the door, she turned, pulled up on the handle and pushed against the weight of the door with her shoulder.

It didn't budge.

She took a step back, pulled on the handle again and pushed a second time, using all her weight and strength. It was a heavy door, and she was no gladiator, but when she tried to push it open a third time without success, she began to get nervous. It had opened without a problem when she'd tested it a minute earlier. She backed up and looked along the seam of the door, wondering if there was a latch or something on the inside. But she saw nothing. She jiggled the handle, pulled and then pushed, shook it, then slammed her shoulder against the door with a grunt, but nothing happened. Heat flushed through her as she realized that she was locked inside. The next thought that entered her mind was whether she was locked in by accident or design?

CHAPTER 22

It was frightening to think that someone would want to lock her inside, but she could not discount it anymore than she was willing to
see only that possibility. It could very well be a sticky door that the staff
knew to be cautious of. Never mind that she'd tried the door when she
first entered the walk-in and it had opened without a problem.

She took a breath to calm herself, determined to be rational, and
then knocked on the inside of the door. "Hello?" she called. "Hello?
I'm stuck in here, please open the door!" She placed her ear against
the cold metal in hopes of hearing something on the other side, but
either no one was there, or the thick door prevented her calls for
help from getting through to the other side. She growled deep in her
throat. This was so annoying. She wasn't scared, really—not about
being inside the cooler. It wasn't cold enough that it would kill her,
but being in here was keeping her from the things she had to do—
report the poker, finish breakfast, cook the crumpets. She jiggled and
pushed and pulled the handle and shoulder-slammed the door for another five full minutes, until her shoulder was aching and her breath
was coming in puffs and she finally admitted that there was no way
out other than someone on the other side of the door letting her out,

which naturally led to the reminder that someone may have wanted to trap her in the first place. But why they would want her locked in a cooler instead of making breakfast was just bizarre. "There's crumpet batter in the oven!" she yelled, banging her fist against the door. "I'll be madder than a plucked hen if it ends up going to waste!"

When even rage didn't get the door to open, she finally let out a breath of surrender, all the more aggravated by the fact that she'd found the poker and couldn't tell anyone. That thought gave her pause. If the poker was in the vegetable pantry, then someone put it here. Anxiety finally began to take root and she looked at the locked door again. Since yesterday afternoon nothing had happened as she'd expected it to and she and Breanna had encountered one strange thing after another. Was something happening on the other side of the door? Panic raced through her at the realization that Breanna was now alone in a house with a murderer on the loose. A murderer that hid weapons and locked kindhearted women in vegetable pantries. She swallowed and turned back to the room. Maybe there was some other way out.

A quick glance showed there was an air vent next to the single lightbulb on the ceiling, but although people made it look easy in the movies, Sadie couldn't fathom how she'd get up there or through that hole. She bent over to scan the back of the wooden shelves, thinking maybe some kind of hatch or something could be behind them. She scanned the right side first, where she'd found the onions and the poker, starting at ground level and working her way up to her tiptoes so she could see on the top shelf. She found nothing but old produce. The back wall had a thick line of various sized metal pipes running across it, but no alternate exits.

On the left side she started at the top, scanning the wall behind each shelf as she made her way to the ground. There was no hatch, access panel, or call button there either, but there were several boxes shoved underneath the final shelf, pushed against the wall. She shook her head as she righted herself. In Colorado that would have earned a health department violation—you couldn't put any food items on the floor. Of course home owners would get away with it. *Did they need a commercial license to run an estate?* she wondered.

She turned away from the boxes before pausing and turning back. There was something not quite right about them. She bent down again and looked at the boxes more closely, trying to determine what it was that had caught her attention. The first thing she noticed was that one box was for toilet paper—not something one would expect in a vegetable pantry, and as she looked closer she realized it wasn't quite square with the floor. Neither was the box next to it, or the box next to that one. They were all a little helter-skelter and didn't seem pushed all the way back. There were four boxes in all, and they covered more than six feet of floor space, but not a one of them was pushed against the wall or sitting flat. There were also two boxes of toilet paper and two boxes with no name on them at all, just a series of numbers—two sets of identical boxes. None of them seemed to belong in the pantry and she thought back to the toilet paper rolls she'd seen scattered around the closet where she'd found the bottle rings.

Hesitation seemed a bit ridiculous at this point so she grabbed the first box with both hands and pulled, not expecting it to be empty. But it was, and the force she'd used to pull sent her scrambling backward into the shelves on the right side. The box in her hand wasn't only empty, it was cut in half. She looked to where she had pulled it from the floor and felt her blood chill as the same black leather shoes she'd seen yesterday from beneath the curtain now lay unveiled, the toes pointing toward the ceiling of the vegetable pantry.

Sadie had just found John Henry.

Chapter 23

"Help me!" Sadie screamed as she ran for the door and began pounding again, this time with far more fervor. "Please," she screamed, her racing heart making the cold room of no consequence. "Please help me!"

As with her earlier attempts to call for help, no one answered her and no one came to her rescue. She felt her throat thicken as tears rose in her eyes. This was no time to give in to a good cry, but another look over her shoulder at those shoes made it even harder to swallow and she clenched her eyes shut as if that could somehow make everything go away. But the attempt at denial did no good; she was still locked in a vegetable pantry with a corpse and the weapon used to kill him. If that wasn't something set to trigger anyone's sensibilities to the breaking point, she didn't know what was.

She banged on the door again. "Please help me," she yelled as loud as she could, but more than ever her words seemed to be sucked into the very walls of the storage room. She had no way of knowing if anyone on the other side could even hear her through the insulation. Her fist was throbbing from where she'd hit the door so many times. She had to calm down and try to think rationally.

"Think," she told herself. "Push away the emotion and just think this through." She closed her eyes and focused on taking deep breaths, hoping to calm herself. Once she was breathing and thinking normally she once again considered her situation and prioritized what she needed to do.

It was a silly exercise since her only priority was to get out of here. It was so early in the morning, and no one other than Austin had been in the kitchen—Austin! Sadie opened her eyes. Would he have come back and locked her inside the vegetable pantry?

Maybe. He had been so antagonistic in the library yesterday, then the inspector said someone had told them the tip was ridiculous, and now, after talking to him in the kitchen, Sadie was a prisoner. She had to get out of here! But how?

Her whistle!

She frantically dug it out of her pocket, smiled gratefully that she'd thought to bring it, and brought it to her mouth. After taking a deep breath, she blew out all the air, immediately gasping at the shrill sound that echoed off the walls of the cooler. She put her hands over her ears and winced at the lingering ringing. In the process the whistle fell to the floor.

"Holy smokes," she whispered, almost unable to hear herself over the ringing. That had not worked out the way she'd thought it would. She looked at the whistle on the floor, feeling betrayed.

Unless she could find some earplugs hiding among the rancid-looking rutabagas, she'd have to come up with another solution. Though she considered leaving the offensive whistle on the floor, she picked it back up and shoved it in her pocket—committing to think hard before using it again.

In desperate need of a better solution, she turned back to the room and scanned it once again in hopes of finding something that could help her—though she hadn't any idea what it would be. She tried not to look at the shoes or think about the rest of John Henry hidden beneath the boxes, but it was nearly impossible not to look. Her chest tightened as she stared at the shoes and finally realized why it had smelled so funny when she'd come in. The thought made her stomach churn and she forced her eyes away from the decomposing corpse and tried again to find a solution to her problem. She looked at the air vent again and rejected it again, then scanned the walls and found nothing but pipes for a second time.

Pipes?

Pipes led somewhere, and they were metal, meaning they would clang and echo if struck. Didn't she live in a house with pipes that sang whenever the sprinkler system turned on? If she could make enough noise, counting on the reverberating metal to help her do so, then certainly someone would come to investigate.

Her eyes were drawn to the poker—the only other metal object in the room. *No,* she told herself, unwilling to compromise the evidence. But after a quick look through the shelves—avoiding looking at John Henry—she felt she had no choice. She wrapped the apron around her hand so as not to get her own prints on the weapon, and then stood on her tiptoes in order to reach up and pick up the poker by the handle. It wasn't very heavy. Gripping the poker firmly, she walked to the edge of the left-hand shelves—only a foot from the box covering John Henry's head—took a breath, and hit the poker against the pipes as hard as she could. The result was fantastic; in fact she could see the pipes vibrate at the impact and her ears rang some more as the poker reverberated in her hands. After waiting for the tinny sound to disappear, she hit the pipes again, cringing at the throbbing in her ears.

And again.

And again.

And again.

She continued hitting the pipes every fifteen seconds or so for nearly five minutes, until her arms felt as though they were going to fall off and she felt sure she'd permanently damaged her hearing. Her brilliant idea no longer seemed so brilliant but she kept going if for no other reason than to keep her mind off where she was and who she was with. She was breathing hard and feeling sufficiently discouraged when she thought she heard someone at the door. She ran for it and began screaming again as she pounded on it with her free hand.

"I'm in here!" she yelled. "Help me!"

There was no answer, and not wanting to miss her chance of alerting someone, she lifted the apron-wrapped poker in her hand and hit it against the door. "I'm in here," she said. "In the vegetable pantry."

This time she was certain that she heard someone. "I'm here!" she shouted again, hitting the door a second time and realizing that each time she hit it, she made a dent in the sheet metal. She cringed, feeling bad about the damage she was inflicting, and yet she lifted her hand again to hit it just as the door opened.

Her own strength caused her to stumble through the door, poker in hand as she tried to regain her balance. Unfortunately she was unable to counteract the laws of physics working against her and she tripped over the bottom seal of the door, falling hard onto the tiled floor of the hallway outside the pantry door. Pain shot through her hip and shoulder, causing her to cry out as she rolled onto her back, her eyes clenched in reaction to the pain radiating through the left side of her body. After a couple of seconds she opened her eyes to look up into the glowering face of Austin Melcalfe.

CHAPTER 24

Sadie scrambled backward until she met up with the wall, then placed one hand on it to help her to her feet, the muscles of her body screaming in protest. The other hand, the one holding the poker, she held out in order to keep Austin at bay.

Austin lifted his eyebrows. "Was that you making that incessant banging noise? You've managed to awaken the entire household and it's not even seven."

"You!" Sadie said, her mind racing. "You locked me in there, didn't you?"

Austin's eyebrows rose. "What?" he questioned, then looked back at the door of the vegetable pantry which was now closed. "Why on earth would I lock you in the cooler?"

"You're the only one who was in the kitchen. I went to get a green pepper out of the pantry and someone locked me inside."

Austin was silent, then looked at the poker. "And found a poker to defend yourself with?"

Sadie looked at the poker as well, remembering that it was a murder weapon and that John Henry was still in the cooler. Suddenly Manny appeared behind Austin's shoulder. "Lord Melcalfe, I . . ." he said, taking in the scene that Sadie admitted didn't look very good. "Mrs. Hoffmiller?"

"Manny," Sadie said, gratefully. "Call the police. Someone locked me in the vegetable pantry and I—"

"I believe you said *I* was responsible for locking you in the pantry," Austin cut in, his voice calm, although his face showed his irritation. "*Someone* implies that it could have been anyone with access to the kitchen, which, as you've proven, can be accessed by anyone." He held up a pen. "I did find this in the latch of the door—but I certainly didn't put it there."

Aha, he was already working on a defense. Could a pen really be responsible for locking her in there? She looked at the handle long enough to see that it could work—the pen would keep the handle from being lifted. Sadie glared at Austin but then looked at Manny again. "I found John Henry."

Both Manny and Austin showed surprise and looked immediately at the cooler door. Austin moved toward it. "Don't open it!" Sadie barked, causing him to pause and look at her as though she were completely deranged. "Fingerprints," she said, only realizing once the word was spoken that if she truly believed Austin was the one who locked her in, it would only be his prints on the handle anyway. She looked at Manny again, pleading with her eyes for him to do what she asked. "Please call the police; tell them we've found the body." She looked down at the poker she was still holding. "And the murder weapon. Ask them to send a *real* detective this time."

Austin was shaking his head. "I'll not have another false report called in," he said. "And my fingerprints are already on the door because I just opened it." He was too fast with his explanation for Sadie to stop him. He took one step inside the walk-in, then startled and pulled back, paused, leaned in again, and then quickly stepped out and shut the door, looking at it for a few seconds. Then he turned to face Sadie, his wide eyes part of his well-acted surprise. He swallowed hard and turned toward the security guard.

"Manny," he said in a dry voice. "Call the police. Tell them to hurry."

Manny hesitated.

"Do it now," Austin said sharply. Manny nodded and disappeared around the wall separating the hallway from the kitchen. Sadie hoped he wasn't going to go far, she didn't want to be alone with Austin again.

"Are you sure that's John Henry?" he asked in a quiet voice.

Sadie was not at all impressed with his act. "I can't help but assume that body is the same one that went missing from the sitting room yesterday. Unless of course you killed someone else."

Austin watched her for a few moments, his expression hardening. "I had nothing to do with this." His voice strengthening with every word as his offense returned to its usual levels. "How dare you make such accusations."

He sounded rather convincing, but Sadie would not be swayed. She opened her mouth to tell him exactly why he'd moved to suspect number one when hurried footsteps startled her. Moments later, Breanna, Liam, and another security guard appeared behind Austin. Even if she felt badly for the reminder that she'd woken everyone up, Sadie was relieved to see familiar faces.

"Mom," Breanna said, looking quite worried. "Are you okay?"

"I'm fine now," Sadie said, smiling as much as she could so Breanna would stop looking so scared. "I was locked in the vegetable pantry," Sadie explained for the second time. "With John Henry."

Breanna gasped loudly and put a hand to her mouth. She was holding her robe together at the neck with her other hand and her fist tightened around the fabric. Liam and the other security guard looked equally shocked.

"With John Henry?" Breanna repeated, lowering her hand from her mouth and looking at the poker in Sadie's hand.

"And she believes I did it," Austin glowered.

Liam looked at Austin in surprise, while Breanna continued to stare at her mother, tears rising in her eyes.

"I'm okay, Bre," Sadie said, taking a couple steps forward so she could put her hand on Breanna's shoulder.

"Because I let you out," Austin added. Sadie glared at him just in case he hadn't figured out that she really didn't like him at all.

Sadie turned to look at Liam and Manny. "He came down to the kitchen just before six o'clock," Sadie said, wondering how much she dared say and then decided she'd lay it all out there. "He was looking for a kitchen maid."

Austin clenched his mouth shut and his neck and face began to turn red. Sadie hurried to continue, making eye contact with Breanna who was still visibly shaken. "The one who ran out yesterday," Sadie said. "He asked all kinds of questions about her and then left. Five minutes later I go into the pantry for a green pepper, find the poker, and the door is locked tight when I try to get out. He used that pen to jam it." She pointed at the pen still in Austin's hand.

"But, uh, why would Austin lock you in?" Liam asked, looking at Breanna. He seemed as worried about her as he did the situation.

"That's a good question," Sadie said. "Ask him. He told the police yesterday that Breanna and I couldn't be trusted, he knew all kinds of details before anyone else did, and he was hanging out in the kitchen looking for Lacy." *And* he'd been looking at the family pedigree while Liam was looking for the family Bible. Maybe the two things weren't related, but Liam had said the earl didn't seem to trust

Austin too much either. An uncomfortable wiggling in her stomach told her she was saying too much and needed to save the rest for the police. However, she couldn't help but make one last plea for her position. "Didn't I tell you he was suspicious?"

Breanna nodded, but it was careful, as if she didn't fully believe Sadie either. She looked at Liam, which Sadie found even more annoying. Was no one on her side?

"You are jumping to false conclusions," Austin spat back. "And I knew the details because Grant told them to me."

"And Lacy?" Sadie accused. "Are you going to deny that you were looking for her this morning?"

They all fell silent, Austin looking equal parts angry and stunned. Sadie wondered if anyone had ever talked to him like this in his life. "You know nothing about me," he finally said.

"I know enough," she said, raising her chin. "I know that you're part of whatever conspiracy is going on here. And I promise you that I am going to figure it out and show you for who you really are."

Austin's nostrils flared, but she had the satisfaction of catching a glimmer of fear cross his face in the process.

Liam stepped forward and took Sadie's arm, pulling her back from where she'd been slowly moving toward Austin. "Sadie," he said, trying to sound authoritative. "I think you should go to your room. I'll have the inspector come up and talk with you as soon as he arrives."

"No," Sadie said, pulling her arm away and shaking her head. "I'm tired of being told what to do." And she was tired of being sent to her room every time something important happened.

"Not that you ever listen to what anyone tells you," Austin retorted.

"And it's a good thing, isn't it?" Sadie spat, wanting very much to slap the man. "If I had done as you said and not come down here, I'd have never found John Henry at all."

"Which brings us back to the part about why I would want you to find him if, as you say, I killed him and hid the body. I would know that locking you in the pantry would ensure you'd find him, right?"

"Stop," Liam said, his neck red with suppressed frustration. "Just stop all of this right now."

"She's a raving lunatic," Austin said, glaring at Sadie and ignoring Liam altogether.

"And you're a deceptive man up to his ears in motive and opportunity, trying to hide behind the skirts of his mother's family name," Sadie countered.

"How dare you speak to me like this," Austin spat. His face turned even darker red and the volume of his voice raised with each word he spoke. "I want you out of my kitchen, out of my house, and out of my country immediately!"

CHAPTER 25

Your house?" Sadie repeated, feeling completely justified by his loss of composure. "Since when was this your house?"

"I have been managing this house for—"

"Yeah, yeah—blah, blah, blah," Sadie cut in, rolling her eyes. "I've been managing the kitchen for an hour, does that make it my kitchen?"

"Stop it," Liam said, putting his hands up and closing his eyes as if he couldn't stand it. "Both of you." They both stopped but continued glaring at one another. Liam opened his eyes, took a breath, and licked his lips. "Austin, were you in the kitchen this morning?" He didn't make eye contact with Austin when he spoke but his voice sounded a little stronger than it had yesterday. Maybe he'd realized that as the heir, he *should* be the one in charge.

"Yes," Austin said. "But I've no reason to lock her in the pantry. She was mixing up eggs in a bowl when I left."

"Why were you here at all?" Liam asked, looking at his cousin.

"Why was she?" Austin returned.

Liam looked at Sadie who answered before she was asked. "Making breakfast," she said. "Obviously." She glared at Austin again. "And I told you why Austin was here," she continued, feeling very smug as the conversation circled back to Austin. "Mrs. Land told me Lacy always did breakfast. Austin didn't know she'd run off yesterday so he came to see her at a time he thought she'd be here. Conveniently it was also a time that no one else would be around."

She waited for Austin to refute it, but he said nothing, simply held Sadie's eyes as his jaw clenched and his face continued to redden. Sadie was sure that if they had been alone, she'd be in big trouble.

"Why were you here to see this girl?" Liam asked. "What is she to you?" Sadie knew he was wondering the same thing Sadie was—did Austin's relationship with this girl have anything to do with the lack of trust his father felt toward him before he had the stroke?

Whether Austin was thrown off by the question or just being stubborn, he refused to answer, which was an answer all its own in Sadie's opinion. After waiting several seconds, Liam took a breath. "Okay," he said. "Never mind. Austin, please go upstairs and wait for the police to arrive."

"What?" Sadie asked, whipping her head back to look at Liam. "You can't let him go!"

"Sadie," Liam said with a kind of pleading frustration. "He's going to go upstairs, that's all."

"He could run off or something," Sadie said. "How do you know he won't?"

"Because I'm a man of my word, Mrs. Hoffmiller," Austin said. "And Liam knows that. I've done nothing to warrant your accusations and you will feel very foolish when you come to that same conclusion." He then walked past her and out of the kitchen by way of the dish room.

Liam turned to Manny. "Please have someone keep an eye on him."

Manny nodded and moved to the side of the room, lifting his walkie-talkie but talking too softly to be overheard.

"I'm not going to my room," Sadie said, trying not to sound like a six-year-old as she turned to face Liam. She was still holding the poker and wished she could put it down somewhere. "I'm in the middle of making breakfast. Everyone needs to eat something and I've already got all the preparations underway."

"Someone else can take over," Liam said. "You've had a horrible shock and you need to—"

"No one else can take over, Liam," Sadie interrupted. "That's why I'm here in the first place. Lacy ran off and Mrs. Land was sent away, which leaves only upstairs maids and footmen—and none of them know anything about cooking. I'm not going to my room, so you can stop trying to make me."

Liam took another deep breath. "Okay, fine," he said, then turned to Breanna. "Will you stay with her?"

Sadie looked at Breanna to see her staring at Liam. Breanna opened her mouth, then looked at Sadie, then back at Liam again. Sadie couldn't tell if Breanna just didn't understand what Liam was saying—or perhaps Liam taking charge of the situation had thrown her off. "I need to talk to you first, Liam," she said, an edge in her voice that surprised Sadie.

Liam swallowed, looking nervous, but he nodded. "Um, okay." He looked toward the security officer who had been hanging back and ran a hand through his disheveled hair as he shifted his weight. "Can, um, one of you guys make sure Mrs. Hoffmiller is safe as well as stand guard over this cooler until the police arrive?"

"Yes, sir," he said.

Liam looked relieved with the answer. Then he turned to Breanna, who spun on her heel and headed out of the room. He sent Sadie a look before hurrying after her. If not for the crumpets, Sadie would have followed. She hated that they were talking without her. It didn't seem fair that after all she'd been through she was still being left out.

A couple minutes later Breanna returned, looking tense and subdued at the same time. She'd retied her robe around her waist.

"What did you talk about?" Sadie said.

"Nothing," Breanna said darkly.

"You seem a little—"

"Dang it, Mom, I said we didn't talk about anything! Will you stop grilling me every time I turn around? You're not the only one experiencing things right now and if I don't want to talk about it, you should accept my answer."

Sadie blinked, stunned by Breanna's reaction. It simply was not in Breanna's nature to be so hotheaded. "O-kay," Sadie said slowly. Then she smiled, hoping it would help Breanna adjust her mood. "What you need are some good homemade crumpets," she said in as bright a voice as she could come up with. "Lucky for you, you're stuck babysitting me in the right kitchen."

CHAPTER 26

Sadie looked around for somewhere she could put the poker she was still holding. She decided on a counter on the far side of the room, an area she didn't plan to use. It was just gross to think that the poker had been skewering John Henry's chest not too long ago. Nasty.

"Will you put a towel down over there?" Sadie asked, nodding toward the section of counter. "So I can put the poker on it. The dish towels are in the second drawer down on the right side of the sink." She braced herself for Breanna yelling at her again, but Breanna just nodded and did as she was asked. It seemed that Breanna's tantrum had used itself up. Thank goodness.

Sadie carefully laid the poker on the dishcloth, then let her apron fall. She flexed her hand a few times to work out the cramps. "I hope I didn't destroy any evidence," she said.

Breanna stared at the poker, letting her eyes travel from the handle to the pointed tip, then back up again. She nodded.

Sadie looked at her daughter with sympathy; Breanna just didn't seem cut out for this kind of intensity. For her sake Sadie hoped the police took care of this quickly and easily so that Breanna wouldn't have to deal with it anymore. She couldn't wait to tell the police what she'd found. There was no doubt in her mind that they would haul Austin off in handcuffs.

"I wonder what John Henry knew that got him killed," Sadie mused as she pulled the crumpet batter out of the oven. Breanna didn't answer, which Sadie took as permission to continue. "He must have known something about Austin, don't you think?" Sadie asked. "Something Austin didn't want anyone to know." She walked over to the stove, where she set the griddle over two of the twelve burners, and turned on the heat. "Do you think he'd kill John Henry in order to hide his relationship with Lacy?"

"I don't know, Mom," Breanna said, picking up the wooden spoon and stirring the casserole mixture Sadie had left on the butcher-block table. "Is there anything else that needs to go into this?"

Sadie looked over her shoulder at the casserole mix. "There were onions in the pantry," she said. "But I don't think I want them in the casserole anymore now that the pantry is a crime scene. See if you can find some onion powder or something. The only meat I could find was ham, and I like a little kick to my casserole."

Breanna complied and went to the spice cupboard, moving different tins out of the way as she looked for something that would work. "How about sage?"

"Sage is good," Sadie agreed. "Even a little basil would help it out."

Breanna nodded and removed a couple of spices while Sadie greased the bottle rings in anticipation of making the crumpets. They worked in silence for a few minutes while Sadie considered why John Henry had been hiding behind the sitting-room curtains in the first place. For the life of her, she could not come up with a valid reason. Especially in light of the argument he'd had with Liam. "I wonder if John Henry was waiting in the sitting room because he wanted to tell Liam something and didn't want anyone else to know he was doing it," Sadie continued.

"Or maybe he was angry with Liam and was planning to kill him," Breanna said, surprising Sadie with her intensity. Sadie looked up at her daughter, who was looking at the poker on the other side of the room. "Someone went in there armed, remember?"

"I guess I hadn't considered self-defense," Sadie said. "But John Henry was behind a curtain panel. How was that threatening?"

"I don't want to talk about this anymore," Breanna suddenly said, returning to the casserole and stirring it with a vengeance, which was hard to do because the mixture was quite thick now that the potatoes had been added.

"Why not?" Sadie asked. They were finally getting somewhere.

Breanna added a bit more basil and began stirring again. "It just seems . . . inappropriate for us to be discussing it." She made a little glance as if trying to look behind her without moving her head. Sadie looked past Breanna and then smiled at the security guard who was still standing exactly where Liam had told him to stand. He was watching them, listening to what they were saying.

Sadie smiled at him politely, then looked at Breanna. "Sorry," she said. "You're right." The very walls of this house had ears; she should use more caution if for no other reason than to make sure the police didn't hear from other people that she talked about the details too much. They might construe it as an unhealthy interest in the case. Sadie didn't want that to happen.

"Let's get these casseroles dished up while we wait for the police," Sadie said, coming over to stand by Breanna.

Breanna looked visibly relieved. "Good idea," she said, leaning over to pull the stack of individual dishes toward them. Sadie leaned into her and whispered so as not to be overheard. "We'll talk about all this stuff later."

Breanna nodded. "Sure," she said. "For now, let's just focus on breakfast."

"Got it," Sadie said with a conspiring wink, hoping that Breanna would be true to her word. Two heads were certainly better than one and Sadie liked having someone to bounce her ideas off of.

The police arrived a few minutes after the breakfast casseroles had been put into the oven. Inspector Dilree wasn't alone this time but he was still several inches shorter than the other men with him and looked at least ten years younger. However, his expression made him look just as official.

The men inspected the cooler first while Breanna washed dishes and Sadie began cooking the crumpets, straining to hear anything she possibly could—but they kept their voices low enough that she didn't pick up a single tidbit of knowledge. A few minutes later, more people arrived at the exterior basement door—a crime scene unit, Sadie assumed. Grant appeared out of nowhere and stood apart from the officers, presumably in order to help them with anything they might need. But Sadie couldn't help but wonder if he weren't also trying to pick up on how much they knew.

"Who checked out the kitchen yesterday?" she asked Breanna when she couldn't silence her thoughts any longer. The first batch of crumpets were cooking, but the book had said it took six or seven minutes for them to get bubbly and dry around the edges so they could be turned over. So far they weren't bubbling at all.

"Checked out the kitchen?" Breanna asked, turning off the sink and facing her mother.

"Remember? Austin paired everyone off and sent them to

check out the house—looking for John Henry. Who was sent to the kitchen?"

"Um, I don't remember," Breanna said, smoothing her hair behind her ear.

"And how did the murderer get him down here?" Sadie continued. "We were in the dish room until we went back up to the sitting room. They would have had to pass us, right?"

"I thought we weren't going to talk about this anymore," Breanna said.

Sadie pointed toward the empty place where the security guard had been. "No one will overhear us," she assured her daughter. "So we're perfectly alright so long as we keep our voices down."

Breanna considered that for a moment before giving in. "Maybe the person who moved the body *isn't* the same person who killed him," she said.

Sadie was confused. "What does that have to do with the fact that no one passed us on their way to the cooler?"

"You said the murderer would have brought John Henry down here and I'm just pointing out that you're jumping to the conclusion that only the murderer would move the body."

"Why would anyone else move it?" Sadie asked, confused by Breanna's point. The tops of the crumpets were completely dry, with only a few holes on the top of each one. They didn't look right and she scowled in discouragement.

Breanna let out a frustrated breath just as a broad-shouldered investigator came around the corner. He looked at a small notebook he held in his hand, then looked up at the two of them, glancing from Breanna to Sadie before letting his eyes stay on Sadie's face. "Mrs. Hoffmiller?" he asked.

Sadie nodded carefully. A gurney with a big black plastic bag passed behind him on its way to the exterior door, pushed by two men in navy blue uniforms. Sadie swallowed. John Henry was in that bag, which she supposed was better than him being behind boxes in the vegetable pantry, but not by much. When the gurney moved out of sight, she met the inspector's eyes again.

"I'd like to have a few words with you, if that would be all right?" he asked.

"Of course," Sadie said. She took one step toward him before remembering the crumpets and looking back at the griddle.

"I'll take care of these," Breanna said, heading toward the stove. "You tell the inspector what you know."

Sadie hesitated. She'd already invested a lot into this morning's crumpets and didn't like the idea of handing over the responsibility to someone else—even if they weren't turning out. However, she didn't imagine the inspector would understand if she tried to beg off the interview for crumpets. There was really little choice in the matter. "Read about how to cook them in the book," she said. "They're tricky."

"Of course," Breanna replied, heading toward the cookbook. She looked at Sadie who was still standing there watching, and then raised her eyebrows, reminding Sadie that the inspector was waiting for her.

Sadie turned quickly and smiled. "Where would you like us to go?"

"I think the staff dining area would work fine," he said.

Sadie nodded and followed him through the doorway. It didn't seem like a very private place to have such a private discussion, especially when the men who had wheeled out the gurney came back through the exterior door and passed not ten feet from where she and the inspector sat. It was raining, again.

"Mrs. Hoffmiller," the inspector said, taking Sadie's attention away from the weather and centering it precisely upon his shoulders. He extended his hand across the table. Sadie took it and gave it a firm shake, pleased to notice that he returned it just as firmly. He wasn't a large man, though he certainly looked that way compared to Inspector Dilree. He was likely in his early forties and for a moment Sadie imagined planting a plaid cap on his head and a pipe in his mouth. He'd make a wonderful Sherlock Holmes. She wondered if the police department ever held costume parties for Halloween.

"My name is Inspector Kent," he said as he withdrew his hand and opened a file on the top of the table. "I reviewed your statement given to Inspector Dilree yesterday and would like to hear your account of what took place this morning."

"Certainly," Sadie said with a nod. "Where would you like me to begin?"

Inspector Kent inclined his head and gave her a small smile. "Wherever you like," he said. "This is your interview. If I need more information, I'll ask for it." He pulled a small recorder from his pocket. "Is it all right if I record this?"

"Of course," she said, feeling far more comfortable with him than she'd felt with Dilree. She decided to start with the very beginning—waking up this morning. But a few minutes into the recounting, she remembered the discussion with Mrs. Land she'd had yesterday, so she went back to that. In addition to the tape recorder, Inspector Kent also took notes.

She finally finished and waited for the inspector to stop scribbling, noticing that she could smell the breakfast casseroles in the kitchen. She hoped Breanna was keeping an eye on them.

"Lord Melcalfe was the only other person you saw in the kitchen this morning?" the inspector asked.

"Yes," Sadie said. "Manny walked me down, but I didn't see anyone else."

"And this staff member who ran out yesterday, do you know her last name?"

Sadie shook her head. "No, just Lacy."

"Well, I'm sure Grant would have that information," the inspector said. He scanned his notes, then looked up at her. "Is there anything else?" he asked.

Sadie scrunched her face and tried to think hard about everything she'd said. She wanted to be as forthcoming as possible, to tell him every detail. She was opening her mouth to tell him that was all when she remembered the argument she'd learned about between Liam and John Henry. She should tell Inspector Kent—she knew she should—and yet she worried that it would take their interest away from Austin, who she felt deserved their scrutiny more than Liam did. After a few seconds she determined not to dilute the implication she'd made toward Austin. "That's everything I can think of," she said, hoping he hadn't read her hesitation.

"Very good, then," Kent said as he stood, shaking her hand a second time. "I have some other interviews to conduct. If I need to ask you any more questions, I assume that would be acceptable?"

"Of course," Sadie said. "I'm happy to help."

She was on her way out of the staff dining room when she had a thought and turned back to the inspector who was sliding the tape recorder back into his pocket. "I was hoping to go into town later today; we need some groceries. Would that be okay?"

The inspector hesitated. "Actually," he said. "We would prefer that everyone stay at the estate until we conclude our investigation of the crime scene."

Sadie hadn't thought of that, but wished she had. "I see," she said. "And how long will that be?"

"I would guess it will take most of today," the inspector said. "I know it's an inconvenience. We'll let you know when you're cleared to leave."

Sadie couldn't help but smile and just hoped the inspector didn't misinterpret it. "That's fine," she said. "I just wanted to be sure I understood."

She headed back into the kitchen quite pleased. There was still the possibility that the answers she wanted wouldn't be discovered at all—she knew that happened sometimes—but she was encouraged by the fact that there was no way Liam or Austin could have her and Breanna shipped out. At least not yet. She was committed to using the time she had as wisely as possible.

CHAPTER 27

Charlotte helped serve breakfast, and each time she entered the room Sadie considered talking to her, trying to see if she would help fill in the blanks Mrs. Land and Austin had left behind. But each time she tried, Grant's lecture from the night before would come to mind and Sadie knew she'd feel horrible if Charlotte was sent away like Mrs. Land or, worse, fired. And then she'd think of how Charlotte had confided in Austin about Liam and John Henry's argument; she'd hate to have Charlotte take whatever they talked about back to Austin. Therefore, she just smiled and thanked the young girl each time she went about another task.

Sadie had pulled the last of the breakfast casseroles from the oven when she looked up to find Austin standing in the doorway with his arms folded across his chest. His sudden arrival startled her, though she tried to hide it as best she could. He glared at her, and she glared right back before determining to ignore him completely. Breanna was speaking to the inspector in the staff dining room.

"You're relieved of your kitchen duties," Austin said bluntly as she put the final ceramic dish on the butcher-block table. Charlotte had already taken half a dozen of them upstairs to set on the buffet, which also held Sadie's crumpets, a variety of fruit and cheese Sadie had found in the refrigerator, and tea brewed by Grant—apparently tea was the responsibility of the butler. Thank goodness. Sadie had no idea how to go about it since the tea was loose-leaf.

"I have breakfast to clean up and lunch to get started," Sadie said in an impassive tone, refusing to let him know how much he bothered her.

"You are not the cook," Austin said. "And you are to leave immediately."

Sadie let out a breath and turned to face him. "We can't leave," she said arrogantly. "The inspector said we have to stay until they have finished their investigation, so although I completely understand why you would love for us to disappear, we aren't going anywhere." She held herself back from tacking on a "So there."

Austin's jaw tightened and his eyes narrowed, which only served to make Sadie feel victorious. "I didn't mean leave the estate," he said, a slight hiss to his words since he didn't seem to part his teeth much when he spoke. "I meant, leave the kitchen."

"Like it or not, you need a cook," she said. "You have three maids and their hands are full. I suppose you could keep ordering in, but without a single kitchen worker who knows how to prepare, warm, and serve the plates—you'll all be eating out of Styrofoam."

"Well, like it or not," he said, copying her own words, "I *have* a cook, a real cook, on her way to Southgate. She will be working in the kitchen until it's time for the staff to leave."

Sadie was stunned. "You found a cook? On New Year's Eve?"

Austin nodded, obviously thrilled by Sadie's disappointment. "Just for a few hours. She's bringing some things in from town and will take care of lunch. You may now go to your room and work on that needlepoint."

He quit the room while Sadie fired silent curses at his retreating back. She had no intention of leaving in the middle of the meal preparation, and turned back to the breakfast casseroles. Because staff ate after the family was served their meal, Sadie moved the casseroles to the warming oven and set about putting out the other items. Mrs. Land had given the impression that the staff didn't necessarily eat the same thing the family did, but that didn't make much sense to Sadie so she'd worked on setting out the same meal for them as had been set out upstairs. She was in the process of arranging the pineapple—from a can, unfortunately—with the grapes and cantaloupe she'd found in the fridge, when Austin's voice startled her for a second time.

"I told you to leave," he said from behind her.

She spun around, knocking the tray in the process, which required her to steady it before she could return his glare. "And I am not done with breakfast yet," she nearly yelled. "When I'm finished, I'll leave."

"You'll leave now," Austin said.

"I will not," Sadie returned.

"Mom?"

Sadie was thrown off guard by Breanna's voice, and looked over her shoulder. Breanna and Inspector Kent stood there watching them.

"What's going on?" Breanna asked, looking between the two of them.

Austin and Sadie were both quiet for a few seconds, then Austin spoke, his tone completely professional. "We have a cook coming in to prepare the kitchen for the weekend and take care of the rest of the day's meals. I have asked Mrs. Hoffmiller to please return upstairs since she is, after all, a guest."

Sadie hated how reasonable he sounded. "And I'm not done with breakfast," she said. "I would like to finish it."

"I thought Charlotte took breakfast upstairs already," Breanna countered.

"Well, yes, she took up the family breakfast, but the staff still has to eat."

"And they can take care of that themselves," Austin added. He looked at Sadie, his face soft, a slight smile on his lips. "We so appreciate all your efforts in our behalf, Mrs. Hoffmiller, but it is no longer necessary for you to shoulder this burden."

"Is this cook you've hired aware of what's transpired here?" the inspector asked.

Austin answered with an easy nod, "Yes, she is. She's a former cook here at Southgate, so she's someone we can trust. I told her she would likely need to speak with you when she arrived."

"Very good," Inspector Kent said. "I'm finished with the dining room and will conduct the remainder of my interviews upstairs. I've posted an officer here to preserve the crime scene until we are finished with it."

"Good," Austin said. "We can all go upstairs, then."

Sadie was thoroughly miffed. "I'd still like to see that the staff gets their breakfast."

"Not to worry," Austin said in his kind, Lord-of-the-Manor voice. "Charlotte will be down shortly to oversee it and the cook will be arriving momentarily."

With three sets of eyes watching her, and no further argument coming to mind, Sadie felt she had no choice but to give in—no matter how badly it burned to do so.

"Fine," she said, untying her apron. She hung it on the hook she'd retrieved it from a couple hours earlier and headed out of the kitchen behind Breanna and the inspector.

"Is that your jacket?" Austin asked, nodding toward her Colorado State University jacket hanging next to the aprons. Sadie had hoped no one would notice it was still there from last night. Even though she was offended to be kicked out of the kitchen, she realized that having Austin bring in a former employee could possibly give her access to even more information. But not unless she had an excuse to visit the kitchen again. So much for that idea. She picked up the jacket, avoiding Austin's eyes so that she wouldn't see the triumph in them.

"Is there anything else?" Austin asked from where he stood in the kitchen, turning so as to watch her every move. "Mrs. Kinsley is rather territorial about *her* kitchen."

Pompous, arrogant, patronizing nitwit, Sadie thought to herself as she shot another glare at Austin and then began putting her arms in the sleeves of her jacket. Austin gave her a smug smile before turning toward the door. Breanna and the inspector pushed through the swinging doors ten feet before Sadie reached them. She was adjusting her shoulders into her jacket when she realized the right side of her jacket felt heavier than the left side. Not recalling if she'd put anything in her jacket pockets recently, she reached her hand into the pocket and wrapped her fingers around what felt like a set of keys.

"Keys?" she muttered to herself as she pulled them from her pocket. Why on earth would she have keys in her pocket? She'd left her car keys at the Park 'n Fly by the Denver Airport so they would change her oil while she was gone. She opened her palm, looking at the ring of keys in her hand. She'd never seen them before.

"Mom?"

Sadie looked up, closing her hand on the keys and lowering her arm. "What?" she asked, realizing she'd stopped at the bottom of the stairs.

"Are you coming?" Breanna said, standing five steps above her. The inspector stood at the top of the stairs, his hand on the knob of the open door Austin must have already passed through.

"Oh, yes," Sadie said, casually putting both hands into her pockets as she started up the stairs. Where had the keys come from? What were they for? A thrill of adventure exploded in her chest. Someone was trying to help her. Someone recognized her pursuit for justice and, though for whatever reason they couldn't find it themselves, they wanted to help her find the answers.

Who had given them to her?

Austin had pointed out her jacket on the wall, but the last thing he would give Sadie was a set of keys—unless, of course, he was trying to get her in trouble somehow.

Once in the foyer, the three of them rounded the Christmas tree to find Austin already gone and Grant standing at the base of the stairs. Sadie wondered if he'd been adequately chewed out for being unavailable during the more dramatic moments of the last couple of days and was now overcompensating. She walked toward the stairs, deep in thought about the significance of the keys now in her possession.

"Aren't you going to eat breakfast with me?" Breanna asked. The inspector was talking to another officer outside of the sitting room door.

Sadie turned around to look at her daughter. "Oh, well, I—"

"You worked so hard on those crumpets," Breanna said, looking at her mother with a slightly pleading look on her face. It wasn't the crumpets Breanna was interested in, Sadie realized, but the fact that she didn't want to eat alone.

"I am looking forward to those crumpets," Sadie said, fingering the keys before removing her hand. She could wait ten minutes before she examined the mystery keys more thoroughly.

Sadie was relieved to find the dining room empty. The inspectors were in the hallway, Liam was probably with his father, and Austin was likely off somewhere gloating about having won the battle over the kitchen. However, as far as Sadie was concerned, the war was still on. She picked up a plate from the sideboard and served herself some fruit, one of the casseroles, and toasted a couple crumpets before taking a seat at the extra-long table.

"You'd think they'd invest in a breakfast nook or something," she said as she spread the napkin over her lap and buttered the crumpets before they got cold. "Don't they get tired of all this fancy-schmancy stuff?"

"It's what they know," Breanna said, sliding her plate onto the table and taking a seat next to Sadie. Sitting next to one another, they both had several empty seats on either side of them. Such largess made Sadie feel rather small and insignificant.

"And we're underdressed," Sadie said, picking up a grape and popping it in her mouth. Her orange Crocs looked downright gaudy against the polished hardwood floor. "Maybe I do understand why you don't want this life," she said thoughtfully. "It would be rather exhausting to try to keep up with it all."

Breanna didn't reply, but the comment seemed to weigh heavy on her, making Sadie worry she'd said the wrong thing. Was Breanna still considering her options? "But I'm sure you'd get used to it if you decided to take that route."

Breanna still didn't say anything.

"Or not," Sadie offered, feeling like she couldn't say anything right.

"Just leave it," Breanna said quietly.

Sadie picked up one of her crumpets, examining it for a moment. It didn't look like the other crumpets she'd had during their trip, but then again it had been made with canning rings. She hoped that was the reason for its poor presentation. She took a bite, fully intending to enjoy every bit of the experience, but after chewing twice, she stopped. The texture was rubbery and the flavor was bland, despite the butter. With no other choice, she finished chewing and swallowed, scowling at the remaining crumpet in her hand. She told herself to take another bite, give it one more chance, but after a few seconds, she returned the offending crumpet to her plate.

"Not good?" Breanna asked. She'd buttered her own crumpet but had yet to take a bite.

"What a waste of my time," Sadie said, thinking about all the effort she'd put into the crumpets. Her mood was decidedly soured.

Breanna took a small bite so as to verify Sadie's pronouncement, then chewed just as carefully as she returned the crumpet to her plate and wiped her fingers on the napkin in her lap. "I think it would be better with jam," she said, but her heart wasn't in it. She was just trying to be polite.

Sadie grumbled and took a bite of the casserole—it helped to soothe her battered ego. "At least the casserole is good," she said after her third bite. Breanna nodded her agreement and they continued eating in silence for a few minutes, both of them seeming to be lost in their thoughts.

"Mom?"

Sadie looked up at Breanna, who had stopped eating and was staring at her plate. "What?" Sadie asked when Breanna didn't continue. She took another bite of her breakfast casserole—it really had turned out quite well. The sage was a perfect touch.

"Um, there's something I need to—" Breanna was cut off by the opening of the door that caused both of them to look toward it.

Inspector Kent walked in while Sadie chewed as fast as she could, so she could speak if he was here to ask her more questions.

"Mrs. Hoffmiller. Miss Hoffmiller," Inspector Kent said, inclining his head first to Sadie, then to Breanna. "I've come to take my leave, but wanted to be sure you had my card."

Sadie swallowed quickly. "Your leave?" she repeated.

"You'll be pleased to know that we did find trace amounts of blood on the wall of the sitting room and that we've completed the investigation of both crime scenes—the sitting room and the pantry. We've left the police lines up in order to keep them intact should we need to return."

"You've got to be kidding me," Sadie said. "A man was murdered and the body was found in the pantry . . . and you're leaving?"

"We've concluded our investigation of the crime scenes and finished collecting our interviews at this time, madam," Inspector Kent said, not seeming the least bit offended by her surprise. "And we've become aware of some rather scandalous dealings in Mr. Tatum's life that are likely the reason he met such an end."

"Mr. Tatum?" Breanna asked.

"Yes, Leon Tatum to be exact—he was working under the assumed name of John Henry Barro. It seems that he was not a nurse at all and, in fact, had some financial trouble in excess of one hundred thousand pounds that it seems he was trying to run away from."

Sadie blinked. "What?" She reflected on Austin's comments that morning about how hiring a caretaker for an earl was not a trite consideration. And John Henry wasn't a nurse at all—he wasn't even John Henry. "How did you discover this so quickly?"

"Much of it was put together by Inspector Dilree," Kent said, "based on the statements he took yesterday. He really is a most efficient recorder. We were planning to come back and follow up on the things he'd discovered, but finding Mr. Tatum's body sped things up exponentially and we have no desire to offset anyone's holiday plans."

"What if you're wrong?" Breanna asked. "What if John Henry's death had nothing to do with his past and everything to do with what's been happening here at the estate?"

Kent turned his eyes toward Breanna. "And what, pray tell, has been happening at the estate?"

Breanna closed her mouth, but Sadie was quick to pick up that line of thought. "Someone moved the body," she said. "Even if some thug killed him, whoever moved the body knew this house well enough to know where to put him—and why do that?"

"As I said, we will continue our investigation, but it is not in anyone's best interest for us to throw off the rhythm of any household—especially that of an earl who is doing poorly."

"Austin told you to leave, didn't he?" Sadie said. "He's the one who doesn't want you here."

The inspector paused before continuing. "He is simply concerned about the effect of our ongoing presence in the house, what with the earl and so on," he said carefully. "But if you're concerned about staying on here, you're welcome to go to London, though we would prefer you don't leave the country for at least another twenty-four hours."

Sadie was stunned, and judging from the look on Breanna's face, she was too.

"Very good, then," the inspector said. "I have your contact information and will let you know if I need anything else."

He exited the room with both Breanna and Sadie looking after him, then they looked at each other. "I need to talk to Liam," Breanna said, pushing back from the table. "He's with his father."

Sadie nodded. She moved to pick up the dirty dishes they were leaving on the table, then remembered that she'd been ordered out of the kitchen. She only wished it was Austin who had to clean up after her. They left the dining room in time to see Austin talking with the inspectors in the foyer, nodding and smiling politely. Grant stood apart from them, but at attention—awaiting his orders, as usual. Sadie knew she was scowling as they passed Austin on the way to the staircase, but she didn't care. If anyone deserved her dirty looks, it was Austin. She had no doubt he was carefully orchestrating every detail of what was taking place.

As she passed, she overheard some of what he was saying, " . . . on behalf of the earl I wish to sincerely thank you for allowing us to . . ."

Oh, she simply couldn't stand that man.

CHAPTER 28

A t the top of the stairs, Breanna turned to her mother. "Um, do you mind if I talk to Liam alone?"

Sadie did in fact mind—not about Breanna talking to him alone so much as the fact that Breanna obviously didn't want Sadie there. It was kinda the same thing, but not really. And yet Sadie still had the keys in her pocket and wasn't sure she wanted Breanna to know about them. "Of course," Sadie said. "I need to change anyway, I smell like . . . the vegetable pantry." She grimaced at the reminder.

"Okay," Breanna said. "You know where to find me."

Sadie nodded as Breanna headed toward the earl's room, then hurried toward her own room, putting her hand in her pocket to ensure the keys were still there and not simply a figment of her imagination. The feel of the cool metal in her hand ignited her excitement and she reached her room within a few seconds of parting ways with Breanna. Once inside her room she hurried to close the door before pulling the keys out of her pocket and looking them over.

There were seven different keys of various sizes on a thick metal ring. She turned them over in her hand and inspected each key carefully. There was little hint as to what door they fit simply by their size and shape, and Sadie hurried to her purse to pull out her reading glasses. She didn't wear them very often because they seemed so old-ladyish, but she was alone and needed the help so she gave in. Six of the keys simply had the name of the company that had made them, but the last key had the words "Room Master" engraved on it. Did that mean it opened all the rooms in the whole house?

Sadie hadn't run into any locked rooms yet, but she'd kept her investigation to the library and kitchen. Certainly whoever had put the keys in her jacket had something they wanted her to accomplish. Did they also know the inspectors were going to be sent packing, leaving no one to figure out what was really going on? Because, despite John Henry's sordid past—or, well, Leon Tatum's—there was more at play than his past catching up with him—she was sure of it. She wondered again who would have slipped her these keys—if not for Mrs. Land being in London she'd assume it had been her. Then again, maybe Mrs. Land had put them there before she left. She had told Sadie to get her jacket. Sadie assumed that Mrs. Land and Grant would be the two people with keys like this—to everything. And certainly Grant wouldn't be the one to give them to her.

The next question was what should she do now?

Her first thought was to get into Austin's room, and it both excited and terrified her. He knew she was on to him, which meant he would be keeping a sharp eye on the things she was doing. Not to mention the close attention Grant would be paying to her as well.

Then she remembered when Austin had showed up in the kitchen. He hadn't used the main stairs and had come in through the staff dining room. That meant there had to be at least one more way to get between floors. She thought of the hallway she'd passed each time she'd gone through the swinging doors of the kitchen. Did the stairs Austin used connect to that hallway?

It made sense that the staff would need more than one way to get around—and if there was an extra set of stairs in the east wing, might there also be an extra set in the west wing, where her room was located? If she could find them, she could go through the basement hallway and then back up the east wing stairs, which would put her close to Austin's room without having to cross any common areas of the house—she was getting a bit tired of hiding behind Christmas trees anyway.

Seeing as how it was ten o'clock in the morning and the staff was likely in the heat of their bed making, floor sweeping, and towel washing—it was the perfect time to do a little digging before Austin managed to have them shipped out of Southgate altogether.

CHAPTER 29

Sadie opened the door to the hallway slowly—grateful for well-greased hinges that allowed the heavy oak door to open nice and smooth. She couldn't see either end of the hallway due to the curve in the overall design, but the portion she could see was clear. She stepped into the hall and closed the door behind her before heading left—away from the main staircase—counting six doorways before the hallway ended in a rounded sitting area. There wasn't an open stairway in sight, but as she headed back the other way, she tried each doorknob she came to.

Though eager to use the keys she'd been given, she assumed that a door leading to the stairs wouldn't be locked—and though the locked doors called to her, tempting her to take a peek—she was a woman of strength and was able to resist the seductive call of her own curiosity. The knob of the last door in the hallway turned easily in her hand and she smiled to herself as she looked down the darkened staircase. There was a light switch on the wall, but even though it was disconcerting to be alone in the dark, she didn't want to turn on the light for fear that someone would see it at the bottom of the staircase. She let the door close behind her and took a few seconds to get used to the dark—it was really, really dark and she wondered why she hadn't packed a flashlight, or better yet, a headlamp.

Holding onto the handrail she carefully made her way down the steps, trying not to think about what would happen if someone decided to take the same stairs up. Her bed hadn't been made yet today, which meant she could very well run smack-dab into who-ever's job it was to make it up. She swallowed and simply hoped that wouldn't happen.

One flight down she encountered a landing and felt around for a switch, flipping it on just long enough to see a door, which she assumed led to the main floor, and another flight of stairs leading down—to the *underside*. In darkness once again, she continued her way down the stairs, slowing her steps as light began seeping in around a corner. There didn't seem to be a door at the bottom.

Assuming she was nearly there, she proceeded carefully forward, straining for any sound that would give away someone being at the bottom. On the final step she paused and listened to the silence for a full minute. Then she poked her head around the corner and scanned the hallway in both directions. Whereas the upper levels were ornate and beautiful, painted rich colors and decorated with what was obviously the finest accents—the below stairs hallway was painted a stark white with a flat gray carpet on the floor and the most basic of light fixtures attached to the ceiling. Surely the nobility was embarrassed by their obvious excess in relation to the staff quarters they provided.

An open door to the left showed a laundry room, but there were several other doors recessed from the hallway walls and she quickly darted across the hall to the first one, peering around the corner to see if anyone was further down the hall. The hallway was still empty so she hurried to the next doorway—this one had a sign attached to the wall that read Grant Contine.

Grant's room?

She peeked around the corner of the doorway, but her attention was drawn back to the sign. Grant's room. Here she was on her way to Austin's room—but she was *at* Grant's room. Maybe she could spare a minute or two just to make sure he wasn't hiding anything. She grabbed the knob to verify it was locked, and then excitedly reached for the keys and let herself in.

Once inside she closed the door behind her and scanned the room, which consisted of a dresser, an armoire, a queen-sized bed, and a chair set opposite a small TV. She walked further into the room, looking at the details such as the made-up bed and the dresser top filled with a collection of colognes and other odds and ends, including an electric razor and a stack of books. Sadie moved carefully, glancing nervously at the door, well aware that Grant could return at any time. She needed to figure out whatever she could before that happened. If she were caught . . . well, she couldn't even imagine what that would be like.

She picked up and replaced several objects on the dresser before realizing she should probably be careful about fingerprints—not that she had to worry about much of an *investigation* or anything. But still, she put her hands in her pockets as she moved to the armoire and pulled open the door with her hand still in her pocket. There were three uniforms as well as a few miscellaneous shirts and sweaters she assumed Grant wore on his days off. She removed her hands from her pockets in order to go through those of the uniform. None of the numerous pockets offered anything other than the fact that Grant liked to suck on hard candies.

Frustrated that she hadn't found anything important, she moved to the small bedside table and pulled on the handle of the drawer. It didn't budge, and on closer inspection Sadie realized it was locked. She frowned at the drawer and considered looking for a key or a hairpin, when she saw a book resting on top of the nightstand. It was a book of poetry, likely from the extensive library upstairs, but the page was marked by what looked like a light green envelope.

Sadie picked up the book and opened it, and removed the envelope while memorizing the page it was on for when she needed to replace it. The address to Southgate was handwritten and the postmark was a week old. It was certainly a personal correspondence and would hopefully help her learn more about Grant, but Sadie knew she couldn't risk taking the time to read it right now. She put it in her back pocket and shut the book, promising herself she'd return the letter as soon as she could. The adrenaline was wearing off, allowing a healthy dose of anxiety to take its place. She'd been here for a few minutes and didn't dare risk a longer stay. Taking a deep breath in hopes it would restore the courage that had allowed her to get this far, she moved carefully toward the door while scanning the room to make sure she hadn't left anything out of place. She still had to get to Austin's room.

She put her ear against the door even though she wasn't sure it would help her hear anything, and then began pulling the door open carefully. In the same moment she noticed two things—the corner of a piece of paper sticking out from beneath a leather shaving kit on Grant's dresser, and the sound of footsteps in the hall.

CHAPTER 30

Sadie's mouth went dry as she considered her present circumstance—standing behind a partially open door to a staff member's bedroom. How on earth would she explain her way out of that?

Her eyes darted around the room, looking for a place to hide but seeing nothing. Even the bed—a favorite hiding place of hers in the past—was too close to the ground to afford her an opportunity. Not daring to shut the door, lest it capture the attention of whoever was in the hallway, she pulled as far to the side of the door as she could and did the only thing she could think of, close her eyes and hold her breath while thinking invisible thoughts.

The footsteps stopped and she felt the hinge moving against her arm as the door was pushed open.

You can't see me, you can't see me, I'm the invisible woman.

"Grant?" a female voice called out quietly. Sadie opened one eye, but the door blocked whoever it was.

Don't come in, don't come in, don't come in.

The mystery visitor paused an inordinate amount of time before the door began to close, allowing Sadie to breathe again, though the rush of blood in her ears made it difficult for her to hear anything else. The door was pulled shut with a snap and Sadie sent a million thank-you prayers to heaven as she opened her eyes and stepped out from the corner she'd wedged herself into. She stared at the door with absolute fear. Did she dare open it again? The thought made her physically ill. That she'd been so close to discovery was proof that she was not invincible and it made her knees shake. What was she doing? It wasn't the first time the thought had crossed her mind, but she must be crazy to be here at all.

Her eyes went to the small window above Grant's bed, but she didn't know how she could get to it. With no other option, she looked back to the doorknob, reminding herself that crazy or not she had to get out of this room before someone found her standing here with Grant's letter shoved in her pocket. She took a deep breath, summoning all her courage and positive thoughts, and turned the knob. She was about to pull the door open when she remembered the paper sticking out from underneath the shaving kit.

Ignoring it was always an option, but even with her renewed concerns toward her current state of mental health, it wasn't in Sadie's nature to ignore something that could be important. With the door opened barely an inch, she reached forward and carefully scooted the paper out from under the kit. It was a half sheet, folded over once, and it only took a flick of her fingers to open it.

Master Liam,

Please allow me to explain myself fully so that you might know I am not the one worthy of the blame you place here—not the only one at least. Meet me in the sitting room while the final tea is being prepared for your guests. Please accept my apology in advance for the things I must tell you.

Sincerely,

John Henry Barro

CHAPTER 31

Sadie read it again and her heart raced. She wanted to believe that Liam had simply had an argument with John Henry and that his recent mood was due to the fact that his father was sick. But with these words in hand she could not ignore the question—could Liam have killed John Henry?

It was a horrible thought and one that part of her rebelled against so strongly she clenched her eyes shut and shook her head. And yet when she opened her eyes and read the note again she had to admit that if she was being truly objective, it was a possibility—in fact it was the strongest possibility she'd encountered thus far. Even more than Austin. Whereas Austin had a bad attitude, a secret, and a suspect nature—there was nothing about the murder that directly pointed to him. Liam, however, had motive—he was angry with John Henry in regard to the earl's care and they had argued, a fact he kept from everyone, including the police. And, if Liam knew John Henry was in the sitting room—per this note—it meant he had opportunity as well.

Even though it broke her heart to do so, Sadie forced herself to look at the possibility. Breanna and Sadie would have been upstairs packing while the final tea was being prepared. The fact that Grant would have been the one preparing the tea meant he wouldn't be on hand to see anyone enter the sitting room. John Henry had something important to tell Liam—could he have hidden behind the curtains to make sure that no one else saw him?

She read the note again. *I am not the one worthy of the blame you place here—not the only one at least.*

Mrs. Land had been blackmailed into doing something against her nature. Was John Henry being blackmailed too? Had he had enough; was he ready to blow it all wide open? And yet the inspector said he was using a borrowed name, was not a nurse, and had outstanding debts. Surely his creditors had a better motive than Liam for killing John Henry in a fit of passion—but that in and of itself bothered her. How did the police find out so much about John Henry in such a short period of time? And how would these phantom creditors know John Henry was hiding behind the curtain? They would dump him in a river or blow up his car, wouldn't they? Breaking into an earl's estate, stabbing a man with a poker, and then sneaking back in to hide the body just did not seem consistent with fringe-of-society killers. Liam, on the other hand, knew the house, he knew the people in it, he was angry with John Henry, and he knew where to find a deadly fireplace poker.

But why would Liam kill John Henry if John Henry was going to tell him the truth?

Maybe Liam hadn't received this note at all. What if it had been intercepted and that person then took matters into their own hands and killed John Henry before he could turn on his co-conspirators?

It was Grant who had sent Mrs. Land away, Grant who hadn't been on hand when they found the body, Grant who managed the house and the people in it, and Grant who warned Sadie away from talking to the other staff. And the note was in *Grant's* room. If a conspiracy was afoot, it seemed ridiculously naïve to imagine that Grant wouldn't be right in the middle of it.

At that moment, Sadie's cell phone vibrated in her pocket, nearly sending her through the roof. Still trying to catch her breath, Sadie pulled her phone from her pocket and flipped it open.

It was a text message from Breanna.

Where r u?

She imagined Breanna's reaction to the answer that she was in Grant's bedroom holding a note that could very well implicate either Liam or Grant in John Henry's murder. She didn't answer the text and instead closed the phone, shoving it into her pocket along with the note. She had to get out of here.

Once again she put her hand on the knob and slowly pulled the door open. Offering a silent prayer, she carefully stuck her head out of the doorway. Realizing it was clear, she stepped out and pulled the door shut. She could breathe again, but was faced with a decision—did she continue on to Austin's room as had been her original goal, or did she go back to her room and review what she'd just discovered.

"Hey!"

Sadie froze with one foot in the air, preparing to take a step. Maybe the unfamiliar voice wasn't talking to her.

"Hey," the voice said again. Sadie turned her head, her eyes stopping on a large gray-haired woman standing several feet away. The woman put her plump hands on her plump hips and stared at Sadie through half-moon glasses that rested on her plump nose. "Whatcha doin' down here?" she asked. "And who are ya?"

She hadn't asked what Sadie was doing in Grant's room, so Sadie forced herself to look a bit more relaxed as she turned to face the woman, assuming she hadn't been there long enough to see where Sadie had come from. Hopefully the dim light of the hallway hid the guilty fear on her face. "I'm S-Sadie Hoffmiller," she said. "I was, well, I'm looking for, uh—I'm lost."

"Darn right yer lost," the woman said. Some of the anger seemed to have left her tone, but Sadie didn't dare trust it completely. The woman continued. "There ain't any common rooms on the bottom level." Then she cocked her head to the side. "Wait, ain't you the woman that made up them hideous crumpets?"

Sadie realized this must be Mrs. Kinsley, the new cook, but having her ego pummeled after everything else that had happened was not a welcome turn to the conversation. "I was only trying to help."

"Right," the woman said with a nod. "Lord Melcalfe warned me you might try to worm yerself into my kitchen."

"I'm not trying to worm my way into the kitchen," Sadie said, not liking that she'd been the subject of gossip. "I'm just lost."

Mrs. Kinsley regarded her thoughtfully. "You want anything special for your meals?" she asked bluntly, surprising Sadie. "I told Lord Melcalfe that there ain't no way I can prepare proper meals on such short notice, but my daughter's bringing up some things from the shop and there's the fixin's for a perfect plowman's lunch in the fridge."

"Plowman's lunch?" Sadie asked.

Mrs. Kinsley shrugged one shoulder. "Bread, chutney, cheese, and a pickle on the side—fill you up right good. Though it's nothing like the fancy stuff Mrs. Land has been shipping in this place." She huffed, showing her obvious disapproval. Sadie couldn't agree more.

"I'll take filling over fancy any day," Sadie said, daring a smile.

She remembered her earlier thoughts about Mrs. Kinsley possibly being able to provide Sadie some information, but it was hard to not run away from the imposing woman. "So, you knew Mrs. Land?"

Mrs. Kinsley's eyes narrowed slightly and it was all Sadie could do not to cower. "They wanted to pass her off as a cook—downright embarassin' if you ask me. When she tried to tell me what to do in my own kitchen, I'd had enough. My daughter told me I had a job in her shop anytime I wanted it—and what with the earl doin' poorly and a maid acting as a cook, it seemed as good a time as any."

"So you left *after* the earl got sick?"

Mrs. Kinsley nodded. "What with Mrs. Land coming down to the kitchen and the earl's lady friend coming to take the place over any time, it just felt like too many changes for me to figure. After the earl's stroke I didn't have much reason to stay."

"Lady friend?" Sadie asked.

"Sure, who do you think he was fixing the countess's bedroom for?"

CHAPTER 32

Countess's bedroom? Sadie repeated in her mind. A door opening further down the hall seemed to make Mrs. Kinsley realize she had other things to do.

"Well, you best get back on up where you're supposed to be. I need to get back to the kitchen—seems everyone's intent that we leave by noon, even though I just got here. I've got lots to do before then and my daughter will be here soon."

Mrs. Kinsley shook her head, then turned and disappeared before Sadie could even find her voice again. Remembering the door they'd heard open, Sadie found herself hurrying to the west stairs. She was halfway up the stairs before realizing that she'd apparently decided to leave Austin's room for later. At the landing for the main floor, Sadie turned on the light so she didn't trip as she ascended to the top level, but she still scanned the hallway before letting herself out of the doorway and then into her room, prepared to find Breanna waiting for her. However, the room was empty. At first she was relieved, then realized that if Breanna wasn't here, she was probably with Liam.

She pulled her cell phone out of her pocket and replied to the text Breanna had sent—it felt as though it took her five minutes. She was the slowest text messager on the planet.

I'm in the room—we need to talk.

She hit send and then tapped her foot while waiting for an answer. She rubbed a hand over her forehead as she considered what to do. Breanna texted her back, causing the phone to vibrate—startling her again. Her nerves weren't up for this.

I'll come when I can.

Sadie clenched her teeth in frustration. Should she demand Breanna return right now? Should she go hunt her down?

Those questions forced her to ask herself if she really thought Liam would hurt her daughter. She clenched her eyes shut and worked hard to push through everything else in order to focus on one thing—did Liam love Breanna?

It took only remembering his face when he looked at Breanna, especially after she'd told him they had no future together, to know that Liam would never do anything to hurt Breanna.

It was a comfort to have an answer to *something.* She would wait for Breanna—and while she waited, she'd get back to work. Before she got started, though, she changed the settings on her phone so that Stevie Wonder's "I Just Called to Say I Love You" would play whenever she got a call or text—no more of those blasted vibrations that sent her blood pressure to the moon.

That taken care of, Sadie pulled the note from her pocket. She read it one more time even though she doubted there was anything else she could learn from it at this point. Then she pulled Grant's letter out of her back pocket, still feeling a teensy bit guilty for taking it, but willing to live with it if it provided her more answers. She pulled a single piece of paper out of the envelope, sincerely hoping it wouldn't turn out to be something lame like a bill.

She unfolded the paper onto the dresser top and smoothed it flat before she started reading.

Dear Grant,

Well, another week has come and gone and I've been given my weekly piece of paper. I realized as I sat down to start this letter that you're the only person who wants to hear from me. For a minute it made me sad—and then I was reminded of the things they've talked about in our group sessions, that every person is priceless. And you are priceless to me. We're having a big Christmas dinner tomorrow and it will be the first Christmas in almost a decade I've spent without you and at least a dozen glasses of eggnog. I'm not looking forward to it and wish I could sleep through the whole thing, but I know that's a big part of my problems— I've wanted to sleep through too many things in my life. Sobriety often feels like I'm the forward in a brutal game of rugby, destined to be run over at any moment. But snoozing in the stands doesn't win a game now, does it?

From your last letter it sounds like things at Southgate are the same as they've always been. It's weird being surrounded by so many lords and ladies here, but proof that not a one of us lives a life free of struggle, eh?

Anyways, I best wrap this up. Remember that I love you, that I can't wait for the day I return to my post and we're together again. You won't get this 'til after Boxing Day at least, but I hope you had a happy Christmas. Next year will be different—better. I promise. I'm looking forward to seeing you next week—it will be the perfect start to a new year.

Love,
Your Essie

When Sadie finished reading she was a bit disappointed to realize that if she'd learned anything, it was to feel a measure of sympathy toward Grant. Though the details were hazy, and she didn't know exactly what the letter meant, she'd gleaned enough to know that this Essie person was important to Grant and that they were apart. She guessed that Essie was in some kind of rehab center, since she'd talked about sobriety and group therapy. Unfortunately there was nothing about the earl's lady friend or a potential motive for murdering John Henry, or even something horrible about Austin she could take to the investigator.

Then again, maybe she'd learned a great deal more than that. Like Mrs. Land, Grant had someone he loved who was in trouble. Was it too far-fetched to assume that Essie could have been used against Grant the same way Rupert had bought Mrs. Land's participation? Assuming that Sadie was assuming correctly—which of course she thought she was—just how far would Grant go? Mrs. Land had been a sentence away from cracking—Grant knew it and sent her to London. John Henry had asked Liam to meet him in the sitting room and although Liam's knowledge of that request was unknown—Grant was the one in possession of the note. And so *Grant* knew John Henry would be waiting for Liam during the time the final tea was being prepared. And what about this "lady friend"? And the countess's bedroom? And where did Lacy fit in? What was everyone trying to hide?

"Wait," she said out loud, forcing her thoughts to take a pause. There was too much in her head, too many directions she needed to pursue. What she needed was a list so she could put it all out there and work through the questions one by one.

She went to the bedside table and opened the drawer for the notebook. It wasn't there. Thinking she may have put it somewhere else, she looked in the other bedside table drawer on Breanna's side—nothing. Then she checked her suitcase, Breanna's backpack, and the drawers of the dresser. When she'd looked everywhere twice, she officially began to panic. She grabbed her phone to text Breanna again, nearly cursing at how slow she was—she really needed to take a class or something.

Do u have the notebook?

While she waited for an answer, she looked everywhere for a third time—just in case.

Stevie Wonder signaled an answer to her text and she hurried back to the bed and picked up her phone.

No, y?

CHAPTER 33

Sadie swallowed hard as she looked around the room one last time. Someone had taken the notebook. She tried to remember everything they'd written down, but had to give up when she realized the notebook simply had everything.

She sat down hard on the bed, letting out a breath. Why hadn't she anticipated that someone could take the notebook? She should have hidden it somewhere—in the toilet tank or under the mattress or in between layers of her underwear—somewhere no one would ever look. And now she'd lost everything because she assumed no one would care what little discoveries she might write down.

She sat up straighter—didn't the fact that someone felt the notebook was valuable enough to steal in fact verify its value? She sat there for a full minute, trying to decide what to do and who to suspect of taking the notebook. Finally, she had to accept that she could either pine and worry about the book, or she could get back to work. It was nearly ten-thirty, which meant the staff would be leaving in a matter of hours.

With no time to waste, she went to her suitcase and pulled out the half-sheet pad of paper and the other ballpoint pen she'd brought—and Breanna had called her neurotic for over-packing. Ha!

She started writing down everything she remembered—but this time she organized it by dedicating one page to each person involved. She had a page for Liam, a page for Grant, Austin, and Mrs. Land. When she finished, she read over what she'd written, asking herself if she'd missed anything. The final page listed the information about Mrs. Land. Sadie studied it harder than the rest because Mrs. Land was the one person no longer available to be questioned. Had Sadie missed anything in their conversation, anything at all?

She relived the entire conversation she'd had in the kitchen without remembering anything that she hadn't already written down. If only Sadie had had a few more minutes with the woman. And not only for Sadie's well-being; Mrs. Land had seemed so relieved to confide in Sadie. Imagine how much better she'd have felt if she'd had the chance to tell Sadie all her secrets. Sadie imagined the lightness that could have entered the woman's countenance, how much more confident and comfortable she'd have felt if she'd been able to truly relieve herself of her burdens.

Wait a minute—Mrs. Land *had* seemed more confident and comfortable during their final conversation. She had made eye contact and her voice had been stronger even though Grant was right there. Sadie had assumed that was because she was excited to see her son. But what was it she'd said?

"Oh, good, you found your book. I asked Grant to make sure you got your book back."

Was Sadie imagining that Mrs. Land might have emphasized the word "sure" in that sentence?

"I asked Grant to make sure you got your book back."

No, she *had* emphasized that word. She'd been trying to tell Sadie something that Grant wouldn't pick up on.

Mrs. Land had written something in the recipe book!

Sadie hopped off the bed as fear gripped her heart. Had someone taken that book too? But a quick sprint for the bedside table assured her that no one felt her recipe book held any clues. She picked up the book, but it slipped out of her hands and fell to the ground, thanks to her eager fingers. She bent down and picked it up by the spine, righted it on the bed and began flipping through the pages, scanning the handwritten recipes in search of handwriting other than her own. When she reached the end and found nothing, she questioned herself. Was all the mystery going to her head? Had Mrs. Land really only been glad Sadie had got her book back?

Sadie went back to the front of the book and turned page after page, slower this time as she looked for something, anything, that indicated Mrs. Land had used the recipe book to tell her what she hadn't had time to say when Grant interrupted their conversation. Sadie reached the end of the book a second time and let out a breath. The adrenaline of the expected discovery was wearing off and Sadie once again felt like an idiot.

She slammed the cover shut. "Ah, crickets," she cursed. *Well, at least Breanna hadn't been a part of this one,* she thought as she turned back toward the bed where she'd left the new clue notebook. She took a step, but her foot slid across the hardwood floor. A dry slide.

Looking down she realized a piece of paper was under her shoe. *Darned stupid piece of paper,* she thought—more than willing to pin all her frustration on it for the moment. Where had it come from anyway?

Then she paused.

Could that darned stupid piece of paper have fallen out of the recipe book when she dropped it?

She snatched up the paper, turning it over in her hand. The words made the breath catch in her throat. She read them twice to make sure she'd read them correctly.

Please return the keys to the drawer next to the sink when you've learned what you need to learn. I'm sorry I can't tell you what I know, but I need to make sure Rupert is safe. I can tell you this much though— Master Liam moved John Henry into the vegetable pantry.

CHAPTER 34

Sadie blinked at the paper and read it again. Mrs. Land *had* given her the keys.

But the last part of the note quickly pushed everything else from her mind.

Liam moved the body.

The very idea made her ill. She grabbed the new notebook, put it in the waistband of her pants, stuffed the notes and letter in her pocket, and hurried out the door, texting Breanna as she hurried toward the east wing. Seconds later she unlocked the door to the earl's sitting room and let herself in, quickly scanning the room. Breanna wasn't here nor had she answered Sadie's text. The room was empty, but still as beautiful as she remembered it from her two previous visits. For the smallest moment she felt a little disappointed that she and Breanna hadn't had their own sitting room too. As her eyes took in the antique desk, silk draperies, and leather chairs, she noticed a door on the opposite side of the room from the door she knew led to the earl's chamber. The room was organized in such a way that the door was behind a chair, and not easily accessed. She'd never noticed it before and immediately wondered if it was perhaps the countess's bedroom Mrs. Kinsley had mentioned. All those Regency romances talked about separate bedrooms and such—would the two rooms, however, share a sitting room?

Distracted by this new discovery, and since Breanna wasn't there anyway, Sadie went to the door and tested the knob. It was locked—of course—and although she had the key, she took a few moments to argue with herself.

Breanna's not here, it would only take a minute.

Liam could be a crazed murderer and Breanna could be with him in the other room.

But he loves her.

But he's been lying all along.

Basically it came down to curiosity vs. Breanna. It was still a hard choice to make, so she forced herself to review the note she'd found in Grant's room, along with Mrs. Land's note that said Liam had moved John Henry's body. In the moment it took to visualize Liam wrenching the poker from the wall and catching the crumpling body of John Henry, Sadie made her decision and turned away, wriggling her hips due to the fact that the notebook tucked into her waistband wasn't very comfortable.

She went to the earl's bedroom door and focused her thoughts before turning the knob. It was also locked—sheesh, you'd think Liam didn't trust anyone at all! She only hesitated a moment before inserting the key, turning it in the lock, and pushing the door open. She saw the earl first and looked away, but only for a moment before her eyes went back to the bed. He was awake! Well, his eyes were open anyway, though he looked rather out of it.

"Mr. Martin?" she asked, then caught herself. "I mean, uh, Earl Martin—or, uh, Lord Garnett or, uh—"

"William."

She snapped her head to the side, having forgotten that she'd entered this room looking for someone. But it wasn't Breanna she saw and Sadie froze as she faced Liam. He wasn't alone. Another man Sadie had never seen before rose to his feet from behind a small desk by the window. Liam turned to him. "It's okay, this is Breanna's mother," he said, passing her so he could shut the door. Then he turned back to Sadie. "How did you get in here?"

Sadie casually put her hand behind her back, hiding the keys. She looked back at the earl to distract Liam from the question he'd asked. "Your father?" she asked. "He's awake?"

Liam and the other man shared a look. After a few more moments, Liam let out a breath. "Dr. Sawyer," he said, waving toward the other man, "this is Sadie Hoffmiller. Sadie; Dr. Sawyer."

The doctor moved toward Sadie and put out his hand, which she shook while taking an appraising look at the man. He was quite attractive, with dark eyes and dark hair just beginning to go gray at the edges. Sadie had a sudden desire to go back in time and fix her hair, touch up her makeup, and lose fifteen pounds. Never mind that she had Detective Pete Cunningham back in Garrison. Pete who?

"A pleasure to meet you," Dr. Sawyer said in a voice so melodic with his accent that it sounded like a song. Sadie grinned for a few seconds before realizing he expected an answer.

"Oh, yes," Sadie said. "The pleasure is all mine." They all paused for a moment, and then her reason for being there in the first place came rushing back and her admiration of a beautiful man was pushed to the back-burner almost as quickly as it had come. "Who are you again?"

"Um, he's my father's doctor," Liam said.

Sadie looked at him, confused. "I thought Austin's father was his doctor?"

"Dr. Sawyer was Dad's doctor before Austin's father took over, and now he's Dad's doctor again."

"Okay," Sadie said slowly, and yet she didn't quite have a handle on it. She cocked her head to the side. "Huh?"

Dr. Sawyer spoke. "I used to be the earl's physician—I practice in London. Until today I hadn't seen the earl for several months, and I didn't know until yesterday about his supposed stroke."

Liam cut in. "When I arrived, John Henry seemed to be trying to keep me away from my father. I was up to my ears in accounts and other estate business, so I didn't push too much, but during our tour of England I determined I wouldn't be so easy to push around when we got back. John Henry and I had several arguments after my return. He didn't want me staying with my father for more than fifteen minutes at a time and he wouldn't let me read my father's medical file. I spoke to Dr. Melcalfe once, and he simply agreed with John Henry on every count. Yesterday, I just lost it and told John Henry to get out. John Henry had told me that Dr. Sawyer agreed that Austin's father would be better prepared to care for Dad due to his close connection to the family, but I wasn't so sure. Basically, I wanted a second opinion in regards to the course of treatment for my father. I left a message with Dr. Sawyer's office yesterday, hoping he could help me understand where to go from there."

"Okay," Sadie said with a nod so that he would know she was keeping up.

"Well, Dr. Sawyer called me back after dinner. He knew nothing about my father's stroke or that he was receiving care from Dr. Melcalfe. As you can imagine, this worried me even more. Dr. Sawyer walked me through some assessments I could make in regards to my father's condition. Turns out that my father doesn't show any signs of having had a stroke at all."

Sadie's eyebrows shot up. "What?" She looked at the earl again who had closed his eyes. "Then what's wrong with him?"

"We aren't certain just yet," Dr. Sawyer said, walking over to the bed and taking his stethoscope from around his neck and putting the earpieces in his ears. A blood pressure cuff was already attached to the earl's arm. Dr. Sawyer took the bulb used to inflate the cuff in one hand and began pumping. "But we're guessing that he's been overmedicated—in a kind of drug-induced coma, if you will."

Sadie was shocked. "Really? But why?"

"That part is still unclear," Liam said, watching the doctor at his father's bedside. "Dr. Sawyer arrived this morning—no one knows he's here but you, me, and Breanna. That's why I didn't argue when Austin sent the inspectors back to the police station to finish the investigation. When you add this to the missing family Bible and Austin's overall attitude—it makes everything going on at Southgate look very suspicious and I think it all comes back to the fact that my father is being kept in a vegetative state for some reason I can't figure out."

"But why not tell the inspectors all this?" Sadie asked. The police had been here all morning and telling them would be the best way to ensure care for his father—right?

Dr. Sawyer looked over his shoulder and raised one eyebrow, indicating that he was wondering the same thing. The blood pressure cuff hissed slightly as he turned his attention back to the gauge on the earl's arm.

Liam let out a breath. "It's complicated," he said. "Austin seems to have the police in his pocket and . . . well, I just want to make sure my father's taken care of before I get them involved—just in case."

"Things will become even more complicated if we don't get your father to a hospital," Dr. Sawyer said. He released all the air out of the cuff and took the stethoscope out of his ears. He even moved nicely, Sadie noticed as the doctor continued speaking. "I need to find out what he's been taking if I'm to give him the proper care without making his condition worse. I've reduced the flow rate on the IV as much as I dare and his blood pressure is rising. I need a full line of tests and the equipment necessary to properly monitor him while we figure out what's been going on. I need another IV bag."

Liam scowled and went to the armoire. He opened the door, revealing shelves of medical supplies, including several bags of IV fluid. "There's something in these bags that isn't on the labels," Liam explained to Sadie as he pulled one off the shelf. "I believe Austin and some of the staff are involved too—John Henry couldn't have done this all by himself."

"That's it!" Sadie said, putting a few pieces together. "That's the conspiracy—that's what Mrs. Land was in on and what had Austin acting so strange."

Liam suddenly looked nervous, instantly reminding Sadie of the note Mrs. Land had left her. There was more going on than the conspiracy against his father and his mystery illness. Sadie considered that Liam's own secrets were probably the real reason he hadn't talked to the inspectors about his suspicions—he knew he'd be implicated in John Henry's murder if they knew the whole story. Would he really come clean once he knew his father was safe? With so many secrets going around, it was hard to say.

She took a step back, looking at Dr. Sawyer and then at the earl—at least they lent credibility to Liam's story. This part of it anyway. "Where's Breanna?"

Liam didn't meet her eyes; he handed the IV to the doctor and then shoved his hands into his pockets. "She went down to get something for us to eat—neither Dr. Sawyer nor myself has had any-thing to eat since Dr. Sawyer arrived this morning. Austin dismissed the security personnel, and then said he had to take care of some things in Exeter. I've told Grant to have the staff ready to leave as soon as possible as well—I want the house cleared before I call an ambulance, hopefully before Austin returns."

Sadie noted that she would have a hard time getting Manny his macaroons now that the security team had been dismissed, but she didn't allow herself to dwell on it right now.

Dr. Sawyer was shaking his head. "He needs medical interven-tion, now," he said again. "Your staff is the least of my concerns."

"Wait—Dr. Sawyer arrived this morning?" Sadie asked, look-ing back to the doctor who was writing down some notes in a small notebook. She'd been in the kitchen all morning, and staff had been everywhere once she was let out of the cooler—how did they get the doctor up here without anyone knowing about it? "What time did you arrive, Dr. Sawyer?" She refused to look at Liam, but felt him tense at her question.

"A little after six-thirty A.M.," Dr. Sawyer said, fiddling with the IV line as he hung the new bag. "I was on call until midnight and unable to leave London before then."

Sadie gasped slightly as her eyes slowly moved back to Liam, who was staring at the floor, his hands still pushed into his pockets. She looked back to the doctor. "How did you get past security?"

Dr. Sawyer looked at Liam. "I didn't see any security," he said. "But we came through the kitchen. Perhaps security was elsewhere."

Dr. Sawyer had come through the kitchen during the exact time Sadie had been locked in the cooler. Her heart sank as she turned her eyes, once more, to the man her daughter had fallen in love with.

"Liam," she said in a low whisper as her heart continued its slow descent. What kind of man does a thing like that? He'd not only moved the body, but he'd removed the poker from John Henry's chest, and then locked her in the cooler with the body? She didn't even know how to verbalize the shock and disappointment and fear she felt as the realization seeped through her skin and began swimming through her veins. She took a step back, watching the understanding blossom into Liam's eyes as well—he knew what she was putting together. They turned fearful and somewhat desperate. She was suddenly glad not to be alone with him right now.

"It's not what you think," he said slowly, taking a step toward her, which caused her to take another step away from him. "It wasn't supposed to happen like that."

"Lord Martin," Dr. Sawyer interrupted, "if you don't call an ambulance, I will have no choice but to do so in your place. Your father is in need of serious medical intervention—decreasing the rate of his medication can have serious complications. Time is of the essence."

A knock caused all of them to look at the bedroom door. Liam hurried toward it, leaving Sadie to stay where she was, though she pivoted to keep him in sight.

"Who is it?" he asked.

"It's me," Breanna's muted voice said from the other side. Liam opened the door and Breanna came in holding a tray. She smiled at Liam as she entered the room, but when she saw Sadie she stopped mid-stride, stumbling slightly. Liam put a hand out to keep her from falling. Sadie tried to ignore the smell of sausage and pastry coming from the tray Breanna held, but even though Sadie had eaten just a couple hours ago, she was suddenly famished. Good food does that to a person—convinces them they're hungry when they have no reason to eat.

"She knows," he said softly. Breanna looked at him with a questioning expression.

"How much?" she whispered back as if Sadie couldn't hear every word.

Liam shrugged apologetically. Breanna looked back at Sadie with guilt and fear in her eyes. Sadie put her hands on her hips and cocked her head to the side as if to say, "Explain your way out of this one, young lady."

Before they had a chance to talk, however, Liam asked Breanna a question. "The staff, are they gone yet?"

Breanna shook her head. "Mrs. Kinsley said some of them were already gone, but I know she and Grant are still here. Her daughter brought in a lot of food and Mrs. Kinsley was finishing up these sausage rolls when I got there." She dared a glance at Sadie, perhaps to see if her mother's steely look was softening. It wasn't, so she looked back to Liam. "She was working on some soup we can heat up for dinner tonight. I wouldn't be surprised if she's gone in another half an hour."

"And Austin?" Liam asked, setting the tray on the dresser top and setting out the plates so he could dish up lunch. "Is he back?"

"No, and Mrs. Kinsley hasn't seen him either," Breanna said, shaking her head. "Maybe you should call him and see where he is."

Liam scowled, but nodded as he began pouring the tea. He glanced at Dr. Sawyer who was taking the earl's pulse, looking at his watch so as to properly calculate it. Liam leaned into Breanna, lowering his voice. "I don't want to call an ambulance until everyone's gone."

Breanna shrugged, indicating that she didn't know when that would be.

Sadie cleared her throat rather loudly and gave Breanna a pointed look. She'd been ignored long enough.

"Um," Breanna said, looking around the room as if searching for help. Her eyes settled on the tray of food and she waved her hand toward it with a shaky smile. "Mrs. Kinsley says she makes the best sausage rolls in Devonshire, Mom—want one?"

Easy Sausage Rolls

1 pound sage sausage (Liam likes onions and green peppers mixed into his)
1 package puff pastry—defrost according to package directions
Mustard
1 egg yolk

Brown sausage in skillet.; drain well (rinse, if desired). Lay sheets of puff pastry on counter and cut into 12 rectangles (6 per sheet of pastry) using a pizza cutter. Spread each rectangle with mustard. Spoon $1/12$ of sausage into the center of each pastry rectangle. Fold over and pinch edges together. Beat egg yolk and brush over the tops of the rolls. Place rolls 2 inches apart on baking sheet. Bake at 400 degrees for 15 to 20 minutes or until tops are golden brown. Allow to cool slightly before eating, but best served warm.

Serves 12.

CHAPTER 35

W ell, that was a dirty trick.

Sadie had come to know and appreciate sausage rolls very much during their trip. It was all she could do to pull her eyes away from the succulent sausage wrapped in flaky pastry. There was also a plate of fresh fruit and cut-up vegetables, as well as tea and more of those yummy lemon cookies from the library.

Must . . . focus . . . must . . . be strong.

She forced her eyes away. "We need to talk," Sadie said, watching Breanna's shoulders slump as she realized her attempt to deflect Sadie's anger hadn't worked.

"Um, how about we go into the sitting room," Breanna said. "That way we won't disturb anyone."

Sadie nodded before leading the way out the door into the earl's sitting room. After she heard the door shut behind Breanna, she turned and faced her, not the least bit interested in wasting any more time—relieved to have a door between her and the distracting sausage rolls.

"Liam moved John Henry and then locked me in the cooler so he could sneak the doctor into the house, didn't he?"

"Oh, Mom," Breanna said—almost wailed, really. She brought her hands up to her face as if she could hide behind them. Sadie wanted to comfort her, but reminded herself that Breanna had been lying all this time. Breanna's chest rose and fell as she took a deep breath and then she lowered her hands, looking at Sadie with a tortured expression. Her shoulders fell in surrender. "I'm so sorry."

"Yeah," Sadie challenged, putting her hands on her hips again—it made her feel powerful. "You're sorry? I'm horrified! I can't believe you're still willing to have anything at all to do with him—I mean, moving the body is bad enough—but locking me in the cooler? I can't believe you're okay with that." She'd hoped Breanna hadn't known, that she'd been an ignorant participant, but she knew from Breanna's reaction that it wasn't true.

"I'm not okay with any of it," Breanna said. Her voice was thick and Sadie noticed tears rising in her eyes. "But it wasn't Liam."

"What?" Sadie said, her hands falling from her waist. If it wasn't Liam, then who was it? And why was Breanna reacting to it so strangely?

"Liam called my phone this morning to tell me you were in the kitchen. I didn't know the extent of his concerns about his father or the arrival of Dr. Sawyer until then, but he needed my help to get the doctor upstairs without anyone seeing them. He'd already managed to distract the security guard posted outside the kitchen door—but Liam needed me to distract you. He told me to take the servant stairs in our wing so that none of the other security people saw me. When I got to the kitchen, you were just walking into the cooler."

Sadie felt her mouth drop open, but it was barely processing in her mind. "*You* locked me in there?" Her entire world tilted on its axis.

Breanna swallowed before continuing. "I was right outside the door when you opened it and shut it again—totally freaked me out. All I knew was that Liam needed me to help him keep Dr. Sawyer a secret. Since I didn't understand everything that was going on, I didn't see how I could explain it to you and I knew you'd ask me a million questions. I put the pen through the place meant for a lock, then helped scout ahead of Liam to make sure no one saw us taking the doctor upstairs. Once Dr. Sawyer was with the earl I totally freaked out on Liam—demanding he fill me in. So he told me everything about his father and why the doctor was here.

"I ran down the stairs to let you out as soon as Liam finished telling me what had been going on behind the scenes, but by the time I got back to the kitchen, Austin was talking to security in the foyer and there was the banging, and I was scared to death about getting caught, and by the time I found Liam to go back with me, Austin was already there and then you were accusing him and then you . . ." She stopped to catch her breath. "Then you said John Henry was in there. I couldn't believe it, Mom. I—I just—"

"*You* locked me in a cooler with a dead man," Sadie said, feeling completely betrayed and not knowing what to do about it. She reviewed how strongly Breanna had reacted to the news that Sadie had been locked in. It hadn't been out of concern for her mother, but guilt at what she'd done. Maybe some of both.

"I didn't know Liam had moved the body and I had no idea John Henry was in there," Breanna said, a tear escaping. She reached out and put her hand on Sadie's arm. Sadie was tempted to shake it off, but this was her daughter. Breanna continued, "That's what I talked to him about before coming back to help you with breakfast—I could tell by the way he reacted that he wasn't surprised that John Henry was in there—horrified at what had happened, but not surprised. And so all the weird things he'd done and said started to click together. I confronted him and he admitted to finding John Henry in the sitting room, panicking, and putting him in the vegetable cooler until he could decide what to do next."

"I hope he felt horrible."

Breanna gave a sharp nod. "He did. I made sure of it." She wiped quickly at her eyes. "It's all so crazy. Gosh, I can't wait to get out of here."

Sadie almost agreed with her—but not quite. Breanna seemed to be missing one very important point. Maybe she just hadn't had time to consider it, or maybe she was avoiding the possibility, but Sadie couldn't do either of those things. "Bre," she said, looking Breanna in the eye. "Did Liam tell you *why* he moved John Henry?"

"He just panicked," Breanna said, shrugging. "A few hours after fighting with John Henry, he ends up dead. Liam felt that if he didn't hide the body then his plan to figure out what was happening with his dad would get totally messed up. I told him he ended up making everything worse and he agrees with me—but it's too late to go back in time. He's just not thinking straight right now."

"I don't think someone broke into this house and just happened to know where John Henry was—I'm not even all that convinced he has the debts the inspector mentioned. I think the murderer is from Southgate—he has to be."

Sadie paused for a moment as she concluded one more thing— Liam was an idiot. "Look at this." She pulled the note she'd found in Grant's room from her pocket and handed it to Breanna who read it. "I know it's hard to consider, but what if Liam's lying to you? What if the real reason he moved the body was because he did in fact kill John Henry in a fit of angry rage and was trying to protect himself?"

Breanna looked up at her mother with wide eyes. "Liam never

received this, Mom. If he had, he'd have listened to what John Henry had to say. All he wanted was answers." She paused. Even though she was angry with Liam, she was still defensive of him. Sadie wasn't sure she liked it anymore. "Where did you get this?"

It was Sadie's turn to hedge, but she stopped herself. If she didn't want Breanna keeping secrets from her, then she needed to stop keeping her own. "Grant's room."

"Grant's room?" Breanna repeated, her eyebrows going up and her eyes going wide. "You went into Grant's room?"

Sadie nodded, and pointed toward the note. "It was on his dresser."

Breanna seemed to stand up straighter once she heard that. "Well, that proves Liam didn't get it. If Liam had received this note he'd have kept it or destroyed it—especially after all of this. And he would have *talked* to John Henry, not killed him. John Henry must have given it to Grant to give to Liam."

Sadie furrowed her eyebrows as she tried to puzzle it out. "I think he'd worry Grant would read it—especially since the note implies that John Henry doesn't want Grant to know he's talking to Liam—Grant's in charge of making the tea, remember?"

Breanna bit her lip as she thought about that for a moment. "Unless he didn't think Grant would open it."

"John Henry was going to spill the beans—why would he chance it?"

"Maybe he left it somewhere, or gave it to someone else to give to Liam and somehow Grant ended up with it."

"Charlotte's been taking care of the earl too," Sadie said, remembering what Austin had said in the kitchen that morning about Charlotte sitting in when John Henry took a break. "Maybe John

Henry gave it to her." They both paused before Sadie continued. "The earl's going to the hospital, right?"

Breanna nodded, glancing at the door to the earl's room. "Liam plans to call the inspector once he gets to the hospital—he doesn't want anything getting in the way of his dad's care."

"Because he moved the body," Sadie added, making sure Breanna was looking at all the facts. "He committed a crime and he knows it. Are you sure he plans to tell the truth once his dad is safe?" She hadn't completely given up the possibility that Liam could have committed the murder too—even with Breanna's assurances, it made the most sense that Liam would move the body because he was guilty of murder.

"He'll tell them," Breanna said, as confidently as she could. "All these . . . things Liam's done aren't Liam and he feels horrible about all of it. He's trying to do the right thing by making sure his dad is okay—then he can deal with the rest of it. I know he'll tell the police everything once his dad is okay—I know he will."

Sadie wasn't nearly as convinced in regard to Liam's good character but decided not to argue. "So, now what?" she asked.

"We're just waiting for the last of the staff to clear out. Once everyone's gone, we'll call an ambulance."

"And are we still going to London?" Sadie asked.

Breanna shrugged. "I don't know what the plan is for getting us to London—we haven't gotten that far yet."

"Well, what can I do to help?"

"Uh, I have no idea," Breanna said.

Sadie scowled and Breanna continued. "I know you hate hearing that," she said. "But I really don't know."

Sadie considered her options. "Well, if Austin isn't around, maybe I'll go see if I can help Mrs. Kinsley in the kitchen."

"Okay," Breanna said, looking toward the door. "I really need to get in there and talk to Liam."

Sadie nearly rolled her eyes. Two days ago she'd thought Liam was the perfect fit for her daughter, now he'd become an annoying part of this whole situation. If he'd just told the truth from the beginning and not acted so rashly, Sadie had little doubt that things would not be as complicated as they were. But that was neither here nor there. "I'll be in the kitchen, then," she said when Breanna turned toward the earl's bedroom.

"Okay," Breanna said again, already distracted from their conversation. "Keep your phone on."

CHAPTER 36

Sadie turned to leave the earl's sitting room once Breanna was gone, but caught sight of the door on the other side of the room. Remembering that she hadn't asked about the earl's lady friend, Sadie decided to take the time to look around that room. Mrs. Kinsley wasn't waiting for her or anything, and who knew when she'd have another chance?

Using her handy-dandy set of keys, she unlocked yet another bedroom door and then quietly entered the mysterious room. Heavy drapes covered the windows. Sadie flipped on the light switch and startled as every shade of purple she could imagine assaulted her eyes. At first glance it was overwhelming and almost cluttered it was so intense. But once she got past the overpowering nature of it, she realized it was actually very well coordinated—just extremely vivid. She moved further into the room, drawn to the large four-poster bed set against the wall opposite the windows. It was covered with a silk bedspread patterned with alternating shades of lavender stripes. At the head of the bed were literally dozens of pillows all different shapes and sizes, covered in various shades of purple and yet all perfectly matched to one another.

The drapes on the window were a pale purple with a floral print valance that swirled and draped across the top, matching some of the pillows on the bed. At the front of the layered pile of pillows was one stitched with the word "Violet." It pretty much summed up the entire room—everything was shades of purple and violet. The furniture looked new—in fact the entire room looked like something Sadie would expect to see in a high-end furniture store. Not that the rest of the house wasn't just as beautiful, but this room was different—modern; specific.

She walked around the room, taking in all the details, imagining the earl picking it out for his sweetheart. What did it mean? Where was this lady friend now? Did Liam know about her? Sadie felt sure he'd have mentioned her if he did, but he was rather good at keeping things to himself, so perhaps not.

She wished she dared talk to him about it—she was very suspicious of the choices Liam had been making—but she didn't think now was the right time. It was definitely something she wanted to know more about, however. And yet there were so many other things she wanted to know more about, this one didn't seem to be much of a priority. She pulled the draperies to the side of the window, filling the room with light. A golden cord attached to the wall held the curtains back. Sadie imagined the kind of life the earl was expecting when he put the room together. He must have been planning to marry the woman, right? It made everything that much more sad. He'd been close to a new life, and had it ripped out from under him.

"Mrs. Hoffmiller?"

Sadie spun around in surprise; she'd thought she was alone. Grant stood in the doorway, arms at his side, regarding her with another of his non-expressive expressions.

"What are you doing in here?" he asked, looking a tiny bit alarmed as he closed the door behind him.

"Um, hi," Sadie said, forcing a smile and ignoring his question. "I, uh, was, uh—" She took a breath and squared her shoulders. There was no reason for her to explain herself to these people any longer. She was certain Grant had played a part in all that had happened with the earl and would not let herself be intimidated by him, or anyone else. "Can I help you?"

"I noticed the door open when I came to take my leave of Master Liam," Grant explained—back straight, chin lifted. "No one is supposed to have access to this room."

"Why?" Sadie asked. "I already know the earl had a lady friend and was planning for her to come live here at Southgate—why not allow access to the room?"

Grant paused, but Sadie had the impression that he was thinking fast. "We were concerned it would be upsetting to Master Liam," Grant finally said. "He hasn't been informed of the earl's lady friend has he?"

"Not by me," Sadie assured him. "The timing doesn't seem right."

Grant looked relieved at that. "Precisely."

"Who is she?" Sadie asked, hungry for more answers.

"I'm sure I don't know," Grant said rigidly. "The earl took great pains to keep her identity a secret."

Sadie wasn't sure she believed him. She already knew he was involved with a conspiracy against the earl, why would he also try to protect the earl's privacy? And yet there was also something in his demeanor that seemed different. Was he more open? Was it simply because he was about to leave on a two-day paid holiday?

"I came to inform Master Liam that the rest of the staff has left, and I'm prepared to depart as well unless he needs anything else."

"I can inform him of that," Sadie said. "If that would help. I know he's quite busy with his father."

"Has the earl taken a bad turn?" Grant asked.

Sadie was trying to feel him out, glean information, determine how much she was willing to tell him in hopes of getting his cooperation. Apparently working for nobility for so long had made him a difficult person to read.

One thing was certain, however, by the time the staff returned, she and Breanna would be back in Colorado. It only took an instant for Sadie to decide to take yet one more risk.

She reached in her pocket. "I found this in your room," she said, holding out the note John Henry had intended for Liam.

CHAPTER 37

Grant's eyes went wide and his mouth opened slightly as he stared at the note in her hand. He made to take it from her, but she pulled it back. "Liam never saw this," Sadie said. "But you did."

Grant stared at the note for several seconds, his eyes looking frantic before he took a deep breath that seemed to calm him, though his expression remained troubled. Sadie questioned her wisdom in confronting him like this, but despite the fact that no one knew where she was, Breanna and Liam were only a room away. Her jogging whistle was still in her pocket and she did a quick review of her Tae Kwon Do. She'd be fine if he tried anything, but she didn't think he would. Austin and Dr. Melcalfe were involved, and certainly Grant had played a part, but he didn't seem to be the person with the most to gain by the earl's failing health, and the conspiracy couldn't have been his idea. He was only the butler.

"Mrs. Hoffmiller," he said, looking at her with fearful eyes. "You have to believe I came about that note only by chance."

"Then you had better explain what chance that was," Sadie said. "Liam is getting his father out of here and then he's coming back for everyone who's been involved in this. You have one chance, right now, to set yourself apart from everyone else. The question is whether or not you'll take it, or if you really think the Melcalfes won't throw you under the bus the first chance they get."

Grant looked away and was silent for several seconds before raising his eyes to meet hers. "Mrs. Hoffmilller," he said, a slight pleading in his voice. "You don't understand what it is you are asking me to do."

Sadie didn't answer immediately. He was probably right, she didn't understand how hard this was for him. But that was because Sadie knew the difference between right and wrong, while this household seemed to operate within a skewed version of ethics. "I am asking you to do the right thing," she responded, "finally."

Grant looked at the note for several seconds and when he looked up at her once more she had the impression that he'd made some kind of decision. "But what is the right thing?" he asked. "I have been asking myself that question for a very long time and have been unable to find the answer."

"It's simple, Grant. The right thing to do is tell the truth."

"And turn my back on my wife?" he asked.

Sadie hedged for a moment on whether or not she should tell him that she knew about Essie. In the end, she chose to let him tell her. "Your wife?" she repeated, technically not lying, like she would have been if she'd said something like "I didn't know you were married" or "What are you talking about?"

Grant regarded her speculatively for a moment. "You have not heard about my wife?" he asked, sounding surprised. Sadie shook her head and noticed that Grant visibly relaxed. So much so that he no longer looked like a butler. The stiffness was gone. Instead he just looked like a careworn old man—though he wasn't much older than Sadie was.

"My Essie has not been well, Mrs. Hoffmiller," Grant said, a softness to his voice. "I was promised that so long as I played my role, she would be cared for."

"So they bought your assistance," Sadie summed up. "But Liam knows what Austin and Dr. Melcalfe have been doing to the earl. He knows that you and Austin, and likely the rest of the staff, were in on it." She held up the note. "And this was in your room. You said you came upon it by chance—what chance was that?"

Grant shook his head. "I can't say."

"Why?" Sadie asked in sharp annoyance. "Because you work for them? Because they blackmailed you into helping with this scheme? Because you have some misguided belief that because they have money and prestige that they truly are better than you? It's not true, Grant, none of it. Liam can help you any way they've been helping you, but you can accept his help with a clear conscience. You can help the man who gave you this job in the first place by coming clean."

Grant shook his head again, making Sadie want to scream, and yet his expression looked truly apologetic. "I'm sorry, Mrs. Hoffmiller, I understand what you want, but I can't give it to you. Essie is expecting me, and I haven't seen her for such a long time."

The holiday. Sadie hadn't thought of that. "You won't tell me because you might not see your wife if you do?"

"I *certainly* won't see my wife if I talk to you now. Everything I've done is for Essie, don't you see? There is so much I can't do for her, but I can do this. She'd have never gotten into Bethelridge without the . . . their assistance."

Though Sadie was anxious to hear more, she had already played dumb in regard to Essie's existence. It would seem suspect if she suddenly knew everything about her now. "Bethelridge?" she repeated. She justified the fact that pretending she didn't know wasn't technically lying. Her pastor might not understand, but she felt sure God would.

"A treatment facility," Grant said. He moved toward the window, looking out at the overcast sky. "Essie is an alcoholic. Bethelridge is the best treatment facility in the UK. I could never have afforded it alone. But they could."

"Austin?"

"Lord Melcalfe and his father," Grant clarified. He stepped back from the curtains and looked across the acres and acres of woods that stretched out behind the estate.

"And they also arranged for legal help for Mrs. Land's son?" Sadie asked, wanting to fill in as many blanks as possible.

"Rupert would have gone to prison without their help—theft," Grant said, still looking out the window. "They knew we would do anything for the people we love."

Sadie held up the note again. "Even kill John Henry?" she asked.

The color drained from Grant's face, which shocked Sadie a little bit because she expected him to defend himself, not look horrified. What if he *had* killed John Henry? He should have been making tea when it happened, but if anyone knew how to sneak through this house it would be him. And yet it still didn't gel in her mind. If he were willing to do all this to protect Essie and keep her in treatment, why would he risk everything by killing John Henry? But maybe he would truly do *anything* for Essie—even murder. Her brilliant idea of getting answers from Grant when no one knew where she was didn't seem so brilliant all of a sudden. But it was too late to turn back now so she pushed forward.

"He was going to tell Liam what was really happening and that would ruin everything, right?" she said. But why would John Henry give the note to Grant to give to Liam? That didn't make sense and Sadie couldn't bring herself to confront Grant directly with the possibility that he'd murdered the other man.

Grant had been staring at the floor, but then he looked up at Sadie. "If I tell you what I know, I won't be able to see Essie. Bethelridge is in Blackpool, several hours from here. I don't know when I'll have another chance to see her if I don't take advantage of it now."

It was ridiculous that the man would put all his morality on one side of the scales, and a visit on the other. And yet she remembered Essie's letter, and she could only imagine how much he missed her. "So, the sticking pin is visiting Essie, not divulging what you know?"

"Essie needs me," Grant said strongly. "I have already determined to go to the police upon my return, after I've made arrangements for Essie in case she has to leave Bethelridge once I confess what I know. I've been feeling for days that things are about to change, that secrets won't be secrets for much longer, but I can't abandon my Essie. She needs me."

She could hear the question he hadn't asked—would Sadie let him leave for his visit with his wife if he told her what he planned to tell the police anyway? It was more temptation than Sadie could turn away from and although it nagged at her to be giving in, to be sidestepping the police, she believed that without Grant's information, Liam would never find the answers he was looking for.

"I won't stop you from your trip," Sadie said. "And I'll talk to

Liam about continuing Essie's care if you will tell me what you know. Where did you find this note?"

Grant visibly relaxed again, and his eyes no longer looked frantic and scared, but rather resigned to whatever might lay ahead. "I came upon that note in the bin in Lord Melcalfe's room last night when I turned down the bed."

Sadie weighed out each word carefully in hopes of discerning whether or not he was telling the truth. "I thought the maids were the ones who turned down the beds," she questioned, still watching him.

"Usually," Grant said, letting out a breath and looking at his shoes. "But I had reason to take care of it myself last night."

"What reason?"

He paused again, then shook his head slightly and turned toward the window. "Lord Melcalfe was at Southgate before he claims to have arrived."

"What do you mean?" Sadie asked, remembering Austin's entrance to the library. "When?"

"After Kevin arrived to take you and Miss Hoffmiller to Heathrow, I had him go up to your room to retrieve your bags," Grant explained. "While Kevin was gone, I saw Lord Melcalfe."

"Where?" Sadie said.

"I don't know where he parked his car, but he came around from the back and was walking down the drive—staying close to the trees on the east side."

"Does he know you saw him?" Sadie asked.

Grant shook his head.

"Did you tell the police?"

Grant shook his head again.

"For heaven's sake, why not?" she exclaimed. Everyone was so busy hiding things that it was a wonder the police had figured out anything at all. Of course she didn't count herself in with the group she was silently berating—she'd only kept back small things.

Grant's face took on some color. "You have to understand, Mrs. Hoffmiller, that in my line of work, keeping secrets is a must. It is an unwritten rule that staff does not report on the comings and goings of the family they serve. It is our job to serve and protect those we work for and we strive to fulfill that expectation."

It was all Sadie could do to keep from berating this man about the *protection* he'd afforded the *earl*—the man who had hired him in the first place. However, she knew his divulging of this information was tenuous at best and she didn't dare put him on the defensive. "So, Austin could have killed John Henry?" Sadie summed up, ignoring his talk about the unwritten rules. She could tell that he knew those rules didn't matter anymore, even if he felt the need to explain them to her. "What time did you see Austin?"

"Lord Melcalfe," Grant corrected automatically. "Just before I began preparing the afternoon tea—I'm afraid we were all running behind. Tea was supposed to be served at 4:00, but it was almost 4:15 before I served you and Miss Hoffmiller in the sitting room. Then I went outside, sent Kevin to your rooms for your bags, and saw Lord Melcalfe. Kevin returned and made a phone call while I watched to see if Lord Melcalfe returned."

"You told us you were smoking," Sadie remembered.

"I would never smoke out front," Grant said, almost as if he was disappointed anyone would believe him capable of such a thing. "But I walked the front grounds for several minutes looking for a sign of Lord Melcalfe—the same time you were calling for help."

"And Austin doesn't—"

"Lord Mel—"

"Oh, stop it!" Sadie said, loosing her cool that these silly titles were getting in the way of this powerful information. "He is not my lord and I will call him Austin if I want to!"

Grant considered this and then nodded his acceptance.

Sadie cleared her throat, in part to cover her embarrassment at completely flying off the handle. In her defense she was rather tense. "And Austin doesn't know you saw him?" she asked again.

Grant shook his head. "When I called him from the kitchen, I asked how far away he was. He claimed to be in Exeter, but he arrived at the estate within only a few minutes and then insisted he hadn't been at the estate earlier. I turned down his bed and looked through his room, wondering if I could find anything else to support his earlier presence at the estate. That's when I found the note in the bin."

Austin had some kind of arrogance to simply throw the note away. Grant continued. "I couldn't tell the police because it would tip off everything else and I'd likely be detained from my visit to Essie."

Sadie had to hand it to the man, he was devoted to his wife. It was sweet, in a twisted and completely unethical sort of way.

"Grant," Sadie asked, turning the conversation slightly. "Why was Austin doing this? The earl had paid for his schooling, hired him on as a manager. Why would he turn on him like this? What was his motive? Was he stealing from him?"

"Not yet," Grant said.

Sadie couldn't have looked more confused if she'd tried.

"The earl was dying, and Lord Melcalfe needed to change certain documents that would ensure his grandmother was cared for and that his position was secure once Master Liam took over the earldom. None of us knew what would happen when Master Liam took the title."

So Grant thought they were keeping the earl alive, not killing him? It was on the tip of Sadie's tongue to tell him the truth—but she wasn't convinced he was worthy of that trust just yet. "Forgery," she summed up. "Forgery that would make sure Liam didn't leave Lady Hane or Austin out in the cold?"

Grant nodded. "Inheritance tax for nobility has gone up a great deal in the last several years, often necessitating that the heir sell off holdings in order to pay the taxes after the title holder dies. The earldom is profitable, but not so much that Lady Hane and Lord Melcalfe didn't have reason to question their own future once Master Liam was in title. They were also working on having Lord Melcalfe become executor of the estate."

"And the earl hadn't already addressed that in his estate planning?"

"The earl didn't expect to die so soon. As I understand it, his will was quite simple and left everything to Liam—with no contingencies."

"Before the earl became ill," Sadie said, "did he seem distrustful of Austin in any way?" In the library last night Liam had said his father wanted him to come back to England—was that because he suspected something might happen? Was keeping his girlfriend a secret the earl's way of protecting her somehow?

Grant paused, and then nodded. "A few weeks before his health turned, I came upon the earl in the library." Grant looked at the floor before continuing and Sadie imagined it was hard for him to part with secrets he felt responsible for keeping. However, she was grateful that he was doing so. "He had moved a section of shelf—something

I'd have thought far too heavy for him to move alone—and beneath it was an open hole."

"A hole? In the floor?" Sadie asked.

"I believe it was a floor safe," Grant added. "A floor safe I knew nothing about. He was putting a book inside of it." He moved his hands to show the dimensions that seemed about six by ten inches or so.

The Martin family Bible?

"Do you know what the book was?" Sadie asked.

Grant shook his head. "No, and because it was obvious that the earl was acting in secret—it was the middle of the night after all—I chose not to disturb him."

"So he doesn't know you know about the safe?"

"I informed the earl the next day that I had seen him. It didn't seem right to keep it from him. I promised him that I would keep his confidence and he said that the items in that safe were no concern of mine, but priceless to him—that he'd had the safe put in at the New Year when the staff took their annual holiday. I guess almost exactly a year ago, wasn't it?" He paused for a moment and then continued. "He asked me not to tell anyone about it, specifically Lord Melcalfe. I agreed and that was the end of it, we never discussed it again."

"And you didn't tell Lord Melcalfe?" Sadie questioned. "Even after the earl was incapacitated and Lord Melcalfe was running things?"

Grant cleared his throat. "I chose to hold onto that information in case it became important—as I said, I had a lot I was protecting." There was a look on his face that seemed to hope this was the right moment to tell this particular secret.

Rather than respond right away, Sadie contemplated the situation. Liam knew his father had the family Bible four months ago.

Grant had seen him putting something "priceless" into the safe a few weeks after that. Both Grant and Liam seemed to suspect that the earl was growing distrustful of Austin. And now, the earl was in an unnatural coma. Was it too far-fetched that perhaps the Bible could have essential information that would cause all of Austin's plans to crumble around his high-polished riding boots? Sadie met Grant's eye again. "Thank you, Grant," she said, smiling, anxious to share this information with Breanna and Liam. "I know it's not easy for you to talk about these things, especially to me. I promise you that I will do everything in my power to see that Essie remains in treatment. Liam will be very grateful for your help."

Grant nodded slightly, and then let out a breath before straightening back to his butler stance. "Thank you, madam, will that be all?" he asked.

"Yes, I think so," Sadie said, even while scanning the corners of her brain to make sure she hadn't missed anything. Oops, she had. "One more thing," she said as Grant's face had begun to relax. It was instantly on guard again. "Tell me about Lacy."

"Lacy," Grant repeated. "What do you want to know?"

"Anything you can tell me."

"Well, I can't say I knew her well," Grant said. "She came to Southgate nearly a year ago. We knew from the start that she was involved with Lord Melcalfe but that we were to pretend we didn't know. She was far below his station, and everyone knew it, but we liked her well enough. Honestly, I believed their relationship would play itself out as most of that type do and one day she would be gone just as easily as she'd arrived."

"Did she know about what was happening here at the estate?"

Grant shook his head. "No, Lord Melcalfe had made it very clear to all of us that Lacy was not to be party to any of this. We understood that he was protecting her from a side of himself he was not proud of, but when you work for nobility you come to expect such duplicity of character."

Well, obviously Sadie had never come to expect such things. She called such *duplicity* hypocrisy. "Do you know why she left yesterday?" Sadie asked. "She said that someone told her to leave if something happened to John Henry." At least, that's what Sadie thought Lacy had meant.

"I'm sure Lord Melcalfe would have left her with that kind of warning," Grant said easily. "As I said, he was protective of her. I'm sure he's seen to it that she's safely uninvolved in everything that's happened in the last twenty-four hours."

"I see," Sadie said. She'd run out of questions and so she changed the subject. "You'll come back, right? If I don't tell the police about this until you're gone, you will come back?"

Grant's face softened, in fact he almost smiled. "Without Essie, this is all I have," he said. "I'm prepared to see that justice is done, I assure you of that."

Sadie considered that and although she dreaded explaining this to the police, and she knew it was likely not the best thing she could do, she'd received valuable information in exchange for her assurances that he could visit his wife. She smiled. "Have a wonderful holiday, Grant," she said. "And give my best to Essie."

CHAPTER 38

Grant left the room first and Sadie followed him a few seconds later, looking around to see if anyone was watching. The earl's sitting room, however, was empty, and the door to his bedroom was closed. It wasn't until Sadie reached the top of the stairs that she learned what had happened while she and Grant had had their tête-à-tête in the countess's bedroom. The front door was open and two paramedics stood alongside a gurney talking to Liam. Grant hurried down the stairs, reminding Sadie of Austin's comment yesterday accusing Grant of being derelict in his duties. At the time she found it a rude thing to say in front of a crowd, now she wondered if he'd said it specifically to cover up his own secrets.

"My apologies, Master Liam," Grant said as he hurried to Liam's side. "What's happened?"

Liam looked at Grant with surprise. "Um, nothing's happened, Grant," he said quickly, nervously, reminding Sadie that he hadn't wanted to transport his father until all the staff had left. He must have assumed Grant had already gone. "I thought you'd left on holiday."

"I can stay, sir, if it would help."

"Thank you, Grant," Liam said with a quick nod. "But everything is fine. Please don't let me keep you." One of the paramedics handed Liam a clipboard with some papers attached to it.

Grant paused a moment, then inclined his head. "Very good, sir. Will I be seeing you when I return?"

"Yes," Liam said, signing the paper. He looked at the butler while handing the clipboard back to the paramedic. "I expect I'll be here for some time. Enjoy your trip."

Grant inclined his head one last time before turning toward the baize door and disappearing around the Christmas tree.

"Ready?" one of the paramedics asked.

Liam nodded and Sadie noted the look of relief on his face. "Yes," he said, heading toward the stairs. "My father's doctor is in his room with him, and we'll both be going with you to the hospital."

As Liam reached the landing, Sadie reached out a hand to stop him. He looked at her, perplexed. "I need to talk to you for a minute," she said. She and Liam were forced to step aside in order to let the gurney go past them. Liam looked after it longingly, but for once Sadie wasn't inclined to give in. "Just for a minute," she said when it looked like he might just cut and run after them.

The gurney disappeared into the east wing and Liam grudgingly turned to her.

"I talked to Grant," she said. "And he says there's a safe in the floor of the library and that he saw your father put a large book into it a few weeks before he got sick."

Liam took several seconds to make sense of that. "A safe?" he said. "My father has two safes and I've looked through both of them."

"This is a new one," Sadie explained. "Your father had it put in during the New Year holiday last year—when no one was around."

It was on the tip of her tongue to also tell him about the countess's bedroom and the lady friend, but it didn't seem directly pertinent to the here and now so she left it out.

"A secret safe," he said under his breath. "Are you sure Grant can be trusted?"

"Not entirely," Sadie said, though she trusted him more than most people right now. "But it's easy enough to disprove."

Liam nodded and scratched his hair. The boy really needed a haircut if he was going to keep messing with his hair all the time. "Okay," he said. "I'll have Dr. Sawyer go with Dad and we can look for the safe before I call the inspector. Breanna and I will meet you in the library."

Sadie agreed and Liam headed up the stairs. But Sadie had another errand to do before meeting up with Breanna and Liam in the library. She headed through the baize door and down the staff hallway.

"Grant?" she called when she reached the door to Grant's room. There was no answer, so she looked both ways and then knocked. "Grant?" she asked again. When he didn't answer again, she took the keys from her pocket and let herself into his room. The poetry book was still on the nightstand—she was glad he hadn't taken it with him—and she slipped the envelope back into place and then locked the door behind her. She was glad that was done and headed to the kitchen to see if there were any sausage rolls left—she might need her strength for the search ahead of them. Mrs. Kinsley was gone when Sadie arrived in the kitchen, but a note on the counter explained what she had left for the next couple of days—including sausage rolls that just needed to be reheated. Sadie's mouth started to water.

At the bottom of the note Sadie was surprised to find her name written next to an arrow that seemed to indicate that she should turn the paper over. She did so, and couldn't help but smile. Mrs. Kinsley had written out, in rather extensive detail, how to make crumpets. The words "A little bit of England to take home with you" were written at the bottom along with a P.S.: "This is the best—and easiest—recipe for crumpets I've found." Things were definitely looking up. Now, if they could just find that safe, figure out what the earl was hiding, and get Austin to confess, they'd be good to go!

Crumpets

2 cups all-purpose flour
1 tablespoon baking powder
1 teaspoon yeast (instant or regular*)
1/2 teaspoon salt
1 teaspoon sugar
2 cups warm water

Sift flour at least twice (this is a very important step in order to get the right density). Add remaining dry ingredients and mix together. Add water and stir with a wooden spoon or a heavy-duty whisk until the batter reaches a consistency similar to pancake batter. Cover with a dishcloth and set aside for about ten minutes or until a few bubbles begin to form on the top of the batter. Heat fry pan or griddle to medium-low heat (not quite as hot as for cooking pancakes).

Grease griddle and crumpet rings very well with non-stick spray. Put rings on griddle and allow to heat along with the pan. When thoroughly heated, add between 1/3 and 1/2 cup batter to each ring (about 1/2- to 3/4-inch thick). Let cook 6 to 8 minutes or until the edges of the top are dry and the bubbles have popped, leaving the standard "holes" in the top of the crumpet. Remove hot rings with tongs and turn crumpets over, cooking 1 to 2 minutes until barely browned. The bottom of the crumpet should be golden-brown but not too crusty. Remove crumpets from griddle and allow to cool on a cooling rack. Grease rings between each use.

To eat, spread butter on the top of the crumpet so the butter is absorbed into the holes. You can also top with jam, honey, maple syrup, or fresh fruit. Once cooled, toast before serving. Warm crumpets are great company for soups, stews, or with melted cheese on top.

Makes 12 to 16 crumpets.

*If using regular yeast, combine $\frac{1}{2}$ cup of the warm water, sugar, and yeast. Let proof 10 minutes, add with the rest of the water when called for in the recipe.

- In lieu of official crumpet rings, flat-bottomed cans like tuna fish and water chestnuts with the tops and bottoms removed can be used. Egg rings and wide-mouth canning jar rings can also be used, but only fill them half-way with batter.

- It's always a good idea to make a test crumpet to ensure that the bubbles form and pop properly. If the bubbles don't pop, resulting in no holes or a "blind" crumpet, add a tablespoon of water to the remaining batter and mix well. If batter is so thin that it seeps out from under the crumpet ring, add a tablespoon of flour to the remaining batter and mix well.

- Try adding $\frac{1}{2}$ cup sugar and 1 teaspoon cinnamon to the batter for a sweeter, cinnamon-roll flavor.

CHAPTER 39

Sadie, Liam, and Breanna looked at the safe door set an inch or two beneath the floor, and then looked at one another.

"I guess Grant knew what he was talking about," Sadie said with satisfaction. When she'd first come into the library—her belly satiated with the yummy sausage roll, grapes, and an éclair Mrs. Kinsley had left—Breanna and Liam were discussing the possibility that the safe didn't exist at all. Apparently they hadn't yet learned that things like this were never easy.

It then took a few more minutes to find the bookshelf Grant had indicated. A small lever of sorts lay against the back of the shelf and triggered some kind of hydraulic system that lifted the entire shelf only a fraction of an inch, but it was high enough that the rollers made contact with the marble floor and allowed the shelf to be easily moved. Sadie found the whole thing ingenious. She hoped whoever came up with such an intricate design made a million dollars—and that they would find a way to implement it on regular furniture like the kind she could afford. It would be lovely to just flip a switch and push her piano wherever she wanted instead of huffing and puffing over the job until finally bribing someone into helping her.

Once they'd moved the bookshelf away from the hidden safe, Liam and Breanna acted as if they'd never doubted her. Aggravating, to be sure, but at least she had the self-satisfaction of knowing she was right. That counted for something.

"Grant didn't know the combination?" Liam asked, standing and running a hand through his hair. He pointed to where the floor had been cut away and cement poured around the safe to hold it in place. "What good does it do us to have a safe we can't open?"

The stress was beginning to show, but Sadie decided not to point it out. "Are you sure your father didn't tell it to you? Send it to you? Somehow give you that information?" Sadie asked. "He's mentioned the family Bible—could he have given you the combination too?"

Liam was shaking his head before she finished. "He's never given me a combination of any kind," he said darkly.

Sadie looked down on the hole with her arms crossed over her chest. "Could a locksmith break into it, do you think?"

"The estate belongs to the earl, and I'm not him; I can't imagine they would simply open it for me—even if they could." He knelt down and grabbed the dial, wiggling it back and forth as if testing how secure the safe was in the hole. It didn't budge. "Aren't there all kinds of safeguards on these things to keep people from breaking in at all?"

Sadly, Sadie's knowledge of safes was terribly limited so she had no answer. They continued to stare at it, but then Breanna, who'd been unusually silent so far, leaned in. "There are instructions," she said. Sadie leaned forward and squinted, but she couldn't see anything but the black surface of the safe.

"'To set a new combination,'" Breanna read out loud. "'One; open safe using current combination. Two; with safe open, program new four-digit combination, pressing the interior "set" button after each number. Three; press the internal "store new combination" button. Four; close safe.'" She looked up.

"It doesn't do us any good to know how to set a new combination if we can't get it open," Liam said.

"Right," Sadie said with a "Duh" in her tone of voice. "But this basically tells us that your father chose his own combination." She turned to Liam, "What's your birthday? I read somewhere that most people use dates for combinations because they're so easy to remember."

"July fourth, nineteen-eighty," Liam said, taking a step closer. Sadie crouched down while Breanna did the numbers exactly, but when she pulled on the handle, nothing happened.

"Try it with the year first," Sadie said.

Breanna nodded and entered the numbers again. Nothing. Then she tried it with the month first, then with an extra turn between each combination of the numbers making up the date. Nothing.

"I didn't think he'd use my birthday anyway," Liam said, unable to hide his disappointment. "He didn't tell me he had a secret safe hidden in the first place—why use numbers I'd figure out so easily?" Liam stood up and shoved his hands in his pockets. Sadie had thought that having his father and the staff gone would make him more comfortable, but he remained tense and on edge.

Sadie felt bad for having been wrong. "What's your father's birthday?"

"I don't know, June sometime," Liam said.

Men! Sadie thought. Shawn never remembered dates either. "Do you have his birth certificate?"

"It's in the desk," Liam said as he headed toward it. Sadie got to her feet and followed, while Breanna kept spinning the dial back and forth in different combinations of Liam's birthday. Liam pulled a key from his pocket and used it to unlock the file drawer before pulling out a file marked "Official Documents" and laying it on the desk.

He opened it and began looking for the birth certificate. An old paper stored in a page protector slid out of the discard pile. Sadie picked it up, noting that it was Liam's parents' marriage certificate. Never having been divorced, she didn't know how people regarded proof of a marriage they had dissolved, but obviously this had been important on some level or the earl wouldn't have taken such pains to keep it.

Sadie glanced at the safe. What would be the most important day in a man's life besides the birth of his child?

"I used my wedding day for years as codes for things," Sadie said absently.

Liam paused and looked at her, then shook his head. "I don't think my parents' wedding date meant much to him."

"Then why keep this?" Sadie said, holding up the page.

"Archiving," Liam said. "It's a legal document and it proves my legitimacy—he'd need it to prove I was heir."

Sadie hadn't thought about that. She was in the process of putting it back when something caught her eye and everything paused for a moment. Written on the line marked "Bride" was the name Violet Amelia Sorenson. The countess's bedroom Sadie had left just twenty minutes ago flashed through her mind—shades of purple, the floral print on the duvet and curtains, the word "Violet" stitched into the pillow. Her mouth went dry, necessitating that she wet her lips before she spoke. Liam beat her to it.

"Found it," he said, heading back to Breanna with the half-sheet of paper in his hand. "It's June 6, 1946."

Breanna nodded and began turning the dial.

"Your mother's name," Sadie said, still holding the marriage certificate. "Violet?"

"Yes," Liam said without looking up.

Sadie nodded thoughtfully. "I bet with a name like Violet, people make purple jokes a lot."

Liam looked at her. "Purple jokes?" he repeated, confused. "She does *like* purple, but I don't think I've ever heard purple jokes." He went back to working on combinations with Breanna.

Sadie looked back at the paper and considered telling him the direction of her thoughts, but then quickly talked herself out of it. Mrs. Kinsley had said the earl was fixing up the countess's bedroom for his lady friend; Austin had said that the earl had never lived at Southgate during the time he was married. "Liam," Sadie said, trying to sound casual. "I'm curious, what's your parents' relationship like these days?"

Liam looked up at her. "Relationship?" he repeated, then shrugged. He seemed a little annoyed that she kept interrupting him. "I don't think they have a relationship. They hadn't seen one another for years until I graduated a few years ago."

"Did they get along at your graduation?"

Liam nodded. "My mom had just separated from Frank—my stepfather; she married him a couple years after my parents divorced. I think it had been long enough that Mom and Dad were over their issues, why?"

It was Sadie's turn to shrug. "Just curious," she said, looking back at the marriage certificate. "Um, could I use your phone, Liam?" she asked after a few seconds. "I left mine up in the room."

"Who are you going to call?" Breanna asked, obviously surprised that after working so hard to get to this point, Sadie was suddenly stepping out of it for something as basic as a phone call.

"Detective Cunningham, I've got a question for him," Sadie lied. She put out her hand for the phone. Instead of Liam complying, Breanna dug her own phone out of her pocket, forcing Sadie to think quick.

"I hate your phone," she said bluntly. Breanna pulled back slightly, shocked by her mother's bold statement.

"You hate my phone?" she repeated while Sadie madly compared her memory of Liam's and Breanna's phones in her head, trying to come up with any feature about Breanna's that she could say was inferior to Liam's somehow.

"Small buttons," she said triumphantly. "I hate those tiny buttons." She looked at Liam. "So can I use your phone or not?" When all else fails, be a bully.

It worked. Liam handed over his phone. Sadie thanked him and headed for the door of the library. The hallway was clear but she started heading for the front door when she remembered that no one was there. Rather than making her feel relieved, it was kinda creepy to think she was alone in this great big house. Not wanting to have such an important conversation out in the open, Sadie moved down the hallway to where it ended with floor-to-ceiling windows where she could look out on the gardens and feel like she had a little more privacy. She then opened up Liam's phone and spent nearly two aggravating minutes trying to access his phone book. Finally she found it and scrolled down until she saw the name she was looking for.

Mom's cell

After taking a breath, Sadie hit the button that would dial the number, quickly trying to come up with the best way to ask what she had no doubt would be a very difficult question.

"Liam," a woman's voice said upon answering the phone, causing Sadie to pause until she realized that his phone number would come up on his mother's caller ID. "How is he?"

The automatic question only cemented Sadie's suspicions. "Mrs. Martin?" she asked, then remembered that Violet had married again and Martin would no longer be her last name.

"Who is this? What's wrong?" Liam's mother asked. "What's happened to Liam?"

Of course she would assume that's why someone was calling her on her son's cell phone. Sadie hurried to explain herself. "Nothing's happened to Liam," she said. "My name is Sadie Hoffmiller; Liam has been dating my daughter."

There was a pause on the other end of the line. "Yes," the woman responded carefully.

"I apologize for contacting you like this, and I'm sorry for the abruptness of what I'm about to ask you, but I beg of you to be honest with me and trust me when I tell you it's absolutely imperative that you tell me the truth."

Violet said nothing for a few seconds. "I'm afraid I don't understand," she finally said. "Is Liam with you?"

"He's here," Sadie said, not wanting to get off track with this conversation. "Well, not *right* here, but here in the house—he's in the library with Breanna." She paused for a breath before continuing. "Violet," she began, hoping she wouldn't offend the woman by using her first name, "were you seeing Liam's father again?"

The line was silent for several seconds, long enough that Sadie feared the other woman had hung up or was shocked by the very suggestion, but then she heard a sniffle which turned into a quiet sob. It was all the answer Sadie needed.

CHAPTER 40

"I'm so sorry," Sadie whispered as Liam's mother broke down three thousand miles away, her own heart breaking for the loss this woman had experienced. Sadie lowered herself into a leather arm-chair while she listened to Violet cry. The secret must have weighed a thousand pounds, getting heavier as the earl's illness progressed. It was almost a full minute before Violet started talking, but then she didn't stop, telling Sadie how she and William had begun talking every few weeks after Liam's graduation. Within six months, they were talking every few days. A year later, William came and spent two weeks with her in Virginia. Fourteen months ago, they met in Paris for ten days.

"He asked me to marry him again during that trip," Violet said. "He said that we were both grown-up now, that we could simply love one another the way we should have back then."

"Why didn't you tell Liam?" Sadie asked when Violet paused for a breath. "He has no idea. The staff knew the earl was seeing some-one, but Liam knows nothing about it, let alone that the *someone* is you."

"We were both just so scared to get his hopes up—anyone's

hopes up, even our own. We took it slowly, knowing that we needed to trust each other completely and have absolute confidence in a future together before we told anyone—especially Liam. We didn't want to break his heart again if we were wrong about us for a second time."

"What did you say?" Sadie asked, watching the first raindrop hit the window. She cast a glance up at the clouds. Once it decided to rain here, it rained buckets. "When William asked you to marry him, what did you say?"

"I said I wasn't ready yet," Violet responded sadly. "But then we talked about living at Southgate instead of London, where we could be away from his sister, away from the noise and intensity of the London life. He agreed; he even moved his office to Southgate. In June we met in New York and he asked me again. This time I said yes." She sniffled again.

"June," Sadie said, trying to calculate everything in her head—June had been more than six months ago. "Did you set a date for the wedding?"

"February first," Violet said in a soft voice. "It would have been our thirtieth wedding anniversary. William was going to invite Liam to come out for Christmas, and I would already be there when he arrived. We anticipated a beautiful moment where we would be a family again—it was our Christmas present to Liam and to each other. And then everything went horribly wrong," she continued. "I had my flights arranged so I'd arrive a few days before Liam would; William and I were talking every day, planning the wedding, anticipating the holiday. Then Liam called me and said William had had a stroke—that's how William's father died, you know. Liam had wanted to go right out, but couldn't arrange for the time off. I wondered if I should go, but with Austin there and Hattie hanging around, I just couldn't bring myself to do it. No one knew about William and me, and for Liam's sake I thought maybe that was best."

"I can understand that," Sadie said. She'd have likely done the same thing in Violet's position. Though a grown man, Liam was still Violet's son, and she would want to protect him from painful realizations. Sadie also noted that Violet still believed William had had a stroke—Liam hadn't shared either his suspicions or his conclusions concerning his father's health. Sadie didn't want to be the one to break the news. "I'm so sorry."

Violet sniffled again. "I also worried about Liam if Hattie knew."

"Hattie—Lady Hane?" Sadie repeated. "William's sister?"

"I can't stand the woman," Violet said without hesitation. "And she didn't care for me either. She saw me as an interloper, a stupid American who had muddied up their blue-blooded line."

Sadie's eyebrows lifted. "Really?" she said. Austin hadn't given that impression at all, either on his behalf or his grandmother's. Neither had Liam.

Violet continued. "It was something William and I fought about a great deal when I was still in England. I swore Hattie was working against me, gossiping about me to people in our social circle so that no one would let me in, throwing me into situations where I didn't know how to behave. Back then William defended his sister—insisting I was using her as an outlet for my own frustrations. I came across as spoiled and pouting, when I was really just overwhelmed and so horribly out of my element that I did nothing rather than risk doing something wrong. Lately, he's come around to see that it's entirely possible I was right. Hattie was definitely one of the reasons I left—only, I thought William would follow me." The sadness had returned to her. "I didn't understand how much England was a part of him. It took a long time before I realized that I had given him an impossible decision—me or the earldom. I would not let him have both, and he could not respect a woman who didn't honor what he felt duty bound to fulfill."

"But he was duty bound to you as well," Sadie added. "He was a husband and father."

"I'm not saying he was right," Violet clarified. "But neither was I, and once our differences began to burn we both threw so many logs on the fire that it was our own Guy Fawkes Day—with a blaze we simply couldn't put out until all the fuel was burned away. When we met up again at Liam's graduation, we understood ourselves and each other better than we had before. We were able to build on that this time, rather than tear one another down because of it. I felt strong enough to come back to England—Hattie and all—and William was prepared to stand up for me this time rather than tell me to stop taking things so personally."

"But you were worried about Liam if Lady Hane found out about the two of you," Sadie said. "Why?"

"William and I could have cushioned him from anything Hattie might have said or done in response to the fact that we were getting back together. But William's stroke left both of us powerless. Liam's the heir and Hattie can't do anything about that, but he didn't need her anger directed toward him. There is no doubt in my mind that Hattie was enraged by the fact that her husband's title went to a distant cousin, while her father's title would land squarely on Liam's shoulders—she treated him well enough, but I believe that she never considered Liam worthy of the title. He wasn't a real Englishman in her eyes and he never would be."

Sadie absorbed all of the information. "Violet," she said, choosing her words carefully, "did you ever think Lady Hane would hurt him?" She implied that she was talking about Liam, but she meant William as well. Someone had orchestrated this conspiracy, but finding a motive had been tricky. Yes, Austin had a management position and a relationship with a kitchen maid to protect, but was that enough to warrant all of this? Grant had said they were forging documents—could that have been Lady Hane's idea instead of Austin's?

Violet was quiet for a few seconds. "I don't know," she said. "When her husband died, Hattie was left with less financial support than she'd have liked. William generously supplements her income so that she's been able to retain her lifestyle. He's also allowed her to live in his London house. I don't think she'd do anything to jeopardize that. However, there *is* something sinister about that woman— and I don't say that only because she didn't like me. There's simply a conniving way about her, a quiet watchfulness that is usually interpreted as simple aristocratic arrogance. William was beginning to see it for what it was, though—anger and resentment."

"Really?" Sadie asked. "What exactly did he see?"

"I don't know exactly," Violet said. "He was very protective of me that way, but there was something he was looking into, something important that he said would bring big changes to the earldom."

"Did he ever mention the Martin family Bible?" Sadie asked, wondering if perhaps that was part of what he was figuring out.

"Well," Violet said thoughtfully, "not recently, no."

"But he'd mentioned it before?"

"Oh, years ago," Violet said in a tone that implied she couldn't imagine how it would be important now. "After we returned to England, when his father was dying, he wanted to put Liam and me in the Bible but couldn't find it."

"Seems like an important item to just come up missing."

"I guess so," Violet said. "But then Hattie had had that big Book of Heraldry put together, so the information was still on record even without the Bible. I don't think anything was lost with the Bible—other than the sentimental value."

Sadie paused and moved the phone to her other ear. "I wonder if Lady Hane would have used the family Bible to get the information for the genealogist who put the compiled book together."

"Maybe," Violet said. "She had the book done before William and I were married—she said that was why I wasn't in it. I know William had talked to her about the Bible and she didn't have any idea where it was—said she hadn't seen it for ages, or something like that."

And yet Hattie's daughters were listed in the book of remembrance with their husbands and children—even Austin had been there. Austin was younger than Liam, which meant that additions had been made to the book after Violet married William. Sadie wondered if Lady Hane oversaw that as well and had left Violet and Liam out of the book on purpose.

"I don't think what William had discovered before he had his stroke had anything to do with finding the family Bible again—I think he'd have told me that," Violet said, taking the subject back to the present. "But whatever it was 'explained a lot'—that's how he said it."

"A lot about what?" Sadie asked, wishing she had her notebook so she could be writing all this down.

"It had something to do with Hattie insisting William apprentice Austin in the managing of his properties, and why she seemed to be questioning William's decisions more and more. I told him it was her way of saying that William wasn't doing a good enough job, that ever since her husband died she had less people to put down."

"Was he planning to confront her with whatever it was he'd discovered?" Sadie asked, wanting to be sure she got ample clarification. "Would he have told her about you and whatever it was he had found out?"

"I don't know," Violet said and Sadie could hear her frustration. "She was coming down for Guy Fawkes Day—I know that much— and he wasn't looking forward to the visit. Whether that was because he just wasn't in the mood for company or because he planned to talk to her about something important, I really don't know. His title and family were a sore spot for both of us, and something we avoided discussing if we could."

"But you and Liam were coming out for Christmas. Would William have told Lady Hane about that early on, so she could get used to the idea?" She paused before continuing, aware that she was treading on fragile emotions and yet recognizing that if she wanted to uncover the truth, she had no choice but to continue. "And what if he had? What if he'd told her about the two of you? How would Lady Hane have reacted?" To herself she asked another question: How far would *Lady* Hane go to prevent it?

"How would Hattie react?" Violet repeated, seeming to pick up on the thoughts going through Sadie's mind. "You're American, so perhaps it's hard for you to understand how seriously some of the British view the Peerage. But for Hattie, I have no doubt that there are few things that would be more devastating than the fact that me—Violet Sorenson—was going to become the Countess of Garnett once again."

Sadie let that roll over her and mingle with the other things she was putting together—Lady Hane overseeing the Book of Heraldry that, without the family Bible, stood as the official documentation of the family line; Austin being in the book, but not Liam; and the fact that Violet was once again going to have an English title—something Lady Hane would be very much against.

"I have one more question," Sadie said. "Did William ever mention having a floor safe put into the library?" She held her breath, hoping and praying that unlike all the things William didn't tell Violet, that he'd have told her about this.

"Oh, yes," Violet said easily. "He said he wanted a place all his own that no one knew about but us. I think he stored our letters and things in there. I thought it was very sweet and romantic. Why, is it important?"

CHAPTER 41

"L iam," Sadie said when she entered the library a minute later. There were so many thoughts exploding in her brain that she worried she wouldn't be able to focus on a single one of them. Breanna and Liam were looking through papers spread out on the desk. Sadie held out the phone toward Liam, knowing that before she moved forward, Liam needed to hear what she had just learned about his parents and that he should hear it from Violet. "Your mother wants to talk to you." She forced herself to accept the time-out for just a few minutes—despite her fingers itching to get her hands on the safe.

"Mom?" he asked, looking at Breanna briefly as he came around the desk, his eyes on the phone in Sadie's outstretched hand. "She called?"

"Sort of," Sadie said, giving him a soft smile. He reached out and took the phone. She let her hand rest on his arm, and smiled at a confused Breanna as Liam lifted the phone to his ear. Sadie wished she could whip up a batch of her Butterfinger cookies—Breanna said Liam loved anything peanut butter and no matter what nutritionists might say, sometimes food was the perfect company for emotional overload, as Sadie knew from experience.

"Hey, Mom," he said into the phone as he walked toward the far end of the library. His words were soon too far away to be heard, but Sadie watched him sympathetically.

"What's going on?" Breanna asked, causing Sadie to look away from Liam and meet her daughter's eyes. For a moment she considered waiting and letting Liam tell her—but that moment passed. If she'd ever held more incredible information than this, she certainly couldn't remember it. By the time she finished telling her story—well, William and Violet's story—Breanna's expression was one of pure surprise.

"Do you think that's why this happened?" she asked. "Would Austin and Lady Hane have gone to these lengths to keep William and Violet apart?"

"It's hard to imagine, isn't it?" Sadie continued. "But after hearing Violet's side of things, it doesn't seem that far-fetched." She headed for the bookshelf where Liam had put the Book of Heraldry last night and pulled the long rectangular book off the shelf, opening it to the pedigree section and looking at the information with a bit more detail. Not sure what exactly she was looking for, she used her finger to trace the line of earls back from William to the very first one—Percible Edward Martin. There had to be a connection between this pedigree and the conspiracy against the earl.

She tapped her foot with anticipation and looked over to where Liam was sitting, taking his time while Sadie and Breanna waited for him.

"She didn't know the combination, did she?" Breanna said, sounding disappointed.

"Oh, she knew it," Sadie nodded. Saying it out loud made her even more eager.

"What?" Breanna replied, her eyebrows shooting up. "Then let's open it."

"Don't you think we should wait for Liam?" A final holdout for doing the right thing and making sure Liam was a part of it.

Breanna lifted one eyebrow. "Um, no," she said bluntly.

It was all Sadie needed to hear. "Oh, thank goodness!" she said with relief, then turned and fairly ran for the safe. "Violet thinks it's the date they were going to get remarried—February first of next year. It was their thirtieth wedding anniversary."

"Oh, that's so sweet," Breanna said as she caught up to Sadie and knelt next to the hole in the floor.

Sadie waved off the sentiment as she too lowered herself to the ground—it hurt. Between falling out of the vegetable cooler and all these blasted stairs, her joints were screaming at her every time she did much more than stand up straight. She grabbed the dial, spun it a few times to make sure it was cleared, and then carefully turned it to the number two.

By the time she got to the final number her heart was beating in her stomach and it seemed she couldn't move her hands fast enough. She paused, took a breath, and pulled on the handle. Having fully prepared herself for the safe to remain locked as it had in all their other attempts, Sadie forgot to breathe as the door swung open. Both of them were frozen for a moment as they realized it had worked. They were in!

They both leaned forward to get a better look into the twelve-inch by twelve-inch hole, banging their heads together in the process. Sadie grunted and raised a hand to her forehead, but Breanna continued as if nothing had happened. Sadie didn't call her daughter hardheaded for nothing.

Breanna reached into the safe and pulled out a book—a big, thick, old, leather-bound book. Beneath it was a bundle of envelopes in every shade of purple imaginable—Violet's correspondence?

"The family Bible?"

They both looked up to see Liam standing above them, putting his phone back in his pocket. He too came down to his knees, but he reached into the safe and removed the stack of envelopes, turning them in his hands. They were held together with a rubber band. Sadie imagined Violet had a similar stack, though hers was likely tied together with a ribbon. After looking at the letters that would likely verify Violet's story, Liam shifted his gaze to the book in Breanna's hands.

The family Bible was incredibly well-maintained for being almost two hundred years old but it would never be mistaken as new by any stretch of the imagination. Breanna carefully pulled back the front cover, revealing a single piece of paper placed between the cover and the first pages that were covered in flourished, albeit, faded, handwritten names. The paper set inside the cover was bright white— made even brighter by the contrasting pages of the rest of the book. Liam put the letters aside and picked up the paper. He unfolded it carefully, while Sadie and Breanna moved their heads in so they could read it with him.

Dear Lord Martin,

Per your request I had a thorough search done of the libraries at both the main house and the Dowager cottage. As you know, though the cottage remains for her use, your sister has not stayed here for some time as she prefers the life in London and the accommodations so graciously supplied by yourself. Though I expected no success in the search, as you can see I did in fact find the Martin family Bible in Dowager Lady Hane's personal library at the cottage. I'm horrified to think it has been here at all, and did not make mention to your sister about its discovery. I trust it is in the same condition you remember it to be. Please let me know if I can be of any other service.

Sincerely,

Anthony Lee Brinton, Sixth Baron Hane

"Your Aunt Hattie had it all this time," Sadie said when Liam finished reading the letter. "And William figured it out."

Liam refolded the paper, then turned it over. One word was handwritten on the paper: *Robert?*

"What does that mean?" Breanna asked, pointing at the name. "Who's Robert?"

Liam lifted his shoulders. "I don't know." He put the paper aside and took the book from Breanna. "Why would Aunt Hattie keep the Bible?" he asked, carefully turning the pages, looking for whatever it was that was so important to be worthy of the deceit. "And what does it have to do with sedating my father?"

Sadie didn't have an answer for those questions—at least not yet—but her eyes were drawn to the open pedigree book she'd left on the desk. "Your father thought it was important enough to hide it where no one could find it," she said. "There has to be something here worth all that effort."

She pulled herself to her feet and headed toward the desk, hoping she wouldn't ever have to sit on the floor again. "The family Bible is the traditional record of your family line," Sadie said, indicating for Breanna and Liam to follow her. "But sometime before your parents returned to England, Lady Hane had this Book of Heraldry put together, and around that same time the family Bible disappeared. Your father found it at the house Lady Hane was left when her husband died."

"Okay," Liam said with an accepting nod. "I get that my father thought it was important—but why?"

"Think about it," Sadie said. "The family Bible is an heirloom, it's an important asset of the earldom. Lady Hane hid it, but was fine having this other book available. Doesn't that tell us that there must be something in the family Bible that she didn't want anyone else to know? Your father was getting his affairs in order because he was about to become a married man again. He'd told your mother that he couldn't understand why Lady Hane was insisting Austin be so involved in his affairs. I think he started looking for answers to that question, knowing that bringing your mother back to England could open a potential hornet's nest of bad blood between his sister and himself. It looks like his concerns led him to make a full-out search for the family Bible."

"And he found it," Breanna added, looking from the book open on the desk to the Bible still in Liam's hands.

Liam didn't respond right away, but he put the family Bible on the desk above the Book of Heraldry. "Well, then, let's find out what he may very well have given his life for." He opened the front cover of the Bible again, then scowled, straightened and reached into his pocket, pulling out his phone which was vibrating in his hand. He looked at the screen, then at Breanna.

"It's Austin," he said. "He wants to talk to me." He quickly typed in a message and then turned toward the door, bending down to pick up the stack of envelopes he'd left on the floor.

"Wait a minute," Breanna said, taking a few steps toward him in order to grab his arm. "You're going?"

"Yes," Liam said with a determined nod as emphasis for his equally determined tone. "You guys finish with this, I'll go talk to Austin."

"Alone?" Breanna asked incredulously.

One side of Liam's mouth pulled into a smile, and he casually reached up and tucked Breanna's hair behind her ear. "He can't hurt me," Liam said with so much confidence that Sadie almost believed him.

"He killed John Henry," Sadie reminded him.

Liam considered that for a moment. "Call Kent and tell him that Austin's here and he's ready to talk—that might diffuse some of his anger that I didn't call him until now. I'll have about fifteen minutes to get what I can out of Austin before the police arrive."

"Um," Breanna said, looking to Sadie for help. "I can do that—but a lot can happen in fifteen minutes. I really don't think you should be alone with him."

Liam took a few steps toward her, until he and Breanna were almost touching. He was only a couple inches taller than Breanna so they were nearly at eye level. He reached out and ran his knuckles across her cheekbone. "I'll be alright," he said in such a sweet, almost sexy voice, that Sadie was inclined to look away. She heard, rather than saw, the sweet kiss he placed on Breanna's lips, and turned back in time to see him turn toward the door. The whole kiss might have been a ruse to get Breanna to stop arguing with him—if it was, it was incredibly clever and worked like a charm.

The door shut before Breanna shook herself back to reality and turned to face her mother, a blush showing through her brown-sugar skin. She cleared her throat. "Well," she said. She pulled out her phone and Inspector Kent's card from her pocket and dialed the number.

A minute later she hung up and put the phone back in her pocket. "Now, where were we?"

"Before the man you refuse to marry made your toes curl?"

Breanna scowled at her mother. "Where do we start?" she said, looking suddenly overwhelmed.

"Well, why don't I take the family Bible," Sadie said, moving around the desk so she could have it in front of her. "And you take the Book of Heraldry—we'll just trace the family line and make sure they match." It was the only thing Sadie could think of, the only reason Lady Hane would keep the family Bible. If the pedigrees matched, Sadie would be out of ideas. However, she had great faith in herself and didn't think she was wrong about this.

"Okay," Breanna said, flipping pages. "Just the earl line, right?"

"Right," Sadie said, squinting at the scrawled words that were hard to read without her glasses. Maybe she'd given Breanna the wrong book.

"Percible Edward Martin—first earl," Breanna said. "What a horrible name."

"I agree," Sadie said. "But he's here in the Bible."

"He had two sons who faired better in the name department," Breanna continued. "Thomas and Edmund." Sadie confirmed them in the Bible, and Breanna continued through another generation that matched the names listed in the Bible. "Abraham Mercer Martin—third earl."

"Yep," Sadie said, her stomach eager to make a discovery.

"Two sons," Breanna continued.

Sadie was already nodding when she stopped. "No, three sons."

Breanna shook her head. "No, two."

Sadie moved to look over her shoulder, where Breanna had her finger between the two sons of the third earl. "I read about these two last night," Sadie said. "The older brother—the fourth earl—died with only daughters. Isn't that sad? I mean, I think of his poor wife and wonder what happened to her. Did she lose her home? Did she ever remarry? Did her daughters—"

"Three sons," Breanna said, cutting Sadie off. "You're sure?"

Sadie looked up at her daughter and went back to the family Bible. "Yes, three sons. The third son is Edgar Horace Martin."

Breanna was scanning the page while shaking her head. "He's not here," she said. "Maybe he died when he was little or something."

"According to Edgar's dates in the Bible, he lived to be almost forty."

"Then he should be here," Breanna said with a nod, still flipping pages in case she missed something.

Sadie nodded her agreement, then focused on the row of books dedicated to the earls' histories. She went to the shelf and pulled out the volume dedicated to the third earl, then flipped immediately to the index in the back. Every reference book had one, and thank goodness they did. She looked up Edgar first and found nothing, so she looked up Martin and found a list of people with the last name Martin, along with the page numbers where they were mentioned. Three names down the list was the name Martin, Edgar Horace.

"He's in here," she said out loud, following the line to the page numbers that referenced information about him. Rather than start at the first page referenced, assuming it would be about birth information and schooling, she went to the last page that mentioned him and scanned the text, having to squint due to the tiny print used in the book.

She found his name and backed up to read the whole sentence. "'On April 22, 1874, Lord Martin was informed of his son Edgar's death on March 31, 1874, in Edinburgh. Following Edgar's marriage to Bethany Melcalfe, the daughter—'"

"Melcalfe," Breanna repeated out loud. It took Sadie a moment to realize why it had caught Breanna's attention.

"As in Austin Melcalfe?" Sadie asked no one in particular.

They were both silent, but Sadie knew Breanna was sharing her thought.

Sadie continued reading. "'Following Edgar's marriage to Bethany Melcalfe, the daughter of a hat maker, Edgar and his family had limited contact with the Martin family. However, Lord Martin was saddened to hear of his son's death, which was reported to have been a result of substantial gambling debts incurred during the last few years of his life. Because Edgar's burial took place in Scotland before the Martin family had received notification, he is not interred in the family plot. He left behind his wife, Bethany Marie Melcalfe Martin, and their three children, Marie, Victoria, and Horace."

And, Sadie added in her mind, *he was left out of the family pedigree.* However, according to both this book and the family Bible, Edgar *should* be there.

Sadie moved toward the desk and set the book down before turning pages in the Book of Heraldry, looking for the end of the Martin direct male line, which, according to this book was William Everet Martin Jr.—Liam's father. "Remember when we talked about the ways titles were transferred and Austin said that if there was no male heir, the title reverted a generation at a time."

"Yeah," Breanna said with a nod. "That's why his grandfather's cousin became the new Baron Hane after his grandfather died."

"Right. Austin's mother was one of three daughters and Baron Hane had no brothers to inherit, which meant the title had to go back another full generation to find a male line." With her finger on

William's name, Sadie traced back one generation to William Sr.—Liam's grandfather, the eighth earl—then traced it back a generation when she saw he had no brothers either. She went back another generation, and another, following any younger sons until they ran out of male heirs—always within a generation or two. The Martin family had far more daughters than sons, it seemed.

When a male line ran out of males, she moved to the previous earl, continuing until she reached the third earl. Because only two sons were listed in the "official" Book of Heraldry, it appeared that there was no other male line not already exhausted and that the title would need to revert yet *another* generation—but the family Bible showed a third son and the personal history of the third earl confirmed it.

"Outside of Liam, Edgar Horace Martin is the next direct male line for the earldom. And his wife was a Melcalfe." Sadie met Breanna's eyes. "We know Edgar had one son—Horace—but we don't know anything more than that."

Breanna looked intrigued. "What if, after Edgar died, his mother changed the family name to Melcalfe—her maiden name?"

"To protect them from his debts?" Sadie supposed.

"Or because the Martin family had disowned them anyway," Breanna offered.

"Or both," Sadie said. It was so far out there, and yet it was impossible not to ignore the possibilities. "And what if Lady Hane figured this out—perhaps when her daughter began dating a medical student with the last name Melcalfe. Didn't Austin say his grandfather was Scottish?"

"And," Sadie continued, flipping the pedigree book back to the front cover, where a handwritten date pulled it all together, "the relationship between Austin's parents would have started right around the time this book was put together—1978." She flipped more pages, until she found the name Harriet Elizabeth Martin—Aunt Hattie. The pedigree showed that Hattie married Andrew Leland Brinton, heir apparent Baron Hane. Three lines linked them to their daughters. Sadie scanned them until landing on the oldest daughter, Rachel Elizabeth Martin, who married Robert Horace Melcalfe in 1980.

"Robert!" Breanna exclaimed. She turned from the desk and hurried to the floor by the safe, where the paper from the Bible had been left behind. She picked it up and brought it back. They both looked at the word written there: *Robert?*

"Dr. *Robert* Melcalfe?" Sadie said out loud, trying to remember if she'd ever heard Austin's father's first name.

"Is there anything else in the Bible that might fill in the blanks?" Breanna asked, flipping pages.

"Careful," Sadie reminded her. "That book is two hundred years old."

Breanna nodded and flipped slower, but reached the end of the Bible without having found anything else to explain what the earl might have discovered. She let out a frustrated huff of air and shut the book.

"If Austin's father is Robert," Sadie said slowly, "and Robert is a direct heir of Edgar Martin Melcalfe . . ."

Breanna finished the sentence. "Austin could be a potential heir to the Earldom of Garnett."

A sudden flash of terror swept over Sadie as she realized the further implication presented by their hypothesis and started moving toward the door. "But only if William and Liam are *both* out of the picture."

CHAPTER 42

Breanna and Sadie raced into the hallway, down the hall, and then screeched to a halt when both Liam and Austin turned to look at them. Sadie wasn't sure what she'd expected, but it wasn't to come across Liam and Austin talking in the foyer. Liam was leaning against the railing of the stairs, with one foot on the bottom step and one foot on the marble floor—the bundle of letters in his right hand. Austin stood a few feet away from him, hands in his pockets and regret lining his face. Sadie had prepared herself for Liam holding Austin by the throat, or Austin having a sword drawn.

"What's wrong?" Liam asked, stepping away from the stairs and coming toward them. Sadie glanced at Austin, who lifted one hand to massage his forehead. He looked exhausted. Sadie didn't even feel bad about not feeling the least bit sympathetic about it.

"Um, nothing's wrong," Breanna said, though she was also looking past Liam to watch Austin. Sadie imagined that if he made a move to get away, she and Breanna would have him tackled to the ground in a matter of seconds. It had been several years, but there was a time when Sadie had a mean half-nelson—left over from when her brother Jack had been on the wrestling team in high school. She was sure it would all come back to her if she needed it.

"You're okay?" Liam asked, touching Breanna's arm and recapturing her attention.

"Yeah," Breanna said, meeting his eyes. Her smile was shaky.

The four of them paused for a moment, then Liam turned to Austin. "Maybe you should tell them your version of things," he said, an edge to his voice. "Get in some practice before the inspector arrives."

Austin looked at the two women. His expression, which had been hard and arrogant in every other encounter Sadie had had with him, was now tired and spent. He looked to have aged five years in the hours since Sadie had last seen him. He dropped his gaze to the floor as he cleared his throat and started talking.

"You have to believe that I didn't know what was happening when all this started—I had no idea."

Right, Sadie thought. She didn't believe that for a second and by the looks of Liam, neither did he.

"Why don't you start at the beginning," Liam suggested. "The way you did for me."

Austin took a deep breath and nodded. "I took a holiday to Dover for Guy Fawkes Day, and when I returned I was informed that William had had a stroke. My father was orchestrating his care, John Henry had been brought from London, and I was to act as trustee of the estate. I was overwhelmed by so many sudden changes but had no reason to believe it was anything other than what I'd been told. A week or so later, my grandmother sent her solicitor asking for access to the earl's private papers. I refused him and that afternoon grandmother showed up and said William had been planning to cut her off, that this woman he was with was giving him bad advice. She explained that her solicitor was only protecting her, assuring there were clauses built into documents pertaining to the earldom that demanded she be cared for once Liam took over. She was worried that Liam's mother held a grudge and that because of her influence, Liam wouldn't honor the existing financial support agreements once William passed away."

"So she knew that he and Violet were seeing each other?"

Austin was quiet for a moment, as if considering the possibility. "Perhaps," he finally conceded, glancing at the letters Liam still held in his hand. "But at the time I believed she was simply talking about her past history with Liam's mother—she said nothing about a current relationship between William and the former countess."

Liam interrupted, putting the discussion back on track. "What happened after she informed you of the intended forgery?"

Austin ran his hand through his hair and his shoulders slumped. Sadie glanced at Liam, who stood straight, his arms folded over his chest and his chin up—finally looking confident and in control. It was a stark contrast to the appearance of both men in the library yesterday. Now Liam looked like an earl, and Austin looked like the powerless cousin. Sadie wished she could tell Liam about what they'd discovered in the Bible before they continued, but she didn't want to interrupt Austin's account.

Austin took a breath. "I told her she needed to take the financial concerns up with Liam, not me, that as trustee I did not have the power to make those kinds of decisions and I would not be party to fraud."

What a hero, Sadie thought, but she kept it to herself so that Austin would keep digging his own grave.

"That's when Grandmother told me that William had not had a stroke. My father had created a scenario through which my grandmother could assure her future—a future that up until now hinged upon the men she was dependent on. She was an old woman, she said, and she deserved to have such assurances that had been denied her all her life because of her gender." Austin looked at the ground. "I'd never seen that side of my grandmother," he said slowly. "I had no idea she felt so beholden to her father and then to her husband; no idea that she was so bitter toward her station that, as she put it, relegated her to nothing more than a bartering chip within the shifting powers of the Crown. When I said I wouldn't be party to the forgery, she told me she knew about my relationship with Lacy." He closed his eyes briefly. "I couldn't believe it. I'd worked so hard to keep Lacy a secret. William had given Lacy a job at Southgate so that I could see her within the course of my working for him—he understood the position I found myself in and was trying to help me navigate what lay ahead of me. To find out my grandmother knew was shocking enough, but then she said that if I went along with this she wouldn't stand in my way of marrying Lacy when it was all over."

"You weren't planning to marry this girl before then?" Liam asked.

"I was," Austin said strongly. "I proposed to her last summer— but I needed to establish myself before I could break away from my family—who I knew would not consent to the match."

"And my father was helping you to do that," Liam added.

Austin let out a long breath, and nodded. "Yes," he said, and the single word seemed painful for him to say. "But he couldn't help me anymore. I was told that if I did not go along with the plan my grandmother and father had put together, I would lose everything. I would be cut out from my inheritance and unable to benefit from any of the advantages associated with my family name and station.

She would see to it that I was removed from my position within the earldom as well."

"That's ridiculous," Sadie said, unable to hold it in. "You have a degree from Oxford, you have two years' work experience with the earl, and you're a grown man." Which in Sadie's mind just made the heir angle that much stronger. He could say that he'd gone along with this because of Lacy and his family, but the truth was that by helping this come together he assured himself the earldom some day. *That* was motive worthy for this conspiracy.

Austin shook his head. "I don't expect you to understand," he said softly. "And saying it out loud makes it sound different than it felt—but I've never had to go at anything alone. I went to Harrow and Oxford because of my family connections. I gained employment because of William. I would need a way to support my own family in the future. Within the offer my grandmother made me was a straight shot to all those things, or a brutal destruction of those same assets. But Lacy was the linchpin. More than anything, I wanted her in my life, but I'd always known I would have to choose her over my family one day. My grandmother was giving me the chance to have both— Lacy *and* a secure future. It was an offer I couldn't resist."

"I don't believe for a second that your grandmother made any kind of deal like that," Sadie said, shaking her head. "She'd already gone to great pains to break up Liam's parents because of Violet's inferiority. There is no way she would accept Lacy as a countess."

"A countess?" Austin said, almost laughing.

"Yes," Sadie said with an arrogant nod. "But not until the three of you figured out how to get rid of Liam."

Sadie had never heard such silence; there was almost a vacuum effect to the air around them. Austin and Liam looked equally stunned.

"What?" Liam finally asked, turning toward her.

Sadie fairly tingled with excitement to relate the rest of what she suspected as if it were fact. "A hundred and fifty years ago there was another man who fell in love with a woman not worthy of his station. He renounced his heritage and married her anyway. After his death, his widow changed her children's names for reasons I can only guess at—imposing her last name instead of the family name of Martin. A boy by the name of Horace Martin became Horace Melcalfe and, aside from Liam, holds the next direct male line for the title. I believe that Dr. Robert Melcalfe is a direct descendant of that boy, which is why he was party to this conspiracy. He is not only a potential heir to the Earldom of Garnett, but so is his son." She turned to look at Liam. "Your Aunt Hattie was willing to kill her own brother, so it only makes sense that your death would be an even easier line for her to cross."

"The Book of Heraldry was altered," Breanna cut in, looking from Liam to Austin and back again. "Horace Martin does not exist within its pages, but the family Bible shows there were three sons born to the third earl and the personal history confirms it." She looked at Austin and her eyes narrowed. "Your grandmother likely learned it when she had the Book of Heraldry compiled and she's held onto this knowledge for thirty years, waiting for her chance to use it to her best advantage."

Sadie picked it up when Breanna stopped talking. "But she was running out of time. William was on to you and your grandmother, Austin. He had found the family Bible at the Dowager cottage, and he was beginning to understand why your grandmother was so determined that you work for him. When she came down with your family for Guy Fawkes Day, I believe he not only confronted her about his suspicions, but he also told her about Violet—that they were getting remarried. Your grandmother realized that this plan she'd put in action years earlier was about to come to nothing. Whether or not Dr. Melcalfe knew about this beforehand, he obviously went along with whatever it took to fake the earl's stroke and keep him in a coma." She shook her head.

Austin was absolutely speechless for several seconds. It was almost disappointing. Sadie expected him to argue, to fight it out, to try to save himself. But he didn't.

"Your motive for participation doesn't hold water, Austin," Sadie continued when it became apparent he was at a loss for words. "Lacy is not and never will be fit to be a countess in your family's eyes—it's my guess that she was simply a dalliance that you have put up as motive. But it's not going to protect you from the truth that is, even now, coming to the surface."

"Are you sure about all this?" Liam said, turning to Breanna. Sadie kept her eyes on Austin; he looked anxious—as well he should, now that everyone knew the extent of his secrets. Liam turned back toward his cousin. "Why were you looking through the pedigree yesterday?"

Sadie glanced at Liam with a bit of concern; he seemed hesitant to accept that the conspiracy against his father was only part of the plan. She could imagine it was hard to swallow—that your father was being murdered and you would be next—but she hoped he wouldn't let the denial overwhelm the facts. That would be dangerous indeed.

Austin closed his eyes slowly, then opened them again. "I knew something was wrong," he said. "I've been on eggshells throughout your whole visit, Liam. I worried you would suspect something, scared that you would ask to review the documents that weren't even on the premises right now. The staff was equally terrified of being discovered, and then John Henry disappeared. I called my father in a panic but he refused to come down. My grandmother assured me that everything would be fine, but she wouldn't come down either. You were protective of your father, the staff was edgy, and you—" He looked at Sadie. "*You* were asking questions, showing up where you didn't belong, and were not the least bit intimidated with my attempts to put you off." Sadie took a little pride in that, but hoped it didn't show on her face. That would be inappropriate.

Austin continued. "In the weeks before William had his stro— became ill, he was spending a great deal of time in the library, poring over the Book of Heraldry and the personal histories of the past earls. I didn't think much of it at the time, but I did wonder why my father and grandmother would do this *now*. They knew Liam was coming for the holidays, they knew he'd be familiarizing himself with matters of the estate, and it didn't make sense that they would instigate all of this right now. There had to be a reason they would take these risks to provide for my grandmother now—not a year ago, not five years in the future, not even after Liam's visit. I was trying to figure that out, but I never did."

Sadie was tired of the story and felt that he was trying a little too hard to look a little too dumb. "I think you were looking in the Book of Heraldry to make sure there was nothing there that would implicate you in that layer of the deception," Sadie said. "You'd worked so hard to pull this off, and even killed John Henry when you realized he was going to blow your cover, and—"

At this Austin shook his head, almost startling Sadie with the quickness of his movements and causing her to lose her train of thought.

"I had nothing to do with John Henry," Austin said strongly. "I didn't kill him and I didn't know anything about being a potential heir." His voice turned pleading. "All I knew was that my grand-mother offered me what I wanted more than anything—Lacy."

Sadie took a step toward him. "Do you honestly believe your grandmother would have let you have her? You were going to be earl someday."

"I didn't know anything about that!" he said, his voice rising. "And it doesn't make sense. She would have told me if I was a po-tential heir—everyone would have known. Things like that don't remain a secret."

"Unless someone is willing to do anything they can to keep it a secret for thirty years. If anyone found out too soon, your plan would never have worked. That your grandmother could also break up Violet and William for a second time was just icing on the cake and perhaps one of the reasons it happened now instead of later."

Austin lifted a hand to his forehead and turned away. "I can't believe this," he muttered. For the smallest moment, Sadie wondered if perhaps he was as ignorant as he claimed to be. He knew the gig was up, why not admit his part? Then again, he stood to lose a lot if he admitted culpability. It was far less serious to be part of a con-spiracy to commit fraud than to murder a man in cold blood because it would help you get a title.

"Did Lacy know?" Sadie asked. Grant and Mrs. Land had both said Lacy didn't know—but Sadie wasn't sure she believed it.

Austin paused, then shook his head, turning back to face Sadie with a morose expression on his face. Breanna and Liam seemed content to let Sadie ask the questions. "She thought William had had a stroke," Austin said. "And she was nervous when my family was around in the beginning, but I didn't want her to know; I didn't want her to feel . . . responsible in any way."

"Does she know now?" Sadie asked.

If possible, he looked even more dejected. "She won't answer my calls. I don't know what happened yesterday, who told her to leave or why. I have no idea where she is, but I've no doubt she's lost to me now." He paused and then turned away. Sadie thought she caught sight of tears in his eyes. "Lacy is a *good* woman," he said, staring at the front door. "When she learns I was part of this, when she understands what I've done—if she doesn't already know—her conscience will demand that she move on without me. I've made a terrible mistake—several terrible mistakes. Lacy will never forgive me, and I'm hard-pressed to think that she should."

Sadie was searching for another question when there was a knock at the front door. She turned to see Inspector Kent open the door and enter the foyer with another officer behind him. She was a little disappointed not to have a few more minutes for her own interrogation—it was going so well.

Sadie moved to the side as the inspector walked toward Austin.

"I believe you and I are due for another chat," the inspector said to Austin, who raised his eyes to look at the men in absolute fear. "Is it necessary for me to remind you of your rights in regard to speaking with us?"

"No," Austin said. "But these women, as well as Liam, have informed me of things I was as yet unaware of. I feel that their information is as important as my own."

"You don't say," Kent said rather dryly. "Well, by all means, let's all go down together."

CHAPTER 43

"Alright," Sadie said Monday morning as she closed the top of her suitcase and wrestled with the zipper. "I'm done." She looked up at Breanna who was still shoving things into her backpack. They'd been at the police station until nearly ten P.M.—but at least they got to leave. Austin was still there, and Lady Hane and Dr. Melcalfe were likely still giving their version of events to Scotland Yard in London while their lawyers began scrambling for a defense. As for Liam, he'd been questioned for several hours about the part he'd played in moving John Henry's body and withholding information from the police. They'd let him go home, but insisted he surrender his passport and remain in Devonshire until they completed the investigation and determined what charges he would need to answer for.

On the way home from the police station, they'd stopped at the hospital for an update on the earl. Dr. Sawyer had identified the medication used to keep the earl incapacitated and was working with a team of other physicians to remedy the situation. The earl was conscious, but not communicative—they said it could take up to a week for the medication to be fully flushed from his system. The three of them hadn't arrived home until midnight, where Sadie had fallen asleep as soon as her head hit the pillow. When morning arrived, Sadie was sure she could have slept the entire day. But they had a plane to catch.

"I'm almost finished," Breanna said, tucking her wet hair behind her ear—she'd just gotten out of the shower and was still dripping all over the place. "Mrs. Kinsley left some things in the fridge for breakfast—but I don't think we have time to cook anything." She looked up and eyed her mother with a visual reprimand.

"I know, I know," Sadie said. "I've already accepted that, but you better hurry, I'm in no mood to save you anything. I'm going to have to start a diet come next week, but I plan to live life to the fullest until then."

Breanna chuckled and went back to her packing, which Sadie thought ought to be called *stuffing* since that's all she did—stuff things into her backpack. Sadie slung her duffel bag over one shoulder, her oversized purse over the other, and pulled both suitcases toward the door, grateful they were on wheels. "I'll see you and Liam in the kitchen," she said.

"Okay," Breanna replied, pushing her pajamas down the side of the canvas. "Liam called Kevin to pick us up. He should be here by 10:30 or so."

Sadie nodded, let herself out into the hallway, and headed toward the stairs. She was missing the staff right about now, which was a sign that she was becoming soft. It took several minutes to wrestle her suitcases down the stairs, but she finally deposited all her luggage in the middle of the foyer. Hopefully Kevin would load them in the car.

She headed for the kitchen to get something to eat.

"Hello?" she called as she entered the kitchen. The lights were off, so she flipped the switch and the room flickered to life. She went to the fridge and pulled out a few items, including several scones that made her smile, even if they were pre-frozen. The diet loomed before her, but she decided that scones wouldn't count—she had a recipe to perfect once she got home and would need something to keep her from feeling sorry for herself.

Sadie went about preparing herself a breakfast of juice, scones—complete with clotted cream and strawberry jam—and a banana. She had just sat down on one of the stools by the butcher-block table in the kitchen when she heard the outside door begin to slowly open.

Sadie's first reaction was instant, mind-numbing panic. No one was supposed to be here and though she was an adventurous girl, she was not in the mood for anymore surprises. Mustering all the courage she had left, she turned in her seat to see who it was—her mind conjuring the possibility that Austin had escaped and come back to the estate to kill them all.

But it wasn't Austin. Instead a petite girl with Asian features stopped when she saw Sadie; the two women stared at each other across the kitchen.

"Lacy?" Sadie asked. Lacy had been dressed in black scrubs with a scarf over her head when Sadie had seen her two days ago. Today she wore jeans, with a white T-shirt underneath a formfitting buttoned-up vest. Her sleek black hair hung loose over her shoulders.

"Mrs. Hoffmiller," Lacy said, coming to a stop. She didn't seem as surprised to see Sadie as Sadie was to see her. "You're still here."

"We're just leaving," Sadie said, standing up from the table. "Are you okay? I've been worried."

Lacy took a breath and then shrugged. "I'm okay," she said. "I guess." She looked around the room. "I need to talk to Aust—Lord Melcalfe, is he here?"

Sadie was quiet for a few moments. "He's at the police station in Exeter," she said.

Lacy's eyes went even wider. "What?" she breathed.

"He's been trying to call you," Sadie said. "A lot has happened since you left. He admitted to the conspiracy against the earl. In fact, I think the police will want to talk to you."

Lacy paled. "Me?" she asked. "Why?"

Sadie watched her for a moment. "You went running out of the estate and were romantically involved with Austin." Sadie noticed the faint blush that colored the girl's cheeks. "Everyone's being questioned, so you're not alone, but they'll need your side of the story. The earl was being overmedicated and his nurse was murdered, that's a pretty big deal." By the last few words she noticed Lacy was looking decidedly pale. "Lacy?" Sadie asked, "are you okay?"

Lacy teetered slightly on her feet and Sadie hurried over to help the girl keep her balance. "Whoa," she said, putting her hands on Lacy's shoulders. "Sit down—I'm sorry, I should have eased you into that."

"This is all my fault," Lacy said, allowing Sadie to lead her to a stool by the table.

"No, it's not your fault, sweetie," Sadie assured her, moving to the sink to get Lacy a glass of water. She put it in front of the young woman and moved to the opposite side of the table so she could see Lacy's face. "Everyone swears you didn't know what was going on with the earl. But someone told you to run, didn't they?"

Lacy closed her beautiful eyes slowly, then opened them again and stared at the cup, wrapping both hands around the glass as if relying on it to keep her upright. "I didn't know," Lacy said softly, shaking her head slightly. "Until John Henry told me Saturday morning, I didn't know anything."

"John Henry told you?" Sadie asked. "That morning?"

"We never really spoke to one another—well, he never spoke to anyone. But on Saturday he came through the kitchen on his way outside. His face was red but I couldn't tell if he was angry exactly. I was cleaning up from lunch when he came back half an hour later. I thought he was on his way back upstairs, but he stopped in the middle of the kitchen and just stood there until I turned to see what he was doing. He told me everything." She paused, and looked past Sadie's shoulder, perhaps trying to find the naïve girl she'd been a few days earlier. "He said, 'Lord Melcalfe did it all for you, ya know?' I couldn't believe it." She looked back at Sadie. "I love Austin," she said, and Sadie could tell she meant it even though the words hurt her. "I met him when he was at Oxford—a school I could never attend. I was a waitress, and pretty soon he was coming in every evening. After awhile he would wait for me outside and we'd talk in his car for hours. He wasn't like the other rich people I'd met—and I'd met plenty. He was kind and confident and when we were together it was like we were our true selves. I know that probably doesn't make sense, but . . . I fell in love with him, even though I knew it was likely the worst decision I could ever make. Our lives were too different and we both knew it would be a struggle for us to make it work." Her voice cracked and she cleared her throat before lifting the glass and taking a sip of water.

"But these last couple months," Lacy said, "things have changed. I thought it was because the earl was sick that Austin was overwhelmed and worried about his family. He's been distracted, short-tempered, and—just not himself. When John Henry told me the truth it all made sense."

"John Henry was the one that warned you to run, wasn't he?"

Lacy nodded. "He asked me to give a note to Liam, and said that if anything happened, I needed to get as far away from here as I could. I thought he was being dramatic, but—"

"The note," Sadie said as a tingle raced down her spine. "You said he gave you a note?"

Lacy nodded.

"What did you do with it?" Sadie asked. Would Lacy have given it to Austin?

"I put it on the tea tray," Lacy said. "That's what we do with correspondence—put it on the tray."

Oh, such a naïve little girl, Sadie thought. She just put it on the tray, where anyone could pick it up . . . Sadie paused.

Anyone?

"Lacy," Sadie said, "did you see Austin on Saturday?"

Lacy shook her head. "No, he'd left to Exeter early that morning. I didn't expect him back until after Liam left—he'd been avoiding Liam all week."

"Grant said he saw Austin here that day—right before tea was served."

Lacy pulled her delicate eyebrows together as if considering that, then she shook her head. "I talked to him on the phone around 4:00—while I was waiting for Grant to come fix the tea. Austin was going into a meeting with one the shopkeepers of one of the earl's properties. He said he wouldn't be back until half-past five at the soonest. Everything John Henry had told me was fresh in my mind—I was so confused, so scared. I told him we needed to talk when he got here."

"Maybe he was lying about where he was," Sadie said. "He could have called you from anywhere."

"I heard the train," Lacy said, looking up at Sadie. "The shop—Arnold's Garage—it's by the train station. Austin had to stop talking until the train passed because I couldn't hear him."

Sadie felt her heart rate begin to increase. If Austin had been in Exeter, he'd have been at least twenty minutes away at the time Grant claimed to have seen him. Sadie couldn't even face the possibility that she could be wrong. "Grant said he saw him," Sadie said, defending her position.

Lacy frowned slightly. "Grant?" she repeated, sounding surprised.

"What?" Sadie asked, feeling the anxiety take over. "What about Grant?"

"Well, I'm sure I don't know how difficult everything has been for him, but he just hasn't been the same since Essie died."

CHAPTER 44

Sadie felt the blood drain from her face as the words landed with a thud in her chest. "Died?" she fairly squeaked.

"It was such a tragic thing," Lacy said. "I didn't know her very well, having just come to Southgate. But I'd seen her drunk a time or two and it was horrible. She'd worked with the earl for a long time, and he'd been very patient with her—but it was getting out of hand. She'd stolen from him and disappeared for days at a time. We all hoped that Bethelridge would help her overcome her addiction, and we knew that if it didn't, she wouldn't be able to stay on at Southgate. Grant struggled with her leaving, though he was gracious in regard to the earl paying for treatment, but we all knew it was hard for him to see her go. When she left treatment, and then died in London a few weeks later, none of us thought Grant would come back."

Sadie could barely breathe. She felt as if her mind were in a blender. She felt sick as Lacy continued. "He was gone for almost two weeks. He didn't even tell us where he was or when the funeral would take place. Then he just came back one day, told the earl that he didn't blame him for what had happened, and that he'd like to continue on at Southgate. The earl, of course, felt horrible, and didn't hesitate to hire him on again. He offered to pay for the funeral expenses, but Grant said it was taken care of—that he just wanted to move forward. But he was never quite the same after that. He kept to himself and seemed to, I don't know, move quieter, if that makes sense." She looked back down at the glass in her hands. "I guess no one would be unaffected by something like that, would they?"

"No," Sadie said numbly. "I guess not." She glanced at the kitchen doors wondering where Breanna and Liam were. It had been nearly twenty minutes since Sadie had left Breanna in the room. She was sick to her stomach at the idea that she'd believed Grant so completely and then let him go. But Grant had been right about the safe and the conspiracy. And yet it was impossible to ignore that if Austin hadn't been at Southgate like Grant said he was, and if Lacy had put the note from John Henry on the tea tray Grant was supposed to take up to Liam, and if Sadie found the note in Grant's room . . .

"Mrs. Hoffmiller?"

Sadie looked at Lacy who was watching her.

"When I left, you said you would help me if you could."

Sadie nodded, trying to push these new discoveries to the side so she could focus on this moment. "Of course."

Lacy nodded, then leaned back so she could pull something out of her pocket. She put a ring on the table between them, staring at it for several seconds before looking at Sadie with tears in her eyes. "Will you see that Austin gets this back?" Her voice shook and Sadie's own throat grew thick as she stared at the symbol of the future these two young people had hoped to share. "After I left I went to stay with a friend in Dover—Austin and I had gone there together in November."

Guy Fawkes Day, Sadie summarized in her mind. Hadn't Austin said he'd gone to Dover on holiday? And that when he'd come back his father had informed him of the earl's stroke?

Lacy wiped at her eyes as she continued. "I left Southgate and went to Dover to think things through. I came to the conclusion that I don't know this man." Her voice was barely a whisper and a tear rolled down her cheek; she didn't try to stop it. "The Austin Melcalfe I fell in love with was a good man. He was kind, and fair, and honest." She paused for a breath. "The Austin Melcalfe I knew would never be part of a plan to hurt someone who had given him so much. He would never have lied to me about it, and he'd have known that if he did, I could never respect him, never share his life, never simply forgive him and move on."

Sadie felt a strange desire to defend Austin, but she couldn't do that in good conscience. She also noted that Austin had verified these exact things—that once Lacy knew of his deceit, she would not continue her relationship with him. It was exactly what Austin deserved, but her heart still ached for Lacy and the loss she was now mourning.

"I'm so sorry, Lacy," she said, offering a sympathetic smile when the girl's glance flickered up for a moment.

Lacy nodded. "I suppose I need to tell the police what I know," she said. She pushed the ring toward Sadie. "But I can't see Austin again. Will you see that he gets this, that he knows my decision, and that I don't want him to contact me?"

Sadie nodded. "I will." She reached across the table and put her hand over Lacy's. "I'm sorry," she whispered. "Please don't think this is your fault. You don't deserve the burden that's been set on your shoulders."

Lacy nodded, but Sadie wondered if she would ever truly believe that she was not the one responsible for all that had happened. Lacy sniffed and wiped at the tears on her cheeks as she stood up. "Is there anyone specific I should talk to when I get to the police station?" Lacy asked.

"Inspector Kent," Sadie said. She wanted to apologize again, but the thoughts about Grant were creeping forward again and the rock in her stomach was getting heavier. She needed to talk to Liam and Breanna—make sense of what she'd learned about Grant. She was hesitant to disregard everything he'd told her based on this discovery, but she couldn't deny that every word of his "confession" was now suspect. And, according to Lacy, Austin couldn't have been at the estate when John Henry was murdered. Lacy might not have drawn the same conclusion from their discussion, but Sadie certainly had. And if it wasn't Austin, and Grant had lied to her . . .

"Thank you," Lacy said with a nod. She headed for the door, while Sadie stared at the ring on the table. When the exterior door shut, she left the ring, and hurried to the drawer where she'd put the keys a few minutes earlier, then fairly ran for Grant's room. There had to be a way she could confirm what Lacy had told her, but her heart was in her throat at the possibilities that were now reopened.

CHAPTER 45

G rant's room was exactly as Sadie remembered it, except that the toiletries were missing from the dresser. She scanned the room and her eyes fell on the nightstand. It was still locked and she took a few seconds to consider her options. After a cursory look for the key in the drawers of the dresser, she gave up on that possibility and took the more destructive choice. A few swift kicks with the heel of her shoe splintered the wood of the nightstand enough that she was able to pull out the drawer and put it on the bed. When she looked inside, she froze for a moment before reaching in and pulling out her notebook—the one that had gone missing from her and Breanna's room yesterday. She'd forgotten all about it.

If Grant had taken the notebook, he would know what she and Breanna had discovered up to that point. She looked back at the stack of papers in his drawer, including several light green envelopes like the one she'd found marking the place in Grant's book the day before.

The first letter she picked up had a postmark for January 6, which confused her. Today was New Year's Day—five days *before* this postmark.

The letter she'd taken yesterday had been postmarked December 22, but until now she hadn't noticed that there was no year on the stamp. Her stomach got heavy. She'd *assumed* that the letter was from this year, and Grant had seemed to confirm that. There were more letters, with postmarks through April. With each one Sadie looked at, her stomach twisted a bit tighter in her belly.

Her hands slowed when she reached the bottom of the drawer and discovered what looked like the bottom layer of a triplicate form—thin pink carbon paper, folded in half. She picked it up and opened it, stiffening as she realized it was a receipt containing the burial information for one Estella Bernice Contine, buried May 18.

The notebook caught her eye again. Grant would have known that she suspected Austin already—and he'd done a good job of tipping the scales right before he was leaving for the holiday. The promise she'd made to him that she'd be sure he still got to go burned in her chest. He'd played her perfectly, giving an eleventh-hour confession and playing upon her sympathies so that she didn't insist he talk to the police right then. She had *wanted* to believe it was all Austin, and so she'd gone against her better judgment and trusted Grant too much, too quickly. He, on the other hand, was a quick thinker. When she'd confronted him in the countess's bedroom yesterday, he'd easily parried each of her questions—leading her toward Austin and away from himself by telling her a jumbled version of the truth.

Her eyes returned to the burial papers in her hand and another name caught her eye, causing her to furrow her brow. Under the portion labeled "Responsible for Payment" was the printed name of Harriet Brinton—Dowager Lady Hane—followed by a swirling signature.

Her stomach sank even lower as the picture in her mind shifted, becoming clearer in the process.

The earl had insisted Essie get help and although Essie might have gone along with it in the beginning, she couldn't do it. After she left treatment, Essie was buried in London and Lady Hane had paid for it. Was Grant in cahoots with Lady Hane before that, or did Lady Hane come to him when he was in need?

She thought back to Austin's adamant denial of having killed John Henry. A denial Sadie didn't believe due solely on the fact that Grant claimed to have seen Austin at the estate earlier than Austin would admit.

"But what if it was Grant who killed John Henry after all?" Sadie said out loud. "What if the butler did it all along?"

CHAPTER 46

Sadie hurried from Grant's room, taking the staff stairs to the main floor. She noticed that Breanna's backpack wasn't in the foyer with Sadie's bags, which hadn't been loaded into the car yet. With any luck Breanna was still packing. She took the stairs two at a time—groaning with each step—reached the second floor, and hurried to their room.

"Breanna, I just—" She cut off when she realized Breanna wasn't there. Her backpack was gone as well.

Sadie pulled out her cell phone and typed a quick message.

Where r u?

When she didn't have a response after ten whole seconds, she hurried toward Liam's room in the east wing while telling herself that she was totally overreacting. *Breanna and Liam are saying good-bye,* she told herself, prepared to perhaps interrupt a farewell kiss very much in need of being interrupted.

Surely Grant, knowing that the truth would come out, would have made quick work of getting as far from Southgate as possible. They weren't in *danger* from Grant, and he certainly wouldn't risk coming back here. Sadie was just tired and overwrought and jumping at shadows.

She told herself all of this, but she didn't believe a single word and her optimism faded quickly.

What if he *had* come back? What if Grant blamed the earl for Essie's death? His going along with the plan wouldn't be blackmail like it was with the others—it would be revenge. He'd have no hesitation telling the truth about the safe because that didn't factor into his own situation. It was one thing to feel foolish about believing him, but what she felt now was more than that.

If Grant were five hundred miles away, then why was she feeling so sick to her stomach? Why wasn't Breanna answering her phone? And why was there so much fear in her chest that she could barely breathe?

Her hand was on the doorknob to Liam's room when she heard the gunshot.

CHAPTER 47

Sadie's entire world came to a halt with the sound of gunfire, only starting again when Breanna screamed Liam's name and Grant said "Don't touch him!"

Sadie's instincts told her to break down the door, but she forced herself to think before she reacted. With her heart thundering in her ears, she looked around the hallway for some kind of weapon. She saw a large, flat bronze bowl on the table next to the earl's suite. She ran for it while digging her phone out of her pocket and then dialing 999—much easier to do than 911—and then ran back to the door to Liam's room. Just before opening the door, she put the phone to her mouth and said as quietly as she could but as loud as she dared, "Gunshots at Southgate estate—tell Inspector Kent." Then she put the phone on the floor near the doorway, dug the whistle out of her pocket, gripped the doorknob, and pushed the door open, blowing into the whistle as hard as she could.

In the instant her foot entered the room at a run, she took in the scene: Liam in a pile in one corner near his luggage and Breanna's backpack; Breanna cowering at the foot of the bed; and Grant, with a gun in his hand, turning in reaction to the shrieking banshee that had just exploded through the door. It took only a fling of Sadie's wrist to send the flat bronze bowl spinning across the room like the Frisbee she believed it was meant to be in the first place.

Grant pulled the trigger of the small black gun he was holding, but just as Sadie hoped, the shot went too high in his panic, hitting the top of the doorframe behind her. A split second later, the bowl caught him in the throat, knocking him backwards as he fired another shot into the ceiling. Sadie dove for Breanna, pulling her away from the bed and back toward the door.

"Liam!" Breanna cried as they reached the threshold. She pulled against Sadie, but Sadie tightened her grip so much that she feared she might break Breanna's arm if she held on any tighter.

"No," Sadie said, dragging her daughter out of the room. "We'll come back." Every action film she'd ever seen showed people crying and comforting each other while their supposedly unconscious pursuer remained in the room with them. Usually it led to one more attempt at the good guy's life. Sadie wouldn't let that happen to the good guys this time. She prayed that Liam was okay, but she would not risk her life or the life of her daughter long enough to see. The bowl was still clattering on the floor as they passed through the doorway and slammed it shut. Sadie bent down to grab the phone she'd left on the floor while Breanna stumbled behind her.

The first door she saw was to the earl's suite across the hall. Afraid that heading toward the stairs made them too vulnerable, Sadie grabbed the doorknob of the earl's sitting room, practically dragged Breanna inside, and then pushed the door closed. She locked the door before talking into the phone. "Hello," she said in a harsh whisper, heading for the door to the countess's bedroom, fumbling in her pocket for her keys.

"They're back on the line," she heard a frantic voice say on the phone. "Hello, hello? Are you there?"

"I'm here," Sadie said breathlessly as she put the key in the lock and turned it before looking back, wondering why Breanna wasn't following her. Breanna was crying and staring at the door they'd come in as she walked backwards toward her mother. Sadie followed Breanna's eyes to see what had captured her daughter's attention and saw the deadbolt turn. How could she have forgotten that Grant was the other person with a key to everything? Moving even faster, she opened the door to the countess's bedroom and both she and Breanna ran inside, closing the door and locking it, but not before she'd seen the earl's sitting room door begin to open.

"The balcony," Sadie whispered, shooing Breanna toward it. "Get down somehow and circle back inside." She placed her phone, still open, on top of the armoire next to the window. If the emergency service was still on the line she hoped they could hear what was happening.

Breanna's face was wet with tears and she looked completely frantic. "But—"

"Go," Sadie hissed. "Liam needs you to get help."

And Sadie needed to know that Breanna was safe. There was little protection Sadie could offer if they were both trying to scamper down the trellis. Breanna would be faster alone anyway, and time was of the essence.

Breanna turned immediately and headed for the French doors. Sadie followed her, releasing the tieback that held the heavy draperies back. The thick fabric fell forward, covering the windows and shrouding the room in muted light she hoped would hide her better. Sadie scanned the room, looking for another Frisbee bowl but finding nothing she could use to defend herself. Everything in the room was obnoxiously soft and the bed was solid wood all the way to the floor. The mountain of pillows on the bed caught her attention and she dove for them, burrowing in through the side, as close to the headboard as possible. She pressed herself against the headboard while wiggling her whole self in, trying to keep from upsetting the pillows too much and hoping like crazy that there were enough of them to cover her. She wished for squeaky hinges that would signal that Grant was coming in, but had to settle for soft footfalls, further muted by the pillows piled above her. She held her breath as she heard him move around the room. She wished she could see what was happening.

"Can you believe this room, Essie?" he said softly, his voice tender and soft, at odds with the man she'd seen pointing a gun at her daughter just minutes earlier. "I'd have given it to you if I could."

Is he talking to me? Sadie wondered.

She felt the bed shift and her breath caught in her throat. After a few seconds, she parted the pillows and her heart jumped to see Grant sitting at the end of the bed—just a few feet from where the pillows ended. He looked at the closed drapes as if they were open windows. He held the gun in his right hand, pressed sideways against the bed while his left hand massaged his neck, presumably where the bowl had hit him. He didn't seem tense or worried that he might need to defend himself. Maybe his coming into this room was a coincidence rather than a pursuit. She hoped so.

"They suffered, Essie. They suffered as much as you did."

Sadie didn't dare move for fear it would give her away but wondered how long he planned to sit here. She hoped the police would hurry. She hoped that Breanna, and maybe Kevin, were helping Liam. Sadie just needed to wait Grant out until help arrived. Waiting had never been her strong suit, but in this case she didn't foresee a problem since the price of impatience was unacceptable. Suddenly Grant's head turned to the side, putting his face in profile against the curtains that seemed to glow in the morning light on the other side of the windows. "I know you're there, Mrs. Hoffmiller," he said. "You should know there's only one bullet left and this one won't go awry."

Sadie went absolutely still.

Grant let out a breath, smiled slightly, and continued talking over his shoulder as though she'd answered him. "Who'd have guessed you'd look behind a curtain panel in the sitting room?" He paused, shaking his head. "Had you left as expected, John Henry would have washed up on a riverbank somewhere; the victim of some anonymous act of foul play. Instead, things got complicated, didn't they?" He sighed and shifted on the bed. Sadie tensed, but listened intently. I can only assume that John Henry went to Lacy with the note because she was the only person with nothing to hide in this whole charade. She actually put that note on the tea tray." He paused and shook his head before continuing. Sadie was still only interested in listening at this point, wondering if he'd tell her anything she didn't already know.

"I take pride in my ability to think on my feet, you see. So it wasn't difficult to put you on the path that led to Lord Melcalfe's deception without implicating myself. It helped that you *wanted* to believe the things I told you—you wanted Lord Melcalfe to be guilty, and in fact he earned that, I think. But I appreciated that you believed me so easily, Mrs. Hoffmiller. Though I spend my life noticing things for others, not many people pay much attention to me. But you did, which is why I'm not going after your daughter even though I know she's gone for help—hasn't she? See, I noticed that the door to the earl's sitting room was locked when it shouldn't be. And then the light changed under this door when you shut the curtains I'd left open after we spoke yesterday. And then I noticed that the pillows weren't just quite right." He looked forward again. "I notice things, that's my job."

He went silent and Sadie swallowed the thick lump in her throat. She didn't know what to do or what to say and hated feeling like a sitting duck doing nothing. Up until a few minutes ago, she'd still believed Austin was the person responsible for all the horrible things that had been happening here—but he wasn't. Or at least he wasn't alone. Perhaps she could figure out why things happened the way they did and how she'd missed it all. She could only hope that asking questions wouldn't be the last thing she did.

"I'm sorry," she managed to whisper though her mouth felt like it was full of sand. She pushed out of the pillows a little bit, watching him carefully in case she would need to make a run for it. "About Essie, I mean. I'm sorry about what happened to her."

She braced herself for his reaction but he didn't move at all, other than let out a breath. "The earl did it," he said after a few seconds, not seeming surprised that Sadie knew. "He said she had to get help or he'd be forced to let her go." He turned his head to the side again, not looking at her but putting his face in profile once more. "He said he didn't want to do it, but he did it anyway. Now what kind of a gentleman does that? I've spent my life watching them, attending to the details of their lives that they can't be bothered with, and I can tell you that not a one of them does what he doesn't want to do. He was angry with my Essie, he was tired of dealing with her imperfections. But not me. I loved her, I took care of her. Did the earl do that?" His voice grew louder and Sadie tried to calm her increasingly panicked heart rate. "Did the earl ever clean her up when she vomited all over herself? Did the earl ever once hide the liquor so she couldn't find it? No, he didn't—not even one time. And yet he said he wanted to help her—by sending her to Bethelridge where she'd be surrounded by aristocrats who couldn't hold their liquor. That would put her in her place, all right. That would show her humility—put her in a room of people whining about their paltry allowance of fifty thousand a year. He sent her there to fail, that's what he did. He wanted her gone and—like any gentleman—he got exactly what he wanted, didn't he?"

"And Lady Hane?" Sadie asked. "Did she always get what she wanted?"

"Lady Hane approached me when I was in London making arrangements for Essie's burial. I was prepared to stay in London, stay near my Essie and find work in another household, but Lady Hane convinced me to stay on at Southgate. She understood what it was like to live in the shadows. She was the firstborn of an earl, but what did it matter? She couldn't inherit, and then when William was born, she was on the sidelines until she was bartered off as a wife to the highest bidder. When she found me in London, she told me that she'd discovered a way to take that title away from William; to pass something down to her own grandson. After what the earl did to my future, I was more than happy to lay in wait, learn whatever I could, and pass it on to her. When I discovered that the earl was seeing his ex-wife again, I knew Lady Hane would be done waiting, and I was right."

"I thought the earl was ready to tell everyone about his relationship," Sadie said.

"Perhaps," Grant said, with a slight shrug of one shoulder. "Things had begun to move quickly about that time. But the important thing was that Lady Hane was ready when the time was right."

"That's why you went along with everything?" Sadie dared ask. "For revenge?"

"For justice," Grant clarified. He stood up from the bed and Sadie tensed again. But he didn't turn toward her, instead he walked to the windows and drew back the curtains, carefully securing the tieback and smoothing the folds of the fabric. Sadie inched out from the pillows a little further.

"I loved her broken," Grant said quietly, running his hand down the fabric as if caressing it. "The earl sent her out to be fixed and it destroyed her. Lady Hane had her own revenge to exact, but mine was no less important."

"And Austin?" Sadie asked. "He didn't kill John Henry, did he?"

"No," Grant said boldly, almost proud. "He couldn't be bothered with such tasks—they are beneath him. As usual, he waits for other people to take care of things—just like his grandmother."

Sadie didn't respond, but moved closer to the edge of the bed nearest the door.

"*Lord* Melcalfe deserves what he gets," Grant said emphatically. "They all do. All they wanted was money and power—there wasn't a noble desire within the whole lot of them. But me—" He put a hand to his chest. "I was fighting for justice, for love."

"You believe that love is worth fighting for?" Sadie asked, thinking of Austin's insistence that he went along with this for love—for Lacy. But she wasn't sure she wanted to debate that fact with Grant right now.

"Of course it is," Grant said with an indulgent smile. "Love is the only thing that matters in the world, which is why taking love away from someone is worthy of the greatest punishment."

"Why did you come back?" Sadie asked, frightened by her own bravery even as she found it impossible to hold back. Yes, he was a deranged lunatic, but if he could see his hypocrisy then perhaps he could be reasoned with.

"It wasn't finished," Grant said. "The earl was not dead, which meant I had to finish my work—an eye for an eye, a life for a life, a love for a love. He took my wife and I thought that playing my role in Lady Hane's revenge would be enough, but then I realized the earl might get better. That meant no one loses but me. That isn't fair; that isn't justice."

"So you shot Liam," Sadie said, glancing toward the open door as she put her legs over the side of the bed. Grant didn't seem to be paying attention to her movements. "You shot the earl's only son." The words nearly stuck in her throat as she thought of Liam crumpled in the corner, possibly dying just as Grant had hoped. She hoped someone other than Breanna would be the one to initially check on him. She pushed the thoughts away and focused. "You've finished your mission then."

That seemed to confuse Grant and he furrowed his eyebrows as he considered that. Sadie placed her feet on the floor as Grant turned back to the windows, the hand holding the gun falling to his side. "I hadn't thought of that," he said. "I suppose there isn't much left for me to do, is there, Essie?"

Sadie scooted her body to the edge of the bed, took a breath, and then ran for the door, expecting at any minute for a bullet to hit her between the shoulder blades. She reached the earl's sitting room. The hallway. The stairs.

On the fourth stair down, she finally heard the shot, and covered her ears as she heard herself scream and fall to the marble steps beneath her. She waited for the burn, to feel the searing pain the bullet would bring, but she felt nothing. Pounding feet came up to meet her from the main level and she realized Grant had never intended that bullet for her at all.

CHAPTER 48

An intense wave of fear and gratitude and sorrow and relief pummeled Sadie as she came to terms with the events of the last several minutes, but as soon as her head broke the surface of reality she began calling for Breanna, who hurried to her side. They sat at the bottom of the stairs. Sadie touched her daughter's face, her shoulders, her hair.

"You're okay," Sadie said, needing someone to say it. "You're okay."

"I'm okay," Breanna repeated, grabbing Sadie's hand and holding it in both of hers. Her eyes were swollen and her cheeks were wet.

"Liam?" Sadie asked.

Breanna managed a smile though she still looked scared. "The police are checking him out right now but he said it was just in his shoulder. He thinks he'll be okay. An ambulance will be here any minute."

"Austin didn't kill John Henry," Sadie said.

"I know," Breanna replied. "You left your phone on, remember? The police heard everything."

Sadie relaxed. "Oh, right," she said, then she looked at her daughter. "I love you, Breanna," she said. "But I never want to take another vacation like this again."

Breanna managed a smile before Sadie pulled her into her arms. "Me neither," she said into Sadie's shoulder. "I've had all the drama I can handle."

Yet as Sadie held her tight she felt Breanna shudder in her arms. "It's going to be okay," Sadie said, her own voice trembling. She said it so as to help herself believe that even when confronted with impossible obstacles, there were always choices. You could allow the bad to drag you under, as Grant had done, or you could fight your way to the top and live to see another day, becoming in the process a stronger, wiser, more humble, and more grateful person than you were the day before.

"It's going to be okay," she whispered again, committing it to memory. "It's going to be okay."

CHAPTER 49

Sadie looked out the plane window Friday morning, watching London disappear beneath them. She kept watching until the river Thames was lost behind a veil of clouds. Then she took a breath; she was a little sad to be leaving, but a lot relieved to be returning to her regular, normal, uneventful life. She turned to Breanna, who had her head rested against the seat. She looked more relaxed than she had for several days. The experience wouldn't be wasted if she learned something about herself, or Liam, or life in general—or perhaps all three. It had been an intense week.

Surgery had removed the bullet lodged in Liam's shoulder six days ago and he was recovering well. Breanna had already missed the first week of the semester and after being assured that Violet—who had arrived to take over as sentry for her two men—would take good care of him, Breanna finally agreed to go back home. Lady Hane and Dr. Melcalfe had been arrested and were facing charges of fraud, conspiracy to attempt murder, and blackmail. Additionally, Dr. Melcalfe was facing an ethics board review as to whether or not he should retain his license to practice medicine. The earl was recovering, albeit slowly. Dr. Sawyer expected it would take a good deal of physical therapy for William to overcome the effects of the drug-induced coma, but everyone was optimistic that he'd be able to go home after another week—with a real nurse this time. And Austin? Well, Sadie had delivered Lacy's ring after Liam came out of surgery. Austin had looked at the ring and finally said he was sorry. Sadie didn't know where Lacy had gone after making her statement to the police. Sadie hoped she was healing.

"So?" Sadie asked, getting herself comfortable as she waited to hear what had happened during the last exchange Breanna and Liam had shared at the hospital that morning. "And don't you dare tell me that it's none of my business or that you didn't talk about anything important."

Breanna let out a breath and opened her eyes. "Believe me, Mom, I've learned my lesson about holding things back. I will never lie to my mother again."

"Or simply mislead her," Sadie added, making sure to cover all the bases. "It never works in your best interest."

"Believe me," Breanna said. "I know."

"So?" Sadie asked again.

A family sat in the row ahead of them and their baby squealed, peeking at Sadie over the seat. She smiled and crinkled her nose at the toddler, but she hoped the child was going to sleep. It was a nine-hour flight to Chicago, but would seem twice as long if the baby screeched the whole time. The mother pulled the baby back onto her lap, provoking another high-pitched squeal in the process. Sadie turned her attention back to her daughter.

"Sooo," she asked for the third time.

"So, he apologized for how horrible the trip turned out and for the things he did," Breanna said. "He's worried about me missing so much school." She lifted her arms above her head and stretched.

"That's it?" Sadie said, feeling her face fall.

"No, not exactly," Breanna said, lowering her arms to the armrests. "He also gave me the name of someone to talk to about possibly getting a job at the London Zoo this summer."

"And you said . . ."

"I said I'd think about it." Breanna batted her eyelashes and smiled at her coy response. "But I was really impressed with the London Zoo—and it would give me a chance to see England in a different way—so I'm going to look into it. Maybe just for the summer. We'll see."

Sadie smiled and patted Breanna's knee. She was glad Breanna wasn't giving up on Liam just yet, but equally glad that she was taking her time to be sure this was the course she wanted to take for the rest of her life. "So, what exactly made you change your mind?" Sadie asked. "A week ago you were ready to walk away."

"It's hard to say what it was that turned the tide," Breanna replied, looking thoughtful. "Maybe it was realizing how much Liam needs me in his life. Maybe it was admitting how much I wanted him in mine. Maybe it was talking to Violet and realizing how much she and William lost because of their determination not to see each other's point of view. Or maybe I'm just not ready to turn my back on the possibilities."

"Maybe," Sadie repeated with a nod. "What England needs more than anything are people on both sides of the divide willing to fight for equality."

"I think I could fight for something like that," Breanna said. She looked at her mother. "Besides, a wise woman once told me that life is a little like English trifle—it comes in layers. I'm too young to regret something this big later on."

"Sounds like good advice to me," Sadie said. "You ought to listen to this wise woman a little more often."

"I'll take that into consideration," Breanna said, leaning back in her seat and closing her eyes. "I'm so tired I think I could sleep for a week."

Sadie agreed, and leaned back in her own seat as well, turning her head to look out the window that was still clothed in clouds. She took a deep breath, feeling her muscles relax. As her mind drifted into sleep a hundred images from the last week played through her mind. Who'd have thought their trip to England would turn out this way? She thought of Pete, who would be eager to hear all about the trip, and she was eager to explore a new level of their relationship—perhaps over a plate of scones . . . once she figured out how to make them.

As much as Sadie appreciated taking things slow, she was invigorated by the reminder that nothing lasted forever and that forces were at play that didn't always make sense at first sight. Life and love were not without risks, but just like Breanna, Sadie was too young to regret something this big later on.

Layers.

Hmmm.

Sadie's Scrumptulicious Scones

1 cup sour cream (light works just as well)
1 teaspoon baking soda
4 cups all-purpose flour
1 cup sugar
2 teaspoons baking powder
1 teaspoon salt
$1/4$ teaspoon cream of tartar

1 cup butter
1 egg

Combine sour cream and baking soda in 2-cup bowl or measuring cup (mixture expands, so you'll want to have extra space). Set aside. Whisk together dry ingredients in a large mixing bowl. Cut butter into dry ingredients using a pastry blender until mixture resembles course cornmeal. Add sour cream mixture and egg. Mix until a soft dough forms—use your hands if necessary. Turn dough onto lightly floured surface and knead a few times, then pat or roll until 1-inch thick. Cut into circles or use pizza cutter to cut into triangles. Place scones two inches apart on lightly greased baking sheet. Glaze, if desired. Bake at 350 degrees for 20 to 25 minutes or until bottom edges are golden brown.

Makes 8 to 14, depending on size of scones.

*Pete likes them cheesy—no sugar or glaze, add 1 cup grated sharp cheese instead.

*If using margarine in place of butter, dough may be sticky. Refrigerate for 30 minutes before rolling out.

Glaze (optional but super yummy)

1 egg
1 tablespoon whipping cream

Mix together egg and cream. Brush on top of unbaked scones and bake as directed. Sprinkle cooked scones with powdered sugar. Set oven to broil but leave oven rack in the center position. Put pan in oven, keeping door open about an inch and watch closely. Sugar takes 30 to 90 seconds to turn a golden brown. Remove scones from oven; serve while still warm.

*To freeze scones: Bake scones as directed. When cool put in zip-top plastic bag, removing as much air as possible to ensure freshness upon defrosting. To defrost, remove from freezer and let thaw at room temperature for 2 hours. Can reheat in microwave.

Acknowledgements

This book would not have happened if not for the help of two British friends, Samantha Humphries and Elsie Beard—thank you both for helping this book come together; details are the difference between good and great and your time and tutoring made all the difference.

Big thanks to my non-British pre-readers—Julie Wright and Breanna Kilpack. You both caught things in need of catching and I so appreciate your help in getting it right. My writing group gave feedback throughout the writing process and kept the story on track: Ronda Hinrichsen, Jody Durfee, Becky Clayson, and Anne Craeger—I'd be lost without you guys. Thank you to the members of LDStorymakers who have created a foundation for my writing over the years and to all those readers who write to me and ask for more.

With this book I started Sadie's Test Kitchen, a closed blog comprised of willing cooks who tried and tested the recipes featured in this book. It was a huge weight off my shoulders to have all of them giving feedback and steering me in the right direction—thank you Don, Sandra, Laree, Annie, Barbara, Shirley, Michelle, Whit, and Danyelle. You guys are priceless.

Acknowledgments

Thank you to the amazing staff at Deseret Book—Jana Erickson for overseeing the process, Shauna Gibby for the beautiful cover, Rachael Ward for the typesetting, and my wonderful editor, Lisa Mangum, who is my continual cheerleader and friend.

Hugs and kisses to my family who suffered through my inability to figure out whodunit for an embarrassing amount of time—patience is a virtue and they are virtuous indeed. Special thanks to my sweetie, Lee, for all that he does for me and our family; he is definitely my better half and I'd have never gotten here on my own.

And of course, thank you to my Father in Heaven for the gifts of a lifetime and the continual help in turning those gifts into talents that bless my life, and hopefully bless other lives as well.

Enjoy this sneak peek of

DEVIL'S FOOD CAKE

Coming Spring 2010

CHAPTER ONE

Have you seen Thom yet?" Sadie asked, craning her neck to see into the corners of the temporary stage set up at the front of the ballroom. Thom Mortinson was supposed to have arrived by 6:30, but had called to say he was running late. Sadie was trying not to show her annoyance at men who had no concept of time. Detective Pete Cunningham—Sadie's date for tonight—was late too. She glanced at her watch: 7:05. Thom was supposed to have begun his presentation at 7:00 sharp.

"Not yet," Gayle answered from where she sat at Sadie's left.

"So, did you two read his book, then?" an increasingly familiar voice said.

Sadie looked past Gayle to the young woman seated next to her—the date of Frank Argula. She was thirty years Frank's junior, with thick brown hair piled on top of her delicate little head. Sadie feared a sneeze might snap her neck completely. Her hair had to weigh twenty-five pounds. Sadie didn't know the girl's name—Trixie or Bambi or something like that, she was sure.

"Sure," Gayle answered, shooting Sadie a look brimming with annoyance. It was the fourth time Trixie had cut into their conversation. Frank was currently involved in an animated discussion with a city councilman.

"It must be really good," the girl said with a floating kind of smile as she looked around the room, "for all these people to want to listen to him talk about it."

"It's good," Gayle said dryly.

Sadie scraped together her last bite of mashed potatoes from her plate. Truth be told, she hadn't loved *Devilish Details*. Thom had published the book a few years after moving away from Garrison and while she was very proud of his accomplishment, the writing just wasn't her style.

Gayle turned back to Sadie. "I still can't believe he agreed to come."

"Why wouldn't he come?" Trixie cut in.

Rather than being annoyed at yet another interruption, Gayle's eyes lit up at the girl's innocence and Sadie took a sip of her drink to hide her smile. Gayle turned back to the girl with a very different expression. *Here we go*, Sadie thought. It wasn't that Gayle was a gossip, per se, but she, well, liked . . . being informed and sharing that information. Of course, any time Sadie pointed that out, Gayle turned the tables and recalled all the times Sadie had been the one to spill a story. A server leaned in to take away their plates.

"Didn't Frank tell you about Thom?" Gayle asked sweetly, once the server moved away.

The girl shook her head.

"Well," Gayle said, wriggling in her seat a little bit and leaning closer, "before Thom wrote *Devilish Details*, he lived here in Garrison with his son—that is until his son killed himself and his girlfriend after their junior prom."

Trixie gasped and put a hand to her mouth. Sadie felt her

stomach tighten just a little bit. Hearing the details laid out so bluntly was a bit of a shock. Even from Gayle. "You're kidding," the girl said, lowering her hand. "A murder-suicide? Here?"

Up until last October, when Sadie's neighbor had been murdered, the Mortinson tragedy had been the most recent homicide in Garrison, Colorado. Damon, Thom's son, had only been a couple years older than Sadie's own daughter and so the tragedy had hit close to home. The school district brought in grief counselors, parents forbade their daughters from dating the bad boys, and Thom Mortinson moved to California. No one blamed him for what happened, of course—Damon had been in and out of trouble since he turned twelve—but no one could fault Thom for wanting to make a fresh start, either. Lost in her thoughts, Sadie didn't realize Gayle was still telling the story.

"So, you can imagine our surprise when a couple years later Thom's name showed up on the cover of a *New York Times* bestseller. Of course we all knew he'd been a bit of a closet writer before Damon's death, but no one expected this kind of success, especially after what had happened."

"Wow," Trixie said. She pulled at the top of her strapless gown and looked toward the stage again. "Has he written any other books?"

"No," Gayle said, shrugging her shoulders. "Just that one book, though he's been saying for years that he has another one in the works."

"Maybe he'll be like Harper Lee," the girl said. "In literary circles the common theory is that she never wrote another book because she'd written the perfect novel right out of the gate. How do you compete with your own greatness?"

Sadie and Gayle both looked at Trixie in surprise. They hadn't expected her to recite scholarly supposition. "Maybe," Gayle said slowly, obviously caught off guard.

"I wonder what it's like for him to come back here," the girl added, unusually serious. "I imagine it's hard."

Sadie was reminded of her own surprise when she'd heard he'd accepted the invitation. What was there to come back to Garrison for but to face old ghosts?

Her thoughts were interrupted as a server placed a white dessert plate in front of Sadie. Every thought of Thom or Trixie disappeared. In the middle of the plate was a most beautiful sight—a thick, gooey piece of devil's food cake. Sadie grabbed her fork and dug in without hesitation.

"I thought you were on a diet," Gayle said.

Sadie looked up, fork poised inches from her open mouth and did her best to scowl at her best friend. Gayle didn't take back the question she'd asked; in fact, she continued to look pointedly at the rich chocolate goodness on Sadie's fork. The rich chocolate goodness that was going straight to Sadie's already ample hips. Trixie turned to converse with Frank, and the clinking of silverware and mingling murmurs of a hundred conversations filled the room. Sadie paid no heed to any of it. Instead, she looked at Gayle and with exaggerated movements put the bite of cake in her mouth and closed her lips around the fork. Sadie closed her eyes and tried not to groan out loud as the decadent chocolate melted on her tongue.

Gayle snickered and Sadie feared she'd failed at her attempts to silently appreciate the deliciousness filling her mouth. It was just wrong that such an amazing culinary creation should have any calories at all.

"You should really attempt a little more self-restraint," Gayle said when Sadie recovered from her chocolate-induced swoon and opened her eyes. No one but Gayle, and maybe Sadie's children, could get away with talking to Sadie like that. However, after twenty years of friendship, there wasn't much they could do to offend each other. "Everyone knows *you* made the cake, so your reaction comes across as rather arrogant."

Sadie used the edge of her fork to cut off another bite. "I have no problem with appearing arrogant when I've done something this magnificent."

In truth, it *was* a little embarrassing to lose control like this— especially in public. Sadie prided herself on her humility, and yet she had no control when it came to good food. She'd returned from England almost six weeks ago and had been existing on salads, fruit smoothies, and baked chicken ever since in hopes of losing not the *seven* pounds she'd thought she'd gained, but the *twelve* pounds the scale said she'd brought home with her. Twelve pounds in two weeks—Sadie didn't know that was even possible.

Unfortunately, the *diet* hadn't been as effective as she'd hoped— possibly due to the fact that despite her strict meal regimen of protein and leafy greens, she'd been baking scones and crumpets a few times a week; she didn't count that as breaking her diet because perfecting the recipes was actually research. Gayle, of course, knew this.

And then Sadie had been asked to supply the dessert of her choice for the library fundraiser. Before she'd even hung up the phone she'd known what she wanted to make—devil's food cake. Since it was commonly understood that diets were left at the door of events like this, she knew it was a perfect opportunity to kill two birds with one stone: she'd make a fabulous contribution to the dinner, and she'd get a piece of otherwise forbidden cake.

"I swear this is the best cake I have ever made in my life," Sadie said reverently after taking her second bite.

Gayle chuckled and Sadie couldn't help but join her, knowing that she was being a little ridiculous. She put a hand on Gayle's arm and leaned in toward her friend. "It's a good thing you're sitting next to me," she said, giving Gayle's arm a squeeze. "I'd be liable to embarrass myself otherwise."

Gayle laughed again and cut a bite from her own piece. She paused for a moment after putting it in her mouth and then turned to Sadie. "This *is* incredible."

Trixie turned toward them both and nodded, her jaw rhythmically moving as she also chewed her cake.

Sadie gave them both a smile, glad to be sharing the moment with people that could appreciate it. She took yet another bite, able to keep from moaning this time—but just barely.

"How many did you end up making?" Gayle asked, hurrying to take another bite as if the cake might disappear at any moment.

"Eighteen," Sadie said. "Thank goodness Shawn came into town last night, so he could help me finish up."

Gayle nodded again, but Sadie noted the distracted look in her friend's eyes. Eyes that were green tonight. Gayle's real eye color was mud—Gayle's word, not Sadie's—so she bought colored contacts. Green was Gayle's favorite since it went so well with her curly red hair, but she also had blue and hazel ones. She even had a pair that were violet, which Sadie found a little bit creepy. Who ever heard of someone with purple eyes? Even a woman as beautiful as Gayle—and she was a beautiful woman—had a hard time pulling off purple lenses.

"Shawn didn't want to come?" Gayle asked once she swallowed yet another bite.

Sadie shook her head. "It's hard to believe, but he thought spending a Saturday night with his mom at a library fundraising dinner sounded boring. In fact, I think his exact words were 'dead boring.'"

Gayle huffed in feigned offense.

Sadie chuckled and lifted yet another bite to her lips.

The rich chocolate threatened to make her weak in the knees again when her eyes caught movement on the stage. Thom had arrived and was fiddling with his wireless microphone, trying to clip it to the lapel of his suit jacket. Another man, shorter and balding, was trying to help.

"Oh, there's Thom," Gayle said, pointing at the stage with her fork. "I'm guessing the little man is his manager? Mr. Ogreski?"

"I would assume so," Sadie said, watching the men with an air of distraction as she cut another bite.

"Thom looks good," Gayle continued in an appraising tone. "He's single, you know."

Sadie rolled her eyes but couldn't help but smile at the same time. After Gayle's divorce five years ago, even the suggestion that she might want to date again was met with thinly veiled violent intents directed at whoever had dared to bring it up. And then, just over a year ago, Gayle accepted a neighbor's invitation to attend a single's dance at her church. Gayle was officially introduced to middle-age single life that night, and she hadn't looked back. Sadie was glad—a woman like Gayle needed people, and people needed women like Gayle. Gayle opened her mouth to say something, but then straightened, dropped her chin coyly, and looked over Sadie's head. "Speaking of single men," she said, then smiled brilliantly and cocked her head to the side.

Sadie swiveled in her seat, then smiled and sat up straight as Detective Pete Cunningham entered the ballroom and headed toward their table. If only she'd been able to fit into her black velvet formal. Instead she was in her navy blue sparkle-dress—which was nice, but not nearly as elegant as the flowing dress Gayle was sporting—green, to match her choice of eye color for the evening.

Sadie stood as Pete approached their table. He undid the button of his tux so it wouldn't wrinkle when he sat down. Dang, but the man looked downright dapper in his patent leather shoes and bow tie. His well-trimmed silver hair and beard were a perfect complement to his formal attire, and for a moment, Sadie thought he might kiss her hello; on the cheek if nothing else. Instead, he gave her a quick hug. "Sorry I'm late—paperwork."

"Not a problem," Sadie said as she sat down and he helped push her chair into the table for her. He was always such a gentleman— too much of one sometimes. In the three months they'd been dating, he had yet to kiss her even once. It was beginning to give Sadie a complex.

Pete had met Gayle twice before and said hello while Sadie introduced the other people at their table, including Trixie, whose real name turned out to be Michele. Apparently she was Frank's niece and an English literature major at CSU. Who knew?

Pete shook hands with the other people at their table—some of whom he already knew—before finally taking his seat. Sadie was nearly bursting with pride to be the girl on his arm. "I'm sorry you missed dinner," she offered. She should probably offer him some of her cake, but she wasn't sure their relationship was at that level just yet. Certainly a little lip-locking was prerequisite to sharing devil's food cake, right? Instead, she waved to get the attention of one of the servers and pointed at her plate and then at Pete. The server nodded and headed toward the doors to the kitchen. Sadie pulled her plate a bit closer to herself in hopes that Pete wouldn't get any ideas before they returned with his food.

"They're getting your dinner," Sadie said.

"Oh, good, I'm starving," Pete said. He looked toward the stage, drawing Sadie's attention back to it as well. "I haven't missed the main event, have I?"

Sadie shook her head. Thom was still fiddling with the microphone. They had someone from the hotel helping him, too. Weird that they were having problems now. The sound system had worked fine for Sadie's introduction of the evening forty-five minutes earlier. The hotel had a wooden podium with a detachable wired microphone offstage as back up, but everyone had agreed the wireless system was better. She wondered how long they would keep trying to make the wireless microphone work before moving to plan B.

"He doesn't look much different, does he?" Pete commented, nodding toward Thom.

"Did you know Thom when he used to live here?" Gayle asked, leaning toward them and speaking in a high, sweet voice. Sadie felt a flash of jealousy that surprised her. Was it her imagination or was Gayle being flirtatious? Or was she just insecure about the no-kissing-for-three-months thing?

Pete looked from the stage to Gayle. "I was one of the detectives on his son's case," he said.

"Oh," Sadie and Gayle said at the same time. Sadie wondered why Pete hadn't told her that before now. But she wasn't about to ask in front of Gayle.

"Maybe you should remind them about the wired microphone?" Sadie heard herself say to Gayle.

"Me?" Gayle said in surprise, dropping her flirtatious smile for a moment. Pete was one of the few men over the age of fifty that Gayle hadn't dated in this town, and Sadie wanted to keep it that way.

"I think they've forgotten about the back-up microphone," Sadie said, giving her friend a pointed look. She'd like a few minutes with Pete to catch up on the day. Surely Gayle could understand that.

Gayle was silent, but put down her fork; correctly interpreting Sadie's look. "Well, I guess I could," she said. Sadie smiled in thanks. Gayle stood up and put her napkin on her chair before heading toward the front of the room. At the same moment, a server set down both a dinner and a dessert plate in front of Pete. By the time Sadie looked up again, Gayle had disappeared behind the curtain to the right of the stage. Sadie owed her one. Michele stood and excused herself to use the ladies' room.

"It's worth the hundred and fifty dollars," Sadie said, nodding toward Pete's dinner now that she had him to herself—for the moment anyway. "I promise." She only wished she could say she'd made it herself. Feeding the people she cared about was one of her favorite things to do.

Pete smiled and winked at her before using his knife to cut off a piece of prime rib. Sadie looked up at the stage in time to see Gayle roll the podium out from the curtains on the right and Thom walk off stage left; he looked frustrated. The hotel worker helped Gayle plug a wire from the floor into a port on the side of the wooden podium. Sadie took another bite of cake in hopes of distracting herself from the guilt of asking Gayle to go up there. Gayle wasn't even on the board this year; Sadie was the one who should be up there.

Suddenly the stage area cleared except for the manager and the podium. An expectant hush fell over the crowd as everyone realized in the same moment that the presentation was about to start. The manager looked out at the crowd as if just remembering they were there. After straightening his suit coat, he made his way to the podium, which was so tall the microphone pointed over his head. He reached up both hands to adjust the snakelike microphone holder so that he could speak into it. However, when his mouth moved, the microphone failed to pick up the sound. *Was there a problem with the entire sound system?* Sadie wondered. After all the committee's work to pull off this dinner, she would be really, really mad if it fell apart now.

Mr. Ogreski continued to wrestle with the microphone, which seemed to be stuck. It was free from the holder now, but the wire, which fed through the hole in the podium, didn't have much give, and he couldn't seem to pull the microphone close enough to his mouth. After a few more seconds, Mr. Ogreski clenched his jaw together, adjusted his grip on the microphone, and yanked it toward him, presumably to free the cord that seemed to be tangled within the wooden podium. It didn't budge. He took a breath and planted his feet, poised to pull again. Sadie let her eyes drift closed—giving herself up to the chocolate ecstasy in her mouth and unable to focus on what was happening onstage for the moment.

In the next instant, a shotgun blast echoed off the walls of the ballroom and all the people in the room screamed in horror while Sadie choked on her cake.

About the Author

J osi was born and raised in Salt Lake City, attended Olympus High School and made an appearance at Salt Lake Community College before marrying her high school sweetheart and starting a family. In addition to her writing, she loves to bake, travel, can her own peaches, watch criminal justice TV, and study the oddness of human nature. *English Trifle* is her tenth published novel, and the second in the Sadie Hoffmiller mystery series that combines many of her great loves into one delicious book.

In her spare time, she likes to overwhelm herself with a multitude of projects and then complain that she never has any spare time; in this way she is rather masochistic. Josi currently lives in Willard, Utah, with her husband, Lee, and their four children.

She also enjoys cheering on her children and sleeping in when the occasion presents itself. She loves to hear from her readers and can be reached at Kilpack@gmail.com.